In Pursuit

"Dear readers of *In Pursuit*, prepare for a literary feast. A novel that is both elegant and electrifying, chock-full of intrigue and suspense, and a love story that is utterly absorbing, I inhaled *In Pursuit* like a decadent meal, unable to slow my delight until the last, delicious page. As she proved in her beautifully-crafted debut *Swimming with Serpents*, Sharman Ramsey knows her history and—more importantly—the hearts and minds of her characters. They shine here once again—and I ponder them, and their remarkable journeys, still."

—Erika Marks, author of *The Guest House*

Historian and author Sharman Ramsey has worked magic with her latest novel *In Pursuit*. Ramsey is a born storyteller and what a tale she has woven with this novel. One part adventure and one part historical fiction, this novel is all parts intrigue. Ramsey reminds us that love, passion and greed are human experiences regardless of the era. Readers are sure to savor this educational and entertaining historical novel.

—Michael Morris, *Man in the Blue Moon*

History comes to life in this rip-roaring novel that starts out in a tearoom in London then sweeps across the seas in a pirate ship to the Spanish territory of Florida soon after the Battle of New Orleans. Sharman Ramsey has spun a rollicking story of kidnappings, lost treasures, Red Stick Creeks and Seminoles, betrayal and revenge, populated with well-known historical figures such as Jean Lafitte, Billy Bowlegs, William Weatherford, and even Old Hickory himself, Andrew Jackson."

—Cassandra King, author of *The Same Sweet Girls*

In Pursuit

A Novel

SHARMAN BURSON RAMSEY

MERCER. UNIVERSITY PRESS
MACON, GEORGIA

MUP/ P473

First Edition

Books published by Mercer University Press are printed on
acid-free paper that meets the requirements of the American
National Standard for Information Sciences—Permanence of
Paper for Printed Library Materials.

Mercer University Press is a member of Green Press
Initiative (greenpressinitiative.org), a nonprofit organization
working to help publishers and printers increase their use of
recycled paper and decrease their use of fiber derived from
endangered forests. This book is printed on recycled paper.

ISBN   978-0-88146-454-2

Cataloging-in-Publication Data is available from the Library
of Congress

Necessity was the plea for every infringement of human freedom. It was the argument of tyrants; it was the creed of slaves.

—William Pitt the Younger:

I dedicate this novel to my husband and dearest friend,

Joel Wardlaw Ramsey

Acknowledgments

Writing this novel has truly taken me on a journey I never expected. I started out studying European history and never thought to find a focus in the Southeast United States and particularly Native American history. Then I discovered my own Native American heritage and recognized that a perspective has been neglected because the victors write the history. Indeed, Josiah Francis is my half third cousin seven times removed through our common Shawnee Cornstalk line (according to genealogist Don Greene and my Legacy genealogy program). While I also have ancestors on the other side of this story, it appears that the voices who are telling me their stories happen to be those of a forgotten people.

I want to acknowledge the assistance given to me by Dale Cox, author of the *History of Jackson County, Florida.* He is a descendant of William Augustus Bowles and the Perrymans, Seminoles of Northwest Florida. Don Greene, author of *Shawnee Heritage I and II,* has once again provided valuable information regarding the relationships of the major players in the novel. Robert Register, blogger at *Zero, Northwest Florid*a, my favorite Renaissance Man, who knows a lot about many things, shared interesting tidbits along the way, guiding me toward interesting facts of the era.

I also want to express my sincere appreciation to dear friends and my favorite bridge partners, Dr. Joe and Cheryl Budd, for tipping me off to the "year there was no summer." It is amazing what an impact climate can have on world events!

You will notice in this series the respect I have for Harry Toulmin. It was a serendipitous discovery to find that he is the ancestor of Rondi Bates Turner, my University of Alabama Tri Delta pledge sister, roommate, and one of my dearest friends. I knew she was extraordinary!

Joie and Godfrey needed to have their story told. But I also wanted to tell the story of the First Seminole War through three different perspectives: the Red Sticks and Blacks, the Americans, and the British. I hoped to do so and still relay Joie and Godfrey's personal drama.

This amazing era in our history has been vastly underrated in its importance to the future of the United States. The Negro Fort mentioned in the story is located just south of the Northwest Florida town of Sumatra and is now called Fort Gadsden. Andrew Jackson had his aide-de-camp Lieutenant James Gadsden build a new fort onto the remaining battery tower of the Negro Fort during the First Seminole War. Jackson then declared that it be called Fort Gadsden. Only in history is this place remembered as the Negro Fort.

My husband and I found the Negro Fort with determination since a bear had demolished the sign. We went during the same time of year that the fort was destroyed. I imagined the fort filled and bustling with the activities of the more than 300 men, women, and children within. Two hundred years ago, a lucky hot shot hit the magazine of the Negro Fort. It came from an American gunboat under the order of General Andrew Jackson that was followed through by command of General Edmund Pendleton Gaines and actually carried out by Colonel Duncan Lamont Clinch on the Apalachicola River in Spanish territory. The instant casualties included 275 men, women, and children. Those people and their story are a part of our history and should not be forgotten.

It is my hope that the Negro Fort, with all the hopes and dreams it represented, can be rebuilt to respect the memory of those who sought the same dream upon which our country was founded—freedom. Call it what it was called then, a name that was their badge of courage and hope. Mow down the weeds and mark the cemetery that holds the remains of those who lost their lives that day as a reminder of the blood, sweat, and tears that have been shed to bring liberty for all the citizens of our country.

I thank my publicist, Kathie Bennett, and my friends Cassandra King, Janis Owens, and Karen Spears Zacharias. Unfortunately, death claimed two of my most cherished friends, Barbara Clemons and Agatha Bennett, before we could have the book signing we had looked forward to. I miss you both.

My appreciation goes out to Marc Jolley of Mercer University Press for believing in the novel—and in me.

Sharman Ramsey
Dothan, Alabama
May 15, 2012

In Pursuit

Chapter 1

S abrina Stapleton and Godfrey Lewis Winkel?
    Joie scrunched up her thick-lashed, Kincaid-blue eyes...and then opened them again trying to clear her vision. Surely she was not seeing clearly. Her heart beat faster. She pressed her nose against the pane fogging the mullioned window directly beneath the sign for Rules in Covent Garden, London's favorite gathering spot. For the past year, the weather had been cold and the days dark. Fowls went to roost at noon, and the candles were lit as if it were midnight.

When sunspots appeared large enough to see with the naked eye, religious zealots expected an apocalypse. The *London Chronicle* reported on the panic: "The large spots which may now be seen upon the sun's disk have given rise to ridiculous apprehensions and absurd predictions. These spots are said to be the cause of the remarkable cold and wet weather we have had this summer; and the increase of these spots is represented to announce a general removal of heat from the globe, the extinction of nature, and the end of the world."

But most people didn't think they were ridiculous or absurd. Everyone around Joie seemed to live in fear. The sudden climate change caused a string of difficulties: disrupted planting and growing cycles, which led to famine, which eventually caused food riots as everyone fought for their share of nourishment. Suicides were rampant and an epidemic of typhus had struck. The streets of London were littered with debris from the waves of immigrants who had come in search of food. Beggars lined the roads, and thieves and cutthroats kept decent folks confined to their homes.

None of it mattered to Joie after what she saw in the tearoom. It started innocently enough. The Duke, her brother Cade's father-in-law, had suddenly decided that their family should leave England. Joie had been determined to see her friend once more before moving away. She felt that she *must* find Sabrina, perhaps the only girl friend she had ever had, and say goodbye. Sabrina's housekeeper tried to be discreet but had let slip where Sabrina had gone. Joie's curiosity was piqued—especially when the housekeeper confided that Sabrina was meeting a man with whom she had been conducting a correspondence.

A man? And Sabrina had not told her?

Her dearest friend!

So Joie had wasted no time in leading her family to think she was heading to the stables to say goodbye to the horses, even slipping on the clothes of a stable boy that she often wore when helping her other brother, Gabriel, work with the animals. Otherwise, they would never have let her roam the streets without a chaperone. She had braved the horrid weather and artfully eluded the challenges in the streets to get a glimpse of this "man."

And yes—that was indeed Sabrina Stapleton, her dear friend, daintily sipping tea by candlelight in the middle of the day. She could see her through the window. And the gentleman? Could it be possible that the tall, spectacled, redheaded dandy dressed like a peacock might be actually be Godfrey Lewis Winkel, the arrogant bastard she and her sister-in-law Lyssa Rendel Kincaid had rescued—five years and an ocean away—from the Fort Mims massacre?

The last time she saw Godfrey Lewis Winkel, she was eleven and he was a tall, skinny, cocky, freckle-faced fifteen-year-old. He'd looked down his nose at her, sniffing at her work-roughened hands and lack of book learning, her always messy black braids, her dusky skin, and the simple fact that she was a "breed," half Creek Indian and half white. Back then, Godfrey had been a city boy coming down the Federal Road from Milledgeville, the capital of Georgia, who got trapped in the Tensaw area at Mims ferry because of the Red Stick scare while on his way to visit family in Mobile. He'd come looking for adventure, experiences he could write about for his family's New York newspaper that would prepare him for the books he would later write. Or so he planned.

He found more than adventure when the fort where they had sought refuge, actually a one-acre enclosure around the Mims home, was attacked by one thousand Red Stick Indians. Nearly all of the five hundred men, women, and children—red, white, and black; militia and civilian; slave and free—were killed, raped, mutilated, and burned. Only a few managed to escape.

So why was he here? At Rules on Maiden Lane in Covent Garden, no less. In London, England, when he should be in America. Having tea and scones (her favorite with clotted cream and strawberry jam) with Joie's very own (at least at one time) best friend.

She would know him anywhere!

She *knew* he would be trouble!

They should have left him there alone on the trail where he had escaped the burning fort, his leg broken and protruding from the skin, staggering, bleeding, and feverish. They should have left him among the rattlesnakes and mosquitoes, alligators and palmetto, pine trees and river oaks!

And they would have, too, but for some crazy reason (she could never explain it to herself) Joie had demanded that Lyssa halt in their flight from the Red Sticks and pull the boy, near dead, onto Beauty and save him along with the other children who straggled out of the palmetto and cane and into their lives.

Godfrey Lewis Winkel was Sabrina's mystery correspondent?

Impossible!

Joie stamped her foot and said aloud, "God damn it all to hell and back, I knew I should never have trusted another female. I'm of a good mind to march right in there and...."

And what?

She pressed her nose against the pane because maybe, just maybe, the fog on the glass had obscured the view inside. Maybe she was wrong.

The well-dressed couple just on the other side of the windowpane turned and pointed, laughing at the urchin with his nose pressed against the window. A woman in an emerald green day dress carrying a matching parasol tut-tutted at Joie's language and pressed a lace handkerchief to her nose as she passed. Even the woman's servant gave Joie a wide berth!

Everyone was fearful these days, what with the 300,000 veterans coming home from Napoleon's wars looking for jobs at a time when Irish and Welsh immigrants were fleeing famine in their countries and crowding the streets. With her dark hair and bright blue eyes, Joie probably did look like what some people called "black Irish." No one would suspect a Creek Indian to be roaming the streets of London.

But she was no ignorant urchin. She knew what was happening in the world because her sister-in-law Lyssa, whom she idolized, often debated those topics over dinner with her father, the Duke. The Duke, the only son of the third son of the former Duke of Penbrooke who'd come to America to seek his fortune, was a graduate of the College of New Jersey. He'd encouraged his daughter Lyssa to learn and speak her mind. And that she did. Vigorously. Sometimes while at the supper table nursing one of her many children. And when she'd caught Joie cringing at her vehement discussions with her father, she'd explained that they were not fighting but debating, and that was healthy. Quite different from the loud voices that had preceded heavy fists in Joie's former life.

Joie caught her reflection in the window and suddenly realized that *she* was the urchin. The tea shop patrons were pointing at *her*! She was attracting too much attention standing there, dressed in boy's clothing, her straight, lustrous, jet-black hair tucked under a cap, with her nose pressed against the window of the popular tearoom. She usually bound her chest but was in too big of a hurry today.

For a moment, fear pierced her stomach. Had Sabrina and her "man" seen her? She chanced another glance. She needn't have worried. Sure as the sun came up in the morning, Godfrey Lewis Winkel, having just tucked a cream-and-strawberry-stuffed scone in his mouth, sat nodding and drinking tea with his pinkie lifted, smiling like a damned Cheshire cat at the girl Joie had once thought her dearest confidant in all the world.

Appalled that she might be spotted spying, Joie Kincaid slipped into the alley, which was dark despite the fact that it was the middle of the day. Leaning against the wall in the alley, Joie mulled over the situation. She had thought her friend, Sabrina Stapleton, would be amused when she saw her in stable clothes. If the Duke's mother found out, of course, *she* would be anything but amused. While the rest of her family had little interest in being accepted by the ton, the Duke's mother had made it her life's goal to gain acceptance into that august group. Joie in boy's clothing would send her into vapors and onto the fainting sofa for sure.

Sabrina was the one thing Joie had thought she would miss about London, besides her brother-in-law, Lancelot Rendel, who was just one year older than she, and her brother, Gabriel Kincaid, both of whom would stay in England. Joie and the rest of the family planned to board a ship to return home to America within a few hours.

At last.

She missed the freedom of home in the Creek Country in America, but the family had certainly needed to recover from the massacre at Fort Mims and the rigors of the Creek Indian War.

The discovery that her brother, Cade, had married not just the granddaughter of Pushmataha, Choctaw chief, but also the daughter of a duke who needed to claim his English estates had come at a time when all were willing to leave the Creek Country…at least for a while.

Lyssa's father, Jacob Rendel, had recently inherited lands and a title, which sounded like a bunch of nonsense to Joie but was very important to the people who inhabited his lands. This son of a Virginia planter who thought he had shed ties to that legacy when he married his Choctaw princess suddenly had to face the challenges of dealing with people who depended on him to accept his responsibilities. Now he had lands and people on both sides of the Atlantic—his father's lands in Virginia and the newly inherited estates in England.

Joie's brother Cade had married Lyssa Rendel right before the massacre at Fort Mims. Lyssa had saved both Joie and baby Jay, who was Cade, Gabe, and Joie's newborn half-brother. Thanks to Lyssa, they had all survived. And in the process, the Rendels had acquired a brood of orphans, survivors of the massacre rescued by Lyssa and Joie. The children had bonded immediately to "Papa Rendel," now the Duke of Penbrooke, who, along with his wife Malee, accepted them all with the same love they showered on their blood relatives, including the twins who were born to Lyssa and Cade just after the couple finally reunited. And thus far, Cade and Lyssa had added to the family in the traditional way: after adopting baby Jay and having the twins, Jace and MaryLyssa, they welcomed Alexander, now nearly two, and baby Oliver, six months.

The Duke and his beautiful Duchess, Malee, the adopted daughter of Choctaw chief, Pushmataha, brought the entire growing family with them to England. Jacob Rendel, Duke of Penbrooke, could not bear to be parted from any of them. The blended family had been the source of much conversation among the ton, shocking them with their disinterest in participating in the artifices of polite English society, which of course made them all the more fascinating.

Jake and Malee's son, Lancelot Rendel, would be heir to the dukedom upon Jake's passing and needed to be indoctrinated into the management of the estate. Since Cade was husband of the Duke's daughter and father of their children, there was no question that he would also go with the Rendels to England. Cade had seen England as a safe haven and was pleased that his twin brother Gabe, their sister Joie, and their half-brother Jay were included in Papa Rendel's affections. Lyssa had actually treated little Jay just as if he were her own baby and nursed him, though he was months older, along with her twins; others even thought she had given birth to triplets.

Little Jay's real mother, Leona Loughman Kincaid, Joie's stepmother, had never wanted a baby in the first place. It was Joie and Lyssa who had kept Jay alive after the massacre.

Joie found it wondrous to watch Cade fall in love with each of the children, but she knew it was because her brother loved Lyssa so much. She was sure that their kind of love would never be her good fortune. After all, she had never *known* love before reuniting with her brothers. She was not sure she would recognize it if she had it. Her stepmother had convinced her that a "breed" was unworthy. When her brothers came

6

along, they told Joie that, other than having her father's startling blue eyes, she was the image of their mother Snow Bird, and they said everyone told them that Snow Bird was the most beautiful woman they had ever seen. Joie had no way to tell. Her mother had died giving birth to her, and shortly afterward she was separated from her brothers.

At age eleven, Joie had seen her stepmother's brand of contempt in the eyes of Godfrey Lewis Winkel. She knew the truth about herself.

It was hard to believe they had been in England for three years. They had left the horrors of war back in America, along with the vengeance of the criminal, Savannah Jack, who had already tried to kill Cade twice. It seemed that everything would be okay if they could just stay together as a family. And they certainly felt safer in London. But now, one in fourteen in the city had died of a dreadful disease called typhus, and it was spreading throughout the countryside. Papa Rendel decided the little ones needed to leave England, and he chose to return to Virginia and see to his father's estates.

It had all happened so fast, which is why Joie felt so anxious to say goodbye to Sabrina.

She stood there with her back against the alley wall, so absorbed in her thoughts that she had no time to react when the burlap sack came down over her head.

When he saw the face pressed against the mullioned window at Rules, Godfrey Lewis Winkel had left Sabrina in mid-sentence. Now, as he stood looking foolishly up and down the street, he wondered what had possessed him to erupt from the London tearoom in such a disreputable manner.

Blue eyes and an urchin's face? Would he forever chase such visions? It was a flaw in his otherwise rational character that he simply must overcome! And a truly embarrassing one, he thought as he recalled the last time he had followed such an impulse down a busy New York street only to be reported to a policeman as a stalker. He had apologized profusely, explaining that he had thought she was someone he knew.

Why could he not be satisfied with the ladies who were truly charmed by his wit and intelligence? Why could he not forget the hoyden who had saved his life?

She had simply disappeared. Dropped off the face of the earth.

Godfrey ran his fingers through his stylishly short, reddish-blond curls, mussing his hour-long effort to tame them as he searched the crowd.

Gad! He was going mad!

Still, he remembered his manners, smiling at a passing lady and tipping his black top hat. He adjusted his fine wool double-breasted tailcoat with turned-back cuffs and a matching high collar of velvet, wondering if he looked as foolish as he felt. The tailor had assured him that this outfit was in the best of taste. Beau Brummel himself would have worn it, the man said.

Godfrey pulled at the canary-yellow waistcoat and bemoaned once again the tight-laced corset the tailor had insisted was a part of every gentleman's dress. The cursed thing made even a simple bow difficult. Though he might be a bit soft—the amusement of those who'd watched him spar with Gentleman Jack had assured him of that—he truly hadn't thought he needed such a garment. Eyeing his reflection in the windowpane, he thought about Sabrina.

She had written him, telling him she admired his article about the map he had found that revealed the location of Captain Kidd's treasure. While the man had died many years earlier, his reputation remained—and his treasure was supposedly still hidden. A brief correspondence had followed regarding Kidd's English appearances near her home in Cornwall. Indeed, the gossip was that Kidd was from a family of Cornish gold miners. When Godfrey mentioned that he would soon speak at the British Museum on the article, which had been published in the *London Examiner*, Sabrina had requested a meeting.

Godfrey's curse and gift was to remember everything he had ever read as well as the date, time, and details of each day of his life (perhaps even back to the womb, though his mother could not confirm it). He sniffed the breeze and mentally recorded his surroundings, imagining them to be much the same as in Kidd's day. Drifting up from the harbor, he identified the scent of the cargoes—cinnabar, ginger, tea, sandalwood, hemp—and, of course, the unmistakable rich whiff of sea-worn ropes and tar. From where he stood, he glimpsed a forest of masts all pressed within the stretch of river from London Bridge all the way down to the first bend. And beneath it all was the acrid stench of human waste and unwashed bodies in addition to the horses and dung from the drays that hauled cargo through the city streets to and from the harbor.

Appalled by his impetuous act, he was about to turn back into Rules to apologize to the attractive and intelligent lady (she did like his work) when he heard a muffled oath and a grunt coming from the alley. Godfrey quickly turned the corner to see two ruffians handling a canvas sea bag that obviously held an unwilling individual attempting to pummel and kick his way loose.

"I say there, you dastardly villains," Godfrey called.

"Myles," said sailor with a decidedly acute case of hog's breath and body odor that even the aroma of the Thames could not mask, even from a distance. "Methinks the man insulted us."

"Well, Cedric, invites the gentleman into our parlor," the other said, showing his blackened teeth in a semblance of a genial grin as he tossed the bag over his shoulder. A loud "Oooof" issued from the bag.

"Ah, so, it will be like that, will it?" Godfrey said, drawing into the boxer's stance that he'd only recently learned from boxing champ Jack Randall. He had to let these villains know what they were up against.

He hoped they could not see how his fists shook. Thinking to catch them off guard with a surprise move, he ran in for a head butt. The villain called Myles stepped quickly aside and threw him an upper cut as he sailed past. Godfrey went down, gasping, confined by the corset, his breath and motion impeded. Suddenly, with a well-aimed kick to the head by the other villain, Cedric, everything went black.

***

Godfrey felt her before he saw her. The cackle of a chicken woke him, and he opened his eyes to confirm that the last person he expected to see and the one person he'd longed to find was lying beside him. She stared at him with a strangely vague look, one of her eyes nearly swollen shut, as they rocked gently on the waves. So they were on a boat, he realized. He saw that he was bound hand and foot with the same rope that bound Joie Kincaid. No doubt she was even now plotting some diabolical scenario to wreak havoc on their captors. And then she would turn her infinite capacity for torment upon him.

He waited.

She said nothing.

She just lay there on her side, grimacing at the mosquito that had hovered and landed on her cheek and staring at Godfrey with the most peculiar expression on her face. He blew a puff of air toward her face, and a red dot of blood marred her smooth skin when at last the mosquito reacted. Unconsciously, he registered the fact that the boat must have originated in some tropical area if it carried mosquitoes in its foul hold.

Finally, he decided to break the uncomfortable silence.

"Well, hello," he said, wondering if Joie noticed the even baritone of his voice amid the cacophony of sounds from the cages around them, provisions for a long voyage, apparently. When she last saw him, he'd been plagued by the cracking speech tones of an adolescent. At the time, it had only added to his mortification at the thought of two females rescuing him and attending to all his bodily needs as he wandered in and out of consciousness for months. One of those females happened to be the very one he used to torment, and now she lay facing him, certain body parts touching him and indicating that she was no longer the little girl he once knew. She still watched him blankly.

Good Lord. What happened to the spitfire?

"Who are you?" she asked in a quavering voice.

"You don't recognize me?" Godfrey asked, crestfallen.

Knowing that her new life as the sister-in-law of the Duke's daughter would probably take her far away, he had caught himself searching for her on every street and corner. He'd last seen her at St.

Stephens after the Creek War had ended with the Battle of Horseshoe Bend and after they had spent months searching for Cade and Lyssa, who had simply disappeared in the Tallapoosa River. Cade Kincaid had brought Lyssa and their twins home at last. Lyssa had survived being kidnapped by Savannah Jack, and Cade lived through Jack's brutal attack.

Through his investigations, Godfrey had learned that Savannah Jack still lived and, as feared, still sought revenge. That was probably why Pushmataha, Lyssa Kincaid's grandfather, had been reluctant to tell anyone where the family had gone. All who had been in the room—Godfrey included—when Jake Rendel discovered he was the heir to a title and estates in England as well as his father's estates in America were sworn to secrecy. Savannah Jack was relentless and brutal, and it was essential that he not know their new location.

Over the past several years, Godfrey had struggled to control his irrational reaction to faces that reminded him of Joie. It was more than an intellectual like himself could bear, but he found that he simply could not help it.

He finally decided that the only reasonable action was to focus his prodigious intellect on finding Joie, confronting her, and apologizing to her for being such an ass. That was the reason Godfrey decided to come to London when the invitation to speak had arrived from the British Museum.

That and the fact that he owed Joie Kincaid so much and wanted to show her that he had been worth saving. He wanted to invite her to the meeting so she could see him well dressed and highly respected. He wanted her to hear how his voice had settled into such a pleasant register, one the local Episcopal Church sought for its choir.

But the note he had sent to the Duke's estate had arrived too late. His messenger had returned, saying the family was no longer residing there.

And she'd forgotten all about him?

"I have been lying here, trying my very best to remember just who *I* am. Should I know *you*?"

Though the light was dim, Godfrey was able to see a bruise on Joie's forehead partially covered by the cap she had pulled over her lustrous blue-black hair. Someone had knocked her in the head with such great force that the blow affected her eye. Godfrey felt an anger rise in him like he'd never known before.

Why was she alone on a London street dressed in the clothes of a stable boy...and her a member of a duke's household? Jake Kincaid, duke or no duke, and Cade and Gabe Kincaid, her muscular, powerful, Creek-warrior brothers, would have to answer to him. His fists clenched, unintentionally tightening the ropes. He saw her wince.

"Oh, I am so sorry!" he said, willing himself to relax.

Her good eye was filled with fear. Was she afraid of him?

He had not realized how tiny she was. Or was it just that he had grown so much larger? His hands, tied there so close to hers, seemed massive next to hers. His anger grew as he saw how the rough rope had chafed her hands. Delicate was not a word he would ever have used for Joie Kincaid! And yet, with her memory gone along with her strong-willed personality, this delicate flower was now his to protect.

He wanted to reassure her, but their environment left him little fodder for optimism. From the casks that surrounded them, it was easy to deduce that they were tied tightly together in the hold of a ship, stuffed amid barrels, casks, and cages of cackling chickens—supplies necessary for a sea voyage. From the steady rocking, it was apparent that the ship was well under way.

"They're awake!" someone yelled from above.

A leg appeared on the top rung of the ladder coming down into the hold. And then another. With each step of that gargantuan bare foot came another length of leg, until the hip appeared on what must be the tallest man on earth, or so it seemed to Godfrey from where he lay at the foot of the ladder. And from the way all light was blocked with the man's descent, the rest of him was proportionately large. His skin was as black as pitch and glistened—with perspiration from his exertions rather than the weather, no doubt, since it had been uncommonly cool for a late August day in England, and the hold in which they were kept was cold and damp. He wore only old canvas slop trousers, a cutlass that hung at his waist, clanking against the wooden stairs with each step, and a huge gold earring that dangled from one ear. His cleanly shaved head made him even more menacing.

"The captain wants to see you," the man announced in a booming bass voice.

"I'm a bit tied up at the moment," said Godfrey, with an attempt at humor. His levity apparently fell quite flat as the man crossed his arms and scowled down at him.

Godfrey glanced at Joie and again saw her fear. The man before him, who was drawing blood from his forearm as he tested the cutlass blade, did not appear to be an official in any common government or familiar private enterprise. He looked more like one of the pirates from Godfrey's writings and talks. Why, he could have stepped straight from the page of his last article published in his father's New York newspaper. Godfrey's articles had caused quite a stir and, he had been told, actually motivated Congress to send ships into the Gulf to end the activities of pirates who threatened life and property. When speaking of economics, it was merely academic.

But this man surely looked like a flesh-and-blood pirate.

Oh, my God. That was it! They had been captured by pirates! But they were taken on land. And Godfrey had no treasure. Though he did have a treasure *map*....

He'd never intended to get *this* close to actual pirates!

Godfrey swallowed hard. There appeared to be a huge lump lodged in his throat, perhaps bile from the fetid stench of the hold. His mouth was as dry as straw.

"Sir," he said. "I am your servant. But, indeed, at the moment, these bonds do impede my effort to accede to your command."

The cutlass came down with a single slashing movement. Godfrey gasped and shut his eyes. He might have passed out with simple shock and fear had he not felt the bonds at his hands fall away. When he dared to look, he saw Joie watching with all color drained from her face.

They still had both hands. He glanced again at the man standing menacingly above them.

Merciful God! Had they *truly* been kidnapped by pirates?

Pirates had become his hobby ever since he found a copy of a treasure map in the New York Society Library. Located in an obscure book of early maps that sketched the lines of Indian treaties, the map appeared to have been created by Captain William Kidd, notorious pirate of the 1700s. If it hadn't been for the research paper he was writing on the early maps to earn his degree at Princeton, he'd have never found Kidd's sketch.

Though college was a hurdle his parents had required of him, Godfrey was impatient enough to start contributing articles to his father's newspaper before he actually graduated. Fortunately, readers had seemed to enjoy the articles he wrote about piracy in the Gulf of Mexico. He received more mail in response to his articles than any other writer at the newspaper…and he had not even joined the staff yet! And then came word from New York's new representative to Congress, James Tallmadge, that Congress was commissioning the ships to combat piracy. (Then again, Tallmadge might have simply hoped for a favorable article to help his efforts to prevent the extension of slavery into Missouri.)

As rewarding as those articles had been, Godfrey's secret desire was to be a novelist. The pirates in Defoe's *Robinson Crusoe* had stirred his imagination. He wanted to write from the pirate's perspective. Surely not all pirates were villains! The British hero, Sir Francis Drake, had been labeled a pirate as he conducted his activities under a letter of marque of the Queen of England. He was more a privateer than a pirate—perhaps a distinction without a difference if you happened to be on the ship he attacked, boarded, pillaged, confiscated, and sold as booty. Even so, Godfrey wanted to create a heroic pirate like Sir Francis Drake.

Or William Kidd! His research on Captain Kidd had led Godfrey to believe that, like Drake, Kidd thought he was also operating under the will of the king's government. Godfrey's theory was that Kidd had been keelhauled, so to speak, by powerful people in England who covered their own involvement by implicating him. A fictional character had already claimed his place in Godfrey's imagination. His name was Caleb Connory, and he was bold and resourceful…and he could read a sextant and a quadrant. As could Godfrey. He had learned the skill from his grandfather's sea captains.

It was fine and dandy to consort with pirates in his mind—in the abstract. But this was flesh and blood. A true reality check for him.

If only it were Caleb Connory lying here instead of Godfrey Lewis Winkel!

Godfrey's one act of courage had been refusing to leave St. Stephens, choosing instead to stay with Judge Harry Toulmin until Cade Kincaid returned with news of Lyssa, who, along with Joie, had saved his life. Only then had Godfrey acceded to his parents' wishes and returned to security of New York civilization, where he immediately fled to the hallowed halls of academia, content to read and write of adventure from the security of his rooms at Princeton and his father's library. He had accepted the invitation from the British Museum merely in the hope that he might find Joie Kincaid on the estate of her brother's father-in-law and thank her in person for her efforts on his behalf.

Perhaps grovel before her and thereby assuage his guilt, expiating himself of his obsession.

Well, he *had* found Joie Kincaid.

But she deserved a hero to rescue her—not the weakling with a useless summa cum laude after his name quivering away at the feet of the looming giant. They would never survive in the world of pirates that he knew so well through his research.

Caleb Connory, on the other hand…maybe Godfrey could act the part.

He had, after all, acquitted himself well on the stage when he had tried his hand at acting, though his greatest contribution was not tripping as he played the rear end of an ass.

He caught Joie's glance and once again felt her confusion and apprehension.

It was worth a try.

Though trembling inwardly, he supported himself on an elbow with casualness he did not feel. He gazed up at the man and, grateful for the deepened timber of his voice that made him sound much more powerful and in control than he felt, said the first thing that popped into his head.

"My servant boy, Joe, will accompany me."

The giant shrugged, and Godfrey assumed he meant yes.

Hmm. That went well. He continued, "The boy has the gift of communicating with horses, though he cannot communicate with people. I intended to check out some horseflesh for racing back home and brought him along."

He should shut up now. Caleb Connory was a man of few words.

Who knew? Joie Kincaid *might have* inherited her brother Gabe's gift with animals. That should provide reason enough for the presence of a lad named Joe to come along with him, while giving the "lad" enough worth to save her life. There was actually a tinge of authority in his words, he thought with surprise.

As Godfrey untangled the two of them from the web of ropes, he whispered to Joie, "Go along with what I say. Our lives may depend on it."

"Caesar! The captain wants to know what's keeping you," a voice called down.

While the giant was distracted, Godfrey whispered, "Keep your hat pulled down with your hair covered and your eyes cast down. Remember, you are unable to speak. Keep behind me and say nothing."

Joie did not know who this young man was, but somehow he seemed familiar. And at that moment in that place, familiarity was something to cling to. She would follow his command.

Godfrey struggled to stand, feeling a thousand pinpricks in his blood-starved feet. Joie stumbled, and he grabbed for her and then realized that, for her own good, he must not treat her like anything but a servant.

Oh, God, he thought, gasping for breath as he took the first step up the ladder, the damned corset had to go!

Chapter 2

The family looked high and low in the Rendels' London townhouse, but Joie had disappeared. Her belongings were packaged and stacked, waiting for the imminent departure. So where was Joie? She had said she was going to say goodbye to the horses, but the others got distracted by the flurry of preparations and had not seen her since. Anxious and perplexed, they sat waiting for her to return before getting into the carriages that would take them to the ship. The smallest children ran around in circles calling, "Joie, Joie," as if it were a game until they wore themselves out and were put in bed for naps. The older children whom Joie and Lyssa had rescued back in America—Rob (the Dowager Duchess's new name for Running Bear), Ben, Sister, Meme, and Andro—sat solemn and white knuckled. They knew well how quickly bad things could happen to good people.

Savannah Jack could have found them. London might have Red Sticks.

Lyssa, Malee, and the Dowager Duchess tried to reassure them. But they huddled together, armed with whatever they could find to defend themselves—a poker, a cane, a broom.

The family's largest trunks were already stowed aboard the ship. But as the planned departure hour passed and night fell, the Duke refused to leave without Joie. Everything that they could get off the ship without delaying it further had been removed, and it had begun its journey across the sea without them.

The following morning, Gabe and Cade accompanied the Duke when he went to inquire of the Bow Street Runners concerning any occurrence that might indicate Joie's involvement. The Duke employed them to pursue a search and then returned home with Cade and Gabe to devise a plan.

Though he was more accustomed to forests than fine homes, Gabe Kincaid could not sit still and wait. He had to do something. He had resisted English society, preferring to stay in the stables with the Duke's horses when not out riding with the Duke and his son, Lance, overseeing the fields. Now he had to make himself presentable and call on the neighbors just as the Duke and his brother Cade would do. Though more comfortable around horses than people and in stables rather than drawing rooms, Gabe fitted himself out in the duds the Duke's mother insisted he must wear to make a good enough impression to get admitted into the homes of Jake Rendel's neighbors and friends.

When they'd first arrived on English soil, the Dowager Duchess had commanded that he and Cade take lessons from the children's tutor. Cade had agreed in order to set an example for Lance, who thought that "talking American" was plenty good enough. But he had encouraged Gabe to take the lessons as well. During sessions on elocution and grammar, Gabe had discovered that he actually had an ear for language. He had never considered that English, Creek, and the lingua franca of trade were actually three different languages. Learning proper English grammar took a bit of effort, but the tutor assured him that he nearly had it; he just needed refining. Gabe still had an accent that was unmistakably *not* British.

Fortunately, asking if anyone had seen Joie wouldn't require many words.

Jake took one side of St. James Square, and Cade took the other. Gabe agreed to venture out of the neighborhood and call on others Joie knew. Since Joie considered Sabrina Stapleton her best friend, she was the logical first choice. Gabe had no problem getting admitted to her home. Though the butler offered to take him to a sitting room, Gabe insisted on waiting in the foyer since his visit must be brief.

He stood nervously crushing his beaver hat with his clenched hand while he admired the beautiful architecture of the cream-colored foyer with its ornately carved ceiling. He always felt like a bull in a china shop in these English homes. His broad shoulders showed to their best advantage in the cropped riding coat and white double-breasted waistcoat that fit snugly on his muscular body. His long black hair was secured with a leather thong. Gabe slapped the unfortunate beaver hat impatiently against his long leg, which was tightly fitted in leather riding breeches that he tucked into tasseled Hessians. He spied an intriguing object sitting on a mahogany carrying case. He knew it was an orrery, but he hadn't a clue as to its purpose. One day he would inquire. Today, however, he was in too much of a hurry to dally with unnecessary conversation.

Gabe Kincaid had called asking for her? Sabrina Stapleton was so excited, she thought her heart would burst from her chest. Joie's brother towered above most Englishmen. His perfect aquiline nose, prominent cheekbones, and unusual amber-colored eyes made him the most perfect specimen of manhood she had ever seen. Unfortunately, he only saw her as another little girl, Joie's friend. She was much too shy to mention her silly infatuation to her friend.

Had Gabriel finally noticed her and come to call? She quickly laid aside the book she had been reading (for at least the third time), *Mansfield Park* by Jane Austen. Fanny Price appealed to Sabrina, seeming much the kindred spirit.

Gabe's back was turned as Sabrina peeked around the entry from the hall into the foyer. The jacket he wore enhanced his broad shoulders, fitting his strong arms like a glove and then tapering down to the most perfect…

Her heart beat faster, and she wished she had worn something more flattering. She glanced behind her to make sure they were alone and took the opportunity to remove her thick, heavy glasses and leave them in her reticule on the hall table. She glimpsed herself in the gilt mirror as she passed and then stepped back, turning to observe her figure at full length. Without her glasses, she could only see the vague image of the prim and proper Miss Sabrina Stapleton. Frowning, she jerked the square-cut bodice of her empire dress lower. She would show him that she was definitely no longer a child! Then she turned quickly, nearly tipping over the imported Blue Willow china umbrella stand brought from one of her father's trips to China; she grabbed it, stilled it, took a deep breath, and then walked purposefully into the foyer.

"Why, Mr. Kincaid, what a delightful surprise," Sabrina said as she approached, her hands outstretched.

Gabe turned and caught his breath. This was not the Sabrina Stapleton he knew from the stables. This young woman was a vision in her softly clinging, cream-colored muslin dress with its high empire waistline. She nearly bumped into him before he took her hands. Her bodice was so low that Gabe could not help noticing a lovely amount of enticing flesh. She looked up at him with sparkling eyes the bright clear color of the forest in spring and flashed him a dimpled smile. The warmth of her welcome took him aback. He'd never been this close to her, and the proximity was unnerving. Mainly, he'd only seen her from the rear as he watched her ride off with Joie. Nothing like the view he was getting looking down her…

"Have you seen Joie in the last twenty-four hours?" he asked abruptly, dropping her hands when he realized he'd held them longer than what was considered polite.

"Why, no, I haven't," she replied, a bit deflated that he had come to inquire about Joie and not to see her.

"Why do you ask?" she continued, taking a step forward, attempting to get close enough to be able read the expression on the blurred image of the face above her.

Gabe took a step back.

"As you know, she was to board a ship to return to America. Yet we cannot find her, and so I must now continue my search." His back hit the wall as she smiled up at him with her beautifully shaped lips.

"Oh, my!" Sabrina exclaimed. "We must find her!"

"Yes…yes…there are others I must question. I must…I must…"

He was stuttering!

"Well, goodbye," he said, sidestepping to stand in front of the door. "Thank you for seeing me," he added as he grabbed the door handle behind him.

He'd rather confront a grizzly any day than a dainty little female like this one who would probably break if you touched her. He was on the verge of making his escape from a woman whose presence had unsettled him in a way that he had never experienced. He'd seen women in Creek Country totally bare-breasted and thought nothing of it. What made the female body so much more alluring when the sight of a woman's chest was a mere tease?

He had almost made it out the door and was pulling a handkerchief from his pocket to wipe his brow when Sabrina said from behind him, "This is all so distressing. People simply disappearing all around me."

Gabe crushed the cloth in the hand that wasn't crushing the beaver hat, stopped in his tracks, and turned back toward her.

He took a deep breath and asked, "Who else has disappeared, Miss Stapleton? What do you mean?"

"Well, yesterday, I was taking tea with a gentleman with whom I have been corresponding. He is an American journalist who writes for a newspaper my father has shipped to him. The gentleman was in London to speak at the Museum on a topic I have long found interesting. You see, the individual about whom he spoke has a connection to my home in Cornwall—Captain Kidd."

Gabe tried not to appear distracted, but he found himself questioning his discomfort again. He had never thought much about the petite blonde standing before him. English ladies seemed fragile and obsessed with the frills of society. Too much like Cade's mother-in-law, the Duke's mother. All he knew was that Sabrina had a good seat on a horse. In fact, her love for horses had brought her and Joie together in the first place. And she enjoyed the odd English tradition of fox hunting, an activity he and Joie thought a bit silly: dressing up to go hunt a single fox that you did not even eat when you caught it.

Joie participated because the Duke's mother insisted. How else would she find a husband? She couldn't sing or play the piano and knew nothing about the rules of society like holding a fan, dancing, making small talk, and such. The Dowager Duchess had decided that Joie would have to marry one of those single-minded, horse-obsessed gentlemen.

The curious friendship between Sabrina and his sister Joie had seemed an unlikely pairing, indeed. But what was this talk of pirates?

"We were having a lovely conversation," Sabrina continued, "when he looked out the window, leaped to his feet, and nearly ran out of the tearoom! And then he just...disappeared! Everyone in Rules turned and stared at me. I was so embarrassed. I ate all of the teacakes by myself while I waited and waited for him to return! He *is* an *American*, I know, but he seemed to be such a gentleman...in spite of those ridiculous clothes...."

Sabrina's voice trailed off and she blushed. She realized that Gabe himself was an American, and he might think she cast aspersions on Americans in general.

She took a deep breath and forged ahead. "But when I finally paid the bill myself—with pin money I had thankfully brought with me to buy ribbons—and departed, I did not see him anywhere!"

"Well, now, that is odd," Gabriel said.

The housekeeper, Mrs. Taylor, appeared at the door. "Would you like some tea, Miss Sabrina?"

"Would you stay for tea, Mr. Kincaid?" Sabrina asked.

"No, thank you, Miss Stapleton. I have to find someone who might have seen Joie yesterday after she left home."

"Miss Sabrina, if I may be so bold as to inquire, did Miss Joie find you yesterday?" Mrs. Taylor inquired.

Gabe and Sabrina looked at each other and turned together toward the housekeeper.

"Why, no, Mrs. Taylor," Sabrina answered, looking confused.

"Joie was here?" Gabe asked.

"Yes, yes, she was here!" the housekeeper said, her head bobbing with every word. "She came to the kitchen dressed as a stable boy and inquired after you." She squirmed a bit and twisted her apron before admitting, "I let slip as you had gone to take tea at Rules in Covent Garden with a fine gentleman friend with whom you had been corresponding."

"Did she say anything else, Mrs. Taylor?" Gabe pressed.

"No, sir, she did not. In a bit of a rush, she was. She let herself out of the garden gate, sir. I was overseeing the polishing of the silver and hurried back to the kitchen."

Gabe, Jake, and Cade had ridden by Rules when they had gone to engage the Bow Street Runners, whose headquarters was close by in Covent Garden. Thinking of his sister alone in that area, Gabe felt a chill run down his spine.

He expected that the two disappearances were unrelated, but he couldn't help asking Sabrina, "Just what is this writer's name?"

"He is an American journalist by the name of Godfrey Lewis Winkel," Sabrina said.

Gabe visibly blanched, and Sabrina reached out to support the man who towered above her by more than a foot.

"Perhaps you should come in and sit a moment," she said, guiding him back through the foyer and into the nearest drawing room toward a Chippendale chair covered in blue damask. Coming to her senses, she changed direction and seated him on a yellow silk loveseat.

And then sat beside him.

As soon as she said the name, Gabe knew that Godfrey's disappearance was connected to Joie's. That the two who were so bound by past events would disappear on the same day and around the same time could be no coincidence. Thinking of it, he felt faint indeed.

"Mrs. Taylor, please bring tea," Sabrina said. "Mr. Kincaid needs something fortifying." She looked toward her father's brandy cabinet but decided against that much fortification.

"Ah, yes, Mrs. Taylor," Gabe said. "And please send someone to summon the Duke. My brother Cade was canvassing houses across the street. Please ask someone to bring him here." He was finding it difficult to think straight.

"Mr. Kincaid," Sabrina began. She was perched so closely to him on the sofa that the fabric of her dress actually covered his knee. "You act as if Mr. Winkel's name is familiar."

Gabe leaned forward and held his head in his hands. "Yes, I know Godfrey fairly well. One might say Joie saved Godfrey's life."

Sabrina leaned toward him eagerly. "Please tell me!" she exclaimed.

When Gabe turned toward her, their proximity cleared all other thoughts from his head. Then he was angry with himself for being distracted by her shifting bodice. Joie was missing, after all!

At that moment, Mrs. Taylor arrived with the tea and clucked under her breath, eyeing Sabrina with persimmon-pursed lips and arms crossed over her ample chest. Sabrina sat back and adjusted her bodice.

Gabe, who had thought about breaking the silence by telling Sabrina everything, caught himself. The Dowager Duchess would split her corset if he were to spill the beans on the family's true background. For now, everyone simply speculated. The Dowager Duchess implied that they had Italian ancestors, though she had trouble explaining Andro, now age seven and named for Androcles from the old story, who was black as coal and just as loved by his family as any of the others. Indeed, some accused Jake of showing him favoritism, but Gabe thought that was only because Andro followed Papa Rendel everywhere he would permit. And if that included his private library, a place off limits to the other whirling dervishes, that was only because Andro treated each book there as if it were holy writ and waited patiently for Papa Rendel to take him on his lap and read aloud of the wonders in those pages.

Fortunately, the family secret was preserved by Mrs. Taylor and the tea tray.

He would wait and let the Duke and his brother Cade decide how much to reveal.

Gabe devoured all the cakes and sandwiches on the plates the housekeeper brought. He was grateful that Sabrina Stapleton was much too polite to make him talk with his mouth full. But when the plate was nearly empty, he felt desperate enough to request another cake and was about to do so when Cade and the Duke arrived. Gabe breathed a sigh of relief and wished he could unbutton his waistcoat.

Cade, Jake, and Gabe questioned Sabrina until they were sure there was nothing more that she could possibly remember. Then they decided to split up. Cade left to find out where Godfrey was staying and question him. Jake took his carriage to canvass the rest of the Square. Gabe was to extend his search to Rules.

"I will go with you to Rules," Sabrina proclaimed, picking up her bonnet.

Dismay was written all over Gabe's face. She knew that he would politely insist that she, a woman, should remain in the safety of her home, while he, a man, should proceed with his manly investigation.

"I shall only follow you in my own carriage if you decline my offer to attend you," she said, adjusting her bonnet and drawing her parasol from a huge oriental vase that stood on the black and white marble floor.

This was Joie's shy, retiring friend?

Holding Gabe's arm as they made their way down the stairs, Sabrina added, "There may be more that I will recall once I get there."

Why was she fluttering her eyelashes? Was there something in her eye?

The carriage ride down the Strand actually turned out to be informative. Sabrina told Gabe the history of the magnificent homes with gardens down to the Thames, who lived where, and how they fit in society.

"I am sure you have already engaged the Bow Street Runners," she said as the carriage turned toward Covent Garden. At Gabe's nod, she continued, "It was a great-uncle of mine—Henry Fielding, the magistrate at the time—who started the Bow Street Runners. Great-uncle John, his brother, continued after Uncle Henry gave up the post and was *amazingly* successful, though he was nearly blind. He could tell whether someone was lying or telling the truth merely by the sound of their voice!"

Gabe could sense her admiration for this uncle, and he silently agreed that such acute hearing would be an excellent gift.

Sabrina surprised Gabe by pulling her spectacles from her reticule as soon as the carriage came to a halt in front of Rules on Maiden Lane. Gone was the provocative young woman who met him in the elegant foyer of her father's fine London home. He realized now that she had pressed him against the wall in the foyer not because of a sudden passion but as the result of poor vision!

Why was he disappointed?

She stepped from the carriage and stood momentarily as if seeing Maiden Lane for the first time. "The last I saw of Mr. Winkel, he was standing in front of the window there, turning right and left as if looking for someone."

She eyed the alley, considering.

"Let us first speak to the staff who were here yesterday," she said, and strode purposefully ahead of him, tapping her foot impatiently as she waited for him to open the door. Gabe followed, allowing her to take the lead.

"Mr. Rule, please," she said to the waiter who met them at the door. The waiter led her through the crowded room back toward the kitchen, where Thomas Rule was shucking oysters, a Rules favorite any time of day, while others were rolling dough and stuffing meat pastries in preparation for the dinner crowd. It was a happy kitchen, with a cacophony of clanking china, clanging silver, and the occasional bell-like tapping of crystal. It was a starving man's finest dream, filled with delicious aromas and shelves loaded with tiny iced cakes and pastries. Though he had eaten his way through Mrs. Taylor's bountiful tea tray until he thought he would never hunger again, Gabe's appetite sat up and took notice.

Mr. Rule led them toward the back door and out into the alley. "Now," he said, pulling his pipe from his pocket, "how can I help you?" He struck a match and puffed on his pipe. Smoke wreathed his face.

"Mr. Rule," Sabrina said, adjusting her spectacles, lifting her chin, and peering down her nose at him. "I was here yesterday about this time taking tea with a gentleman. That gentleman has gone missing, as has a friend of mine who might have come looking for me. We would like to know if you or any of your employees might have seen something… curious…yesterday that might help us."

Rule took another draw on his pipe. He was obviously a patriotic man, Sabrina noted. Perhaps he had fought Napoleon. The white clay pipe he held so familiarly boasted a carving of Nelson with a lowered flag on one side and Britannia on the other.

Thomas Rule perused them thoughtfully through the wreath of smoke. "I usually step out here for a smoke and a breath of air about this time each afternoon," he said. "I must say, I did observe something yesterday, now that I think of it. A very tall, thin man and a short, squat fellow carrying something ungainly in a burlap bag that they both struggled to put on a cart that already contained another bag. The short fellow appeared to be the one in charge, giving orders to the tall one, who complained with every step. I assumed it was a bag of oysters that had been refused until the man the other called Cedric took a cudgel and walloped the bag that was already in the cart. I was called back into the kitchen when the new boy tripped on the bucket of oysters and spilled them underneath the feet of the pastry chef, who fell and started a series of disasters."

"That would be the commotion I heard in the kitchen," Sabrina said.

"Yes," Mr. Rule agreed, tapping his pipe. "And I must return to the kitchen before another calamity befalls us this afternoon."

"One more thing," Gabriel insisted. "Could you show us exactly where the cart was?"

Sabrina nodded approvingly. Thomas Rule led them down the alley and indicated the spot.

"Now, if you will excuse me," he said, just as someone stuck his head out the door calling for him. He hurried back into his restaurant.

"Here are their footprints," Gabe said, pointing. "You can see that someone is walking backward, carrying something with someone walking forward."

Sabrina pulled a magnifying glass from her reticule. She then proceeded to backtrack the footprints into the alley.

Gabe couldn't help being amused. Fortunately, he had learned from the best how to school one's countenance. Creek warriors were models of stoicism. He had also been taught by the best trackers in the world, so it was amusing to him to watch this proper young lady bend close to the ground with her magnifying glass, looking for what he had already observed—the point of the scuffle.

But, surprisingly, it was Sabrina who spotted the dot of turquoise amid the mud and animal droppings in the cart tracks. Sabrina pulled on the bit of color and lifted out Godfrey's turquoise cravat.

Gabe realized that he had neglected asking her to describe Godfrey's clothing. He was slipping. Too long away from home. His amusement turned into frustration with himself.

He took another look about him. The imprint of a pair of small boots caught his attention. He knew they would match the prints in the stable back at the Duke's town home and on his estate. Joie *had* been here. Suddenly, the tracks began to make sense. She had run into the alley from the front of Rules and had been surprised by the owners of those two pair of boots. Both she and Godfrey must have been stuffed into the burlap bags. Gabe wondered which of them had been struck by the cudgel.

"Sabrina, please take the carriage home. I need to track the cart," Gabe said.

Sabrina sniffed and hurried back to the cart. "You need me," she said. "Detecting runs in my veins."

Once again, he hid his amusement. Without revealing his family's secret, how could he tell her that tracking had been his life before he came to London?

He followed her along the alley and then right down Southampton to where the cart had turned left onto the Strand. There the tracks were quickly lost among the many others on the pockmarked, ill-paved, well-traveled road.

"It is my considered opinion that the cart is headed toward Wapping and the docks," Sabrina said, looking eastward. Gabe followed her glance. Wapping was a continual straight road with Wapping Marsh to the north and the Thames to the south. It was home to sailors, mast-makers, boat-builders, block-makers, instrument-makers, victuallers, and representatives of all the other trades that supported the seafarer. Mazes of alleys consisting of small tenements and cottages housing laborers, street sellers, loafers, criminals, and semi-criminals crossed the area as well.

The Strand was the end of their walk. They headed back to Rules, where they had left the carriage.

"Back to Miss Stapleton's home, please," Gabe told the driver.

"No, to Wapping now, James," Sabrina countermanded.

"Enough now, Miss Stapleton," Gabe said. "The docks are much too rough for a lady."

She opened her mouth to object, and he touched her lips. "I will learn much more with the freedom to move and question. I can fit in. You will not."

The surprising effect of his simple touch silenced her. She could object and force the issue, but she knew in her heart that he was right.

After taking leave of Sabrina, Gabe returned to the Duke's home and changed into his roughest clothing. He added a scarlet kerchief about his head, strapped on an eye patch, and rolled in the dirt a bit before following the cart tracks down to Wapping Wall, known as a gathering spot for sailors, pirates, cutthroats, footpads, and smugglers. It was after midnight when he wound up at the Prospect of Whitby, at the Wapping Old Stairs leading down to the Thames. At that very spot, Captain Kidd had been tied to the posts at low tide and left to drown when the tide came in over one hundred years ago. The stairs were part of the network of stairs, causeways, and alleys providing access to the Thames since the series of shallow walls were built on the formerly sloping banks of the river.

The Prospect of Whitby was one of the two- to six-story houses and shops constructed on the wall. Its location as a public house next to the steps at which the watermen would dock to pick up and let off passengers made it a popular location—and helpful when some hapless soul might happen to fall into the water. It was also a logical meeting place for someone who wanted to plot a kidnapping.

But why Joie? Why Godfrey, for that matter?

Gabe pushed into the boisterous, smoke-filled, dark-paneled pub with cut limestone floors and took a seat at a corner table.

"You're a big'un, luv," the barmaid exclaimed, eying him appreciatively. Gabe ordered a pint of ale.

When she returned, Gabe pulled the thin but buxom girl onto his lap and, in his best Cockney accent, feigning anger and frustration, asked, "'As me friend, Cedric, left me a message? 'E said 'e 'ad a job fer me and would leave a message with the prettiest maid at the Prospect of Whitby."

The girl giggled. "No message, luv, but I spotted Cedric with 'is buddy Myles pulling bags o' somethin' down the Wapping Stairs," she said, suddenly serious. Looking around and then turning to whisper in his ear, she said, "'E'd been bragging about a big take when 'e delivered the goods."

"I knows about the 'big take'! Part of that big take was s'posed t' be mine!" Gabe said, fishing for more information. He pulled a guinea from his pocket and slipped it down the depths of the barmaid's cleavage. "Did ye 'ear where they was 'eaded? Cedric owes me."

The girl's slender hand dove down and retrieved the coin. She curled her fingers around the guinea and weighed it in her hand. "Falmouth," she whispered. Then, in a normal voice, she added, "Say, luv, I gots to get back to work, but if ye wants to wait 'til I close things up...."

She leaned low, her dress loose about her slender frame, and let him view what she had to offer. Then, with a peck and a longing glance backward, she headed off.

Gabe watched her sashay away before taking his leave. He lingered in the black dark just beyond the glow of the Prospect of Whitby at the top of the Wapping Stairs and looked down at the Thames. More than twenty rough-cut, algae-covered steps led down to the bank of the river, above which hung an empty noose. He felt a chill of fear for Joie.

The villains had no doubt had a boat waiting.

There were so many ships in the water that you could almost walk from one to another and cross the Thames! Boats arrived and departed at all times of day and night.

My God, Gabe thought. They'd been kidnapped and carried out to sea. But where? And by whom? He would have Jake and Cade coordinate the Bow Street Runners and the Thames River Police to continue the search, but they would waste precious time if Joie and Godfrey had already been transported to Falmouth. From what he had heard of Myles and Cedric, they might have been smart enough for petty thievery. But surely Joie had not looked like a logical target in the shabby clothing Mrs. Taylor had said she was wearing. And if Godfrey was a just a target for theft, why go to the trouble to take them both away?

Gabe knew there was more to this. Someone besides the two cutthroats was involved. Sabrina had said that Godfrey was in England to deliver a talk at the British Museum on Captain Kidd. Kidd met his end at the end of a gibbet like the one that hung on this very spot. Was that the reason for bringing Joie—and likely Godfrey—here?

He would go home and see if Jake had gotten a ransom note for Joie, which would at least give some sense to the kidnapping. He could find out whether they had located Godfrey and discovered the purpose of his visit to England, though by this point he doubted that Godfrey was still around any more than Joie was.

The barmaid said the villains were headed for Falmouth, a place with fewer people and fewer ships. Perhaps Gabe could intercept them there! He was determined to go to Falmouth.

Chapter 3

Reflecting off the open sea, the brilliant sun assaulted Godfrey's eyes as soon as the man called Caesar preceded them onto the deck and no longer blocked the light. Godfrey stepped out of the hold and breathed in deeply, inhaling the bracing salt-sea air, a blessed relief from the musty dank of the hold. Looking up, he spotted a flock of Manx Shearwaters, genus *Puffinus puffinus*, which he knew should already have begun their winter migration to South America. He watched as they cleared the white aft mast and dove into a school of fish starboard of the bow. He stood shivering for a moment to catch the rhythm of the ship's roll. His eyes soon adjusted to the sunlight that still manifested the strange yellowish glow that had been present since the 1815 eruption of Mount Tambora in the Dutch East Indies.

He resisted the urge to reach back and help Joie when he heard her stumble. Could her injury be more severe than he imagined, affecting more than her memory?

"Molly on deck," someone yelled. Catcalls and whistles followed him, carried on the crisp wind from the men above him in the two masts of the ship and from men on deck who were clad in a motley array of slops, Monmouth caps or brightly colored bandanas, and long linen shirts. Most of them were barefoot, a necessity despite the cold, he knew, for maneuvering the timbers for the sails. Their hair was loose, braided, or bound with a leather thong or ribbon, certainly not fashioned in the Titus style Godfrey had spent so much time creating before going to meet Sabrina Stapleton. Many wore gold earrings.

He now knew with certainty that the outfit sold to him by the much-vaunted Schweitzer and Davidson of Cork Street was more than just a fashion mistake. Mentally, he damned the double-breasted tailcoat with turned-back cuffs, the matching high collar of velvet, and the canary-yellow waistcoat, and he *double damned* the tight-laced corset. The once white, stiffly starched shirt was spattered with mud, and upon further inspection he found his ruffled cuffs were ripped. The turquoise cravat and beaver top hat were long gone. He would gladly trade his form-fitting, fawn-colored pantaloons for the loose slops of the sailors who mocked him.

The important things in life had suddenly been winnowed down to essentials, and that included survival. Mainly, the survival of the young woman with her head lowered and her hands in the pockets of the stable boy's pants who stood so close behind him that he could almost feel her breath.

Though Godfrey's heart pounded like the Creek Indian drums he'd once heard, he affected an air of Caleb Connory-like casual observation, all the while cataloguing the details of his surroundings in his mental journal as he made his way aft on the main deck that ran stem to stern without a break. Godfrey would be able to remember the date, along with every face he saw and everything that happened on that date, just as he remembered every word on every page he'd ever read. As always, it was both his gift and his curse.

Like a breeze through a field of grain, heads nodded as they passed, a sign of respect for the black man whose powerful demeanor could have intimidated even the bravest of men. But Godfrey did not discount fear as the motivator of the sailors' respect.

Just how many men were on the two-masted schooner? Godfrey estimated that it would take sixty to eighty to man a ship that large, even with a single gun deck. He noted four guns on each side, sixteen gun ports, and numerous swivel guns/blunderbusses mounted atop the bulwarks. Three hatchways led below decks, and there was a wheel for steering. Small portholes were situated above the scuppers for oars. Windlass, mast, yardarms, storage boxes for tools, water barrels for drinking water, a bilge pump, ropes, cleats, and batons, all necessary for ocean-going vessels, were neatly tucked in their places about the meticulously cleaned deck.

Godfrey was impressed. One did not live in New York City without learning a bit of seamanship. And although his knowledge came mainly through observation (his grandfather had owned a fleet of merchant ships and took Godfrey, a precocious child filled with questions, with him to the docks) and books, he recognized a well-run ship when he saw it. A few of his grandfather's ship captains had allowed him to take the wheel. The captain of this ship, whoever he was, ran a tight ship.

Caesar led them to the farthest hatchway, painted red, and down to the second deck. With another step down, he knocked on the door to the captain's cabin, which, according to Godfrey's observation, took up approximately one-fourth of the space on this deck.

"Enter!" came a voice on the other side of the door. Caesar ducked his head, pushed the door open, and led them down a short corridor and into the teak-paneled captain's quarters. The captain himself lounged back in an intricately carved, tapestry-covered Jacobean armchair. His feet were propped on the glistening, recently polished (if the smell of lemon and beeswax were any indication) teakwood desk ornamented with carved lion's heads and cluttered with charts held down by a quadrant and sextant on one side and the newest edition of Falconer's *Universal Dictionary of the Marine* on the other. Brilliant white teeth glistened in the disarmingly unexpected smile of the olive-complexioned man. Spanish, Godfrey thought, as he continued his perusal of his surroundings.

Remembering the architecture of similarly styled schooners docked in New York, Godfrey knew that the bread room encompassed the space created by the turndown of the hull at the rear of the ship directly behind the Titian-style portrait of a nude woman hanging on the wall behind the captain. The bread room held the ship's biscuits, keeping them (as much as possible) from molding in the damp of the hold.

Two elegant windows on either side of the captain's desk lent a natural light to the cabin, making the silver candelabras on the table and captain's desk sparkle. The windows were framed in rare yellow silk that pooled decadently on the silk Khotan carpet, probably from East Turkestan. Godfrey had seen similar items aboard one of his grandfather's ships. An intricately carved mahogany bed draped with red velvet and covered with snowy white silk-cased pillows and a red silk coverlet was secured against the bulkhead separating the captain's cabin

34

from what Godfrey supposed was one of his officers' cabins. The captain apparently wanted guests to be impressed with his success.

And Godfrey was indeed impressed.

The captain made an indolent gesture indicating that Godfrey should take one of the other two Jacobean chairs in the room.

Godfrey sat.

Joie, thankfully in character, slouched against the cabin's back wall. Caesar left to get back to his other duties, whatever they might be. Godfrey remained aware of Joie's every movement, could almost hear the pounding of her heart and feel her every sigh. She'd saved his worthless life, and now it was time to return the favor. Though why and how they'd wound up here he could not imagine. It must have been a terrible mistake. Myles and Cedric were not thieves. Godfrey's gold chronometer remained in his waistcoat pocket, and the watch key remained attached to its intricately fashioned gold fob and was secure in the pocket of his pantaloons. He had not seen the two kidnappers among the crew of the ship.

The captain leaned forward and folded his hands on top of the charts, focusing his sparkling brown eyes on Godfrey. Godfrey was reminded of his mother's small spaniel. More than once, he had found himself the victim of this dog and had learned not to trust the sincerity and innocence of big brown eyes. He'd reached out and gotten his hand bitten, learning the hard way the difference between appearance and reality.

Wrinkles creased the captain's eyes, and his skin was leathered by years in the sun. In spite of his silver-streaked hair, he was still a handsome man. But even more, he had an air of power that made him a man who would captivate women and draw the admiration of men.

Godfrey immediately recognized him as the intense man who had sat near the exit at the British Museum the day he'd given his presentation on Captain Kidd.

"The speech you delivered on Captain Kidd," the captain began, his heavy accent confirming Godfrey's suspicion of his Spanish heritage, "was very interesting. I have also read your articles in the American papers about pirates in the Caribbean."

He suddenly slammed his hands against the desk and pushed back in his chair. "Why do you focus on this Captain Kidd? I began my career in 1783 and captured and burned thirty-six ships in just my first twelve years, amassing a fortune that I have buried throughout the Gulf and Caribbean. Yet I have no mention in your writing! You write of that inconsequential William Augustus Bowles, waste ink and paper on Jean and Pierre Lafitte, flatter Luis Aury…and ignore the greatest pirate of all time! And yet, it is I who focused my efforts on Spanish ships, weakening a nation that could have helped defeat that fledgling United States of America. Your country, no? That praise you heap upon that pissant Lafitte!"

The captain was jealous? Godfrey and Joie had been captured because a pirate hadn't gained the notoriety he felt he deserved?

"You have me at a disadvantage, sir. You know who I am. May I know your name as well?" Godfrey asked daringly.

The captain gesticulated. "I am *José Gaspar*! Formerly a hero in the Spanish navy! I am now known…and feared…by the name 'Gasparilla,'" he growled. The spaniel's eyes were no longer warm and friendly. Indeed, they had turned cold as flint. The madness in them chilled Godfrey.

"You will write my story."

At that moment, Joie slid down the wall and vomited all over herself and on the rare Khotan carpet.

Godfrey jumped from his chair and ran to where she now lay unconscious, nearly blocking the door. He lifted her awkwardly, encumbered as he was by the hellish corset. "This…boy," he stuttered, thinking quickly to explain his reaction, "is worth a chest of gold. His gift with horses has the potential to make me a very rich man. He may have been seriously injured when your kidnapper hit him on the head. As your *biographer*, I need a cabin with a desk. And the boy will stay with me."

"Augustus!" Gaspar yelled. His face had taken on a greenish tinge as the smell permeated the room. He looked in disgust at his precious carpet, a major prize from the recent capture of a merchant ship on its return voyage from the Orient, now soaked with vomit.

Another Spaniard, with black hair, beard, and mustache, rushed into the room with cutlass raised. Joie, her shirt soiled and smelling, lolled lifelessly in Godfrey's arms.

"Clear your belongings from the chart room. My biographer will use that space," Gasparilla said to Augustus in a combination of Spanish and Portuguese. Both happened to be among the eight languages Godfrey spoke and read fluently, if one did not count Latin, Greek, and Arabic, which most people considered academic languages.

But at the moment he looked at the two men questioningly, figuring it might be best if they thought he only spoke English.

Augustus indicated that Godfrey should follow him into the small adjoining space off the captain's cabin. The door, which Godfrey noted had a lock on the outside, opened onto a small corridor with a similar cabin directly across the way. Holding his breath, Augustus stuffed a few personal items into a canvas bag and quickly left Godfrey to tend to the boy who had heaved all over himself and the captain's prized carpet.

Godfrey laid Joie gently on the bunk. The bed coverings were tucked tightly about the thin mattress, military style. Perhaps Augustus had seen military action as well. That seemed to be the history of many pirates, particularly now in a world filled war veterans, pestilence, and famine.

Godfrey poured water into the basin from the pitcher and grabbed the cloth hanging nearby. He dampened it and wiped Joie's pale face. She was breathing normally, thank God. Her soiled shirt rose and fell with every breath.

The reeking garment had to go.

Godfrey was a gentleman, and a gentleman would not undress a lady. But this was a desperate situation. There was no one else to tend her! Just as she'd had no one else to tend him those weeks after the massacre at Fort Mims.

He grabbed a shirt that hung from the hook behind him. Now what? He closed his eyes as he slowly gathered the nasty shirt, folding it as he went and finally pulling it over her head. And then his hands brushed her breasts, startling him so that his eyes popped open. Not that he was an expert, but what he saw was a glimpse of a man's vision (at least this man's vision) of perfection. Joie was no longer the little girl she had once been. She was all woman, and a beautiful one at that.

Dear God. He gulped and hurried to complete his task before someone burst through the thin barrier between the two of them and those licentious, amoral pirates!

With no need to keep his eyes closed any longer, he quickly drew her arms through the sleeves of the clean shirt, which he presumed belonged to Augustus. As he pulled off her boots, preparing to tuck her under the covers, a knife fell from one of them.

Bless be.

Godfrey could not get out of his fancy garments fast enough. With Joie's knife, he slashed through the strings of his blasted corset and sucked in the first full breath of air since he had put the damned thing on. How long ago? He allowed himself a moment to scratch his belly with pure pleasure but stopped when Joie moaned and twisted on the bed.

He pulled his shirt back on, letting it hang loose over his trousers and wishing he had slouch pants like the crewmen. Then he turned his attention back to Joie. He felt under her cap to assess her injuries and found an egg-sized lump beneath the mass of silken black hair, the reason for her blackened eye. After adjusting the cap, he dampened the cloth once more and replaced it on her forehead.

A loud commotion played in the corridor outside the cabin door. He heard the captain threaten to shoot whoever broke something getting the damned carpet out onto the deck. From the sound of it, there was a whole herd of clumsy pirates banging against the walls and up the stairs. Godfrey heard a piece of heavy crystal hit the wooden floor and shatter.

A gunshot exploded from the cabin next door.

Good God almighty. Had Captain José Gaspar actually *killed* one of his men for breaking a piece of crystal?

After a moment of stunned silence, there was even louder thumping and bumping out in the hall as they all tried to lift the heavy Oriental carpet through the hold to fresh air on the deck.

Would there be blood on the wood floor to clean as well?

Looking back down at Joie, he chided himself. It was a hell of a time to become obsessed with the vision he had glimpsed of her breasts. He reasoned that his interest was purely for her own security: he had to address her womanly figure in order to keep her safe. Her chest would require binding to keep the crew from noticing that she was indeed not a boy. He was her friend, her guardian, the reason she was in this fix. *That* was the reason for his extreme emotions.

The soiled shirt had to be disposed of, anyway. He ripped the back of it into strips and proceeded to wrap Joie's chest as quickly as possible. Hearing a banging in the hall as the men carried the heavy carpet past the door, he pulled on Augustus's shirt to cover her as quickly as he could and then sat on the end of the bunk at her feet, attempting to look as if he were not watching the door. They were in a terrible predicament, and it was up to him to deal with the madman who had gone to so much effort to kidnap him.

Joie was an innocent bystander. He longed to know how and why she happened to be in the wrong place at the wrong time. But if she could not remember her name, how could she remember what brought her to the alley outside Rules?

He rested his elbows on his knees and leaned his head against the hull of the ship, closing his eyes in an effort to dull the shooting pain in his own head. Then, lulled by the rocking of the ship and Joie's even breathing, he fell asleep.

Chapter 4

When Gabe returned to the Duke's townhome, he found the Duke, his brother Cade, Lyssa, Sabrina Stapleton, and her father, a well-to-do merchant associated with the East India Company who had close connections to the Colonial Office, sitting around the table in the small dining room. They were all picking at their kippers and eggs, breakfast food to which the Duke's family was not yet accustomed. The cook was befuddled by their preference for the cornmeal porridge they called sofkee and was probably relieved to have some native-born English to eat her cooking. They looked up hopefully as he walked into the room, but he could see the hope die in their eyes when he shook his head. Unconsciously, Gabe's eyes went directly to Sabrina Stapleton seated at the far end of the table next to her father. She smiled at him reassuringly, her beautiful eyes now distorted behind the thick lenses of her glasses.

Lyssa's violet eyes swam with tears as he settled into the chair left empty for him at his usual place beside her. He knew they were tears of worry for Joie. Joie and Lyssa had bonded like real sisters after Lyssa saved Joie's life, and then the two of them had worked together to care for the orphans they rescued from the Fort Mims massacre, along with a badly wounded Godfrey Lewis Winkel. Gabe and Cade had actually known Lyssa since they were children on a Twiggs pack train coming into the 'Bigbee territory deep in Creek Country more than ten years before the Creek War.

Cade had once thought Lyssa and Gabe belonged together. But for Lyssa, Cade had always been the one. She was an exceptional woman who not only shared Gabe's gift as a *whisperer*, an instinctive communicator with most animals, but was also brilliant, educated by her father from a early age when she had surprised him with her intellect.

Gabe was dirty and exhausted. He smelled of cheap perfume and cheaper gin that had splashed upon him amid the boisterous revels of the taverns. He had known the desperation the painted faces were meant to hide. Though his own belly was full these days, he knew that hunger drove the skeletal barmaid to offer her services; she was driven by fear that she would not eat and could not feed her hungry children. He'd rubbed elbows with drunken sailors now blinded, paralyzed, or limbless—still with families who looked to them to provide—who found release in a bottle from nightmares of the battlefields. That sensitivity was the curse of the whisperer's gift. Lyssa stroked his back in loving concern, and he knew she sensed his pain. He also knew that she worried not only about Joie but also about him being in an environment so far beyond what they had known just three years ago.

It was true that nothing about Gabe escaped Lyssa's attention. She had even noted a telling glance between Gabe and Sabrina when he entered the dining room. Could it be? Ever since they had met as children, traveling with Twigg's pack train into the Creek Country, Lyssa had taken both men into her heart. Though Cade was the love of her life, Gabe had become a true brother, and they shared a bond forged stronger by the love they both bore for Cade.

Theirs was a tragic story, but at least it had a happy ending thus far. Cade and Gabe had grown up like every other Creek warrior, disciplined by their Creek mother's male relatives, who had also taught them skills of war and hunting—not necessarily skills favored in London drawing rooms. Their white father was a trader who was present in their lives but not prominent in rearing them. And when their mother, Snow Bird, died giving birth to Joie, their father tormented them in his drunken grief and then took up with another woman, abandoned his sons, and had a third son with their stepmother. Ten years later, Jason Kincaid and his second wife were viciously killed and mutilated at the massacre at Fort Mims on August 30, 1813. Fortunately, Lyssa had arrived in time to save Joie and Jay, the newborn infant brother Joie refused to leave behind in the burning fort.

Lyssa Rendel Kincaid was more than his brother's wife to Gabe. Both Gabe and Cade adored her. But Gabe's feelings had never been romantic. He had simply sensed a kindred spirit in Lyssa, creating a special bond between the two of them from the beginning.

Gabe reached for the cup of coffee Lyssa set before him. He downed the rich black liquid gratefully and then leaned back to share his news. "I lost them at the stairs to the Thames at the Prospect of Whitby. A barmaid there recognized the names and descriptions of Myles and Cedric, who apparently frequent the pub. She saw them pulling two large bags down the stairs. She also heard them mention Falmouth. I assume they took a small sloop to meet up with a larger ship to set sail immediately from Falmouth."

Falmouth was well known as the port with the best winds for setting sail across the Atlantic, a fact that sobered them all.

"Who would have done this? Where are they taking them?" Lyssa asked, voicing the questions they were all asking.

Gabe looked at Cade. "What did you find out about Godfrey?"

Cade, sitting on the other side of Lyssa, gently took Lyssa's clenching hand and said, nodding toward Sabrina, "As you know, Godfrey was here at the British Museum to deliver a talk on one of his pirates and, most particularly, William Kidd. He is supposed to have a map drawn by Kidd that might lead to his treasure."

He lifted his hand to silence Gabe's next question. "And yes, I did go to his rooms at the George Inn. They were in total disarray. Someone had been there, obviously searching for something."

Sabrina whispered, "The map...."

Gabe stood. "There is no time to waste. I must go to Falmouth. I need to find Myles and Cedric or at least learn more about them and perhaps their motivation." He nodded toward Sabrina and added, "I think Miss Stapleton and I share the impression that someone else hired the two of them to kidnap Godfrey. I would assume our sister happened to be in the wrong place at the wrong time."

"I would prefer to join you, Gabe!" Cade said.

Gabe patted him on the shoulder. "I know, Brother."

He looked at the hand Cade held so tightly. Gabe remembered the anxious days they had spent not knowing if Lyssa and Joie were alive or dead, and then the days after they had found Joie, Godfrey, and the orphans. He remembered Cade's agony when they learned that Lyssa had been captured by the Red Sticks and had no way of knowing if she lived.

"I will travel faster alone," he finally said. "Your responsibility is here."

Cade nodded reluctantly. Lyssa's fingers tightened around his hand, and she looked at Gabe, her eyes round with fear as she remembered all that she and Joie had endured together. Gabe and Cade knew that if it had not been for the six-month-old nursing infant who needed Lyssa, in addition to the other children, she would insist on helping them search.

Jake agreed for Gabe to head to Falmouth alone. "We'll continue the search here," he said. "Our trip to America will be postponed. Cade will take Malee, Lyssa, and the children to the country estates, where they should be safer than here in London. I will remain here. Should other clues surface, we will be prepared to pursue them."

Sabrina Stapleton took her father's arm and leaned closer to whisper in his ear. Her father, now a respected member of Parliament, looked at her, considering. Sabrina's father had raised her much like the son he never had, training her in the management of their estates as well as having her educated by the best available tutors. She accompanied him frequently when he attended meetings throughout his district, and he held her opinions in high regard. Her words had obviously motivated him toward immediate action. He nodded at Sabrina and then took her hand to help her to her feet.

To Gabe he said, "While you prepare, I will go to Lord Bathurst and see if any curious events have come to his attention that might shed light upon this apparent kidnapping."

After the Stapletons took their leave, Jake turned to Cade and Gabe and explained, "Apparently, Sir Phillip Stapleton earned his fortune through his association with the East India Company. He has a close relationship with Lord Bathurst, the Secretary of State for War and the Colonies. I once asked Sir Phillip if he was acquainted with Zachary and Colin MacCauley, and his face lit up. They are sons of John MacCauley, an old friend of John Witherspoon, who was President of the College of New Jersey, as well as my professor and mentor. John MacCauley and

John Witherspoon were both ministers in the Church of Scotland before Witherspoon agreed to come to America and take on the challenge of educating a bunch of colonists."

Putting a hand on his daughter Lyssa's shoulder, he continued, "I have learned that both brothers are associated with the Clapham crowd." Lyssa nodded, used to her father's connecting the dots in governmental circles. She had grown up with his explanations of the intricacies of government and politics.

"Zachary publishes the *Christian Journal*, and Colin is a general with the East India Company. Both are abolitionists. William Pitt the Younger, Prime Minister during the American Revolution, who died only recently, was a member of that group. William Wilberforce, whom everyone acknowledges is the most steadfast and ardent of abolitionists, was a leader in pushing for the Slave Trade Act of 1807 that abolished the slave *trade* throughout the British Empire, though not slavery itself. Lord Bathurst is sympathetic to their cause."

The Duke made eye contact with each individual sitting at the table. "These are names with which you should all be familiar. Such networks often work outside official policy. With connections like those of Sir Phillip, we should have the choice of ships and the best intelligence in order to pursue the kidnappers."

Cade and Gabe glanced at each other. They were fast becoming educated in the politics of the age. Simply sitting at the dinner table with Jake Rendel and Cade's wife Lyssa never failed to be a learning experience.

The brothers knew that one of the Duke's primary concerns upon his return to Virginia would be to address the problem of the slaves he had inherited from his father. He had thought little of it until Andros became part of the family. Now, however, Jake Rendel had become familiar with the history and participants of the Clapham group; he had developed a personal interest in their philosophy and their answers to the dilemma he now faced.

When the Duke finished his speech, Gabe bustled around the house, making final preparations to leave for Falmouth. In time, Sir Phillip

Stapleton returned with a letter of introduction and orders to assist signed by the colonial undersecretary, Sir James Stephens.

"Should the information you acquire in Falmouth require further pursuit," Sir Phillip told Gabe, "Sir James recommends that you find the schooner *Venus* and Captain George Woodbine. If there is a connection between pirates and the kidnapping, he is most likely to be acquainted with those who might assist you. There is a sloop at your disposal at Wapping Stairs to take you to Falmouth."

Once Gabe made his way to Falmouth, he found Myles and Cedric easily at the Swans Nest Inn, toasting their good fortune and attempting to lure twin barmaids into a celebratory orgy. Gabe stowed his possessions in a storeroom behind the bar and prepared himself for a battle. He painted his face red and black in the tradition of the Creek warrior. Then he hid in the shadows outside the Swans Nest and settled in to watch, listen, and wait. Eventually, Myles stepped out to relieve himself. Gabe grabbed him in a chokehold and pulled him unconscious against the wall, where he tied a rag about his mouth and secured his hands and feet. He dragged him into the storeroom and waited again. It did not take long for Cedric to come searching for his partner. Gabe also bound and gagged him.

The scant light from the moon illumined Gabe's painted face. His bare muscled chest glistened as he loomed menacingly over the two men who lay quivering beneath him. He pulled his hunting knife from the loose trousers and ran his finger down the edge, drawing blood. "Make a noise," he challenged, flipping the razor-sharp knife skillfully in his hands. The two men's eyes bulged when he untied the gags.

"Where are the two you kidnapped in London?" he asked in a deep, gruff voice.

"Who are you?" Myles asked, his own voice trembling.

"Oh, God! It's a demon!" Cedric whispered, his eyes wide and white with fright, his breath loaded with the stench of alcohol and rotten teeth.

"I am your worst nightmare if you do not answer me quickly. I will begin here," he said as he caressed Cedric's nose with the tip of the knife as if tracing where it would cut.

"We *don't know* where they are!" he cried out.

"Who paid you to kidnap them?" Gabe asked.

"It was the biggest man I ever seed...taller'n you!" Cedric whimpered. "He was coal black." He cocked his head to the side and said, "He speech had a French sound, though I'd swear he was with a Spanish man."

"Hush, Cedric," Myles pleaded. "He said he would kill us if we told!"

"*I* will kill you if you do not," Gabe said, his tone chillingly calm. "You are two worthless lumps of clay and don't deserve to live. But, if you give me names and tell me where they are now, I will not kill you."

"They be already t'sea," Cedric whispered to Myles. "What good does it do not to tell?"

"Names," Gabe growled.

Myles gulped. "The big black man who was dressed in the garb of a sailor was called Caesar. Big gold earring in his ear. All we know is that he came ashore from a big schooner that had a mermaid with big tits on the bow and was flying a Spanish flag. He did the talking, but he was with a man who wore fancy clothes."

"That man was average size with dark hair and eyes," Cedric offered. "He looked Spanish. They went ta London ta show us who to kidnap. They paid us half up front. Caesar pointed ta the fancy man at the British Museum and told us ta bring him to the Wapping Stairs where a boat would be waiting for us ta bring him to Falmouth. The fancy man didn't go back ta the inn but went ta a tearoom in Covent Garden. Some damn fool boy got in the way. We had ta deal with him, and the noise brought the fancy man into the alley. We didn't know what ta do with the boy, so we handed him over as well. Caesar said they needed hands, and he'd make a sailor out of him."

"He give us a bonus for the boy," Myles reminisced with a toothless grin.

The boy. That would have been Joie.

Before Gabe realized what he was doing, he pulled back his fist and punched Myles. He heard the nose bone break, and Myles lay silent as Cedric's eyes got big. He drew himself up in a ball, pushing away from the man who looked like an enraged demon.

"Where are they taking them?" Gabe demanded.

"I don't know," Cedric said, whimpering. "Maybe it has something ta do with the map they kept talking about. The map they went ta search for at the inn whilst we kept an eye on the fancy man."

"What did they find at the inn?" Gabe pressed.

"Nuthin'. No notes, no papers, just his belongin's. Regular stuff, I heard them say. That's when they got so desperate to grab the man. Couldn't see as how that dandified gentl'mun could be so important, meself," Cedric chortled.

Gabe pulled back his fist and punched Cedric in the nose. Both ruffians were now unconscious, and Gabe rifled through their pockets. He found the gold and took it. He might need it in his search.

The next morning, dressed once again as an English gentleman, Gabe carried a duffle and a small satchel that held his letters of introduction down to the docks, looking for the ship *Venus* and Captain George Woodbine. The crew was provisioning the ship as Gabe approached. He threw his duffle bag over his shoulder and proceeded up the ramp, where he was stopped by the quartermaster.

"Is Captain Woodbine about?" Gabe inquired.

More supplies were headed up the ramp, so the mate tossed his head in the direction of the captain's quarters. Gabe nearly had to double over to enter the open door, where he stood waiting to be recognized. He had time to study the captain sitting at a large, dark-stained plank table that was currently covered with maps. There was no desk or dining table, so that table apparently served many purposes. The captain's accommodations were spare, providing necessities of fine quality but without luxury.

Woodbine was a man of middle age, his thinning hair combed to give the appearance of having more, and was of average height for an

Englishman, which was nearly a foot shorter than Gabe. He was clean-shaven and meticulously groomed in the red jacket of the Royal Marines with gold epaulets and buttons. A cabin boy knelt in the corner polishing boots. Silence fell among the officers with whom he was conversing, alerting the captain to Gabe's presence. Woodbine leaned back in his chair, lifting two legs off the ground. He eyed Gabe seriously as he twined his fingers together on the small paunch that the fine suit could not camouflage completely.

Gabe bowed gracefully, a product of long hours of instruction by a demanding tutor and the Dowager Duchess, and produced his papers. "I am Gabriel Kincaid. The Duke of Penbrooke is my brother's father-in-law."

Woodbine lifted an eyebrow, noting Gabe's copper skin and long black hair tied with a leather thong. He accepted the proffered papers and indicated that Gabe should sit while he perused them.

He soon dismissed the other men.

"Give me the short version, Mr. Kincaid," Woodbine barked.

"The Duke of Penbrooke, my brother Cade Kincaid, Sir Phillip Stapleton"—Gabe noted that Woodbine's eyebrows lifted at this name—"and I believe that Joie Kincaid, my sister, has been kidnapped along with a gentleman, Godfrey Lewis Winkel, who came to England to deliver a talk to the British Museum on the pirate, Captain Kidd. We also believe there may be a connection between their kidnapping and a map the man claimed to have. I followed their tracks to a sloop at Wapping Stairs and then to Falmouth, where I have learned they were taken aboard a ship. Sir James Stephens provided me with these letters in hopes that your understanding of such things might be of assistance. And that you might permit me to pursue my sister as a passenger upon your ship."

"Why do you believe they have left Falmouth?" Woodbine asked in his no-nonsense voice of command.

"I tracked their kidnappers, a pair of ne'er-do-wells by the name of Myles and Cedric, to a tavern frequented by pirates and fugitives. They admitted their involvement and gave me the name of one and the descriptions of two who seemed to be conducting the kidnapping."

Woodbine nodded and said, "Proceed."

"They described one as the biggest man they had ever seen. That man was coal black, went by the name of Caesar, and was dressed in the slops of a sailor. He wore a single huge gold earring in one ear."

Once again, Woodbine's eyebrows lifted. Reading the man's physical reactions Gabe realized that he knew something about the huge black man with the gold earring.

"The other man appeared slight with the look of a Spaniard, dressed as a gentleman in fine, expensive clothes. The ship on which they sailed had a bare-breasted mermaid on the helm and flew a Spanish flag."

"Well, sir. It sounds like your sister is caught up in a fine kettle of fish, if I do say so. There is one man that jumps out with that description. He is referred to as Black Caesar, but his real name is Henri Caesar. He led a slave revolt in Haiti before stealing a Spanish ship and becoming one of the most feared pirates in the Gulf of Mexico. I have heard he often associates with the pirate, Gasparilla, in the Tampa Bay area of Spanish Florida." Woodbine looked at Gabe and shook his head sympathetically. Then, seeing the dismay on Gabe's face, he added, "These men went to quite a bit of effort to come to England to capture your sister and Mr. Winkel. Have you any idea what might be worth such an effort?"

"Godfrey's lodgings were ransacked," Gabe explained. "Cedric said they did not find the item for which they were searching. Miss Sabrina Stapleton said that Godfrey's purpose in coming to England was to discuss a treasure map that he had discovered. She says he has written of many of the pirates in the Gulf and is known as somewhat of an expert. The map is what they sought, I would imagine. When they could not find it, they needed Godfrey, it would appear. I think my sister just happened to be in the wrong place at the wrong time."

"Forgive me for looking at you so curiously, Mr. Kincaid. You remind me very much of someone who recently visited England with

Colonel Edward Nicholls, who is a friend of mine. In fact, I delivered him to New Providence only a few months ago."

"Sir, I think you have performed admirably in restraining yourself in asking questions about me. I assumed that you are acquainted with the Colonies since I was recommended to you by the colonial under-secretary, Sir James Stephens. Let me tell you that I am Creek. My brother married the Duke of Penbrooke's daughter, Lyssa. My brother, our sister Joie, and I have a Creek mother of the Clan of the Wind."

Woodbine leaned forward with his hands folded on the table. "Tell me more of your interesting family, Mr. Kincaid," he said.

Woodbine indicated a bottle of wine, but Gabe shook his head. "The Duke, Jake Rendel, was then merely the son of a Virginia planter who chose to trade among the Choctaw and Creek and race his horses at a track in St. Stephens. He found out that he had inherited the title and lands and was desperately needed by the people living on those properties. The Creek War had been hard on us all, and he insisted that we accompany him to England."

Woodbine arched a brow with interest. He stood, however, and said, "I would like to continue this conversation, but at the moment I must check and make sure all is stored properly and get the *Venus* underway. This is my merchant ship, and I am its captain. My official title is Captain in the Corps of Colonial Marines, though I am not at the moment involved in *active* service. I have spent quite a bit of time among your people." He paused and looked at Gabe thoughtfully. "Yes, indeed," he said.

Woodbine lingered a moment and then prodded himself to proceed with his responsibilities. "As you know, aboard ship there are limited private accommodations. You are welcome to sail with us, but I am afraid a hammock with the sailors is all I can offer you."

"Sir, I am Creek. A hammock is luxury compared to some places I have slept."

Woodbine's personal servant had long ceased polishing boots to stare at the big man sitting with the captain. He jumped when the Woodbine commanded him to show Mr. Kincaid around.

"And what's your name?" Gabe asked, a bit amused at how the boy skittered around him to lead him to the quarterdeck.

"Trilby, sir," the young man replied with a gulp.

"You needn't be afraid, Trilby. I left my scalping knife back home."

The boy gawked and Gabe laughed.

"I'm just kidding," he assured him.

Trilby showed him where to stow his bag, demonstrated how to hang the hammock, and then taught him to roll it in the morning the required seven turns so that it would be snug enough to pass through the ring measure for storage along the bulwark nettings.

"Extra protection should we be attacked," the grinning boy told Gabe, who had commented on the number of hammocks pressed along the side of the ship.

"Tell me about yourself," Gabe said. It didn't take much to open that floodgate. Trilby was a chatterer. He told Gabe that his father had brought him to the ship's captain when he was six to train as a sailor. Vice Admiral Cochrane, commander-in-chief of the North American Station at the dock yard in Bermuda, had told Trilby that his own father, a Scottish peer, the Duke of Dundonald, had put him aboard a ship about the same age, and look at the heights he had achieved.

Trilby grinned at Gabe and said, "Perhaps someday I will also be an admiral."

By the time he left Gabe, the two of them were fast friends. "Wait till I tell the others that I now know a real live Indian!" the boy exclaimed as he hurried away.

Gabe supposed there was no way he could have kept it secret. The truth would have come out. His height, coppery skin, and hawk-nose features had reminded the captain of someone, though Gabe realized he had forgottento ask who. He would surely have an opportunity to do so at some time during their voyage.

Later, Trilby brought Gabe an invitation to sup with Captain Woodbine.

At supper they were joined by the quartermaster, first mate, and ship's surgeon. As it was early in the voyage and the stores were fresh and plentiful, the cook had prepared a delicious leg of lamb with mint jelly and potatoes and peas. Ale was offered, but Gabe requested boiled hot water to prepare the coffee he had brought with him (he had never developed a fondness for tea, despite the Dowager Duchess's efforts to adapt them all to the habits of their new English lifestyle). He had observed fewer stomach ailments in those who drank tea and coffee with the boiled water. After observing the foolishness of so many of their kin, he and Cade had made it their practice not to partake of anything alcoholic. A man needed to keep his wits about him.

After the meal, the other three men returned to their duties, but Woodbine indicated that Gabriel should remain.

The captain was in a mood to reminisce, assisted by a pipe and fine wine from his private stock. He leaned back in his chair and said, "I know you must wonder whom I meant when I said earlier that you remind me of someone."

Gabe nodded, glad that he had brought up the subject on his own.

"I told you earlier that my captain's commission is with the Corps of Colonial Marines. In August of 1814, I was among a group of British solders who were sent to aid and train our allies, Seminoles and Red Stick Creeks who had escaped the battle of Horseshoe Bend. I was serving under Colonel Edward Nicholls with a detached company of the Corps of Colonial Marines when I was ordered to build a fort on the Apalachicola River in East Florida as a refuge for Indians who looked to Britain to follow through on their promises after the War of 1812. Nicholls was by then an experienced leader, having already served in one hundred engagements with the enemy. Because England does not recognize slavery, there were many runaway slaves who also joined us. In fact, the Corps of Colonial Marines was originally raised by Vice-Admiral Sir Alexander Cochrane and was composed of former slaves. These men fought on the Atlantic and Gulf coasts in the War of 1812."

Gabe nodded, encouraging the captain to continue.

"We decided to build the fort on a strategic bluff on the Apalachicola River on a site where Forbes and Company was doing business with the Indians. It was then known as Prospect Bluff. There, our Corps of Colonial Marines, including Indians, free blacks, and escaped slaves, built an earthen parapet 125 feet in diameter, 15 feet high, and 18 feet thick. We dug a moat around it 14 feet wide and 4 feet deep with a palisade consisting of a double row of pine logs surrounding it. A 30-foot octagon-shaped powder magazine built of earth and logs sat in the center of the fort. I recall the dimensions well. With the river in front, a swamp in the rear, and a small stream to the south, that fort was as impregnable as I could possibly make it."

He shook his head, remembering. "It was hot as hell there on the Apalachicola River. My blood and sweat *truly* went into building that fort!"

Gabe was well acquainted with the Apalachicola River. In 1803, when he and his twin brother Cade were captured by Savannah Jack and William Augustus Bowles, they were taken to St. Marks. Through the single act of kindness and courage of one woman, Cade had managed to escape from the cage in which they were kept and get Gabe, unconscious, into a canoe, down the St. Marks River, across the Apalachicola Bay, and up the Apalachicola River, where they were rescued by High Head Jim probably quite near Prospect Bluff.

"Nicholls promised our Indian allies that the British would defend them and force adherence to Article Nine of the Treaty of Ghent signed 14 December 1814," Woodbine went on. "That article promised the restoration of Creek lands lost to the United States with the Treaty of Fort Jackson that had been signed by less than a handful of the Creek chiefs. Nicholls went further than that, however. He told the Creeks that should they *not* have their lands returned to them, the British would support an Indian state carved from East and West Florida. It was about then that I first met Josiah Francis." With these words, Woodbine looked about the small cabin and lowered his eyes with a sigh.

"I do have a relationship of sorts with Josiah Francis," Gabe said. "My mother was the granddaughter of Red Shoes. Red Shoes married the second daughter of James McQueen, whose first husband was a Shawnee, Young Rising Sun. They were the grandparents of Josiah

53

Francis's father, David Francis. Red Shoes, my great-grandfather, raised David Francis, I was told."

Woodbine had had many conversations with his Red Stick allies. He knew that Red Shoes of the Clan of the Wind, son of Choctaw chief Red Shoes and the Creek woman Sehoy, was related to many prominent Red Sticks, including William Weatherford. Weatherford had led the Red Sticks at the massacre at Fort Mims and, unfortunately, had later been one of the signers of the Treaty of Fort Jackson. Woodbine knew Weatherford well. The two of them had actually strategized the attack on Floyd's troops at Camp Defiance on January 27, 1814. Woodbine realized that the relationship with James McQueen's daughter gave Gabriel Kincaid a special relationship with the Red Stick Peter McQueen as well as Josiah Francis because he was a blood relative of both of their wives. Francis's wife Hannah was William Weatherford's half-sister, and Peter McQueen was married to Elizabeth McGillivray, William Weatherford and Hannah Francis's aunt. Captain Woodbine viewed these Red Sticks as his allies.

His hands tightened on the stem of his wine glass and his eyes narrowed speculatively. "We left William Hambly, an agent for John Forbes Company at his Apalachicola trading post, in charge of the fort that held at least two hundred. He had come to us assuring us of his loyalty. There was a longtime settlement of nearly five hundred free and runaway blacks who settled for more than fifty miles north and south of the fort. I found out later that Hambly was sending information on our moves to John Innerarity, his boss at Forbes Company, who operated out of the Pensacola office. Innerarity apparently passed information on to the Americans, though we thought he was on our side."

Gabe took note of the contempt in Woodbine's voice when he spoke of Hambly.

"For some reason, the Red Sticks pretty much left the fort to the blacks and joined some of the Seminole villages throughout the area. The Creek and Seminole have close ties, as you know."

It could have been the effects of the wine on Woodbine, but Gabe thought he detected a hint of eagerness in the way the captain leaned toward him.

"The Spanish, who are the legal rulers of East and West Florida, have been weakened by the wars of Napoleon and revolutions in their Central and South American holdings. It's to the point that they have no power to put teeth to American protests that the runaway slaves should be returned to their masters. When we originally came to Florida, the Spanish welcomed us in training Indians as allies because they felt the threat of United States expansion.

"Unfortunately, the British government, now also weakened by the wars with Napoleon and afraid to rock the boat with the tenuous peace over the border with Canada, has chosen not to support Nicholls's promises."

Gabe could hear Woodbine's contempt for the British. He steepled his fingers with his elbows propped on the table, determined to pay close attention to the captain's words. Gabe knew the danger of considering oneself an island apart from the swirling currents of politics. His family had done that for far too long and had suffered because of it.

Woodbine took another sip of wine, cleared his throat, and continued. "The Americans insist that the treaty Andrew Jackson forced the Creek chiefs to sign at Fort Jackson justifies their claim to lands that actually belong to the Creeks, at least according to Article IX of the Treaty of Ghent. And while the Spanish would actually love to have an Indian buffer state between them and the Americans, they are now toothless tigers with filibusters, freebooters, and pirates running rampant through their holdings in the Caribbean, Latin America, and East and West Florida."

Woodbine sounded frustrated, and Gabe couldn't blame him.

"I sailed with Nicholls when he brought Francis as spokesman for the Creeks to plead his cause before the Regent. The Regent made Francis a brigadier general in the British army and gave him a splendid uniform, 325 pounds, a gold-mounted tomahawk, and a snuffbox set with diamonds."

Woodbine shifted his eyes from Gabe and took another swallow of wine. His face had reddened—from the wine, Gabe supposed. Or was it discomfort?

"He considered me a friend," Woodbine said.

"Considered?" Gabe asked. "Is Josiah Francis dead?"

Woodbine shook his head with tears in his eyes. "He lives as far as I know." Then his voice took on a morose tone. "In July of 1816, Hambly turned traitor to the men at Prospect Bluff, though the inhabitants of the fort had suspected him and cast him out. He then led the Americans in a barrage of the fort—by then called the Negro Fort. A lucky hot shot struck the powder magazine in which we had left 300 stands of muskets, ammunition, and other ordinance. The blast was felt all the way to Pensacola, and all 100 men and 200 women and children were killed. A handful were captured and executed. Only a few escaped to Chief Bowlegs on the Suwannee. Slave raiding ensued, and most were returned to slavery."

He shook his head in disgust and, opening a drawer in the side of the table, pulled out a newspaper article that he slid toward Gabe. "Edward Nicholls sent me this copy of the Savannah *Journal* containing an article about the Negro Fort prior to its destruction."

Gabe took the paper and read silently,

It was not to be expected, that an establishment so pernicious to the Southern States, holding out to a part of their population temptations to insubordination, would have been suffered to exist after the close of the war. In the course of last winter, several slaves from this neighborhood fled to that fort; others have lately gone from Tennessee and the Mississippi Territory. How long shall this evil, requiring immediate remedy, be permitted to exist?

"Of course, articles like that caught Andrew Jackson's attention," Woodbine said when Gabe looked up, "and it was he who ordered Brigadier General Edmund Pendleton Gaines to send forces to destroy the fort."

Woodbine closed his eyes, remembering the men with whom he had toiled and sweated in the sweltering heat of the semi-tropical environment. They had worked together to build the fort fifteen miles above the mouth of the Apalachicola and sixty miles below United States territory on a strategic bluff at the bend of the river—a British promise of security.

Now maudlin in his cups, Woodbine went on speaking of those he could see as they appeared in his memory. "Garcon, whom we had left as sergeant major and commandant of the fort, was thirty years old—a carpenter and former slave of Don Antonio Montero. He followed me and Nicholls from Pensacola. The British had been invited by the Creek Indians there to defend Pensacola from the Americans. Miraculously, Garcon survived the explosion at the fort along with a Choctaw chief, but they were executed immediately when captured.

"Unless they were in the village behind the fort, Tom and twenty-three-year-old Augustine, Billy and Lally and their children—Cressy, Flora, Beck, Cynthia, Nero, Congo Tom, Carlos Congo, and Carlos Mayumba—are all dead."

Woodbine chuckled through his tears. "Lally made the best gumbo I have ever tasted! She also made these little balls of fried bread she called hushpuppies. She tossed a few to the dogs that yapped at the door and shouted 'Hush! Puppy!' I laughed so hard as they tumbled over each other that all the children were rolling on the floor, laughing at me laughing!"

He paused a moment and wiped his eyes.

"Harry was a caulker and navigator who could also read and write. He had a baby son. Ambrosio, the shoemaker, made me these boots to show his appreciation. They were carpenters, coopers, ironsmiths, bakers, servants, masons, and cooks. They worked along with me building that damned fort—their home built on sand, it so happened—that represented their dream of freedom. Their dream for their children. They'd worked so hard to build it so that husbands and wives could grow old together, and so their children would not be sold away from them but could play and grow in the community of friends and family—safe.

"The blast was so devastating that the forty who had survived did not live long," he said, staring into space. Each face was forever ingrained into his memory.

After a long pause during which he struggled to restore his composure, Woodbine said, "Abraham, who followed us from Pensacola, survived and made his way to Bowlegs Town on the Suwannee River. There is a Scots trader there, Alexander Arbuthnot, who writes to me." He poured himself another glass of wine.

With his eyes swimming, Woodbine leaned forward and struck the table forcefully, nearly upsetting his goblet. "I had recruited among the blacks at Angola on the Manatee River at Tampa Bay, the largest settlement of free blacks and runaway slaves in Florida, for the Corps of Royal Marines. Some settled at the fort at Prospect Bluff *at my urging*. Many of those who trusted me died there!" He shook his head, despairing of the fact that it was he who had basically led them to their deaths.

"The Spanish are weak. The Americans are spread thin. Unfortunately, there is also unrest in England with the famine and food riots, so the government has lost its heart for conflict in America. Still, a force could land at Tampa Bay. Joined by the forces from Angola and across the state, we could establish a truly free colony."

Realizing he had said too much, Woodbine pushed his wine glass away and dismissed Gabe, saying, "Morning comes early. It's time to call it a night."

It would never do for anyone to think he was driven by something more than profit. That was what motivated men. Profit—and power.

Gabe looked at the captain and sensed his struggle. Woodbine was more than he seemed. A soldier of fortune with empire in his blood? Perhaps. But there was more. Much more. He had not seemed surprised that a letter might come to him from Sir James Stephens. Interesting.

Though the captain's past intrigued him, what Gabe wanted above all was to find Joie and take her home safely. He felt the tides of world events swirling about them and longed to get them all back to a place where they felt secure.

Chapter 5

She knew she wasn't who he said she was. But who was she, and why was she dressed in men's clothing? And who was this young man named Godfrey who spoke to her so tenderly, telling her to take it easy and please remember to pretend that she was a he? Was she some sort of simpleton? Why could she not remember who she was? Why did Godfrey seem so familiar? And, perhaps most important, why did she instinctively trust him?

Joie heard a collective gasp from the pirates, and in spite of her pounding head and Godfrey's insistence that she remain below decks, she could not resist stepping out into the sunlight. The rough assortment of pirates, all sizes, ages, and ethnicities, stood gawking up at the mainmast, where a man was clinging to the shroud by his fingers and toes. He was attempting to scramble up the outside angle in order to gain the top platform. Joie felt dizzy as she watched the tiny figure so far up the mast thrust an arm between the topmast and the halyards and stand on the cap. There the figure gripped the mast with both arms as if his very life depended on it. Indeed, it did. Joie's head swam as the ship swayed and rolled, pitched and heaved.

The man pointed and yelled something that got caught on the wind.

They all shook their heads and muttered, "Did ye hear that?"

"Probly beggin' somun to come git him down!"

They all laughed.

Where was her benefactor? His red, curly head was nowhere to be found. She chanced another look at the shirtless man dangling from the topmast. He had reddish-blond hair. She shook her head in disbelief. Surely that was not Godfrey, the scholarly man who had set himself up as her protector.

By this point, he was dangling from the mainmast. Her heart lurched. Somehow she knew this was not the kind of thing Godfrey ordinarily did. A man who wore a canary-yellow waistcoat did not climb to the top of a mainmast on a schooner at sea.

The men nodded as one in approval. "He's coming down the backstays," one whispered, as if that were a good thing.

Joie watched as Godfrey crossed his legs over the stay and let himself down hand over hand. Her heart pounded and her head still swam, but she could not tear her eyes from the man swaying above her in his descent from the top of the mast. And then he started to slip down the tarred rope. He wound the rope around his arm and Joie could almost feel the rope burn, but his speed was too fast. Before he could lose his grip, she dived toward the pile of tattered sail being mended on the main deck and rolled the canvas to the point where he dropped, landing with a thump and a groan. She was sure her actions saved him from a severe injury.

She didn't notice that her cap now lay on the deck. Her long black hair hung in waves down her back and lifted about her like Medusa's in the wind. Her azure eyes, startling against her dusky skin, glittered beneath her thick lashes.

Before she could help herself, she started shouting at him. "God damn it all to hell and back. What kind of a son of a bitch, jackass, pen-pushing, waistcoat-wearing fool would do a damn thing like climb up the top mast of a sailing ship?"

All the pirates looked at each other and then at Joie. "He's a she," one said.

"And a beauty she be," said another, smacking his lips.

"Sounds like me old wife," said Black Bart with nostalgia.

"Ye have a wife?" asked Dirty Dick in surprise.

Black Bart drew a finger across his throat. "She gives the Devil hell these days," he said with a chuckle, showing his gap-toothed smile and blackened gums.

The atmosphere changed suddenly. Men long deprived of female companionship focused their lustful attentions on the single woman upon their deck. Joie felt like the lone chicken in a pack of foxes sizing up what they should have for dinner. As one foul-smelling pirate leapt for her, Joie did a back flip and wound up beside Black Augustus, a black-haired, shaggy-bearded man, one of Gasparilla's right-hand men, who was now divested of his cutlass, a weapon Joie currently wielded with apparent skill. She stood over Godfrey, who struggled to stand from where he lay on the canvas pile, gaping up at her in astonishment. He still gasped for breath.

"Where did you learn that?" Godfrey finally managed to ask.

Joie swallowed hard as she watched this young man, her protector, get slowly to his feet. Apparently, she had been recovering down below for some time, as Godfrey now looked less like a decorated scholar than a true seaman. His red hair had bleached in the sun, and muscles rippled under his tanned skin.

Joie shrugged and shook her head, surprised at her actions—and reactions.

"Ye knew she be female?" Diego growled.

Dear God. They all looked ready to pounce. Godfrey knew he needed to act quickly. What would Caleb Connory do? With as much savoir-faire as he could muster after his speedy descent and harrowing fall, he stomped over to her and declared, "She is my wife!"

And then he pulled her to him, planting his lips firmly on hers and staking his claim.

Joie was so surprised that she forgot to move, and then she found she didn't want to move. By then, they both forgot they were playing a role. His tongue teased her lips, and instinctively she opened to him. His tongue touched her own, and then his mouth opened over hers for a kiss more intimate than she had ever thought possible. He lifted her, and her legs wrapped tightly around him. The cutlass clattered to the deck. When the hoots of the pirates finally registered and Godfrey allowed her to slide gently back to her own feet, for a moment they looked at each other with something akin to shock.

His wife? This was definitely not familiar! Joie clung to him, realizing that her legs barely supported her.

Godfrey, finding it hard to breathe, pulled her tight against him and tucked her under his arm.

"Mebbe I shoulda tried that to shut her up," muttered Black Bart.

Godfrey took a deep breath and willed his heart to stop racing. "I did not know if pirates respected the sanctity of marriage," he said. "But that was before I heard our captain's brother speak of his dear wife Ramona."

Godfrey smiled at Leon Gaspar. Was he laying it on too thick?

"And since I have now become a pirate myself, passing your test," he continued, inclining his head toward the mast he'd just climbed, "indeed, we are now all brothers. Is that not so?"

The pirates looked at each other. Brothers? They'd as soon knife each other as the enemy. But then, they'd knife their own blood brothers just as easily, so some actually nodded. Godfrey *had* been quite entertaining the past two weeks as he had challenged them all to teach him what they knew so he could become one of them. A pirate! Like those he'd made so famous in his articles. Perhaps he would write of them in those articles and make *them* famous. Like Captain Kidd...and Blackbeard...and Jack Rackham.

Gasparilla had gone along with it because Godfrey had convinced him that he would be a better biographer if he experienced just a little of what the great and glorious Gasparilla had experienced. An "if you cannot beat them, join them" philosophy. A strategy to buy them time. And in the meantime, it had distracted them all from the "boy" recuperating in the cabin.

Godfrey looked to Gaspar and then to Black Caesar. Were they buying it?

"Oh! And by the way...ship ahoy!" he added, gesturing to the east, where a ship that he had spotted while in the crow's nest approached on the horizon.

Suddenly galvanized, the mass of men met the challenge of their experience and assumed battle posts, just in case this ship proved to be a worthy target. Pirates lived for the moment a potential prize might wander into range. Many of these men had served various European navies during the Napoleonic Wars. Peace had produced a surfeit of sailors who had to find another way to make a living. What was a pirate but a sailor with no (or very selective) national loyalty?

Some had been privateers on ships, holding letters of marque from one country that made them representatives who could attack that country's enemy and confiscate the goods and ships. Privateers were allowed to share in the booty. Pirates, on the other hand, had to share with no one. The booty was split between the crew.

So now, in a world not officially at war, unemployed sailors were free to pillage at will. Today they flew a Spanish flag. They had others to fly should the need arise.

Gasparilla sent his fleetest climber to the top of the mast. Godfrey thanked God that he hadn't called him to make that climb again.

"Spanish!" the climber yelled.

Gasparilla smiled. Though he was Spanish and had himself once been a darling of the Spanish navy, Spain was now his favored target. That was a story he had promised to tell Godfrey. But for now, his crew knew the drill and was in the process of drawing closer to the supposedly friendly ship. Rodriguez, the master gunner, called for readying the cannons and ordered the powder monkeys to position the powder and cannon balls. Black Caesar armed himself with daggers, a cutlass, and six loaded pistols.

As they closed in, all the pirates sent winning smiles toward the sailors on the other vessel. Their captain hailed the pirate ship and requested permission to board.

Gasparailla ordered the ship to heave to, and then he gave the signal to fire the cannon. Now that the ships were barely three feet apart in the light sea, Black Caesar shouted, "Aboard ye maties!" and leapt onto the Spanish ship, where a melee was soon underway on the deck.

Barely able to see with the smoke from the cannon and the gunfire, Godfrey knew he must follow. His loyalty was being tested. He grabbed at a rope, imitating the others, and swung out over the separation between the boats. Unfortunately, he did not have enough play on the rope and for a moment dangled above the sea in trouble. Suddenly, another pirate came swinging behind him on another rope and gave him a push that took him onto the other deck, where he landed with an inelegant roll. When he turned to thank the man who gave him the timely push, he saw Joie release the rope and land near him. He reached out and thrust her behind him. Back to back they stood, cutlasses ready, pistols cocked.

"You fool!" he said. "You were to stay on deck."

"Yeah, and watch you fall off the damned rope and get crushed between the ships!" she cried over the din.

He knocked a cutlass from an attacker's hand.

"I'm not—"

"I know. You're no more a pirate than I'm a parrot! And a wife does not let her husband go into a dangerous place like this without her protection!"

Wife! She really thought she was his wife!

"Protection! A man is supposed to protect his woman," Godfrey countered. He parried a cutlass, and with a thrust he disabled his attacker—though not with a death wound, Godfrey was grateful to see. Balanced and waiting, he pushed Joie behind him once again with the gunwale of the ship at her back.

"His woman!" Joie jumped around him and kicked at a strategic spot on the attacker who appeared through the cloud of smoke. The sailor went sprawling in pain onto the deck. Godfrey now stood at her side with a dagger in one hand and the cutlass in the other. He was, without a doubt, the handsomest pirate she had ever seen.

Legs apart, tossing the cutlass from one hand to the other while scanning the smoke surrounding them, alert and ready, she looked at Godfrey and said, "What the hell did you think I was going to do? Stand there on the deck while you danced into danger? Twiddle my thumbs and wait to see you in pieces on the deck here? What kind of ninny did you think you married?"

"But I didn't—" Godfrey stopped, noticing that the smoke had lifted. For some reason, the action had ceased. And once again he and Joie were the center of attention.

"Kiss her and shut her up!" commanded Gasparilla. "This battle is over. The captain of this ship is an old friend, and he has surrendered the ship."

The captain looked none too happy about the reunion.

"José," a voice called out from the sailors guarded by Gasparilla's men. Gasparilla looked toward them. "Soy yo! Su cuñado!"

"¿Es Gomez?" Gasparilla shouted, sounding overwhelmed at hearing that voice from his past. "¿De dónde es usted?"

"Estoy aquí, José," Gomez said. "I am here." The two men embraced, crying.

"¿Mi hermana?" Gasparilla whispered.

"She is dead," Gomez told him. "My beloved, your sister, died trying to give me a son. He was too young. She was too old. Your sister is gone. We now have no one left in Spain. I was forced into Napoleon's service and wound up here upon this ship from hell."

The two men held one another in their grief.

"What is the cargo of this ship?" Gasparilla asked.

"The hold is filled with slaves."

"The British have forced Spain to agree to end the slave trade within three years," Gasparvilla said gleefully. "These will bring us top dollar!"

The smell of the ship would have told the cargo. Cries for help lifted to the deck in a language they could not translate but also could not misinterpret. Babies' cries. Children's high-pitched pleas. Deep male and desperate female voices. Joie looked at Godfrey, and he knew her desire to rush to their aid. It was killing her to stand there helpless on the deck.

Gasparvilla's men cheered at their good fortune.

But Joie and Godfrey watched Black Caesar. Though his countenance did not change, his eyes glittered, and Godfrey sensed his inner turmoil. The man reminded him of a cobra ready to strike.

Godfrey reached out and grabbed Joie's arm before she could do something impulsive. He knew her. Though her memory had not returned, her spirit had. Her first instinct would be to charge into the hold and unchain every poor soul in there. And she would be killed without a moment's thought by Gasparilla.

"We're prisoners as well. Don't forget it!" he hissed, holding her tightly.

He looked up and found Black Caesar watching their every move. He, apparently, could sense Joie's determination to free the human beings chained in their own filth below them. Her tear-filled eyes looked into Caesar's, and Godfrey could have sworn there was a private communication between them.

"You men have the choice of joining me and my crew, or you may take your chance in that rowboat," Gasparilla announced to the defeated sailors. Most chose the pirate life over certain death in the thimble of a boat on the vast sea. Amazingly, a handful of men did settle in the rowboat, taking their chances with nature or a passing boat rather than a pirate ship.

Gasparilla divided his crew. Part of the crew of the prize ship joined them on the *Floridablanca*. (Curiously, Gaspar referred to whatever ship he sailed as the *Floridablanca*, the name of his greatest enemy, a fact Godfrey discovered when he asked Caesar why he kept calling the *Mary Rose*, on which they sailed, *Floridablanca*.) He left a pirate named Roderigo in charge of half of his men so they could man the prize. They would take the slave ship to the nearest port to sell and dispose of the cargo as quickly as possible. That port would be Amelia Island, recently taken from the Spanish in East Florida by the adventurer Sir Gregor MacGregor. The United States had passed a law prohibiting the importation of slaves, but that only made Gasparilla's prize cargo more valuable. MacGregor had the connections to smuggle the valuable slaves into Georgia through nearby Amelia Island.

Perhaps the battle had taken longer than Godfrey realized. While the drama of determining who would stay and who would go took place on the deck, Joie paled and started to weave where she stood. Godfrey believed it was the thought of the poor unfortunates below deck. Perhaps the odor. But when her eyes rolled back in her head and she buckled unconscious onto the deck, Godfrey feared there was something more serious at play. He lifted her and called her name. Black Caesar seized a rope dangling from the yardarm and grabbed Joie from Godfrey, swinging her back with him to the deck of their ship.

Godfrey jumped for the rope when it came back his way, and this time he made a successful landing. By then, Black Caesar had returned Joie to the cabin and stood sentry until Godfrey arrived. Something inexplicable had happened aboard the captured ship. They had acquired an ally.

Hours passed, and Joie did not awaken. Lying there on the cot, she held her aching head and moaned. Tears slipped down her cheeks in her sleep. Godfrey worried. He had thought her memory loss would make her docile. But as she recovered her strength, she also recovered her strong spirit. What they had seen on the slave ship had taken her beyond her strength, and she seemed to be having a relapse. Now she was soul sick at a situation she was helpless to fix.

Godfrey sighed with frustration, knowing how headstrong and determined Joie could be. He cringed at the memory of her holding her own with the cutlass in the middle of a pirate attack. The two of them had *fought* alongside the *pirates*! Those were words he'd never thought to put in a sentence about himself: fighting and pirates! Add *Joie* to those words, and it was even more amazing. He, Godfrey Lewis Winkel, had fought alongside bloodthirsty pirates and Joie Kincaid. He shut his eyes, and the image grew even more vivid—and more frightening.

Gasparilla summoned Godfrey to dine with him that evening. Joie was still sleeping when he left. Godfrey made a point of sitting where he could watch the door to their cabin. All four men were well into their cups. Several empty wine bottles lay on the table.

Gasparilla introduced him to his brother-in-law, Juan Gomez, and his friend and fellow graduate of the Spanish Naval Academy, Menendez, captain of the captured slave ship. Gasparilla gave this man no other name. Godfrey had already become acquainted with Gaspar's brother Leon, who dwelt endlessly on the charms of his wife Ramona.

After the introductions, Gasparilla narrowed his eyes at Godfrey. "Tell us how this Amazon you say is your wife was captured in the garb of a stable boy," he demanded.

67

Godfrey gazed at his folded hands. Lord help me, he thought. What reason could possibly make sense? Stay as close to the truth as possible, he reminded himself.

"I was seeing another woman at a tea shop. A woman who had written me, admiring my work. Joie suspected something and followed me."

Another woman. Jealous wife. That they understood.

"Why was there no women's clothing in your room at the inn?" Gaspar asked.

"I thought she was still in the country visiting her friends," Godfrey responded. His hands were sweating, and he only hoped he had schooled his visage and looked convincing. "My wife is…unpredictable, shall we say? I could not believe it when I saw her face pressed against the window there at Rules. I rushed out to confront her and assure her that the woman was merely a fan of my writing."

That brought a knowing chuckle and a slap on the back.

"Anyway, that was when your two…representatives…captured us."

Gaspar and Gomez smiled appreciatively.

"Women can be trying," Gaspar said. He took a sip of wine and leaned back in his chair. "You may take notes for my biography tonight," he commanded, glancing at Menendez to make sure he heard that he, José Gaspar, had a biographer to record his grand and glorious deeds.

Gaspar nodded toward the paper, quill, and ink located close by. Godfrey reached for them. It was better, he supposed, that Gaspar was unaware that Godfrey did not need paper and ink for recall. He would remember everything said and done as well as every detail of their surroundings. When Gaspar began to dictate the details of his life, though, Godfrey wrote.

"I was born José Gaspar near Seville, Spain, in 1756. A young woman with whom I was caught in a dalliance"—here he threw Godfrey, who happened to glance up from the paper, a wink—"claimed that I had made unwanted advances toward her. It was a lie, of course. No woman has ever been unwilling."

He looked at his friends as if awaiting a challenge. None of them were so foolish. Gaspar tossed a charming smile, his perfect teeth gleaming, toward Godfrey who, by his own recent admission, was expected to understand such things. Godfrey could easily believe that this charming, handsome man with his thick, once black mane of hair, expressive chocolate eyes, and deep sensuous voice could very well have set many a woman's heart aflame.

"My father sent me away to the Naval Academy," Gaspar went on. "It was there I met Menendez. ¡Que conocía a muchas mujeres! ¿No es así mi amigo?" He nudged his friend, who nodded and managed a smile in remembrance.

Gaspar then looked back at Godfrey, whom he thought did not know Spanish, and said, "Many women. We knew many women. I found my calling in the navy and rose quickly in the ranks." He looked to Menendez for confirmation.

Menendez nodded. "There was no better naval officer than Gaspar," he confirmed. "A skilled tactician and a born leader." It appeared that Menendez admired Gaspar, but Godfrey sensed that he did not approve of him.

Gaspar laid his hand upon that of his old friend and squeezed. The candle sputtered, casting a sudden shadow. Gaspar lit another so Godfrey could see to write.

"Wine?" he asked Godfrey.

Godfrey shook his head. Gaspar filled his own glass and leaned back, remembering.

"I was twenty-seven years old, already an admiral serving as a naval attaché in the court of Charles IV. By this time I had married my beautiful Rosa, and we had a son. But the court of King Charles was a web of intrigue. Manuel Godoy was jealous of my success and my relationship with King Charles and his wife Mary Louisa. Mary Louisa was not a woman who would be denied." Gaspar smiled once more.

"She wanted *me* as a lover, but Godoy wanted her. To get her, he had to get rid of me. A furor arose while I was in the queen's chambers, and before I knew it I heard someone yelling that I had stolen the crown jewels. I escaped through a secret exit and rushed out of town and back to my mother's home, where Rosa and my son were staying. I was followed. My son ran into the house yelling that soldiers were coming. My Rosa kissed me and pushed me out the back door. Somehow I managed to evade Godoy's men and hid in the bushes behind the house. Godoy ordered my mother's home burned." Here he paused, and Godfrey was surprised to see tears rolling down the pirate's face.

"I heard the cries of my Rosa, my son, and my mother, but I knew they feared I would return to save them and Godoy would capture me as well. I could only hide and listen." His hand shook as he lifted the wine glass to his lips. "I assumed many disguises and eluded Godoy as I made my way to Cadiz. I made a pretty convincing whore," he said, forcing a laugh, a poor attempt at covering his emotion. Gomez chuckled obligingly.

"I rounded up a crew in bares along the way and commandeered Godoy's pride of the Spanish navy, the *Floridablanca*, and headed toward the Americas. I then began my war with Spain."

Gaspar took time to refill his wine glass and to top off those of Leon, Menendez, and Gomez. Godfrey was busy scribbling away to please his host.

"Since then, I have captured many Spanish ships. Over 400. The country of my birth has enriched me many times over. Had they not betrayed me, my loyalty and those riches would have been theirs. My fortune lies buried, and one day I will retire to live off of those riches."

Godfrey could see that Gasparilla was driven not by wealth but by revenge, though the wealth was a measure of how effective his revenge had been. Gaspar was a complex man.

"I have taken their women," he said. "Dark-haired, dark-eyed beauties."

"Like Sheba?" Gomez chuckled knowingly, trying to lift Gaspar's maudlin mood.

Godfrey caught a glimpse of Black Caesar in the hall. At the mention of Sheba, he stilled and flinched.

Gaspar smiled and continued, "Sunny-haired women with sky eyes." Then he hunched over his wine glass. "But none have been able to replace my Rosa."

Gomez was his only friend in the world who shared the memory of Rosa with Gaspar and his brother Leon. That made him a treasured friend to Gaspar.

"She was beautiful inside and out, my friend," Gomez said. "She is irreplaceable. As was my Angelina." The two men embraced.

The emotion returned to Gaspar's eyes. "My son never had a chance to experience life. They took everything from me, and I have taken everything I could from them." It was painful to watch him still grieving for the family forty years gone.

Gaspar leaned forward and whispered, "I sent a man to assassinate Godoy. Perhaps he will succeed."

Then he lifted his hand and flapped it at Godfrey. "Enough for tonight," he said. "I am tired. Gomez, take Menendez with you to the hammocks. Watch him. He would take a knife to me if he could," he said, patting Menendez on the shoulder. "I do not want to have to kill him."

At last Godfrey could return to Joie. It was cold in the cabin, and she was shivering. He touched her cheek lightly and was surprised to find her skin hot to the touch. Worried, he lifted her and had her take a sip of the hot tea, sweetened with the captain's precious store of sugar, that had mysteriously appeared in their cabin. He suspected Black Caesar had procured it. She barely woke to drink, but still she drank thirstily. Her eyes were bloodshot and her skin flushed.

Godfrey had never been a praying man, but kneeling there beside her it seemed appropriate. "Please, God. Give me the strength and wits to get Joie out of this mess safely."

He covered her with a blanket and his fine wool double-breasted tailcoat. Then he made a pillow from an extra shirt and lay on the hard wooden floor so that he blocked the door. It took a while, but sleep finally came to him with the rocking of the boat.

Chapter 6

Joie was truly ill. Godfrey had to play the part of a pirate rogue during the day and an admiring biographer of Gasparilla at night, mastering swordplay and seamanship to impress their captor. All the while, he would rush back to the cabin to tend her as frequently as he could without calling attention to her illness. It was typhus, he had no doubt.

There was seldom a moment of peace and quiet with bells ringing every half hour to regulate the sailors' watch and a pirate crew that constantly shouted, sang, fought, farted and belched competitively, cursed, and laughed. They were a rough lot. Using abject humility and admiration as his tool, Godfrey learned to navigate the personalities of those aboard the ship. As a result, he learned to tie knots from the Portuguese Black Augustus, who was perhaps the cruelest of Gaspar's crew, so named because of his bushy black beard. Augustus informed him he needed to "know the ropes." So he taught Godfrey a variety of sailors' knots…and how to use a garotte, though with the latter came fond tales of remembered victims that Godfrey would just as soon never have heard.

It was from Leon, Gaspar's brother, that he learned to climb the mast so that he didn't end up crashing onto the deck. Godfrey found a bit of a masochist in Leon because he seemed to think it amusing to see Godfrey tiptoe across the mast and climb the netting into the crow's nest. Especially in a brisk wind. The brothers shared a ghoulish sense of humor.

One afternoon, Arturo de Mirada handed him a cutlass, and Godfrey knew he would either learn to use it or die. His lessons with boxing champ Jack Randal did him little good. He discovered that the desire to live was a powerful motivator for learning a new skill. It became great entertainment for the men to find out who was teaching Godfrey what each day, and a crowd would gather.

After the humiliating beginning of his voice change several years before, Godfrey had to admit that the sin of pride was upon him now regarding the wondrous timbre of his fine baritone voice. So, when taking a break from Black Augustus and the cutlass, he asked Black Bart to teach him one of the shanties they sang. He decided to sing out, much to the delight of the crowd that had already gathered to watch him bleed as the result of Miranda's tutelage. Perhaps the song might at least distract them long enough for him to catch his breath. Singing aboard the ship was the sailors' favorite entertainment, though Godfrey had never participated.

Black Bart started, and Godfrey soon joined in, picking up the melody easily.

Oh, a little swig of gin wouldn't do us any harm,
Oh, a little swig of gin wouldn't do us any harm,
Oh, a little swig of gin wouldn't do us any harm,
An' we'll all hang on behind!

So we'll ro-o-oll the old chariot along!
An' we'll roll the golden chariot along!
So we'll ro-o-oll the old chariot along!
An' we'll all hang on behind!

Black Bart picked up his hornpipe and started playing.

Oh, a plate of Irish stew wouldn't do us any harm,
Oh, a plate of Irish stew wouldn't do us any harm,
Oh, a plate of Irish stew wouldn't do us any harm,
An' we'll all hang on behind!

Cook, in his apron with his pipe hanging from his lips, and Diego, the beefy carpenter with his beard braided in three braids with one long braid down his back, danced a jig.

73

So we'll ro-o-oll the old chariot along!
An' we'll roll the golden chariot along!
So we'll ro-o-oll the old chariot along!
An' we'll all hang on behind!

Several verses later, Godfrey was their new best friend. Fortunately, he discovered he knew many songs acquired from his visits aboard ships with his grandfather, and the party continued into the night. Black Caesar would occasionally disappear into the hold to check on Joie and would reappear to nod that all was well, and Godfrey could continue with the merry making. By the end of the evening, he was the recipient of numerous black-toothed or gap-toothed, hogs' breath smiles. Black Bart rewarded him with a bear hug that nearly knocked Godfrey out with the godawful odor from under his armpits.

He knew they'd just as soon gut him.

Back in his cabin, it seemed that Godfrey had just closed his eyes for a moment when Black Augustus yelled down that Gaspar requested Godfrey's presence on deck. The ship cut through the cobalt waves in the crisp, sun-washed day. Gaspar stood at the bulwark, one with the ship, his long, silver-streaked hair blowing in the wind and his legs bent, catching the sea spray as he rode the waves through the pass into the harbor. Waves curled and crashed in rows of foam against the white-sand beach ahead of them on the east coast of Amelia Island. Godfrey shivered as he went to stand on the deck beside Gaspar. It was much colder than he'd imagined Florida could be in early September.

While Godfrey waited for Gaspar to speak, his mind wandered to the porpoises that had been attracted to the ship. They frolicked about the protruding breasts of the crimson-nippled mermaid figurehead, making Godfrey smile. They gamboled in the foam of the windswept sound like sailors on shore leave. Godfrey envied their freedom. Life living life. He took a deep breath and for a moment forgot his own fears and simply relished being alive.

Then Gaspar spoke. "Those slaves will make this a very profitable voyage," he gloated.

Godfrey's moment crashed like a wave against a rock.

It seemed incredible that in the midst of the beauty and joie de vivre about them, a slave ship sailed into Fernandina Harbor with a cargo of human beings stolen from *their* lives to become notations in a ledger...human capital. Right before Joie had collapsed on the slave ship, there had been a baby's cry. It sounded as if it could have been the child's *first* cry. Godfrey had actually thought Joie had fainted in response to that cry. It had obviously registered because now, in her delirium and burning with fever, Joie often struggled with him to get out of the bed and go save the baby. "I must find the baby," she'd sob. "Help me find the baby!" It broke his heart. She would have rushed into hell to save those people without a second thought.

He simply could not focus on what Gaspar was saying! His thoughts were never far from the woman in his bed below.

He thought about her symptoms. Because of the famine, many Welsh and Irish had come to London, and soon the epidemic began. They called typhus the "Irish disease." Godfrey had heard that as many as one in every fourteen people had died of it that year in London. For most of the time before coming to London, Joie had lived on the Duke's estate. But, since the incubation period was from one to two weeks, she could have been exposed right before getting kidnapped, or perhaps it was caused by something in the hold where they were kept.

Godfrey quickly recognized the symptoms—the rapidly spreading rash; pain in the abdomen, joints, back, and head; a high fever, perhaps lasting up to two weeks; a dry, hacking cough; nausea; and vomiting. Godfrey was now nearly as familiar with her body as he was his own, having bathed her frequently with cool water to try to keep the fever down. Fortunately, Joie was quiet with her suffering. He had no doubt that Gasparilla would toss her overboard if he suspected that she might harbor some infectious disease. It was their good fortune that Gaspar was distracted by Gomez and Menendez and seemed to have forgotten about Joie.

Godfrey learned much about Joie's life since leaving Creek Country through her mumbled ramblings. The lonely orphan girl had escaped the rigors of the tutors hired by the Dowager Duchess to find friends in the gypsy caravan encamped on the Duke's estate in Cornwall. It was there she'd learned swordplay, how to throw a knife, how to do back flips on the back of a galloping white Arabian (that had caused him to go weak in the knees just thinking about it), and how to dance with many veils.

But his heart broke over the tears of a little girl who longed for the mother who'd died giving her life and the love of the father who rejected her and abused her. She appeared to relive these events in her delirium. He knew she only wanted to belong somewhere with someone. And he, the arrogant Godfrey Lewis Winkel, appeared in her dreams to once again torment the little girl whose love and loyalty would not let her leave a burning fort and ravaging Red Sticks without her baby brother. That brave little girl had insisted on saving his own worthless hide.

Her heart had been broken by the unintentional faithlessness of the only friend she'd ever had and by the desolation of knowing that the man she could never admit she loved would never be hers. At least, that was how she had perceived his presence with Sabrina in the tearoom. She did not know that he had only come to London to find her.

Godfrey bowed his head. He did not deserve her love. She was beautiful, brave, and loyal. And because of him she was now a prisoner of the mad pirate, Gasparilla.

With effort, he drew his thoughts back to the man who had commanded his presence on the deck. Gaspar was droning on about his opinions on the current affairs at Amelia Island. Though the slave ship would surely bring profit to be divided among all the pirates, it did pose a problem in that it was taking precious time to dispose of the individuals within.

Godfrey was repulsed. Profit on *human beings*. What kind of world was it where human beings became entries in a ledger?

"Amelia Island is the closest spot," Gaspar said. "So many die in the hold that when you've got a cargo of slaves, it is best to find the closest point of sale. Thank goodness Amelia Island is now a place friendly to pirates and privateers."

Gaspar held the lapels of his jacket and, unconsciously, Godfrey supposed, struck a pose at the railing much like a portrait Godfrey had seen of Napoleon, Gaspar's hero, whom he saw as a kindred spirit, another bold adventurer. Perhaps he was right, Godfrey thought. Like Napoleon, Gaspar was a dictator of all he controlled and was at least a hero in his *own* mind.

He shook his head at the irony. The French Revolution that had given Napoleon his opportunity had been fought for concepts like "liberty, equality, fraternity," and yet Gaspar saw no hypocrisy in selling human beings into slavery. It was only in 1815, years *after* the Revolution, that France had prohibited slave trading. But who was he to judge? The American Constitution had also protected the slave trade. By 1804, however, slavery was illegal everywhere north of the Mason-Dixon line and in territories north of the Ohio River.

Realizing that Gaspar was now expecting his full attention, Godfrey brought his thoughts back to his captor.

The captain paused a moment as if concentrating on what to say, imagining it being read by a broad audience in the biography he envisioned Godfrey writing. Others of whom he spoke were bit players in the great masterpiece that was his life.

"I approve of Gregor MacGregor. Like me, he is aiding the cause of liberation. He has been much involved in Spain's colonies, particularly with Simon Bolivar. As they say, 'The enemy of my enemy is my friend.'"

Familiar to Godfrey, this was an old proverb both in ancient Arabic and Chinese. One Gaspar might have learned in Spain at the Naval Academy.

What a revelation! Gaspar saw himself as a liberator! A freedom fighter, perhaps?

Gaspar filled Godfrey in on the details of the man who had just taken Amelia Island from the Spanish. Gregor MacGregor, a veteran of the Napoleonic Wars and a hero of the South American struggle to liberate itself from Spain, had recently traveled to the United States seeking support for his continued efforts in Florida. In March of 1817, deputies in the United States from Venezuela, New Granada, Mexico, and Rio de la Plata gave him commissions authorizing him to take possession of East and West Florida.

These commissions gave him a cover of legality while he sought financing and attempted to recruit more men to his cause. He had the unofficial blessing of the United States government to further weaken Spanish hold on the area and make it easier to annex with promises of reinforcement.

"But is MacGregor's loyalty to the United States?" the captain asked.

Godfrey was about to answer, but the question turned out to be rhetorical, and Gaspar continued, answering himself.

"I think not. I have heard from the Cuban fishermen in Charlotte Harbor that something is afoot with some old British officers who plan an expedition of sorts. Just rumblings, but from people who know what they're talking about."

Gaspar then chuckled as he related how MacGregor tricked the Spanish garrison on Amelia Island into thinking he had many more troops than he actually had, and the Spanish surrendered. MacGregor had managed a swift, successful conquest of Amelia Island. He now titled himself the brigadier-general of the United Provinces of the New Granada and Venezuela and general-in-chief of the armies of the two Floridas.

Gaspar was impressed with MacGregor's audacity.

For a while, he and Gaspar stood watching the great blue heron and snow white egrets float on the wind.

"This is the finest natural harbor on the east coast of Florida," Gaspar finally commented. "I considered setting Amelia Island up as my base once, but it is too close to the United States, as I think MacGregor will discover. Cumberland Island"—he gestured to the shore to the north—"is part of the United States. The St. Mary's River just ahead is the southern boundary of Georgia, and Fernandina Harbor is just around the bend to our left." Gaspar indicated each spot as they sailed into the harbor.

The Green Cross of Florida flew over Fernandina. It looked a lot like the Union Jack in green rather than red. To Gasparilla, the most important asset was the court there that could condemn prizes captured by those who flew flags of Venezuela, Granada, or Mexico (all of which were among Gasparilla's collection). The admiralty court would collect a 16.5 percent fee of the gross revenue of the prize. But, perhaps even more important, some on the island had direct connections to enable them to immediately dispose of the cargo of the slave ship through the permeable Georgia borders and into the hands of land-hungry, labor-deprived Georgians.

"Roderigo, my man who took over Menendez's slave ship that we captured, is already ashore negotiating with Charleston attorney John Heath, who runs the admiralty court."

Godfrey could not help being impressed with Gaspar's knowledge and said so.

"I have a network of contacts," the pirate explained. "There is a community of free and runaway slaves at Angola on the Manatee River near my base of operations. Cuban fisherman operate camps there and in Tampa Bay nearby. Seminole and Red Sticks make frequent hunting and trading trips to the Tampa Bay area, and the British continue to supply them." It was then Gaspar realized he might be saying too much. Part of his control over Godfrey was Godfrey's ignorance of the area into which he was being taken. He stopped talking abruptly.

The anchor had been set, and the men awaited his orders.

Gaspar turned to Black Caesar, who approached them. "Purchase supplies to replenish those we have used. I leave it up to you." Gaspar handed Black Caesar a bag of coins, as the large man was serving as quartermaster for this voyage. "Gomez, Menendez, and I will visit Madame Bonet. She runs a very high-class whorehouse on Lady Street and keeps tight security."

Then Gaspar looked back toward Godfrey and dug his elbow into the younger man's side. "You will stay with your wife, eh?" He said, winking in a show of camaraderie. "Perhaps she is *embarazada*?" he said with a knowing smile.

Godfrey felt relieved. So Gaspar thought Joie's faint and her seclusion was because of a pregnancy. Godfrey had not considered that, but it was a pretty good cover.

The Spanish sailors from the captured ship would stay on Amelia Island, either as welcome recruits for MacGregor or to make their way to St. Augustine and join the Spanish colony there. Most of the pirates were allowed a brief shore leave. Godfrey, of course, was ordered to keep to his quarters, and Black Augustus was stationed nearby.

That was fine. He did not want to leave the ship, except to bring a doctor back with him. But Joie's condition was dire and he could not leave her, even if Gaspar would let him go, and Godfrey knew enough of the captain's character not to confide in him.

He must pretend that he had all the time in the world and only wanted to listen to Gaspar. If Gaspar knew that Joie was ill, his own aversion to illness and would demand her removal from the ship. And without Godfrey, as sick as she was, Joie would likely die. Her health had deteriorated to the point that her lips were parched and cracked and her eyes appeared sunken and glowed with the fever.

The cook made a thin gruel that Godfrey managed to feed her along with constant sips of the sweetened tea that he prayed would sustain her. Joie had nursed him for weeks after Fort Mims, and everyone had told him they had feared he would not survive the protruding bone and fracture with its resultant infection and fever. Lyssa had given him willow bark for the fever and made poultice after poultice to pull the infection from his body. Unfortunately, the surgeon, in this case also the ship's carpenter, had no willow bark, though he had the right tools to deal with most problems on a pirate ship, particularly amputating limbs, the most frequent consequence of pirate battles. Godfrey bathed Joie as frequently as possible to cool her feverish body.

Georgia was so close. He'd come through Georgia to Creek Country in 1813, excited about his adventure with his aunt and uncle. That adventure had turned into disaster when his aunt and uncle died at Fort Mims and Godfrey himself was seriously injured. He imagined jumping off the boat and swimming to Georgia. But he could not leave Joie. She would never survive.

No. Godfrey had to bide his time. He knew that Joie's family was frantic with worry. How could they possibly find her? It must appear that she had simply dropped off the face of the earth! It was up to him to save the two of them.

Joie needed a doctor. How could he get her to one?

Unasked, Black Caesar did the next best thing. While ashore getting supplies, he consulted a medicine woman, relating Joie's symptoms in hopes of a diagnosis and advice.

"I go to one of Madame Bonet's house servants, a voodoo woman from my home in Haiti," he told Godfrey. "I tell her symptoms. She say typhus and give me vervain, garlic, and guinea-hen weed to make as tea. She give me pepper also and say use vinegar to wipe things down and add to water."

Black Caesar handed him another packet that Godfrey recognized as willow bark. That familiar addition calmed his fears slightly, though he felt wary about working with the other strange items. Still, he convinced himself that a voodoo priestess couldn't be too different from a medicine woman like Lyssa Rendel. Anyway, it was surely worth a try. Godfrey immediately mixed the ingredients, brewed them into a tea, and added sugar to make it palatable. Joie drank greedily in spite of her sore throat.

"Oh, God, don't let me be poisoning her!" he prayed.

By morning, all were aboard once more, and the ship headed south to round the Florida peninsula and go up the other side. The closer they came to his base, the more frequently Gaspar commanded Godfrey's presence. He continued to shatter Godfrey's bias regarding pirates being illiterate, dissolute ne'er-do-wells. Godfrey actually thought the educated, disciplined, and successful Gaspar was much more dangerous than the stereotypical pirate. Though the captain often acquired dated news, he had learned about Godfrey's visit to the British Museum early enough to sail to England and then make his return trip to meet with his colleagues in the Gulf of Mexico.

Black Caesar, Godfrey had discovered, was a Gulf pirate who usually sailed independently of Gaspar. His base was on Pine Island, not far from Gaspar, and when Gaspar had mentioned his intent to capture the writer who chronicled pirates, Black Caesar had decided to come along for the adventure.

Or so Gaspar said.

But Godfrey suspected there was an ulterior motive for Black Caesar's presence. He thought of the woman named Sheba whom Gomez had mentioned. Why hadn't Caesar stayed behind and taken advantage of Gaspar's absence? With Gaspar gone, he could have had the woman if he wanted her. Perhaps Gaspar had known of Caesar's interest and had encouraged him to come to England so as not to leave Sheba vulnerable to Caesar.

Apparently, Gaspar was also well acquainted with the most well-known pirates of the Gulf, Jean and Pierre Lafitte and Luis Aury. They had recently shifted their privateering base to the island of Campeche, also known as Snake Island, off the coast of Texas. The settlement on the island was named Galveston.

Each evening, Gaspar held court in his elegant cabin, enlightening his two friends, Gomez and Menendez, and his brother, Leon, as to the events that had transpired in the Gulf of Mexico. The discourse became an extended lecture on people, politics, and whatever else provoked or interested Gaspar. He had a captive audience.

Though Godfrey hated leaving Joie alone at what now seemed a critical point in her illness, he knew his presence at the table with the quill in hand was necessary. They had sailed around the keys of Florida and were headed up the west coast when Gaspar began telling tales of those whom he expected to arrive soon at his island.

The other men nodded in agreement at most of Gaspar's dissertations, and eventually the wine he imbibed slowed his speech, though Godfrey thought they were more immersed in Gaspar's excellent selection of wines than his thoughts. When Gaspar's head dropped on his chest, they all were at last released to their beds.

Gaspar was fascinated with Jean Lafitte and Luis Aury. They were his favorite topic of conversation, and Godfrey suspected that he was envious of their notoriety. Maybe Gaspar had only used Captain Kidd's map as a ruse. It seemed to Godfrey that Gaspar had actually sailed around the world to capture his own biographer—or for some other, more sinister reason that he could not quite fathom at the moment. One thing he knew: Gaspar was not an easy man to read. It seemed important to Gaspar that Godfrey meet the Lafitte brothers and Aury in person. After all, Godfrey had used every bit of information leaked to him by authorities in pursuit of pirates in order to write articles for his father's newspaper. Maybe Gaspar, realizing how much Godfrey knew, was anxious for him to encounter these men in the flesh.

On a night shortly thereafter, Gaspar spent most of their evening gathering pondering Luis Aury, his thoughts lubricated by wine. "Galveston is nearly on the same latitude as my island, almost straight sailing across the Gulf of Mexico," Gasparilla began. "The Mexican ambassador to the United States, José Manuel de Herrera, originally ordered Aury to occupy Galveston. Aury was a Jacobin who supported the radicalism of the French Revolution. He served in the French navy, and Herrera apparently found him qualified for the titles of civil and military leader of Mexico. Last year, Herrera commissioned Aury's small squadron of twelve to fifteen ships and 500 veteran Haitian sailors with letters of marque to raid Spanish shipping."

Gaspar's eyes turned to Godfrey's notes. Godfrey dipped his quill in the ink and looked up expectantly. Satisfied, Gaspar continued.

"Aury had often taken advantage of Lafitte's operation at Barataria, and so he used Lafitte's operation as the model for setting up his base at Galveston. It was to be a place where privateers might refit and dispose of their cargoes, and, of course, Aury would make a commission.

"With a few hundred men and some lumber, Black Caesar told me that Aury set up a ramshackle village that he called the capital of the independent nation of Texas, claiming to have conquered Texas from the Spanish." Gaspar chuckled. "His court of admiralty condemned vessels and their cargoes could lawfully be admitted to the United States as condemned prizes from actual nations."

"¡Cojonudo!" Gomez exclaimed.

Gaspar nodded and smiled broadly. "Here comes the funny part. When Aury left Galveston to transport Francis Javier Mina and his men to the Santander River in Mexico, Lafitte, angry with the Americans for running him out of Barataria, became an agent for Mexico and moved into Aury's beautifully appointed red-painted mansion that also has *its own moat.*"

"US revenue cutters had broken up the Lafitte brothers' very profitable smuggling operation around New Orleans using the many bayous in that area," Gomez added. "Jean agreed to become a paid Spanish agent. He was ordered by Spain to occupy Galveston and turned coat to accept Mexico's offer." Gomez shook his head in disbelief.

"Details such as this have not been included in your resources, have they, Mr. Winkel?" Gaspar said, giving Godfrey an unreadable look.

As the boat groaned and creaked its way up the west side of the Florida peninsula, Godfrey focused on his scribbled notes to avoid the tension of Gaspar's glance. His attention never strayed far from the cabin where Joie lay.

Gaspar continued, "Lafitte requested that I host a meeting of the pirates of the Caribbean to discuss the United States' revenue cutters in the Gulf of Mexico. President Monroe insists that Galveston is part of the Louisiana Purchase and therefore Lafitte must abandon the island. They have already lost Barataria. The United States navy is becoming a nuisance to our continued, shall we say…endeavors?"

He eyed Godfrey pointedly. By bringing Godfrey into this meeting, he could demonstrate how well he was aligned with the most famous (and infamous) pirates currently sailing the seas. That should make for good material for a writer to write. But was Gaspar truly staging this event for Godfrey's benefit?

Godfrey reminded himself that it was never good to underestimate one's enemies. Still, he wondered what other reason Gaspar could have for going to the trouble to capture him?

What if Godfrey was there for the pirates' entertainment? If they knew *he* was the infamous writer who had stirred the Americans to military action in the Gulf, Gaspar might see him as a significant bear to throw into the pirate's den for entertainment.

Oh, God!

He would have to prove to Gaspar that he—and therefore Joie— were worth more alive than dead!

Gaspar wound up the evening by delivering a detailed report on the talents of the whore at Madame Bonet's. He also gave a comparison between the woman he was considering as his next "companion" and the women kept in his compound on Captiva Island. He described one beauty that he called Sheba, who was "like the Queen of Sheba" because of her "ebony beauty."

Godfrey tensed. He had heard that name before. Unconsciously his eyes turned to the corridor where he sensed Caesar's presence. A slight movement outside the cabin where Joie lay confirmed his suspicion.

Black Caesar stood there in the shadows, almost lurking. Godfrey knew that the mention of Sheba had brought him closer. Gomez and Menendez had suddenly become a rapt audience as Gaspar waxed eloquent on the physical attributes of a long list of women he had once had on Captiva Island. He reminisced graphically about the sex acts he had performed on those women and had them perform on him in his room in the mansion with mirrored ceilings. He mentioned many women, and then coldly and off-handedly mentioned that, once they no longer interested him, he disposed of them. Gaspar finally passed out with his happy thoughts about the women who were now waiting for him to select them.

The shadows cast by the sputtering candle were no longer cozy. The darkness grew menacing. Godfrey shivered now, not with cold but with greater fear for Joie. He sensed that they were in terrible danger. And he hadn't a clue how they could escape.

Perhaps her illness and necessary seclusion had been a blessing. Godfrey resolved to redouble his physical activities. He *must stay strong* for both of them. It was up to him to come up with a way to get out of this.

When at last he could return to the cabin, he gently bathed Joie's face and arms with the cool, wet cloth. Then he brought the cup of honey-sweetened tea to her lips, and she drank obediently. She looked at him briefly, and perhaps it was his imagination, but for a second he thought he saw a glimmer of recognition. She did seem less agitated, and her skin was not so hot.

Eight bells rang. Godfrey heard the chief mate with the larboard watch call for the starboard watch.

Propriety had been damned when he had removed Joie's shirt and bound her chest weeks ago. Now took her in his arms and cocooned around her, pulling the woolen blanket and his topcoat over both of them for warmth. He was exhausted and needed to feel her safe within his arms before he could succumb to sleep. She unconsciously curled to fit perfectly against him and sighed. He hugged her tighter and slept.

Chapter 7

It was nothing short of a miracle that the sailor in the crow's nest of Woodbine's ship, the *Venus,* spotted the small dinghy. The desperate, severely dehydrated sailors from the slave ship had been adrift for days upon the vast expanse of empty sea. Fortunately, those sailors provided the information needed to direct Woodbine and crew toward Joie and Godfrey.

Only Gabe would have recognized the beautiful, black-haired, blue-eyed female pirate the incredulous sailors described. They said she had swung onto the ship and wielded a cutlass in the battle at the back of a big, red-headed pirate. There was no question in Gabe's mind that this was his sister, Joie Kincaid.

"And then, battle over, she, being a woman, fainted and had to be carried back to the pirate ship by the biggest black man I ever seen!" the sailor declared.

Gabe paled at the thought of his little sister battling alongside pirates against those villainous slavers.

"They will be heading to the closest port to dispose of their slave cargo," Woodbine assured Gabe. "And that just happens to be right where we are headed…Amelia Island."

It was a bright, sunny morning, still oddly cool for the season, when at last they arrived at Amelia Island. Gabe anxiously scanned Fernandina Harbor. His heart fell. No ship with a bare-breasted mermaid on the helm. And none of the ships matched the description of the one described by Myles, Cedric, and the slavers. When at last they were anchored, Gabe jumped aboard the dinghy, deciding to go ashore with the sailors who intended to resupply. Once again he checked out the inns and taverns—only these were built of coquina and tabby. The town was filled with adventurers, Irish and French refugees, Scots, Mexican and Spanish patriots, several of Lafitte's Baratarian band, and the original inhabitants of Fernandina, along with privateers, slavers, and other seafaring scoundrels.

It did not take long for someone to remember having seen the extremely large black man with gold hoops in his ears. He'd been ashore inquiring about a doctor, but the only healer on the island was the voodoo priestess at Madame Bonet's. Gabe asked for directions and hurried over to conduct his own investigation. He made his way around back to question the silent servants whom he knew were often able to contribute more information than the owners of an establishment. The voodoo priestess, who was also the cook at Madame Bonet's, remembered the black man well.

"Mais oui," she said. "Très bien je m'en souviens très bien. Zees brave man led an insurrection on my home island of Haiti. Nous avons beaucoup d'amis en commun."

"In English, please," Gabe requested. "I am afraid I do not speak French."

She smiled. "Hees name is Henri Caesar, and he is the brave man who led an insurrection on my home island of Haiti. He needs ze medicine for a woman weez—how you say?—typhus?"

Gabe reeled. Typhus! So many in London had died of that disease! It was the main reason Jake Kincaid had decided to take his family back to the United States.

The priestess continued, "I give him ze medicine and he leave. Ze captain and heez amis leave Madame soon after and ze boat sail zees morning."

Dear God. If only they had arrived sooner.

Gabe could hardly wait to get back to the ship. He climbed the ladder and nearly ran to the captain's quarters.

"We must sail immediately!" he demanded.

Woodbine shot Gabe a quelling look. "Gregor Macgregor," he said to the man sitting beside him, "may I introduce my impetuous guest, Gabriel Kincaid. Kincaid here is searching for his sister, who has apparently been abducted by a pirate recently anchored here. The pirate seized a slave ship that they presented to your admiralty court and arranged for sale."

Though he spoke the words matter-of-factly and lounged in his chair as if only interested in a convivial visit, Gabe sensed the captain's disgust at the thought of marketing human beings. There were serious issues at stake here. As Gabe was merely a passenger hitching a ride with Woodbine, who himself was apparently on a special mission, he calmed himself and prepared to listen. Gabe sensed that Woodbine intended for MacGregor to play a role in his own quest. Impatient as Gabe was, he must allow the game to play out.

Woodbine indicated a chair at the table and asked, "What did you find out?"

Gabe pulled out the chair and sat. Then he sighed and shrugged. "They have surely been here but have already sailed." He kept the information about typhus to himself. He would not want fear of illness to impede his search.

"What ship would that be?" MacGregor inquired.

"José Gaspar is the pirate," Gabe responded. "Henri Caesar is the black man most people remember."

"Ah, yes, MacGregor said, nodding. "Roderigo, his representative, negotiated well for the disposition of the prize. The profit for our government will be a nice addition to our coffers. Gaspar will be returning to his base on the west coast of Florida." MacGregor paused, looking thoughtful. "Some of Lafitte's men from Barataria are here at Fernandina, and, according to them, Lafitte is considering aligning himself with Gaspar. They plan to meet soon, though I am not sure exactly where."

"You have excellent sources," Woodbine said.

MacGregor inclined his head, acknowledging the compliment. "I have found it pays to have eyes and ears everywhere."

For some reason, Gregor MacGregor, Scottish adventurer and aspiring empire builder, reminded Gabe of Tecumseh's brother, the prophet Tenskatawa. He was about thirty-five years old with an inclination toward corpulence, much like Gabe remembered Tenskatawa.

They both had an indefinable air that gave them consequence. Tenskatawa had gone from being a misshapen, alcoholic, womanizing scoundrel to a prophet of the Shawnee, telling all that the Great Spirit had come to him and given him visions for a new world if only they would listen and repent. Calling Americans spawn of the Great Serpent, he preached their death. Full of his own importance, he organized witch hunts against Christian Indians.

Gabe had actually gone to the Creek Grand Council meeting at Tukabatchee with William Weatherford, Sam Moniac, and his brother to hear Tecumseh speak. Tecumseh had come south to attempt to forge a united Indian force to repel the white man, leaving instructions for his brother to avoid any confrontation with the white man until he returned. Ignoring the command from his brother, whom he'd always envied for his natural leadership and abilities, Tenskatawa had ordered the warriors of his village, Prophetstown, to attack the Indiana force under the leadership of William Henry Harrison. Tenskatawa was defeated along with Tecumseh's dream.

Tecumseh and Tenskatawa's great-grandfather on their father's side was James McQueen, who had come with James Oglethorpe to Georgia and wound up marrying a Creek woman and living there until he died at 128 years old. Their mother, Metheotaske, was a Souvanogee (Shawnee) Creek. They visited their family in Creek country for extended periods when times were hard up north. Their Creek relatives, including Gabe, though he was much younger, were well acquainted with these northern cousins.

Gabe decided that MacGregor had the same air of self-importance as Tenskatawa—the confidence that destiny had decreed great things for him. Unfortunately, as Gabe had seen firsthand, madmen with visions wound up getting people killed.

Unlike Tenskatawa, though, who was blind in one eye and misshapen, MacGregor was handsome—tall and dark with thick eyebrows, muttonchop sideburns, and soft, plump, womanly lips. Women of the ton would have found his brooding good looks enchanting. Seated in Woodbine's cabin with MacGregor, Gabe listened as he described his miraculous conquest of Amelia Island in a deep voice with distinctive Scottish brogue.

"You know," Woodbine said to Gabe, "the Georgians call Florida Satan's backyard. That opinion led those self-proclaimed 'patriots' from Georgia under George Matthews to capture Fernandina in 1811. They were just following the model of the filibusters in Baton Rouge."

"Matthews planned to offer it up to the United States and achieve a coup similar to that accomplished with Baton Rouge, when American settlers seized that city and expelled the Spanish garrison," MacGregor said. "When the filibusterers in Baton Rouge requested annexation to the United States, President Madison immediately granted it."

"Unfortunately for Matthews," Woodbine interjected, "the timing for his venture here at Amelia Island was bad. The Americans and British were headed toward war, and when Great Britain protested, the Americans were afraid to stir up the Spanish at the same time they would be fighting us Brits. So Matthews had to go home to Georgia with his tail between his legs."

MacGregor leaned forward, his eyes glistening. "But that was then, and now Florida is ripe for conquest. We marched ten miles two abreast through the swamps and were successful in surprising the Spanish when we stormed their garrison here," he said, recalling the ease of his glorious victory.

He flicked an invisible bit of lint from the cloth of his crossed leg, an affectation of humility. "One shot was fired, but that was an accident. Seventy prisoners surrendered to us. We took two schooners at Fernandina." At this, he leaned back with a self-satisfied smirk on his face. He made it sound like a walk in the park.

"That was an amazing victory," Woodbine said admiringly.

Gabe got the feeling that Woodbine was sitting calmly, listening and waiting—like a fisherman teasing a fish to take the bait.

MacGregor shrugged and then admitted, "I have been promised many more men from my sponsors in the United States, but they have yet to arrive."

Woodbine refused to fill the vacuum of silence. Waiting. Challenging.

"The truth is that I must secure reinforcements, or this endeavor will fail," MacGregor admitted ruefully, his eyes lowered now. That was the opening Woodbine had awaited.

"I appreciate your lofty goal, MacGregor. Should you and I unite, we could be a real force with which to be reckoned. I myself have been given great tracts of land by the Indians that I must secure. The huge grant of land that Forbes claims the Indians awarded him in payment of their debt on the Apalachicola River in North Florida is illegal. It could be ours!

"Forbes is already selling that land and settling Americans on it. It won't be long before those Americans will be asking to be annexed to the United States just as they did with Baton Rouge. If you would join me in going to New Providence where a British regiment has been recently disbanded, I believe we might secure the men and funds we need."

MacGregor's eyes lifted, bright with interest.

With the hook set, Woodbine continued. "Add those troops to the 1,500 Indians who have committed to our cause and the blacks that will join us to drive out the Spanish and resist the incursions of the Americans."

Woodbine spoke calmly and determinedly. "We will set up our base in Tampa Bay and then set out overland to take St. Augustine. The buffer of an Indian nation between us and the Americans would make that land secure."

MacGregor had grown restless. Clearly, he was seeing fortune once again at hand.

Gabe could not believe what he was hearing. He thought he'd joined a merchant voyage. But it seemed that Woodbine was set on nothing less than the conquest of Florida!

MacGregor leaned back in his chair. His fingers tapped on the tabletop.

The hook was surely set. Had Woodbine succeeded in reeling him in?

Minutes passed, and Woodbine calmly sipped his wine. He offered more to MacGregor, who refused.

"I sail now to New Providence," Woodbine finally said. "Will you sail with me?"

MacGregor hesitated only a moment. "My wife and I will follow soon upon my ship, the *General MacGregor*. I will meet you in New Providence."

MacGregor left the *Venus* after much hand pumping and backslapping between the two men. Together they would build an empire. Gabe wondered how two men with such egos could possibly cooperate to achieve that goal.

Three days later, the *Venus* sailed through the Florida Straits across azure seas to the sugar-sand beaches of New Providence Island, dropping anchor in the fine protected harbor of its capital, Nassau. Woodbine would stay here to enlist recruits for his venture in Florida, while Gabe would find passage with one of his associates who would take supplies to Josiah Francis, as Woodbine had promised. The Red Sticks would play an integral part in Woodbine's grand endeavor.

Robert Chrystie Armbrister was to meet Gabe and Woodbine at the Green Shutters Pub on Parliament Street down near the wharf. They arrived at the pub as the sun was setting and the sky had become a striation of purples and pinks, pastel colors recreated on the coquina and tabby buildings about them. It was a pleasant evening with balmy breezes filled with the musky scent of the tropics, salt and sea as well as the ripe smells of fish and offal.

Woodbine took a table in the exotic courtyard lit with lanterns built around a flaming Royal Poinciana tree. The bright pink and white five-petalled butterfly flowers emitted a pleasant light scent that attracted hummingbirds even in the fading light of day. A jacaranda had done with its summer blooming and now filled one corner beautifully with its fern-like foliage. Lush bougainvillea spilled from the palm-thatched roof of the pub and from the many terra-cotta pots scattered about. Agapanthus, anthurium, and the exotic bird of paradise bloomed beneath the Royal Poinciana and jacaranda trees. The sweet scent of night-blooming jasmine, punctuated by the spicy smells of Caribbean cooking, filled the air.

"Armbrister is notorious for being late," Woodbine commented as they were seated. "I have no intention of waiting for him to eat."

If Gabe hadn't been so worried about Joie, he might have appreciated the rare beauty of Nassau. Now he knew that his sister had not only been kidnapped by pirates but also had typhus. He needed to get to her now! But in order to do that, he had to wait and depend on the help of Woodbine and his friend.

Woodbine was apparently well known in the area. As soon as he was seated, the barmaid greeted him flirtatiously and placed a jug of dark ale before him. Gabe asked for coffee but settled for tea, the favorite of their usual clientele. New Providence was an important base for the British.

They were soon served conch cut in strips and seasoned with salt, red pepper, and lime juice—a dish the barmaid called scorched conch. Cracked conch, he discovered, was pounded, lathered in egg and flour mix, and then deep-fried. When conch was mixed in spicy herbed batter and deep-fried in balls, it was called conch fritters. Large boiled lobsters and melted butter arrived, along with huge servings of peas and rice, fried plantains, and a Bahamian bread the barmaid called johnnycake. She set a plate of *bunuelos de viento* before them just as Woodbine's associate, Robert Armbrister, arrived.

Armbrister strode into the courtyard with the eager swagger of confident youth. His magnetic midnight-blue eyes fairly sparkled with anticipation. A wave of greetings welcomed him, and the handsome young officer dressed in his full scarlet uniform stopped to visit each table of military men in the courtyard as a hail-fellow-well-met.

Woodbine watched him with approval. "He has many friends. He's a natural leader. Surely some of these men will be willing to follow Armbrister into the expedition," he said, almost like a proud papa.

Armbrister was a jovial man who seemed much younger than Gabe, though Gabe was not yet twenty-five years old. The officer held his tricorn hat under his arm and absentmindedly brushed back an unruly lock of black hair from where it constantly fell to cover his eyes. His dark muttonchops and eyebrows set off his startling blue eyes, which were nearly obscured by thick, almost womanly lashes. Gabe observed that here was a man who paid attention to details—particularly of his attire. His boots shone. Gabe wondered if the more serious issues of his life received the same attention.

All eyes followed Armbrister as he finally made his way to Woodbine's table and made a courtly bow. Woodbine stood to shake his hand, and Gabe stood as well, waiting to be introduced.

"Lieutenant Armbrister, may I introduce to you Gabriel Kincaid," Woodbine said.

Armbrister, nearly a head shorter, lifted his chin and eyed Gabe curiously. He presented his hand, and Gabe took it, noting the man's firm grip. The two men sized each other up.

"My pleasure, sir," Armbrister said.

"And mine as well," Gabe responded.

Woodbine indicated that they should resume their seats. "Armbrister here is quite familiar with your people and your land, Kincaid. He and I served together in the Creek Nation under Captain Edward Nicholls at Pensacola and later at Apalachicola during the war with the Americans. Together with Seminoles, Creeks who had fled to Florida, and blacks, both free and runaway slaves, we built a fort at Prospect Bluff as officers in command of a detached group of the Corps of Colonial Marines."

"Ah, so you are Creek?" Armbrister asked.

Gabe inclined his head slightly in assent.

"When I first landed with Nicholls at Pensacola in May of 1814, we found Red Sticks in swamps near Pensacola near starvation. We shared our supplies with them and then began arming them to fight against the Americans," Armbrister said.

Woodbine shook his head. "I attempted to enlist the pirate Lafitte to fight with us against the Americans. I could have raised a force of about

2,800 Indians, but Lafitte chose to join the Americans. We were drilling Indians and ex-slaves in the streets of Pensacola when Jackson arrived with 3,000 men and cannons. We blew up Fort Barrancas and San Miguel and, with our Indian friends, many of them Red Sticks, and the free blacks and former slaves, we made our way to the Apalachicola, where we built the fort at Prospect Bluff."

The barmaid appeard with another glass for ale, and Armbrister helped himself from the plates before them.

They spent a moment in silent reflection before Armbrister broke the silence again, nodding toward Gabe "And now, Mr. Kincaid, may I inquire as to the purpose of your visit here in New Providence?"

"Kincaid here is in pursuit of his sister who has been kidnapped by the pirate José Gaspar," Woodbine supplied. "He arrived at the ship in Falmouth with letters of introduction from Lord Bathurst."

Armbrister lifted his eyebrows and with a nod acknowledged Woodbine's explanation for the inclusion of a stranger at this point in their preparations. Then his countenance fell into one of grave concern. "I am sorry to hear about your sister's kidnapping, Mr. Kincaid. I have heard it said that José Gaspar is one of the Gulf's most bloodthirsty pirates."

"My sister was not the primary target, Lieutenant Armbrister," Gabe explained. "She was captured along with a friend of hers who writes about pirates and was supposed to be in the possession of a treasure map that we have assumed was the purpose of the kidnapping. I know my sister was alive when they anchored at Amelia Island. I have hope that she still lives."

"I understand that Gasparilla's base is an island in Charlotte Harbor, near Tampa Bay," Armbrister said.

The mention of Tampa Bay Woodbine to the purpose of their meeting. He leaned forward. "MacGregor has joined forces with us. We need you to sail as soon as possible to Tampa Bay to set up a base of operations for our expeditions."

"As you know, my father is the governor's secretary," Armbrister said. "He has been receiving letters from Alexander Arbuthnot, who, in

Nicholls's absence, has become their spokesperson for our Creek friends and their dire situation."

Woodbine explained to Gabe, "Francis traveled with me back to Nassau. But it is Arbuthnot who in July brought Josiah Francis from Grand Providence back to St. Marks aboard his ship the *Chance*. Arbuthnot has become quite influential with the Indians, Red Sticks and Seminoles, in the short time he has been in Florida."

"Francis has settled three miles west of the Spanish fort at St. Marks on the Wakulla River," Armbrister said to Woodbine. "I have heard that he thought of resettling his family in Nassau, but Arbuthnot convinced him he could do his people more good remaining there."

"Gabriel Kincaid and his sister, Joie, are related to Hannah Francis, Josiah's wife, as well as Betsy McQueen, Peter McQueen's wife," Woodbine said. "But the Kincaids left Creek country immediately after the Creek War and have been living in England, where their brother's father-in-law inherited a title and estates."

Woodbine turned to Gabe and said, "Arbuthnot has been extremely successful at his store, which is located uncomfortably near Forbes' store. The Indians trust Arbuthnot and trade with him, making enemies of Nimrod Doyle and William Hambly, representatives of Forbes Company. Hambly turned traitor of the fort at Prospect Bluff, by then referred to as the Negro Fort," he added with contempt. "It was Hambly who directed the American gunboat as to the perfect place, the magazine, to direct their hot shot.

Armbrister, Arbuthnot, and I plan to make it even more uncomfortable when we open another store on the Suwannee near Bowlegs Town. Florida is ripe for the taking and we must move now to take Florida from the Spanish for the good of all."

Woodbine sat up straighter and adjusted his coat. Armbrister unconsciously emulated his mentor.

"Robert," Woodbine said, "it is important that those supplies reach Francis, either at St. Marks or through Bowlegs at Suwannee Old Town 100 miles east of St. Marks. We must ensure that Bowlegs is friendly to our cause before we march across Florida to take St. Augustine. We have a friend at Bowlegs Town in Abraham, one of those who joined us at Pensacola and helped build the fort at Prospect Bluff.

"After helping me garner some more supporters and a bit of financing, Robert will sail with some of our black recruits." Though this last sentence was addressed to Gabe, Armbrister nodded, taking the direction.

Woodbine told Gabe, "Many of these recruits are from Angola, a large black settlement near my plantation south of Tampa Bay on the Manatee River. The harbor at Tampa Bay is superb—suitable for ships of any size. Cubans have operated a fishery out of nearby Charlotte Harbor for years. A settlement of Red Stick Creeks is close by on the Peace River, and other Indians have settled nearby in an area referred to as the Hammocks, so opportunities for trade are most favorable. So is our opportunity to recruit from these groups."

The barmaid returned once more to ask if anything else was needed, and the men soon took their leave.

When they entered the dark street, Armbrister took Woodbine aside for a private conversation.

Upon his return, Woodbine said, "You will understand that your silence is critical. I do not want to put it like this, Mr. Kincaid, but our assistance hinges upon your accommodating the needs of this expedition. Your timing is unfortunate."

Gabe was in a fix. The reason he had hitched a ride with Woodbine was to follow Joie and rescue her. Who would have known he would end up in the middle of international intrigue? He was now caught in a plot to wrest Florida from the Spanish—a plot apparently supported by influential people in the government in England. And now he knew too much for them to let him go!

Gabe nodded. What choice did he have?

He had thought that he and Armbrister would leave New Providence quickly. But, much to his dismay, Armbrister would have been just as much at home in the social scene Gabe had left in England, where dawdling was a social grace! Armbrister called it developing contacts.

To Gabe's thinking, the young officer was a blustering, posturing fool in his captain's red coat. He tried to give Armbrister the benefit of the doubt. There was surely more to the man that he could see; Woodbine held him high regard. Perhaps he made a better impression on the battlefield. Gabe grew more and more impatient as they faced continued delays while Woodbine and Armbrister tried to raise recruits and financial support. Gregor MacGregor arrived in his *General MacGregor*. Gabe did not know whether Joie had survived typhus, and there was absolutely nothing he could do to hurry things along.

He was trapped, and he was desperate.

Chapter 8

She heard his voice first, the familiar rumble that had soothed her fevered dreams. A stranger's voice that she knew. That voice reached down beneath her unconscious mind and brought Joie slowly awake. She shivered with cold but stayed very still. Just beyond was a glimmer of something. A thought that must not be lost. She focused on the thought that was there beyond her memory. And then suddenly, she knew who she was! Joie Kincaid! In a rush, all of her memories came flooding back!

The last she really remembered was being attacked when she went to hide in the alley beside the tearoom. She had looked into the window at Rules, and there sat Godfrey Lewis Winkel with his pinkie lifted, drinking tea with her supposed best friend, Sabrina Stapleton. Her anger surged with the memory, and then her head started hurting.

Calm down, she told herself. She looked around and realized she was on board a ship, but she sensed that she wasn't alone. The voice she heard was familiar—older, but familiar. Slowly it all came back to her. She and Godfrey were together on a pirate ship. Sabrina Stapleton was *not* with them.

Joie was afraid to move, though her need to use the terra-cotta pot there in the corner brought her off the cot briefly before she burrowed back under the blanket and pile of coats that had kept her from freezing. Her head pounded, so she covered her eyes against the flickering candlelight and focused on the voice, willing herself not to drift back into the soft cloud of darkness. The voice calmed her, soothed her, washing over her like the warm water of the fancy copper bathtub at the Duke's townhouse. Slowly the pain receded.

A montage of memories proceeded through her mind, scenes of times past. She remembered the Godfrey who had taunted her at Fort Mims; Godfrey on the path injured and afraid where they found him, sick with fever, for her and Lyssa to nurse back to health; Godfrey surprising them all by embracing the tiny toddlers Meme and Mo; Godfrey jumping to shield and protect her from Pushmataha and her brother Gabriel when they surprised them in the cabin where they'd taken refuge after the Fort Mims massacre; the Godfrey she had last seen in St. Stephens when Pushmataha and Gabe had brought Cade and Lyssa home, beet red at seeing Lyssa nurse the newborn twins. That Godfrey Lewis Winkel had little resemblance to the man who only recently, on the deck of the pirate ship, had pulled her into his arms and kissed her, claiming to be her husband. That kiss had shocked them both, and Joie grew warm with the memory of it.

Pirate ship. They were on a pirate ship! They had been attacked and kidnapped by pirates! Her family must be frantic! A headache threatened to take her back into the blackness. Joie calmed herself and struggled to focus on the voice.

"...and so the story goes that when Captain Kidd's wife was allowed to see him for only seconds before he was hung, he handed her a strip of pasteboard with the numbers 44106818 written upon it, a fact known to all who study pirate lore. If you look at that as 44 degrees 10 minutes as a latitude and 68 degrees 18 minutes as a longitude, that takes you very close to Oak Island off the coast of Maine, an island owned by the Olmstead family, who sold a parcel of it in 1801 to Jacques Cartier, an employee of John Jacob Astor. Astor's deposits from his fur business *had* averaged about 4,000 dollars a year before 1801. Then, in 1801 Astor paid Cartier 5,000 dollars, though he had never before paid Cartier any more than 500 dollars for the furs and pelts Cartier brought him. Suddenly, that same year, Astor's account with the Manhattan Company jumped to 500,000 dollars."

A shadow passed in front of the door to the cabin. Black Caesar! Listening. Unseen.

"How do you know that?" came Gaspar's voice, challenging.

"My mother's father is his banker. I sometimes accompanied him to the bank after hours and had to entertain myself," she heard Godfrey answer. "Astor came into the bank frequently, and I befriended his mentally disabled son."

"Are you saying that John Jacob Astor, that very wealthy man now buying up New York City, found Captain Kidd's treasure?" Gaspar said, sounding incredulous.

"I have seen the box with the initials WK chiseled into the top," Godfrey assured him. "I had been playing in Astor's attic with his son and saw the rusty iron chest. We were playing pirate with toy swords, and J.J. told me that the chest was a real pirate chest. I asked him where it had come from, and J.J. said his father had bought the chest from a fur trader named Cartier who found it on an island.

"I remembered that, of course, and set about to learn of a man named Cartier who might have owned property at a place associated with those numbers. That they were coordinates was obvious."

There were long moments of silence where Joie envisioned the men around Godfrey nodding, though she knew they had no idea how he figured out what seemed so obvious to him. It surely was not obvious to her!

Godfrey rambled on. "I asked my grandfather to give me an astrolabe for my birthday and requested that he take me fishing and teach me to use it. He was too busy to go himself, but he sent me off with a captain he trusted and one of his small sailing ships. Of course, I guided our trip to that island and asked the Olmsteds if they minded me doing a little exploring. They had a son about my age who was eager to show me his favorite spots on the island. I figured the coordinates, give or take a bit, and he led me to a cave that we explored. We found a hole in that cave the exact dimensions of the iron chest in the Astors' attic. Imprinted on the bottom of that cave was the same WK as on the chest."

Joie heard Godfrey's audience exclaim in amazement.

"I, of course, never told my new friend about their lost fortune," Godfrey said.

Then came Gaspar's voice. "Well, I had dreams of being the one who found Kidd's fortune. I plotted and planned your capture for just that purpose. Why then should I now keep you alive?"

It sounded as though he were intentionally provoking the others.

"What a futile trip around the world!" said Gomez.

Joie's heart clenched.

"Lead him to the plank!" Gomez shouted. "Feed him to the fish!"

Joie looked about desperately. Where was the nearest cutlass? Her eyes fell on the terra-cotta pot, filled to brimming with her urine and excrement.

Menendez's calm voice reminded Gomez, "You would not have been reunited with your brother-in-law had this young captive not made the trip. And I would have disposed of the slave ship and gone home a rich man instead of making my friend Gaspar here even richer."

"There is that," Gomez agreed.

"You did not tell the rest of the story at your presentation at the British Museum," Gaspar accused. "If the mystery has been solved and the treasure found, why not tell the world and stop futile efforts at finding the treasure?"

"It would betray my friend," Godfrey responded, his voice smooth as butter. "But *not* telling *you* would be to betray a new friend, the brilliant pirate Gasparilla for whom I am the official biographer and with whom I would like to search for another...a greater treasure...the treasure of William Augustus Bowles."

Ever since he found himself on this ship, Godfrey had suspected that his life, and therefore Joie's, depended on making himself more important to his captors alive than dead. How better to appeal to a pirate than through treasure?

Joie could barely contain herself. Godfrey had built to the moment as well as any showman she had ever seen. Her friend Ronaldo, the gypsy king, could not have done any better. Had Godfrey had this scheme up his sleeve when he told the story of Captain Kidd's treasure? Or was it a spur-of-the-moment invention? He had mentioned the treasure of her father's greatest enemy, William Augustus Bowles, the man who, along with Savannah Jack, had kidnapped her brothers Cade and Gabe right before she was born. Joie knew the story well now.

Bowles had proclaimed himself emperor of the Muscogee nation, called himself Eastajoca, and boldly claimed Joie's father's trading privileges, in effect attempting to run Jason Kincaid out of Creek country. Her father had left his pregnant wife, Snow Bird, and his ten-year-old twin sons at his trading post on the Oconee River near his wife's people in order to track Bowles. Bowles had simply waited for Jason to leave and, along with Savannah Jack, kidnapped her brothers as they ran to the nearby village to get help for their mother, who had gone into labor not long after her father left.

By then, Bowles had captured the fort at St. Marks and operated his navy, actually a piracy operation, from there. Bowles and Savannah Jack took Joie's brothers to St. Marks and kept them in cages, where the women of the village tortured them with sharp sticks. At last a compassionate woman left a sharpened stick in their cage. When Savannah Jack was drunk and Bowles was away, Cade used the stick on a keeper and escaped. Somehow Cade managed to get Gabe, delirious with fever, into a sailboat, down the river, and across the bay to the Apalachicola River, where they were discovered, both of them sick and unconscious by then, by High Head Jim, their cousin Polly Durant's husband.

William Weatherford, one of their own Clan of the Wind, had known of the psychological trauma the boys suffered from those events. He took them with him when Bowles was captured at Tukabatchee, capital of the Upper Creek villages located at a sharp bend of the Tallapoosa River, taken to Pensacola, and delivered to the Spanish whose ships he had plundered. The Spanish jailed him at Morro Castle in Cuba, where he died. It was then that Savannah Jack had sworn a blood oath to exterminate Jason Kincaid and all of his children. Savannah Jack had brutally killed their father and stepmother at Fort Mims and left behind his signature—a knife with his personally carved handle that he had plunged into Joie's father's chest.

For years, Joie had nightmares that Savannah Jack would someday come for her. She was still horrified that he had captured and unwittingly sheltered Lyssa, the pregnant wife of Cade Kincaid, when she was out foraging for food for Joie, Godfrey, Jay, and the orphans they had rescued. Jack had held Lyssa for some time, thinking she was the pregnant widow of a warrior killed in the battle of Fort Mims. Finally,

Cade rescued her at Horseshoe Bend, nearly getting killed in the process. Savannah Jack, however, survived to dominate Joie's dreams.

Now it sounded as if Godfrey were leading the pirates back to the site of her brothers' torture. Closer to her mother's people.

Just where *were* the Red Sticks who had survived Horseshoe Bend? Joie knew that Savannah Jack would be with them. She shuddered with foreboding.

Satisfied for the moment, Gasparilla dismissed Godfrey, Gomez, and Menendez. Godfrey helped Menendez get the drunken Gomez to his hammock and noticed an interesting collection of reading material when he lifted the blanket. Menendez turned to climb into his own hammock while Godfrey unconsciously scanned the pages of *Harris's List of Covent Garden Ladies*, a publication that was brand new to him.

His first inclination as he perused the collection of pocketbooks—each with nearly 150 pages on thin paper—was that he didn't realize Gomez could read English. But then the details distracted him—these were books of prostitutes operating in Covent Garden.

The curse of Godfrey's gift was that, as swiftly as the pages flipped by, they were burned into his memory:

Miss Kilpin, who offers her favours inside the privacy of hackney carriages, but who is in reality a married city lady, who takes this method of getting home deficiencies supplied abroad.

...a well-shaped girl, about twenty-three, good-natured and said to be thoroughly experienced in the whole art and mysterie of Venus's tactics and as soon reduce a perpendicular to less than the curve of a parabola. She is rather generous and you may sometimes find your way in there free of expence.

...many a man of war hath been her willing prisoner, and paid a proper ransom...she is so brave, that she is ever ready for an engagement, cares not how soon she comes to close quarters, and loves to fight yard arm and yard arm, and be briskly boarded.

Menendez noticed Godfrey's absorption with the books. "Gomez found those in Gaspar's cook's possession. He tells us that he made frequent use of the information. The latest there is 1795. Gomez has been stirred to learn English," he said with a wink. "I, *fortunately,* already read English! *Un*fortunately, the ladies are twenty years older now, probably dead from their activities. But the writing is truly inspirational." With that, Menendez turned his back on Godfrey and proceeded to operate from memory.

Godfrey dropped the books like a hot potato. But the words and images remained vivid in his mind, particularly a certain passage.

He gazed on her a while with eyes of transport and fondness, and gave her a world of kisses; at the close of which, in a pretended struggle, she contrived matters so artfully, that the bed-cloaths having fallen off, her naked beauties lay exposed at full length. The snowy orbs on her breast, by their frequent rising and failing, beat Cupid's alarm-drum to storm instantly, in case an immediate surrender should be refused. The coral-lipped mouth of love seemed with kind movements to invite, nay, to provoke an attack; while her sighs, and eyes half-closed, denoted that no farther resistance was intended. What followed, may be better imagined than described; but if we may credit Miss W-lm-t's account, she never experienced a more extensive protrusion in any amorous conflict either before or since.

He returned to their cabin with the words burning through his thoughts, his heart beating rapidly and his face flushed.

Joie heard his return but kept still, feigning sleep as he used a lantern to light his way. She resisted peeking when she heard him taking his clothes off, only keeping the long shirt on to sleep. He touched her forehead, feeling for fever, perhaps letting his touch linger a bit too long, and then she heard him sigh in relief when it felt cool. He lifted her and put the cup of cool water to her lips. She drank obligingly. He laid her gently back down on the bed and arranged the pile of thin blanket and jackets over her. And then he lay down himself, spooning with her and pulling her close to share his body heat. She heard him whisper a prayer in her ear, pleading with God about something.

"Oh, God. Oh, God," he said.

If only Godfrey could love her like Cade loved Lyssa. But Joie would never forget the constant harping of her stepmother—and eventually her father—telling her over and over that she was a worthless breed, not white and not Indian. She had tried so hard to earn her father's love. However, deeply wounded by the death of his beloved wife, Snow Bird, Jacob Kincaid had allowed his heart to grow hard and cold. When he saw his three children, he saw his wife, and so he distanced himself from them with a bottle and emotional withdrawal. The only person who had truly loved her unconditionally was the baby her stepmother had never wanted. The first time J.J., or "Jay" as she and Lyssa often called him, was placed in her arms and looked at her with his innocent blue eyes, she felt that he was sent just for her—someone at last who would love her. But now Jay had Lyssa, Cade, Gabe, and all the children. He no longer needed her.

Joie knew that Godfrey did not love her. He simply felt responsible for her. It was a matter of gratitude rather than love.

But when he took her into his arms and gave her his warmth and comfort during the night, she felt loved and secure. Perhaps these moments were all she would ever have of that feeling. She surely would not hold him to his claim that she was his wife.

There was something different tonight, though. When she heard his footsteps coming closer, Joie decided to take advantage of the opportunity to experience the closest thing to love that she would ever know. Should they escape, Godfrey would remember that he was a gentleman and would go back to the life he knew before they were kidnapped. Should they die at the hands of the madman Gasparilla, at least she would know for a brief moment what being loved was actually like.

Joie's heart beat faster. This was Godfrey, the boy she loved. Yes, she could finally admit to herself that she did indeed love him. She'd loved him when he was a pompous know-it-all at Fort Mims who only wanted to talk to Sally Carson, the belle of the Bigbee, trying to impress her with his education. Sally had spent her time looking beyond Godfrey to the uniformed militiamen. But Joie was impressed. Godfrey used such big words and read fat books that she longed to be able to read. She'd loved him, even when the first hesitant smile she gave him was returned with his offhanded remark that she was an ignorant breed, much like her stepmother had said. Despite that, she'd loved him then.

And now she loved him as the beautiful boy who'd converted himself into a powerful, muscular, fearless man who was smart enough to manipulate the bloodthirsty pirate and save her. She remembered his gentle touch as he bathed her through her fever, talking softly to her all the while, encouraging her, calling *her* the bravest, strongest, most courageous person he had ever known. Willing her to live.

And he had called her his wife.

Joie would claim the rights of that title tonight and demand nothing else. One night. Then she would tell him that her memory had returned, and she would let him go.

Smiling to herself, she wiggled into his embrace.

She could almost feel his eyes pop open. With little encouragement, she felt him stiffen against her buttocks. She snuggled closer. He groaned and rolled over onto his back, gentleman that he was, putting distance between them. Joie knew that he would fear taking advantage of her. So she climbed on top of him where he lay flat on his back. She took his face between her hands and leaned down to kiss him.

It must be a dream! Those damned books. Those images in his mind! Godfrey was so shocked he didn't know what to do. He dared not make any noise and bring Joie to Gasparilla's attention. The captain was just yards away on the other side of the bulwark. But this kiss was just as powerful as the public one they had shared on the deck.

Their one and only kiss. Until now.

Surely Joie was delirious. Or a figment of his imagination and he was dreaming. She must be. But her skin felt cool to his touch, while his own was now burning. Burning with the heat she brought to his body. And now she was moving and he was aroused and aching. She pulled his shirt off and then pressed her "snowy orbs" against his chest, caressing him everywhere, stroking him while her tongue teased him, reacting to his own response to her kiss.

Godfrey was not experienced in lovemaking. His reaction surprised him as much as it surprised her.

He wanted her with an all-consuming lust. But he retained enough control to hold back. At the moment, she was his to protect. He refused to take advantage of her in her weakened state.

And then she pulled her shirt (which was actually his shirt) over her head and put his hands on her breast.

"I am your wife," she whispered.

"Joie," Godfrey croaked. "I just said that because…"

She reached down his body and took him into her hand, and Godfrey couldn't think…couldn't speak. She stroked him, watching him grow bigger and feeling herself respond with a raw and powerful longing. She kissed him there and all the way back up his body to his lips, which suddenly and passionately claimed her own.

She felt him close, teasing, and before either of them had time to think, she positioned herself so that her "coral-lipped mouth of love seemed with kind movements to invite, nay, to provoke an attack." Carried away by the lascivious prose that ran through his mind, Godfrey entered her.

Her single indrawn breath stilled them both.

"Oh, God," Godfrey moaned. "What have I done?"

After the initial pain, the pleasure set in. Joie wiggled and pulled his face to hers. He rolled over and held himself above her. She wrapped her legs around him, refusing to let him go.

"Cupid's alarm-drum" pounded with urgency.

"I am your wife," Joie whispered, though she knew it was a lie. She felt herself clenching around him. No power on earth could take him from her in that moment or steal the memory of once, just once, belonging totally and completely to the man she loved.

And, God help her, she did love Godfrey. Unexplainably. Undeniably. Unreasonably.

Giving herself completely to the moment, even though she knew it was pretend, she nipped at his lip as he thrust into her again and again. She breathed in his scent and ran her hands down his back, reveling in the hard muscular feel of him, pulling him closer and urging him on.

He nuzzled her neck, teased her breasts, kissed her lips. She felt like a goddess, and he was worshipping at her altar.

At last she reached a point where every cell of her body was aware of him, and the feeling was overpowering. His own body clenched, and she felt the pulsing of his seed enter her as the two of them came together in that single lightning moment.

He lay gasping on top of her until she pushed him away so she could breathe, and then he rolled, taking her with him. She sprawled on his chest, happier than she had ever been. But she could sense the wheels of his mind, and she knew he now felt guilty for having taken her…thinking she did not know who she was. She pretended to sleep to keep him silent.

Godfrey was exhausted. He wanted to talk, to tell her how much he loved her, admired her, adored her, but that could wait until morning. He pulled her close, her ear next to his heart with her leg across his body.

At last, his even breathing told her that he slept.

Chapter 9

Godfrey felt eyes upon him. He was warm and cozy tucked under the pile of blankets and coats on Joie's bed, with Joie wrapped tightly in his arms. His eyes popped open with shock at the realization that he was actually flesh to flesh with her. Another part of him had come awake as well. There she was, entwined with him, her beautiful face covered by her long, dark hair that was spread with abandon over his chest. He had made love to Joie Kincaid. It hadn't been a dream.

But Gaspar's sly grin and lascivious expression quelled Godfrey's lust and replaced it with alarm. Godfrey had heard whispers of Gaspar's predilections. His usual randy habits and cruel treatment of women had led several of the sailors to warn Godfrey to keep his *wife* away from the captain.

Now, waking to Gaspar's face turned the dream into a nightmare. With only one glance, Godfrey knew that Gaspar wanted Joie.

The pirate licked his lips and inhaled deeply, appreciatively, as if the musky scent of their nocturnal activities was a fine perfume. He quirked his eyebrow at Godfrey, hesitating as if considering something, and then shook his head as if in answer to an internal question.

"Dress quickly and follow me," he whispered. "Leave the woman here."

When Godfrey slipped from Joie's embrace, she moaned and snuggled into the smell of him and the warmth he left behind.

He dressed hurriedly and followed Gaspar onto the deck.

"Unfortunately, there are no women in my home to welcome my return," Gaspar complained as he settled into the dinghy to transport them from the anchored boat to the shore. "My last *amante* is gone, and I have yet to decide upon her replacement." He gave Godfrey a telling look.

Gaspar's eyes were a soulless void. A chill ran down Godfrey's spine. He had to get Joie away—and soon!

Godfrey followed Gaspar into the boat and onto the island in the grey of the fog-shrouded day. The wind had whipped up, and sand stung his face and eyes. As he approached the pinnacle of the hill where Gaspar's expansive mansion stood, he looked back toward the ship bobbing about in the inlet but saw only Caesar climbing into a boat that was rocking dangerously next to the ship. For the moment, Godfrey felt that Joie was safe while she slept. He would keep an eye on Gaspar and not give him the opportunity to return to the boat.

Godfrey wished he'd had the chance to awaken her this morning—to see her beautiful blue eyes in the morning light. To tell her what he'd tried to say with his body the night before. He longed to go back to her now.

Instead, he followed Gaspar into the vast, green-shuttered house built on what appeared to be an old Indian mound. Gaspar's home could have been the home of Spanish royalty. They entered through an oiled pine front door, one of many in the home, to see red tile floors with blue and white tile wainscoting and oiled, dark-paneled, coffered ceilings. The house was furnished with walnut tables, elegant and intricate with detail; chairs of walnut, some painted and gilded, some upholstered with Cordova leather or intricate tapestry; ornate ironwork; walnut cupboards with boxwood inlay; red silk draperies with yellow silk linings; and a magnificent marble staircase with intricate ironwork rails, along with armorial hangings and needlepoint tapestries. Godfrey had been in fine homes, but never one so fine as this—and here it was, situated on a sand mound on a barrier island. Gaspar had created his own empire where he lived the life of a Spanish grandee in luxury stolen from the Spanish themselves. As long as the scrub oak, saw palmetto, and sea grass held the sand in place, Gaspar was secure.

All that day, Gaspar held Godfrey captive with him, keeping him away from the ship and Joie. Not long after they entered the house, the wind began to beat against the wooden shutters, which soon shielded the elegant furnishings against the onslaught of the driving rain that had followed the wind. Gaspar had led Godfrey into the library lined with walnut-stained bookcases with a walnut vaulted ceiling, a cozy room that Godfrey would have welcomed if he were not concerned about Joie.

This was the first time Godfrey had been completely alone with Gaspar. The captain ordered Godfrey to sit opposite him at the desk in one of the two chestnut arm chairs. Then he handed him a quill pen, pen knife, paper, and ink.

"This is the perfect day for us to be inside and for you to hear of the exploits of José Gaspar," Gaspar said to Godfrey with a smile, his eyes glittering with pleasure.

Then he kicked back in his mahogany lolling chair with his feet propped on the carved walnut desk and began to talk of his youth, his adventures, his naval career, his disillusionment, and a detailed recollection of his life as a pirate.

Godfrey's mind wandered as Gaspar talked. He wondered if Joie was comfortable. Did she know that he was thinking of her?

Gaspar lifted glass after glass of the four bottles of Barolo, a red wine that sparkled in the fine crystal goblet he dangled between his fingers. The crystal glass was unusual and worthy of a footnote in a mind that catalogued details. It consisted of a round funnel bowl finely engraved with a bunch of hops and two pairs of crossed barley ears, set on an airtwist stem with a single spiral cable. Details, Godfrey had discovered, made writing come to life, but these particular details seemed curiously familiar in his mind.

It would come to him.

Bread, fruit, and cheese were delivered on a tray set with Sevres china meant for John Jacob Astor, Gaspar told him with a wink.

Godfrey realized then that the crystal and china were familiar because he had read a description of them on the manifest for one of his grandfather's ships that had been lost at sea, or so they had supposed. Godfrey now knew better. He wondered what had happened to the ship's captain, the same captain who had taken Godfrey on his quest to find the truth of Captain Kidd's treasure. Unfortunately, Godfrey thought he knew the man's fate.

As night fell, Gaspar continued his drunken recall of his life's adventures. When at last he began to nod, Godfrey saw his chance to retire for the evening.

"May I now return to the ship and my wife?" Godfrey asked.

Gaspar lifted one hand and beckoned to the guards who had appeared at the door. He gestured that they take him.

They took him indeed, protesting, to a bedroom where he was thrown upon a carved mahogany tester bed with a burgundy sunburst under the canopy. Then they left, barring the door behind them. He could only lie there and listen to the screams of the wind lashing against the shutters. He wished he could escape to join Joie on the ship anchored in the inlet. The banshee-like howls of the tempest sounded like the cries of a woman in distress. He tried every window and every door, frantic with the need to see Joie to assure himself that she was safe, but everywhere he looked, there was a guard or a lock—on the outside.

He could think of nothing but Joie. Her beautiful face above him, watching him, loving him, was more than he had ever expected. Her love was in every gesture, every nuance. He did not deserve her. He had to let her know how beautiful, how courageous, how full of every quality that makes someone extraordinary she truly was. He knew that her stepmother had beaten her down. He knew that he had done so as well, and the knowledge of it nearly killed him. How could she love him after he had said such things to her when she was so vulnerable? He would never forgive himself, but if she would let him, he would spend a lifetime trying to shower her with all the love she deserved. He finally fell into a fitful sleep, anxious for the morning.

When the sun rose, the guards brought him servants' clothing and then allowed him to leave the room. They led him to the courtyard at the side of the house where bougainvillea climbed the arches of an arbor of roses, which were under-planted with rosemary and thyme. Lavender poured from terra-cotta pots. Godfrey smelled coffee, beignets, and bacon and spotted quiche on the table. He looked east beyond the patio and saw their ship, now peacefully anchored on the clear turquoise waters that lapped lazily on the wind-swept, wave-washed, white-sand beach. There was no trace of the night's storm. To the west he saw what looked like white clouds on the horizon. Ships approached.

Gaspar followed Godfrey's eyes and said, "My—colleagues—fortunately sailed behind the squall." He rubbed his hands together with satisfaction and added, "They will arrive on time."

"I want to see my wife," Godfrey said.

Gaspar looked at him quizzically. "You are here at my bidding. You will do as I say. You have been fascinated by pirates, and now you will meet them because of my hospitality. A woman can only distract." His eyes were cold and full of venom. "You should be grateful."

Godfrey swallowed hard but maintained his Caleb Connory calm. He leaned back in his chair and casually gazed down at the ship. He did not let Gaspar know that he was affected by intimidation, though the captain's look had chilled him. He dared say no more. He did not want Gaspar's attention on Joie. He had to play the game, though he hoped to catch a glimpse of the one who was never far from his thoughts. His anxiety had only increased overnight. The banshee wailing of the wind had such an ominous sound!

Guards stood at a distance but watched his every move. They had seen Gaspar's punishment of those who failed at fulfilling his commands.

"She is being taken care of," Gaspar said dismissively. He flipped the ruffles back on the fine lawn shirt that he wore loose and open and lifted the steaming cup of black coffee to his lips. He sniffed, enjoying its aroma.

"This is more than a cup of coffee. It is a memory of a great victory. The memory of a Spanish ship I captured sailing from Martinique."

Godfrey had seen another of Gaspar's victories. The memory of the day he captured Menendez's ship would be of misery and human flesh. Would that aroma bring Gaspar pleasure as well?

Godfrey accepted a cup of coffee and said casually, "The seeds of the coffee from Martinique originated in the Royal Botanical Gardens in Paris. Louis XIV was given a young coffee plant by the Mayor of Amsterdam. A French naval office *acquired*, shall we say, a seedling from that plant and then survived a hurricane, sabotage, and a pirate attack to bring it to the island of Martinique. There the coffee plant flourished."

"Well, I for one am glad *that* pirate was unsuccessful," Gaspar commented. "He would not have known what to do with a plant, and then no coffee would have been grown on Martinique and I would not have been able to steal the coffee from the ship I captured. So God works in mysterious ways." Gaspar chuckled and settled back in his chair, lifting his face to the warmth of the morning sun and basking in the light breeze of the rain-washed day.

"I should keep you around," he said to Godfrey. "You amuse me."

Suddenly Godfrey could almost feel Gaspar's mood shift. The charming companion of moments before disappeared. No longer slouching in his chair, the captain commanded, "You are not to mention Bowles's treasure to anyone. Is that understood?" Both of his feet were now planted firmly on the tile floor of the lush patio. His hand caressed the cutlass he wore at his waist, a subtle threat, and his eyes glittered gold, reminding Godfrey of a coiled snake.

Godfrey swallowed hard and nodded his agreement. He looked beyond Gaspar to where the approaching sails grew larger. "Who are you expecting?" he asked, calmly changing the subject.

Gaspar settled back once more. "Jean Lafitte and his brother Pierre, though Pierre claims to be retired from the family business. He lives with his mulatto wife in New Orleans. There is a bit of irony in their occupation, considering the heritage of Pierre's wife and their background—they came to New Orleans from Santo Domingo. And they have made most of their money circumventing the outlawed slave trade.

"Their half-brother Dominique You will be here as well. He doesn't trust me, you see," Gaspar said with a satisfied smile. "He is quite the protective older brother. You is very proud of his role in the revolution in France. Later he came with General Victor LeClerc to Haiti to quell the revolution there. You is crafty and skillful in his use of artillery."

Godfrey wondered if Gaspar caught the further irony there. Slaves rebelling against oppression, wanting freedom, which was supposed to have been the reason for the revolution in which LeClerc and You had fought.

"Yes, I think that is You's ship, *Le Pandoure*. Knowing the ships he has taken and their captains, I would say that of all of this group, he comes closest to being as bold as I am."

"I hear Jean Lafitte is at loose ends at the moment," Godfrey remarked. "Their business underwent some reverses when Daniel Patterson led the American naval assault on their Baratarian enterprise."

Gaspar paused before saying, "That is partially the reason for our gathering."

He looked at Godfrey meaningfully, and Godfrey sensed that his usefulness was being assessed. By now Godfrey had concluded that Gaspar had used the map and the treasure merely as a ruse, though a plausible one, because he was half serious about finding Kidd's treasure. But Godfrey thought his true intent was likely to present him to his fellow cutthroats and watch the wolves play. Of course, with the new possibility of Bowles's treasure, Gaspar was reassessing Godfrey's worth.

Gaspar's fingers played upon the table. His threat delivered, he picked up the strand of their earlier conversation.

"For a while, they were quite successful. Jean outfitted privateers and arranged for the distribution of the captured cargoes through the swamps around Barataria Bay and New Orleans. Pierre was well respected in New Orleans society and handled the public aspects of their business mainly in New Orleans. I'm sure you know it was Pierre who commanded the artillery provided by the Lafittes to Andrew Jackson at the Battle of New Orleans, in spite of the stroke he had in 1809 and the paralysis on his left side. I myself have entrusted many cargoes to them for disposal."

Gaspar squinted in the sun, watching the first of the ships anchor near his own. "That is Charles Gibbs's ship. I personally witnessed him chop the arms and legs off a captured Spanish captain," he said with a smile of approval and a significant look at Godfrey. Godfrey sensed that the man was nearly licking his chops with anticipation should he decide to expose Godfrey's true role to his colleagues.

"It was a day much like this," Gaspar said, sweeping his arms to indicate the glorious sun, brilliant blue sky, and smooth, clear waters. From the look on his face, it was obviously a fond memory. "Lots of slaves on that ship. One of the many slave ships I delivered to the Lafittes to sell."

Gaspar went on listing his expected guests. A pleasant breeze blew from the Gulf, rippling the palm fronds. "Victor Gambi is Italian," Gaspar said, with typical Spanish disdain. "He never parts company with his axe and is known as perhaps the most bloodthirsty of all who will be gathered. But he respects Lafitte."

Godfrey hoped sweat wasn't breaking out on his forehead like it was under his arms in spite of the pleasant breeze. He lowered his arms.

Gaspar chuckled. "Early in their association, Jean Lafitte issued an order to Gambi and his men. One of Gambi's men challenged Lafitte by saying, 'Gambi's men take orders only from Gambi.' Lafitte drew his pistol and shot the man." He narrowed his eyes. While Gaspar had never come straight out and said he knew Godfrey had written the condemning articles, Godfrey had a feeling he did.

Godfrey swallowed hard and kept his outward composure with great effort.

"Jean Lafitte had sailed with me once when something similar happened. I did just as Lafitte later did. He has told me that I am his hero." Gaspar spoke of Lafitte like a fond papa. From what Godfrey had discerned considering his knowledge of the two, Gaspar was at least twenty years older than Lafitte. Little grey colored Gaspar's thick black hair, but Godfrey knew the man was closing in on sixty—quite old for his line of work.

The pirates climbed the stairs up the mound and were welcomed to Gaspar's grand home by one of Gaspar's male slaves dressed as an English butler. He showed them to Gaspar's library, now elegantly appointed with a collection of leather lolling chairs so that it resembled an aristocratic men's club. Gaspar and Godfrey met the visitors there.

They found seats around a wooden table that included a rotating serving element much like the wheel of a ship with nuts, fruits, dates, meats, boiled shrimp, scallops, oysters, breads, sauces, condiments, and confections.

The *piece de resistance*, an Orange Fool, was the specialty at Boodle's, London's exclusive men's club. Gaspar could not resist boasting that his cook had once been the chef at Boodle's—before being captured when Gaspar and his men seized the ship on which he sailed. He had been traveling with an aristocratic patron of the club who had arranged for him to serve as a private chef on his honeymoon voyage with his forty-years-younger bride. The Orange Fool had a sponge cake base that was covered with thick cream beaten with orange juice and rind, lemon juice and rind, and sugar. It was all arranged in a trifle bowl so that the juices soaked into the sponge cake for at least two hours, and it was simply delicious. A hit with Gaspar's guests. Godfrey wondered if Gaspar might possibly be displaying a little humor with his choice of dessert.

Pierre Lafitte had bought a pipe, more than 100 gallons, of white wine from Champlin as a gift to Gaspar to fuel the meeting. "When we left New Orleans for Galveston, we celebrated the departure of Aury with a pipe of this wine," Pierre said jovially to Gaspar.

The men mingled after the meal, pounding each other on the back. They complained of the dirth of treasure now being transported by Spanish ships and the intrusion of the presence of the American navy in the Gulf.

Gaspar left the room to question his men on the whereabouts of Black Caesar, for whom they were waiting to begin.

"Have you noticed that there are no women?" Jean Lafitte asked his brothers in a low voice.

Jean was tall and lean, around six feet, two inches, while his brother Pierre was at least four inches shorter. Jean had strong Gallic features, with dark, thickly lashed hazel eyes, thick dark hair, a beard partway down his cheek, and startling white teeth. Pierre was more muscular, light complexioned with light brown hair that fell over his low forehead, and slightly crossed dark brown eyes. His smile was also brilliant with remarkably white teeth. Their brother, Dominique You, was of a height between Jean and Pierre, with the same Gallic features as Jean, though coarsened by his being eleven years older and perhaps twenty pounds heavier than Pierre.

Dominique You wore a brace of musket pistols at his waist and stood with an unconsciously protective stance near his brothers. Godfrey got the impression that You had not been in favor of his little brothers attending this conclave. He'd stayed in New Orleans when his brothers went to Galveston and tried to get them to retire and stay with him. He kept glancing out the open doors at the horizon as if expecting Matthew Perry and Lawrence Kearney to arrive at any moment with the entire American navy.

Jean Lafitte indicated an island in the distance. "Isn't that the island the Cuban fishermen call Captiva?"

"Did you notice the huts on that island as we sailed into Charlotte Harbor?" Pierre asked. "It looked as if they were devastated by the storm last night. I hope there were no women there!"

Jean and Dominique shook their heads. Jean bent forward to speak softly. "The Cuban fishermen say that Gaspar once captured the daughter of the viceroy of New Spain, who was on a voyage from Mexico City back to Spain. Gaspar kept her on that island, attempting to seduce her. Eventually, her persistent refusal enraged him, and he lashed out at her with his cutlass, beheading her. Legend has it that her headless body haunts that island."

Listening to the men talk from the anonymity of his place behind the desk dressed in servants' clothing, Godfrey felt the bile rise as his fear for Joie increased.

"Great story, brother," You said. "That makes me much more comfortable visiting here with your…friend."

Victor Gambi had overheard the conversation and looked across the sound to the island with interest. "I've killed many men and women, but as far as I know, their spirits have not chosen to linger."

"You do not stick around the same place long enough for the spirits to haunt you," Charles Gibbs joked.

"Since then," Jean continued, undaunted, "it is said that he will keep women captives there and eventually bring one to his home on this island to be his woman. When he tires of her, he sends her back to the island to be executed and buried."

"Do you really believe that of our charming host?" Gambi looked about him. It all seemed so civilized, much different than Lafitte's own base at Barataria had been.

Jean Lafitte shrugged. "I believe it well enough that I am reluctant to inquire of the beautiful woman who was his companion last time I was here."

Godfrey's blood ran cold. Where was Joie? It had been more than a day since he had seen her.

Gambi looked toward the island once more. He accepted the rum and fruit drink decorated with a twist of orange from the servant's tray, lifted his glass, and toasted Gaspar. Godfrey thought that Gambi, whose nose was half slashed off, looked the most like a pirate of any of the Lafitte group. The others were too polished.

"Ah," Gambi said, smacking his lips, "this is a vast improvement over me rations of grog on the *Petite Milon*!"

Gaspar returned and said, "Black Caesar cannot be found at the moment. He made a delivery for me yesterday and has not been seen since. He may show up at any time. Only Luis Aury is missing."

They made a serious dent in the pipe of wine, and, with them thus lubricated, the official part of the meeting began. Godfrey remained apart, not yet introduced, and was assumed to be a servant.

"Our friends Aury and Caesar must be detained," Gaspar said, affecting casual disregard. But the tendons in his neck stood out as he strained for self-control. They dared to ignore his *invitation*?

Godfrey had a feeling that Gaspar would express his disappointment when the opportunity arose. For now, though, he indicated the chairs and said, "Please be seated."

Gaspar introduced Godfrey as his biographer with no name given. He was positioned inconspicuously behind Gaspar's massive desk that had been provisioned with quills, ink, and paper. The opportunity to record the appearance of these men who were legendary for their exploits, despicable though many of those exploits were, was irresistible. Though the quill and ink were unnecessary, he accommodated Gaspar by jotting down details.

If Godfrey were not aware of the true reputations of those men, he might have thought he had stumbled upon a gentleman's club rather than a coven of bloodthirsty pirates. These men were dressed finely to impress. Perhaps flashy might be more descriptive—fine to excess and dripping in jewels, most with jewel-handled daggers, finely crafted swords of Toledo steel, and pearl-handled pistols. It was an intimidating display of power. He knew they could use them.

Big Rene picked up on Gaspar's comment about Aury being the only one missing. "Aury is on another adventure," he explained. "When Jean here decided to move in on Aury's Galveston venture, Aury was convoying Mina to the Satander River. Mina joined forces with revolutionaries in Mexico under Guadaloupe Victoria. So then Aury decided to join forces with Gregor McGregor at Amelia Island. He has probably arrived there by now."

Godfrey recalled that Big Rene, Renato Beluche, had served with You as an artillerist fighting the British under Andrew Jackson. He had then gone to join Simon Bolivar and the Venezuelan patriots to free them from the yoke of Spain, though he frequently joined the Lafittes and the Baratarian smugglers in their piratical activities against Spain and England.

Godfrey was conflicted. His morality was being challenged. His own country had fought and won their freedom from old country monarchies. These men had played a part in weakening those countries so that the colonies could win their freedom. Some had actually fought in the American Revolution. Godfrey sensed the fine line between being a privateer with a letter of marque from a country involved in an official war against another country and being a pirate who took ships due to personal grudge or mere greed. This group of men was driven for many reasons.

For Gaspar, Godfrey felt no such ambivalence. His feelings were simple. Hatred. He hated the man who had put Joie's life in danger.

How long would this drag on? He must find Joie!

Godfrey pulled his mind back to the meeting.

Dominique You said, "Our friend Aury can't resist a revolution or an opportunity to strike a blow against Spain and King Ferdinand VII."

"I knew I liked Aury," Gaspar said, laughing.

"Guadeloupe Victoria got captured and was executed in October," Jean Lafitte said.

Silence fell upon them, and then Lafitte spoke. "Since Stephen Decatur defeated the Barbary pirates and things have calmed over in the Mediterranean, the Americans have turned their attention to us."

Godfrey tensed. He knew that the American navy being more involved in the Gulf angered the Lafittes since they had reestablished their base at Galveston, supplanting Aury after the destruction of their enterprise at Barataria. They called the colony "Campeche," from which they issued letters of marque and flew the Mexican flag.

"I rather like my new headquarters at Maison Rouge," Jean said with a chuckle. "Aury moved out, and I moved into his old dwelling." For those who did not know he added, "It is painted red and surrounded by a moat."

They all laughed, imagining such a dwelling on a sand island.

Pierre Lafitte said, "Jim Bowie, one of our associates, tells us that there is talk in the United States of passing a law prohibiting the importation of slaves into any port in the United States. He isn't worried, however. The loopholes would make those we manage to get to him even more valuable."

Gaspar decided it was time to shift topics and called on Godfrey to deliver the talk on William Kidd that he had given at the British Museum.

"My biographer here has done a bit of research on someone we are all familiar with—Captain William Kidd. We've all wondered about that treasure of his. I thought you might be interested in hearing what he has to say…might help you in hiding your own treasures, eh?"

"Hide it? I spend it…on important things like wine and wenches!" Gibbs jested.

They were all deep in their cups by now, so Gibbs's quip was deemed the epitome of wit, and they all laughed heartily.

Gaspar was obviously not concerned that the rest of his colleagues might be as well read as he. None seemed to suspect that the same expert on William Kidd was also the author of the articles that had helped stir the American government to move on the pirates in the Gulf. With amazing self-possession, surprising himself since he knew how his legs shook, Godfrey managed to deliver his museum talk.

The pirates were intrigued with the treasure, the clue, and its possible discovery. They were appalled by the perfidy of a nation that would have sent Kidd on a mission—and then hung him!

"No honor whatever," opined Big Rene as he sprawled drunkenly in the lounging chair, licking the spoon from a last bowl of Orange Fool.

The meeting lasted late into the night, at which point most made their way back to their ships. A few were helped to guest accommodations in Gaspar's large house. They all left cursing the American government and an anonymous writer for stirring things up. After Godfrey's presentation, they felt justified in their many attacks on the English ships and unappreciated for their contributions to the Americans. Beyond that, Godfrey could not see that much was accomplished in the meeting other than simple pirate gossip…and perhaps the conclusion that the days of successful piracy were numbered. The effectiveness and power of the American navy was growing and had the pirates of the Gulf worried.

If he weren't so scared, he might actually feel vindicated.

"I think I'll go down to the ship now," Godfrey said, driven by anxiety at not seeing Joie in nearly two days.

"You'll stay in the hacienda tonight," Gaspar ordered with a chill in his voice.

Godfrey's uneasiness multiplied. When he opened his mouth to protest, Gaspar nodded to two of his henchmen, who took Godfrey by the arms and pushed him toward his room of the previous night, where he was once again imprisoned. He beat on the thick, eight-foot door until he no longer had the strength to do so.

Chapter 10

When Joie opened her eyes the morning after her amazing night with Godfrey, she saw the dark face of Black Caesar.

"Dress quick," he said. "We are in the inlet at Gasparilla's Island. Lafitte's ship, *The Pride*, arrive soon."

Instinctively trusting Black Caesar, Joie pulled on her only clothing, the stable boy's clothing in which she had been captured and joined Caesar on deck.

She stood back warily as Caesar approached Black Bart, who was fighting the waves in an attempt to secure the small rowboat to the side of the ship.

"I take the woman to the island of women," Caesar told him.

"But, Gaspar said *I* was to…"

Caesar glowered threateningly at him, and Black Bart handed him the rope without another word.

"Where is Godfrey?" Joie asked as she stepped into the small boat. Caesar tossed a glance over his shoulder. Joie followed his eyes across the water and caught a glimpse of Godfrey, tall and bronze, his reddish-blond hair reflecting the one ray of sunshine not obscured by the fast-approaching dark clouds. She could just make him out as he strode up some stairs behind Gaspar to the top of what looked like an Indian burial mound about fifty feet high. An elegant stucco home, painted white to blend with the white sand that covered the island, stood on the mound.

"Is that a tower?" she asked, noting the tall structure attached to the house.

"An observatory, Gaspar calls it," Caesar answered. "He watches for ships from the Spanish fleet to target."

Even before they left the turquoise waters of the sheltered inlet, the boat began rocking dangerously. The wind whipped about them as the dark clouds blew in swiftly from the west, soon obscuring the island. A curtain of fog veiled the bay on which Caesar struggled to travel. The rowboat bobbed about on the white-capped, wind-whipped waves. In the fog, it was hard to tell where one ended and the other began. Joie held on tightly, fearful that the boat would surely capsize. It took all of Caesar's strength to make it across that treacherous water. Finally, they found themselves in a secluded inlet, and another island came into view. One of Gasparilla's men was waiting for them. It seemed to Joie that they had come quite a distance from the captain's island, but their approach had been so rough that she couldn't be certain.

As the guard approached, Caesar whispered to Joie, "Tell Sheba '*tonight*.'"

Puzzled, she watched him turn back to the boat and produce a couple of bottles of wine. The guard slapped Caesar affectionately on the shoulder and pulled the cork from a bottle. He offered a drink to Caesar, who declined. And then the guard helped Caesar turn his boat around and gave him a push. Joie's heart plummeted when Black Caesar disappeared in the fog. She was all alone. As if the weather sensed her sadness, a light drizzle of rain began to fall.

The guard escorted her to a semicircle of five palmetto huts on the beach. A group of raggedly dressed white women huddled together at the door of the first one. Seeing her, they turned their backs and went inside together. But one woman, black, beautiful, and regal, stood apart at the door of the middle hut. The guard shoved a frightened Joie toward the door of an empty hut between the one where the black woman stood watching her and the first hut where the three women ignored her.

Once more, Joie looked behind her at the shore where Caesar had vanished. The waves crashed upon the beach like powerful claws shredding the pristine sand.

Steeling herself, Joie remembered that she had a message to deliver. She figured Sheba must be the beautiful black woman who, moments before, had been standing at the door, wearing a yellow turban and a dress of brilliant colors. She, too, had seemed very much alone.

The guard entered the last hut to get out of the rain. Quickly, Joie ran into the hut that must be Sheba's. The woman sat cross-legged on a woven mat in the center, solemnly watching the rain and the pounding surf.

"Are you Sheba?" Joie asked tentatively.

The woman nodded, still staring out the door.

"Black Caesar sent a message," Joie said. At that, the woman finally looked at her with sad, chocolate-brown eyes. "He said, '*tonight.*' Do you know what that means?"

Sheba nodded again. "*Asseyez-vou,*" she said. "Seet," she repeated in accented English, realizing that Joie did not understand.

Joie sat and joined the woman in her silent watch. The rain fell harder, becoming a dark curtain and obscuring the water that now seemed part and parcel with the sky. It might well have been nighttime.

Sheba pointed outside the hut to a place in the sand where a white protrusion was growing visible as the waves clawed at the beach.

"That is a skull," she said matter-of-factly. "Gaspar takes a woman, one of his captives…just as *we* are." She indicated herself, Joie, and the hut next door. "She becomes his plaything. They try to please him, for they know their life depends upon his favor. But—when he's tired of her—he has her killed and buries her there in the sand." She sighed and added hopelessly, "I have seen several skulls and bones that the guards quickly rebury."

"But, Caesar's message?" Joie asked with a lump in her throat.

"Like Caesar, I am from Haiti. He and I are…friends. He makes promises, but…." Her voiced trailed off, and she shrugged helplessly.

Joie looked at the skull. More of it was uncovered now. Was that what the women huddled in the first hut had been watching with such horror?

Sheba handed Joie a portion of bread. "Food is sent from Gasparilla's home by boat, but in bad weather…." She shrugged again.

They did not see the guard for the rest of the day.

"They usually trade guard duty," Sheba explained, "but with the weather so bad, his replacement will probably stay on the other island. That means no more food will come."

Joie had thought it could not get much darker than it had been all day, but when night truly descended upon them, it was so black that she could not see where the land ended and the water began. No candles were provided for the women. The guard's cabin, however, could have been a beacon, he had it so brightly lit. They knew he was there and, judging from the bawdy songs he sang loudly in Spanish, he was drunk. Sheba translated some of them to keep them entertained and distract them from the high-pitched, hysterical crying that came from the first hut.

When the guard's candles had melted down and only his snoring could be heard, Joie and Sheba settled onto their grass mats to sleep. Suddenly, they heard a voice from out of nowhere.

"It is I, Caesar," he whispered. "Follow me."

Sheba took Caesar's hand and reached for Joie. Joie let herself be led away, knowing instinctively that this was her one chance to live. Gaspar had no use for her—perhaps besides one. It was Godfrey he had wanted. She shuddered when she stumbled on the skull they had watched the waves uncover. Caesar led them behind the huts to a small cove, where two rowboats were pulled up on the shore. By the light of a lantern they saw others of Caesar's men pulling the struggling women from the first hut into one of the boats. Apparently, Caesar had realized the guard was loyal to Gaspar, and so with foresight he had dispatched him with the two bottles of wine.

A woman screamed, and Joie saw one of the pirates lash out, striking her so that she fell and hit her head on one of the boats. She sank lifelessly to the shore. The other two women crouched together in the bottom of the boat. Caesar helped Sheba into the other boat, while Joie climbed in on her own. She did not know how much she could trust Caesar, but she knew for certain that she did not trust the other pirates. She wondered if Caesar would have brought her at all if she had not been in the hut with Sheba.

As soon as they left the comparatively calm water of the small cove, the waves whipped about the boat. Joie could not see the other boat. It took all of Caesar's strength to pull the oars to give them some headway.

Fortunately, the tide was going in, and so the boat made some forward motion. She had no idea where she was.

Caesar fought the waves for what seemed like an eternity. Joie and Sheba were tossed mercilessly about. They held on tightly to the sides of the boat. She knew Sheba was as frightened as she, for at one point, in the middle of a particularly high wave, she heard Sheba yell to Caesar, "I cannot swim!"

With the rain and the waves, Joie did not think she could get much wetter or colder. And then came the rogue wave that sent the boat shooting straight up in the air and over. The three of them tumbled out.

Sheba disappeared.

"Sheba!" Joie yelled, praying that she would break the surface. The woman's clothing could have taken her under and kept her down. Treading the rough water, Joie felt Caesar beside her. He immediately dove down. At last he broke the surface, pulling Sheba with him.

"Help me get her out of these clothes," he pleaded with Joie. "Don't struggle, Sheba," he added.

Somehow Sheba managed to do as he said in spite of her fear. While Caesar wrapped the yellow length of cloth that had been Sheba's turban under her arms and made a loop through which to wrap his own arm, Joie wrestled with the rest of her clothes.

"I can swim," Joie assured Caesar, though she wasn't sure whether he cared. "Save Sheba."

The waves were already separating them.

"Joie!" she heard Sheba call. And then silence. There in the inky black darkness where sky, land, and sea virtually became one, Joie knew an isolation totally foreign to anything she had ever experienced. There was no moon or stars to keep her company, just the peril of the water that threatened to envelope her with each mighty wave. Suddenly, she was frozen with fear, her heart clenched within her chest, and she couldn't breathe.

Yet, in her soul, she felt a presence. She focused on that single ray of inner light, which grew brighter as she allowed it to manifest itself in her consciousness.

"Yahola, Father God, I am in your hands," she said aloud, simply wanting to hear a sound in the darkness, reaching out to the one she knew was always there. She was no longer alone.

With that thought, she was comforted.

"Well, where do we go from here?" she asked. No voice came down from heaven, but she was freed from the paralyzing fear.

Joie had no idea which way to swim and had no energy to fight the tide, so she merely tried to keep her head above water and grab a breath of air whenever she could. She shed her trousers and now wore only the long boy's shirt. She was exhausted. Though she was an excellent swimmer, the illness had drained her. She did not know how long she could keep her head above water.

It would be easy to give up. She was so tired.

She thought of Godfrey and the night they had experienced and was grateful. Loving him had brought her so much joy. In that moment, she had thought that it would be enough for a lifetime, though she had believed the lifetime would be much longer.

Soon Joie felt a peacefulness envelope her—and then intense pain when the spar hit her in the head.

Millea Francis had left the rest of her band to walk on the beach. They had come to trade with the Cubans at the Fisheries—and to see if Woodbine had returned or sent a message. She had seen sails on the horizon as ships entered the bay, but they anchored at an island inlet near the mouth of Charlotte Harbor. She lifted her face, letting the slight breeze blow her thick black hair from her tawny face, and held her hand above thickly lashed brown eyes to shield them from the blazing sun.

None of the ships were the *Venus*. Her heart fell.

A snowy egret perched on driftwood caught her attention. It seemed to direct its beady black eyes purposefully her way. She watched as the bird soared and then landed once again in the pile of driftwood, kelp, and seaweed. Millea had accompanied other Red Sticks to see if the British officer, Captain George Woodbine, might have returned with the supplies he and Edward Nicholls had promised. They needed ammunition to hunt—and for defense. The greedy Georgians were outrageous in their boldness, intruding on lands promised by treaty to the Creeks.

Though her father, Josiah Francis, had actually traveled to England to see the Prince Regent and had sent letter after letter through Alexander Arbuthnot complaining about the Georgians' incursions and violation of treaties, those letters went unheeded. It would almost seem that the American government *condoned* the aggressions of those who perpetrated crimes against Indians and settled on land on the southern side of the border.

The relationship between her father and Alexander Arbuthnot had begun when Woodbine had Arbuthnot bring Francis back to St. Marks from Nassau after her father's trip to England. Arbuthnot benefitted from his association with her father because the refugee Red Sticks and their Seminole friends, along with the blacks who lived alongside them, now traded with Arbuthnot instead of with Forbes and Company. Arbuthnot seemed sincere in his advocacy concerning their plight, but experience had made Millea cynical as to his motives.

Tears came to her eyes when she thought of how hopeful her father had been. The Prince Regent had given him the red jacket of the Corps of Colonial Marines in recognition of his service as an ally and a colonel during the war now known as the War of 1812. Then, after the ceremony, her father had told his family that Lord Bathurst informed him that it was now official British policy not to press for the fulfillment of Article Nine of the Treaty of Ghent. Nicholls's assurances would not be supported by the British government.

They were on their own.

Woodbine had assured her father, however, that there was still support among those who felt badly about making promises to his people and then abandoning them. George Woodbine, Edward Nicholls, Alexander Arbuthnot, and Robert Armbrister had plans. Abuthnot told her father that the new president, James Monroe, seemed in accord with the unofficial policy of expansionism that their enemy Andrew Jackson seemed all too willing to continue no matter how far they fled. Indeed,

Jackson threatened to follow them into what they had thought was the safety of Seminole lands in Spanish-controlled Florida. The Spanish, unfortunately, did not seem willing to engage the Americans over their disregard for borders or promises.

Though the British had basically abandoned the Indians who were their one-time allies, for some reason her father, Josiah Francis, maintained his belief that his British friends, Colonel Edward Nicholls, who had arranged for him to meet the Prince Regent, and Captain George Woodbine, would live up to *their* promises.

Millea pulled her shawl about her in the chill of the morning. She shook her head sadly as she thought and walked the beach. She kicked a sand dollar back toward a gentle wave.

Edward Nicholls had assured them that the Treaty of Ghent that had ended the War of 1812 guaranteed the return of their lands. When that did not happen, he promised them their own nation that would be carved out of what was now Spanish-controlled Florida. Woodbine had taken the gifts given to her father by the Prince Regent, and her father believed that he intended to use them to purchase supplies needed to engage the bellicose Americans.

They had all, the Seminoles and other Red Sticks, simply hoped to live peacefully. Just till the soil and put down roots. But their neighbors to the north kept stealing their cattle and initiating conflict. Their complaints to Benjamin Hawkins were ineffectual. The Beloved Man of the Creeks, as Hawkins had been known when he became Indian Agent in 1796, was now old and sick. Friendly Creeks profited from enforcing the policy that emanated from Washington under President James Monroe. Though she was only sixteen years old, Millea had been in the center of the conflict from the time she was born.

She remembered well when her father's cousin, Tecumseh, had visited with them when he came south. Tecumseh's mother Methoataske—"Turtle Laying its Eggs"—was a Tukabatchee Creek, and his father, Puckenshinwa, was the grandson of James McQueen, as was Millea's father, Josiah Francis. She was only ten years old at the time of

Tecumseh's visit, but Tecumseh had made a vivid impression on her. She was proud of her family.

She remembered everything Tecumseh had said. He came to solicit their support for a united Indian front to fight the "Long Knives," as he called the Americans. He had seen how they pushed further and further into the lands of the Shawnee, forcing them out of Ohio. Millea's father had taken his talk—allied with him—and become a major prophet of the Red Sticks.

"The British, our former friends, have sent me from the Big Lakes to procure our help in expelling the Americans from all Indian soil," Tecumseh had said. "The King of England is ready handsomely to reward all who would fight for his cause." Millea's father believed him. And trusted the British to live up to their promises.

Just as Tecumseh had predicted, a comet appeared in the sky about the time he would have made it home to the Lakes. Tecumseh had told them he would stomp his foot upon his arrival home, and the earth would shake. Sure enough, the earth shook. Captain Sam Isaacs, husband of her mother's cousin, said it made the mighty Mississippi flow backwards. He had been an unbeliever before that. But afterward, he told everyone that he had been taken to the depths of the sea, where he had gone swimming with serpents. Isaacs later became a prophet, but a false one, according to her father.

After the Red Stick defeat at Horseshoe Bend, those who survived and had taken to the canebrake made their way south and were welcomed by the Spanish governor, Maurequez, in Pensacola. They were also courted by British officers Edward Nicholls and George Woodbine. The British needed allies on the American southern border, and they promised their support to the now landless Red Sticks. Only a few former Red Sticks had signed the Treaty of Fort Jackson; yet Jackson now claimed that *his* treaty was the binding one, not the Treaty of Ghent that returned their lands. In Pensacola, Woodbine gave the Red Sticks gold, guns, gin, and red coats, promising them continued British support. They drilled in Pensacola Square as members of the British Corps of Colonial Marines.

Nicholls and Woodbine accompanied Captain Perry of the *Hermes*, one of seven British ships at their disposal, to Mobile Point to take Fort Bowyer. The Americans defended the fort well, and Nicholls lost an eye while commanding the howitzer he had pulled over the white sand dunes. The Americans held the fort against the superior forces of the British, who retreated to Pensacola, where they discovered that Jackson approached. The announcement of Sharp Knife's (their name for Andrew Jackson) approach made the Red Sticks cast aside their red coats, guzzle the rest of the gin, grab their new guns, and head for the Everglades.

And that's pretty much where they were now—ragged and wandering. The people without their land. Millea's family was living on the Wakulla River in North Florida, near Arbuthnot's trading post close to St. Marks, on land that Nicholls and Woodbine had said would be theirs, just as the British had promised.

Millea lifted her face to the sun and allowed the wind and the waves to soothe her. But the snowy white egret was persistent in attracting her attention with its rising and diving. She shook the memories from her head and walked forward, squinting in the sunlight.

The bird was diving at a spar, not driftwood! And lying there where the water lapped shallowly and gently against the sandy beach, tightly clasping that spar, was a woman wearing only a white linen shirt.

Millea moved closer. Was the woman dead? Kneeling beside her, she found a girl near her own age. She was breathing but also bled from a huge gash on her head. Millea pulled the girl from the shallow waves onto the dry white sand. She then looked all about her. There was no sign of other debris that might indicate how she might have come there.

She needed help. Millea ran back to the group loading supplies at the Fisheries.

When Joie awoke to a raging headache, she saw a crowd of Indians surrounding her. A girl about her age leaned over her, pressing a rag against Joie's head. And there—directly behind that girl—stood Savannah Jack.

Oh, God! It had to be him! She would recognize that man anywhere, though she had never actually seen him.

Savannah Jack was the madman who had killed her father and stepmother, thought he had killed her newborn brother, and would have killed *her* if she had not hidden under a canoe at Fort Mims. Years earlier, he had kidnapped her brothers, tortured and nearly killed them; and he had taken her sister-in-law Lyssa and would have killed her if Cade had not rescued her at Horseshoe Bend. Joie had heard tales of that demon-possessed man all her life!

From where she lay, he loomed ominously large and muscular, with a body crisscrossed by tattoos and battle scars. He scowled menacingly at her. His deep facial scars and cropped ears only added to her conviction that he truly was the avowed enemy of everyone in her family. And he was standing only feet from her!

Her heart raced.

She had always sworn that if she ever saw the man who had harmed her loved ones, she would take the knife he'd carved and gut him like a sturgeon. Suddenly, the blood rushed from her head, and she felt dizzy. She was weak, so weak. She must be strong.

But first she must stay awake and alert!

"Are you all right?" the young woman asked in a gentle voice. Then, looking where Joie stared with wide and startled eyes, the girl said, "Stand back, Jack. You are frightening her."

Jack, the girl had said.

Dear God. There was no mistake.

Jack was staring at her as well. "She looks familiar," he muttered. Those odd blue eyes. That face.

"I am Millea Francis," the girl said, turning back to Joie. "What is your name?"

If Savannah Jack found out that her name was Kincaid, he would kill her. And the name Joie was so unusual that it would tip him off immediately.

After being captured by pirates and nearly drowning in freezing water, she'd only thought that her situation couldn't get any worse. She was wrong.

Joie's head pounded. She turned on her side and vomited the water she had swallowed. Darkness clouded her vision, and, no matter how hard she tried to stay awake, she passed out.

Joie awoke to the gentle roll of a horse's gait, with powerful arms supporting her. Reluctant to open her eyes, fearful that those arms might belong to her family's greatest enemy, she pretended to be unconscious and simply listened. Eventually, as the conversation progressed, she came to recognize the different voices. Millea was the beautiful girl whose face she had awoken to earlier.

"We are fortunate that you came to the Fisheries while we were there, Abraham," Millea said. "You can tell us news from Bowlegs Town. Have your people at Angola seen or heard from Armbrister or Woodbine? I have not been to Angola, but I know that many people there are as anxious for their return as we are."

The man behind Joie, who must be Abraham, laughed and said, "One question at a time."

His voice was deep and calming. She heard it and felt it rumbling in his chest. He sounded like a young man. She could feel the strength of his arms around her. Thank God she was *not* in the arms of Savannah Jack like her sister-in-law Lyssa had been when he captured her.

"No, but we look for them to return soon," Abraham answered. "I have visited their plantation, and they expect them soon. I have many friends there. As I am sure you know, the two hundred who work on Woodbine and Armbrister's plantation there where the Manatee and the Braden rivers flow into Charlotte Harbor came with Nicholls, Woodbine, Armbrister, and myself when we left Pensacola. Many are survivors of the explosion of the fort at Prospect Bluff."

He paused, and when he spoke again, his voice quavered with emotion. "I have also come to visit old friends in Angola. We lost cherished friends, family—mothers and fathers, daughters and wives there, husbands and sons—that we speak of so they are not forgotten."

Joie sensed that his loss was even more personal than he revealed.

A boy's voice piped up then. "It was Sharp Knife's men who blew up the Negro Fort. You were lucky to escape!"

"Yes," said Abraham.

A simple word that carried great sorrow. A moment of silence settled upon them then as Abraham remembered the awful day when he survived the explosion that ripped apart nearly 375 of his friends. Yet he had survived. Why him?

"Many of my friends were captured and turned over to Indians friendly to Jackson—and were executed by them."

With her ear pressed to his chest, Lyssa heard the rhythm of his heart now beating faster. His body tensed and his voice hardened. "The free blacks and runaway slaves at Angola and at Bowlegs Village are eager to join Woodbine and seize Florida from the Spanish. The Spanish, after all, are so weakened that they can no longer protect themselves or defend their territory, much less fulfill their promises to shelter us. The Americans will not leave us in peace. Even here, on Spanish land hundreds of miles from the border, the Americans and especially Jackson threaten to capture us and return us to those who claim to own us. Their own laws and treaties mean nothing to those Americans.

"My people feel as though Angola is their last refuge before abandoning this land and sailing to an island in the Caribbean, though I fear they would pursue us there as well." Abraham sighed. "I tell them of how comfortable we are, settled near Bowlegs Village. They tell me that is too close to the Americans. Eventually they will come for us to take us back into slavery."

"They are right!" came another voice that Joie now recognized as belonging to Savannah Jack. His hatred and contempt were evident.

She was beginning to understand what her friend Sabrina had said about the other senses being enhanced when one lost one's sight. Maybe it was a good thing to hear people speak before their appearances caused bias. Abraham's voice was well modulated, cultured. Joie could tell he was an educated man. She liked him because of the kindness in his voice.

The boy spoke up again. "We Red Sticks do not feel safe even on our winter hunting grounds along the Talakchopcohatchee, so far from the border. Isn't that right, Uncle Peter?"

"Billy speaks the truth," came the voice of an older man from up ahead, rough with experience and, like Abraham's, edged with sadness. He spoke with authority. "Sharp Knife is land hungry and will not forget that we escaped him at Horseshoe Bend. He merely bides his time until he finds an excuse to pursue us." Joie also heard the man's fondness and pride for the boy.

Horseshoe Bend. That was where her brother Cade had fought Savannah Jack and rescued Lyssa. Lyssa knew the names, though she had not met the people. Cade and Lyssa had told the family their story and explained how Joie was related to all these people. Since she had been separated from her brothers as an infant and raised by her father and abusive stepmother, she had learned nothing of her Indian ancestry. When she was reunited with the brothers who had lived among their people, she was hungry to learn of their many connections to others.

Joie realized that the Peter who spoke must be her kinsman, Peter McQueen, the Red Stick Tallassee chief and son of James McQueen. Probably now around fifty years old, Peter married Betsy Durant, daughter of Sophia McGillivray Durant, the aunt with whom Joie's mother, Snow Bird, lived after the death of her own mother.

Billy, the boy, would be Peter McQueen's nephew, Billy Powell, the grandson of another of McQueen's sisters, whom they all called Queen Ann. He was the son of Polly, Queen Ann's daughter by Don José Copinger, whom the king of Spain had appointed governor of East Florida in order to divide the lands of Florida for the Spanish land grants.

As her father, James McQueen, often said, Don José was practically the only man his "little queen" would have considered a fitting mate. Cade usually told those stories with a smile and sometimes a chuckle as he remembered Nicey, a woman for whom family meant so much. She was also of the Clan of the Wind and had taken care of him and Gabe after their father abandoned them. She loved telling stories of their people. Whenever Cade thought of Nicey, a haunted look would come over his face, and Joie knew that his mind had returned to Fort Mims. He would never forget the horror of his last glimpse of Herman and Nicey Potts, the couple who had loved him better than his own father had.

Joie always begged Cade to tell her more. She had been eager to learn of her Indian heritage—something her father and stepmother had used to shame her.

"Grandmother did not want to be left at Ekanachatte," she heard Billy say.

"You know she was too old and sick to make the trip, Billy," Peter said. "Econchattemicco promised to take good care of her."

Had Savannah Jack not been in the middle of the group, Joie might have felt secure in revealing who she was, even though her brothers had fought on the other side in the Creek War.

But he was with them. And if there was anyone in the world she feared and hated with equal fervor, it was Savannah Jack. The Creek War in which brothers had fought brothers proved that hatred knew no family constraints, and, though Joie thought she could trust Millea—her voice was gentle and caring and she had insisted they bring her, a stranger, with them—perhaps it was now time to *pretend* she had amnesia.

There were times when it was safer *not* knowing who you were.

Joie desperately wanted to see Godfrey. But there was no way to get word to him of *where* she was without revealing *who* she was. And, even if she did, she might put him in more danger.

The voice of the man who carried her made her feel safe from Savannah Jack. Unaware of the tears that seeped from her eyes, Joie allowed herself to slip once again into the darkness.

It was night when she awoke on a pallet inside a cypress-framed, palmetto-thatched chickee elevated on stilts about three feet above the ground. Millea sat close by her side. She was indeed a beautiful young woman, with her black hair cut with bangs about her face and now done up in a bun in the back. Millea had awaken Joie to feed her sofkee, a creamy concoction of coarsely ground corn boiled with water and salted, from a beautifully decorated and fired pottery bowl.

"So pretty," Joie said, indicating the bowl.

"My mother is quite talented," Millea said.

Joie opened her mouth and welcomed the first food she had eaten in over a day.

"Can you tell me your name—or how you came to be washed up on the beach like that?" Millea asked.

Joie looked at her in honest bewilderment. She wasn't exactly sure how she wound up on that shore. The last she remembered, the spar hit her in the head. She must have instinctively grabbed hold of it and clung to it, though she could not remember doing so.

Millea read the bewilderment on her face and accepted her shrug as an admission that she couldn't remember. In Joie's weakness, the tears returned. Millea patted her hand and offered another spoonful of sofkee.

"Eat. Regain your strength. You're awfully thin. Have you been sick?" she asked.

Once again Joie gave a weak shrug, but she continued opening her mouth for the offered sofkee until she turned her head in exhaustion. With a soft "Thank you," she fell asleep once more.

Millea persisted in feeding Joie back to health and believed her claim of amnesia. The name was no longer a problem. Millea called her "Niña," Spanish for girl, and seemed satisfied.

They slept together, ate together, worked together, and grew closer with each passing day. They found more and more in common, and if it weren't for those Joie loved and knew were missing her—and the desperate ache in her heart that only Godfrey could soothe—she could be happy.

Chilly days passed with Joie sitting in the sun in front of the chickee, looking out over the Red Stick village on the Peace River. She also joined in the preparations for the people's return to the villages in North Florida. Alongside Millea and Sanie, Billy Powell's sister, and Billy and Sanie's mother Polly, she helped pack barrels with dried fish, deer meat, bear, curlew, wild hog, heart of palm cabbage, coco plums, wild grapes, guavas, papaya fruits, and vegetables to take back to family on the Wakulla River. The odd weather had devastated the corn crops

141

further north, so McQueen had come south to procure foodstuffs from a more temperate climate.

Thus far Savannah Jack kept his distance, though she often caught him looking at her as if trying to remember where he had seen her before. Surely she did not look that much like her brothers! Joie kept an eye on him, hoping he would leave his knife somewhere so she could hide it for the right moment. She went to sleep at night plotting ways to kill the man who had tormented her family for so long.

In her spare time, Joie occupied herself by whittling a flute just as her brother Gabe used to do. She'd not gotten one far enough along to play as of yet. She had little energy to do anything other than pack a few items and whittle, so she might as well do something productive while she awaited her opportunity to fulfill her destiny as Jack's killer. For some reason she thought of Jonah in the story the Duke had read to them. There was a reason for her being spit up on the shore where she was.

She'd been with McQueen's band for about two months when at last she felt like herself again. She had raw energy and wanted to clean, so she led Millea to the stables, where they watered the horses and brushed their coats.

Oh, she would love to mount a horse and ride like the wind, though she hadn't a clue where she would go. She remembered the days on the Duke's estate when she ran down to the field where the gypsies were camped and watched them practice their stunts. They caught her practicing on Francine, her favorite horse in the stable, and took her under their wing, teaching her to dance on the horse's back. She amazed them by jumping over jumps and through hoops, and doing back bends and back flips.

"I can show you a trick," Joie said impulsively.

"You remember something! Do you remember your name?"

Joie pursed her lips, trying to give the appearance of deep thought, and then shook her head. "No. I like your name for me just fine."

Millea smiled and said, "Show me your trick."

Joie took the beautiful Arabian from the corral. She nuzzled it, whispered to it. She guided the horse around the corral a few times, and then she jumped on his back, singing to him. He unconsciously trotted to the rhythm of her song. Millea was afraid to move or make a noise because she feared she might spook the horse.

Finally, Joie sat on the horse's back and leaned over his neck, whispering to him and stroking him. The horse threw his head back and whinnied in ecstasy. Joie stood up, in her element for the first time in a long, long while. Her black hair blew in the wind, her skin flushed with excitement, and her blue eyes sparkled. Amazingly, she jumped and flipped backwards. Millea stifled a scream.

Joie actually stumbled on her landing but righted herself just in time. Balancing quickly, she flashed Millea a brilliant smile and then leaped down.

"Where did you learn that?" Millea asked.

At that moment, Joie was tempted to tell Millea everything. But then she registered the applause coming from behind her friend. A crowd had gathered, watching her perform with the horses. Among them was Savannah Jack, who eyed her intently.

"I think he thinks you are interested in him," Millea said.

Joie was speechless.

"You watch him all the time. At one time I thought you were frightened of him. But I think he thinks you are awed by his magnificent body. That's the kind of man he is." Millea shrugged.

Then she assumed that Joie was embarrassed to be discovered. "Many girls are," she assured Joie. "Awed by his body, that is. It is nothing to be embarrassed about. I would think he was too old for you, but many older warriors have young wives. He already has one wife, but he might want another."

Awed by him? Repulsed by him was more like it. His wife? He *would* be so arrogant as to think that any woman who noticed him desired him. But she *could* get closer to him if he thought she was interested in him that way. Then she could get his knife. She would have to think about it.

For now, she would bide her time. Follow him to the horses and surprise him there. That was her plan.

Unfortunately, after her exertions on the horse, Joie experienced abdominal cramps and had to go back to the chickee to lie down. Then she saw that she was bleeding.

Millea followed her and sat cross-legged next to her. "I know your secret," she said.

Joie's eyes widened.

"You're going to have a baby, and you can't remember who you are so you don't know who the baby's father is. I think you're interested in Jack because you think he could keep you safe."

Safe? Good God! If Millea only knew!

But could she possibly be pregnant? With Godfrey's baby? And now she was about to lose it?

Tears spilled down her cheeks. She did not want to lose all she had left of Godfrey.

"I know someone who can help," Millea said, and she headed off to Billy's mother Polly, who mixed up a tea that calmed the cramps and put Joie to sleep.

Millea sat back and studied her new friend. When she'd first found her, she'd wondered if the bruises on her head were signs of abuse. Perhaps the girl had been raped. The bruises had healed, and Millea never questioned her claim to amnesia. Until she could remember, Millea resolved keep her close.

That afternoon, a messenger from Peter McQueen's daughters at Tukabatchee arrived. It had taken him a while to find Peter and the rest of the group, so his news was months old. Chief Neamathla of Fowl Town had gotten into a dispute with the commander at Fort Crawford just north of Ellicott's line over the use of land east of the Flint River, which the chief claimed belonged to his people, the Miccosukee. He had protested to General Edmund Gaines that the white settlers on those lands were in violation of treaty.

The messenger said that Neamathla was infuriated by the general's response that the land belonged to the United States as a part of the treaty signed by the Creeks at Fort Jackson. Neamathla protested that the

Miccosukee had not participated in the Creek War. Neither he nor his people had signed that treaty, and therefore it could not possibly apply to them. In response, General Gaines sent 250 men under Major David Twiggs to capture him. Though Gaines's first attack was beaten back, he was successful in his second attempt and ran the Miccosukee off their land.

Two regiments of Indian troops led by William McIntosh, Taskanugi Hatke, of Coweta had volunteered to serve the US Army at Fort Crawford and had attacked the Creek village of Fowl Town, fifteen miles east near the mouth of the Flint close to the Spanish Florida border and nearly sixty miles north of the site of the old Negro Fort on the Apalachicola River.

That night after the messenger delivered the news, Peter McQueen and his band huddled around fires, covered with all the blankets they could find. Tree frogs chirped and a gator bellowed, complaining of the cold from the den it had dug and flapping its tail in the stand of bamboo in the nearby cypress swamp. A bobcat screamed, and the bugle-sounding cry of a whooping crane pierced the night. The old ones said that the past two winters had delivered a cold like none they had seen. The ground was frosted, and ice covered some of the swampland. Fruit had frozen on the trees.

Joie shared a blanket with Millea as they sat in their chickee, listening to the men talk. She wished she were tucked into her soft canopy bed with silken sheets beside the nice big fire burning in the fireplace back in England.

"The people of Fowl Town probably fled to Ekanachatte, where we left Queen Ann," she heard Peter McQueen say. "Or perhaps they have gone on to Miccosukee. Econchattemicco has been a good friend to us, welcoming us into his village when we left the Negro Fort. It looks as if we are once again in the crosshairs of another war."

"The attack on Fowl Town requires retribution," Savannah Jack insisted. He had finished another knife, and Joie could hear the sound of its blade scraping against a stone as he sharpened it.

"Sharp Knife will come," Billy Powell said grimly.

The talk went on late into the night, and Joie's mind wandered. What had happened when Gaspar found out that Black Caesar had taken Sheba? Where were Black Caesar and Sheba now? She figured Gaspar didn't care what happened to her. Godfrey had probably cared—at first. By now, though, he had probably decided that she had either died in the storm or gone with Caesar. It was probably best if he felt that way. She missed him so much that she would have cried if Millea were not so close. Crying, of course, would have ruined Joie's amnesia ruse.

Shifting so that she could see through the doorway of the chickee, Joie studied Peter McQueen, who was sitting cross-legged on the ground and wrapped in a blanket before the fire. The responsibility of his family rested heavily on his shoulders. He was the youngest of his father's many children. Much of his family had fled Creek country with him, and, as their chief, it fell to him to keep them safe. He blew a plume of smoke from his long pipe, and Joie watched it lift skyward. It went with a prayer, she supposed. His people needed them. His piercing black eyes were dark ringed and heavily hooded with fatigue.

At the Fort Mims massacre, Joie had seen the bestial results of zealots goaded by religious fanaticism and the bloodlust of war—a blinding horror where a child was not a niece or nephew and a woman neither sister nor aunt, a man not uncle, brother, or son, but all were enemies to be scourged from the land. She had traveled far from Fort Mims.

Now she saw these frightened human beings dispossessed of all they had known before: their traditions, their land, their heritage. They were wayfarers desperate for a stable place to start again. But land-hungry Americans and greedy men who thought one human being could own another pursued them beyond the boundaries of international law, and they were helpless. Betrayed by the British who had promised aid and loyalty, the Creek people knew they must stand and fight once again until they could fight no more. These were her mother's people. She was of their blood, though they did not know it.

The fire crackled. "The weather will turn warmer. Sharp Knife will soon be at our village," McQueen said, breaking the silence.

The unusually cold weather brought them all together before the fire. The men in the first circle nodded. The women sat further away, near their men but in an almost concentric circle behind them, huddled in blankets and listening closely.

Young Billy Powell, grandson of McQueen's sister, squatted close to Sandy and John Durant, Peter McQueen's brothers-in-law. Sandy Durant's eyes were sunken deep into his head, burning with fever. A cough rattled deep in his chest. Joie saw that he was not long for this world, but he refused to give in. The weak would be left behind on the Peace River, but only death would keep Sandy from another encounter with Sharp Knife.

In the time that she had been with them, Joie had learned much about these people through Millea's constant chattering. She supposed Millea was determined to fill in her lack of past memories with new ones.

In spite of his age, McQueen, now in his fifties, remained fit and vigorous. His pale complexion told of his Scottish heritage. Three of his daughters by Betsy Durant—Millie, Tallassee, and Nancy—had married Chacartha Yargee, son of Big Warrior, who was himself chief of Tukabatchee and had remained friendly to the Americans. Sometimes the daughters managed to get word to their father about what was going on in the Creek councils. Chacartha's friend, Timothy Barnard, often translated for Indian Agent Benjamin Hawkins, sharing information. This latest difficult news about Neamathla's trouble had come through the messenger from McQueen's daughters.

"I am told that the new president has called upon Sharp Knife to invade Florida in pursuit," McQueen said. "He has sent word to William McIntosh and those friendly to the Americans to pursue our brothers who were attacked at Fowl Town and had to flee."

"Does Weatherford now ride with McIntosh, Talmuches Hadjo?" Savannah Jack asked McQueen with contempt. Joie had never seen him smile. His scarred visage merely shifted from scowl to deeper scowl while he carved the handle of yet another knife. Joie shivered.

William Weatherford, aware of their clan connections, had befriended Joie's brothers when they had come into the Creek country after their mother died and their father abandoned them. Cade and Gabriel probably knew Millea and her family well. Gabriel had actually lived with Weatherford, who raised horses and ran a racetrack. Gabe's gift as a "whisperer" had garnered Weatherford's trust and respect. It was Weatherford who had taken Joie's brothers with him when he captured William Augustus Bowles, pirate and adventurer, and turned him over to the Spanish for punishment and ultimate death in Morro Castle, a prison in Cuba. Sadly, Weatherford had also led the attack on Fort Mims and later surrendered to Andrew Jackson, signing the Treaty at Fort Jackson.

William McIntosh, White Warrior of the Creek village of Coweta, ran a ferry over the Chattahoochee River. He also was of the Wind clan. He led the friendly Indians as an ally of the Americans. McIntosh had fared well with his perfidy and was extremely wealthy.

"That has not been confirmed," McQueen responded to Jack. "It is said that he lived with Jackson on his plantation after the war."

Kind Abraham, who had returned from his visit to Angola to join the Red Sticks on their journey back north, said, "Runners from St. Augustine have brought the news that Americans have seized Amelia Island. We know our so-called masters in Georgia and elsewhere have been demanding the return of their slaves. They fear rebellion like that of Prosser's slave Gabriel in Virginia, at Chatham Manor in Georgia, and in New Orleans in 1811. Having a growing number of free slaves south of the border makes them afraid of another rebellion like that in Saint-Domingue, where 500,000 blacks rose up against the 40,000 whites on the island. They fear our growing numbers and power."

"How do you know this?" asked Billy.

"I read," Abraham answered, laughing. "Dr. Sienna had me read newspapers to him. I still read them when I can find them." Then, suddenly serious, Abraham added, "That is why my people are forbidden an education. Knowledge and ideas are dangerous in the hands of a slave."

McQueen looked at Billy meaningfully, and the boy ducked his head.

"So, young Billy," McQueen said, "talking paper is not a white man's silliness. Knowledge is power, just as I have told you."

Turning to Abraham, he said, "I told Billy that Tecumseh learned to read from the daughter of a settler in western Ohio that he befriended. It did nothing to diminish Tecumseh's courage or standing among his people."

"I will teach you, young warrior," Abraham said. "We need every weapon at our disposal to resist our enemies. We have planted fields with corn, beans, and squash, felled trees and sawn timber to build comfortable plank homes. Our children run free. Nicholls gave us the word of the English people that if we fought with them, they would protect us. He has given his oath to us that they will not betray us and will insist on the enforcement of the Treaty of Ghent. We will fight with whatever weapons we can find to remain free."

Joie had heard grumbling among Red Sticks who wondered at the wisdom of their association with free blacks and runaway slaves. Some believed that if they were not so closely associated with those whom the Americans considered their property, then the Americans might not be so interested in invading Spanish Florida and pursuing the former Red Sticks who only wanted to be left alone. The British had welcomed them all, red and black, as allies in the Corps of Colonial Militia. But seeing former slaves and Red Stick enemies in British uniforms fueled American fears. Both the Red Sticks and their black allies considered themselves victims, targets for the land-hungry Americans. There was strength in numbers.

"Talmuches Hadjo, you cannot trust a white man's promise," growled Savannah Jack, reminding McQueen of their past neglect.

"Woodbine promised powder and weapons," Abraham said. "Perhaps they have delivered what they promised to St. Marks. Perhaps he is already at St. Marks."

Later, Millea told Joie that Abraham had been the slave of a Dr. Sierra in Pensacola when Colonel Edward Nicholls enlisted him and

Millea's father, Josiah Francis, in the British Colonial Corps of Marines. Abraham had followed Nicholls to Apalachicola and helped build the fort at Prospect Bluff that many came to know as the Negro Fort. Then, in June of 1816, the villain William Hambly, an employee of Panton and Leslie whom Nicholls had left in charge of the fort, led the Americans fifteen miles up the river to Prospect Bluff. When Hambly mysteriously disappeared, Garcon had taken charge of the fort.

Their confidence had run high then. They flew a red flag above the Negro Fort, indicating a fight of no quarter under the Union Jack, and shot insults along with cannonballs at the Americans in the flotilla. But the traitor Hambly had told the Americans exactly where to aim a volley in order to hit the fort's magazine, which produced an explosion felt all the way to Pensacola. Abraham had just left the fort with Garcon, who, unfortunately, wound up being captured and executed by "friendly" Indians.

Abraham himself was not a physically impressive man. But he had an extraordinary intellect and spoke several languages. He had obviously been well educated and served as a translator between the Red Sticks and the British and Americans many times. Abraham was still young and relatively new to Bowlegs Town, Millea told Joie. She said that, though many among them referred to Abraham as a slave of the chief of Miccosukee, he and Nero, also a black man who was Bowlegs's chief advisor, represented Chief Bowlegs frequently as Abraham had done on this trip to the Cuban Fisheries. Nero and Abraham saw themselves as sense bearers to the chief.

Joie observed that the condition of the blacks who lived with the Indians was somewhere between that of servitude and freedom. Millea said that there were 300 who lived in Pilaklakaha, a separate settlement of blacks free of Indians that was close to Bowlegs. They lived with their own families and occupied their time as they pleased, paying Bowlegs a small annual stipend of corn. The Spanish and their slaves in St. Augustine had a similar arrangement. The settlement of blacks lived under a different type of governance than did the Seminoles and Red

Sticks. Millea said that even the homes they built were of a different style.

Once, in what seemed like a lifetime ago, Joie had heard Jackson's name and felt hopeful. But then, she had lived among the white man and hoped for Lyssa's safe return. Now, living among her mother's people and sharing Millea's anxiety over the safety of her loved ones, particularly the children for whom Joie had become so fond, Joie felt their fear and understood their frustration at being forever pursued and finding nowhere safe.

She could hear Sandy Durant's labored breathing above the sobs of the women. Children, unaware of what disturbed their parents, clung to their mothers. They had hoped to live peacefully on the lands they had settled and cultivated. But war loomed once again. More devastation, death, and destruction, and they were already living on the edge of subsistence. But the Americans, goaded by Jackson, would never be happy until they possessed all the land in the South, beginning with Florida and then extending to Texas and Mexico. Millea's father had so prophesied, though it was probably less a prophecy than a sigh of despair based on his experience.

"Americans want our land. But they will have to fight for it," Peter McQueen declared, his voice rumbling like an approaching thundercloud.

Little Sanie said, "Granny must be scared!

Billy looked at his Uncle Peter and insisted, "She needs us!"

Chapter 11

Godfrey beat against the door until his hands were black and blue. Days passed and no one came. The house seemed ominously silent, except for the occasional footfall that sounded outside his door. He would then yell once more, demanding his release. His water pitcher was empty.

There were no ships in the inlet. Godfrey looked desperately about him for any sign, any clue, of where Joie might be. He should have insisted that she come with him wherever Gaspar was taking him! Why had he thought Black Caesar had her best interests at heart and would protect her there on the ship? How stupid could he be? He berated himself over and over again.

He might well have died in that mansion on the sandy hill in Charlotte Harbor, alone amid the sea oats and scrub oak, if not for the intervention of Gaspar's friend Captain Menendez. He finally insisted to Gaspar's guards that Gaspar would be unhappy if Godfrey were found dead upon his return.

"Do you know where my wife is?" Godfrey asked Menendez, who had come and opened his door.

The ship was gone. He had last seen Joie on the cabin bed, beautiful and love tousled. He envisioned her being ravaged by the pirate who had kidnapped them—the man who hated women.

Menendez eyed Godfrey speculatively. How much to tell him?

"Gaspar is angry because Black Caesar took Sheba. Gaspar is in pursuit."

Godfrey recalled the look in Gaspar's eyes when he saw Godfrey and Joie the morning after they made love. He had left her on that ship! Now Gaspar had Joie, and he was not there to protect her!

Menendez sat leisurely watching him, sipping coffee and breakfasting on sugar dusted beignets on the piazza like a man on holiday. Cabbage palms swayed behind them in the slight breeze. The smell of fresh-frying beignets joined with the sweet smell of a fragrant bougainvillea. Godfrey's stomach cramped with both nausea and hunger.

Frantic though he was, he sat resignedly at the table with Menendez and searched the surrounding seas for a returning sail.

"The slave said I had you to thank for my freedom," Godfrey said as he poured water from the pitcher on the table.

More beignets and fresh coffee were brought from the kitchen.

Menendez nodded, pouring himself another cup of coffee, and waited for Godfrey to slake his thirst. "Our friend, Gaspar, departed in a fit of anger at the deceitfulness of his friend, Black Caesar. I restrained myself from commenting upon the irony of his dependence on honor among thieves."

Godfrey drank another full glass of water.

"I finally convinced the guards that he merely forgot to mention releasing his valued guest and would not appreciate losing the one who would lead him to treasure."

"Where is Joie?" Godfrey asked again.

Menendez shrugged and then gestured toward the beignets and coffee. "Join me?"

Godfrey took a hot beignet dripping with oil and covered in sugar. He relished the sweet delicacy, feeling his strength return and the pounding of his head ease as he was brought back from thirst and the frantic weakness of hunger. He tried to eat slowly to avoid being sick, but it was not easy.

Menendez talked while he ate. "Gaspar was once a dashing, devil-may-care companion. He played free and easy with women, enjoying them, pleasuring them, but only really loving his beautiful wife. He adored their son. He was a skillful officer, honored for his successes, courageous in battle, the man you wanted at your side or leading your battles. When he was betrayed in the royal household and his wife and son were brutally killed, he went mad. Every woman has now become the she-devil who betrayed him. He uses them and then slays them as he wishes he could do the woman he now confuses for each and every woman since. Every ship of Spain represents the king who ordered his capture and his family's murder."

Menendez paused, remembering the man he had once known. "I know this. He was my friend and my companion in enough devilries while we were in the academy, and he was at my side in enough battles for me to be in his debt." Menendez followed Godfrey's glance across the turquoise waters, watching the dip and dive of the sea birds and the porpoises frolicking before them.

"He came to me a broken man when the soldiers pursued him. He was this close to killing himself." Menendez indicated a fraction of an inch between his thumb and pointer finger. Then he shrugged. "Anger and hatred kicked in, and vengeance saved his life. I do not approve, but I do understand."

Godfrey watched a cormorant dive into a school of fish and then fly to the shore with its catch. Life was a battle. The strong devoured the weak.

Days passed. During the day, Godfrey was allowed on the piazza with Captain Menendez. At night, he was once more locked in his room. He had to find Joie. And when he did, he would need to be strong and ready. He rigged the ropes that had held the draperies throughout the room around the rafters, attached some rings, and, during those long hours when he could not sleep, he practiced rope dancing like he had seen years ago at the Royal Circus in London with his grandfather. At least it kept him from going crazy.

The guards walked with him about the island, convincing him that there was no way off. Gaspar and his men had taken all boats to search the shores and Pine Island, Black Caesar's usual lair, looking for Caesar and the women.

At last Gaspar returned. Godfrey rushed with the guards and Menendez to the dock at the inlet.

"Where is Joie?" Godfrey demanded.

"Black Caesar took her!" Gaspar said, trembling with anger. "And he took Sheba."

Gaspar strode up the steps to his house on the hill. He shook with anger. After a brief hesitation, Godfrey ran after him.

Caesar took her? She hadn't been with Gaspar all this time? Godfrey was incredulous.

If Caesar took her, then there was hope.

"But where would he have taken them?" Godfrey entreated.

Gaspar held up a bright yellow length of cloth. "I do not know, I tell you! This is all that was found. Sheba's turban. We found it washed ashore, barely visible in a clump of seaweed."

Gaspar stomped past them toward the house, ordering that hot water be brought for a bath. Everyone around Godfrey held his breath. The mercurial man might suddenly turn and cut off all their heads.

"Black Caesar better hope that Gaspar never finds him," said Juan Gomez, coming abreast of them. "He has not raged with such anger since..." His voice trailed off as he looked at Menendez. "You remember."

Menendez nodded.

"Was this Sheba a woman he truly cared for?" Godfrey asked.

Gomez shrugged. "He thinks so now, at this moment. But, then, he always does—until he tires of them. We found one body on Captiva Island. One body not yet a skeleton, that is."

"Captiva Island?" Godfrey asked.

Gomez indicated an island in the distance. "There. That is where he keeps his female captives."

Godfrey grabbed Gomez by his shirt. "Please, tell me what happened!"

Holding up his hands as if to push Godfrey away, Gomez explained, "Gaspar had told Black Bart to take her to Captiva Island as soon as we reached this island, and he brought you with him here. But Bart says Caesar countermanded those orders and took her himself."

All the blood left Godfrey's head, and he tightened his grip on Gomez, though this time not to threaten but to keep from falling. His knees had gone weak with fear. "And the body?"

"No, we are sure it wasn't your woman."

Godfrey released Gomez's shirt and stood in front of him, a haunted man. His eyes were bloodshot with lack of sleep and worry. He could barely process the horror of what had happened to Joie during the night of that monstrous storm.

"We found the bodies of two other women ravaged almost beyond recognition a short way up one of the creeks," Gomez added. "Gaspar said they were two of the women he held captive on the island."

"Joie?" Godfrey asked once again, his voice a mere croak.

"No, both were blonde and much too fair skinned," Gomez assured him.

For some reason Godfrey felt hopeful. Black Caesar had seemed more ally than enemy. There was still a chance Joie was alive. If he could just get free, he would search for Black Caesar and find Joie.

Gaspar called for Godfrey later in the day.

"Where is Bowles's treasure?" the captain asked with no ado. "Be careful now, your life depends on it. I have little use for you otherwise." Gaspar lifted the bottle of wine before him. Dispensing with the glass on the table, he put the bottle to his lips and drank deeply.

"I saved your worthless hide by *not telling* the others that you are the writer that led the US Navy to focus on piracy in the Gulf." His eyes glittered dangerously.

They heard someone at the door, and Gaspar yelled, "Away! No one is to come near this room until I call for you!" The footsteps scurried away.

Godfrey had prepared for this. The hunt for William Bowles's treasure would probably be his best opportunity for escape.

"I am waiting," Gaspar said with a threat in his voice.

Godfrey hesitated and then took the plunge. "Bowles's father-in-law was Thomas Perryman, principal chief of the lower Creek towns that some call Seminoles, whose village was on the east bank of the Apalachicola River. Bowles married Perryman's daughter, so he had a close association with the Indians in that area. When he embarked on his quest to create the State of Muskogee, a nation that he envisioned would compete with the United States and European powers, he enlisted Perryman's help and that of the Bully, then-chief of_Ekanachatte; Kenhega of Miccosukee; and James Burgess, a Georgia trader. I'm sure you remember that Bowles declared war on Spain after the Spanish attacked and burned his headquarters. He then used his so-called navy to attack the ships of John Forbes and Company as well as Spanish ships.

"It is said that he cached his loot at Ekanachatte with his friend, the Bully. He'd had a falling out with Thomas Perryman, his father-in-law, and with William, his wife's brother. The Bully and now his successor, his nephew Econchattemicco, are well known as being richer than anyone in Creek country."

"How do you know all of this?" Gaspar asked. "You're a New Yorker, aren't you?"

Godfrey turned his back to Gaspar and looked out the window west and north, remembering. "I was one of the few survivors of the Creek massacre at Fort Mims. I was rescued by a couple of very brave people."

Lyssa. Joie.

The beauty of the sun-kissed day eluded him. His mind had drifted back to the weeks after that horrible day. He had been unconscious for a long time. He would never forget the excruciating pain of the leg so badly broken that his bone protruded through the skin. Lyssa and Joie had set the leg and then tended the series of infections that set in, all while eluding the marauding Red Sticks. Nor would Godfrey forget the humiliation of his total dependence on Joie and Lyssa, who cared for his most basic needs. It was only through their extraordinary care that he was alive today.

And now he had failed Joie.

He cleared his throat, realizing that Gaspar expected more. "After I was rescued, I spent time with Judge Harry Toulmin, the superior court judge for the Tombigbee District of the Mississippi Territory, on his plantation at Fort Stoddard. I continued to correspond with him once I returned home. As a writer gathering research, I learned a lot from him about the history of this area and its major players. I corresponded with the Indian Agent, Benjamin Hawkins, as well."

He did not mention his ulterior motive for writing those letters—keeping up with the Kincaid family, particularly Joie. She had become his obsession. She was an enigma to him. He'd treated her like a worthless leper, and then she'd saved his life. What kind of person risked her life for a stranger who had abused her? Joie's example had changed his life.

He had written Judge Toulmin, inquiring about happenings in the area and hoping he would drop a word or two about Joie. He never did. That was when Godfrey decided to track down Jacob Rendel, father-in-law of Joie's brother, at the estate he had inherited. It was the reason he had accepted the invitation to speak at the British Museum. It was also how he and Joie had ended up being kidnapped. And Joie had now disappeared.

"I've never been much of a letter writer," Gaspar said. He reached for the bellpull behind him, and there was an immediate sound of feet and a tap at the door.

"Take Mr. Winkel here to his room and secure his door," Gaspar commanded. "He'll take his supper there. Then summon Captain Menendez."

Two guards accompanied Godfrey back to his room.

"I'm really hungry tonight," he told them. "Could you bring me some extra bread...and water for a bath?"

As they lowered the bar to secure the door, Godfrey overheard one whisper nervously, "Tonight?"

The food was brought to Godfrey later in the evening, and he thought the guards acted strangely. As had been his habit since the long days in isolation before Captain Menendez remembered him, he hid a portion of the food.

He, who had always had plenty and had never known hunger, had suddenly become a hoarder. But never before had he been a prisoner! If he should ever find a way to escape, he would need food to survive. From now on, he would be prepared.

Was Joie hungry and lost? Godfrey ached to go and find her. He was supposed to protect her! He pulled on the ropes suspended from the rafters and worked his body until he was exhausted. Concentrating on the intense physicality of the rope dance helped clear his mind.

The candle had burned itself out and the room was uncommonly chilly by the time Godfrey finished. He burrowed down under the covers and slept.

The sound of a gunshot awoke him. He heard shouts, and more guns fired; it sounded as if a brawl were taking place in the direction of Gaspar's library.

Feet pounded on the tile floor outside the bedroom.

"Gomez! Mutiny!" Menendez's cry rang out.

Then came the clash of cutlasses.

The sounds of shattering glass, pottery, and wood followed. Then came yet another gunshot, and the shrill cry of a man mortally wounded resounded through the echoing halls.

Who?

Gaspar's agonized voice sounded above all. "My friend! My dear Menendez! No!" The wail of despair.

"He needs a doctor!" Gomez yelled. "Help me get him to the ship!"

He. Who? Menendez?

And then silence.

What had happened?

Godfrey beat against the door, but no one heard.

From the barred window, he watched the *Floridablanca* set its sails and head landward to the interior Charlotte Harbor and the Cuban Fisheries. He heard the footsteps of those he knew were slaves cleaning up after the battle he had heard.

Was Gaspar dead? Was Menendez shot? A mutiny? What had happened?

Days passed. Godfrey was glad that he had been wise enough to ration himself on the water and food he had hoarded. But it was nearly gone. Would he die there and be found later—a mere skeleton?

When he heard footsteps in the hall beyond, he beat loudly on the door, but the slaves just shuffled faster. Soon he would no longer have the strength to beat on the door. He had already given up on his exercise.

With so little food, he no longer had the energy. Godfrey figured that they'd received no order concerning him, and they were too frightened to do anything beyond what they were commanded.

Perhaps Gaspar had abandoned his lair. Forever.

Godfrey was so thirsty he began hallucinating, losing himself in dreams. One minute Joie was there. A hazy figure, but there. And then she disappeared.

The water was gone. Had been for nearly a day. He would die here, and no one would ever know.

Caleb Connory would have figured a way out. Godfrey looked at the ropes in the rafters and wondered why he had ever thought keeping strong would help him escape. Caleb Connory was a hero. Godfrey Lewis Winkel was not. Godfrey turned his head to the wall.

Was that Joie standing beside his bed?

"Come to me," he whispered. She smiled. He reached out to touch her, but she had no substance. She was merely a figment of his imagination. If he had not been so dehydrated, he would have cried. Instead, he drifted into oblivion.

The next morning, he struggled to sit. He looked hopelessly toward the window. What was that? During the night, the *Floridablanca* had reappeared in the inlet. Godfrey forced himself to his feet and stumbled to the window. He grabbed at the bars and began yelling as loudly as his dry, aching throat would allow. At last, someone came to the door. He heard the bar lifted and the door pushed open.

There stood Gomez, looking at the feverish, nearly delirious Godfrey in shock. A beard had grown over Godfrey's now pale, gaunt face.

"Man, haven't they been feeding you?" Gomez asked.

Godfrey shook his head, almost too weak to speak. "Too afraid," he managed to respond in a raspy whisper. Light-headed with hunger, his lips parched and cracking, Godfrey wavered where he stood.

Gomez reached out to hold him up. He pulled a blanket from the bed and wrapped it around Godfrey's shoulders.

"Come, you must eat! Gaspar is asking for you. When some of his men mutinied, he was dealt a nearly mortal wound," Gomez explained. "We had to take him to the medicine woman at Angola. It took all of her skill to keep him alive."

"Menendez?" Godfrey whispered.

"He threw himself between his friend and a man wielding a pistol. He took the shot and died immediately. I was there by then and killed his attacker. Others loyal to Gaspar rallied to our aid, and we fought off the mutineers."

Supporting Godfrey as they walked, Gomez guided his faltering steps down the hall and out into the sun. He seated Godfrey on the piazza in the first bit of sunshine Godfrey had seen in weeks. Leaning back in his chair, Godfrey welcomed the feel of the sun in spite of the continued chill in the air.

"Drink slowly, now," Gomez ordered. He lifted a mug of water to Godfrey's mouth, and Godfrey drank so deeply that the water sloshed all over his body. A wave of nausea assaulted him. He shivered, and Gomez ordered another blanket.

"This is a rare cold winter," Gomez commented. His face mirrored his concern.

A servant brought Godfrey a boiled cornmeal concoction, salted and dripping with butter, much like the sofkee Lyssa had made when she and Joie rescued him after Fort Mims.

"We must rebuild your strength," Gomez told him, spooning the gruel into Godfrey's mouth. "I think the idea of finding Bowles's treasure is what has kept Gaspar alive. The medicine woman said his recuperation will be slow, and he must not leave his bed for quite a while. He lost a lot of blood, and there are bones that must heal, broken by the musket ball he took before Menendez arrived. Menendez took the shot that would have finished José off."

Godfrey did not have the strength for more questions. He applied himself to the sofkee and longed for his bed. Perhaps he would see Joie once again.

His mind drifted, and he wondered if Joie had enough to eat. He could not let himself imagine that she might be dead. Surely he would know if she were.

"Must find Joie," Godfrey said, and then he slipped away, finding the blessed oblivion once more.

Chapter 12

After getting word about the attack on Fowl Town, Peter McQueen debated whether they needed to complete their mission or head back to their village. His wife, Elizabeth Durant, was reluctant to leave her ailing brother, Sandy. Though McQueen expected Sharp Knife to intervene in some way, he reasoned it would take a while for him to gather his army. In addition, he did not expect Jackson to venture out with an army in that weather before March. Woodbine had May as the projected date for his expedition. If Woodbine would appear with the arms and ammunition and the volunteers he promised, they could defeat Jackson once and for all.

But they might have to hold him off until Woodbine arrived.

Deciding, McQueen had them collect the supplies they needed. They would wait as long as they could in hopes that Woodbine would come with the promised arms and ammunitions. If they had to fight Sharp Knife once more, they would need it. Sandy Durant had hoped for another chance to face Sharp Knife in battle, but after a long time struggling for each breath, at last his chest rose and fell no more.

Unsure of what he would find when he made it back to Ekanachatte, where they had left Queen Ann, Peter convinced Elizabeth, whom he feared had acquired the same cough that killed her brother, to stay at Talakchopco, their winter camp on the Peace River, until he sent for her. They left most of the women and children, including Sanie and her mother Polly, with Elizabeth.

Eventually, they could wait no longer for Armbrister or Woodbine to arrive. They knew they must return as soon as possible to their village on the Wakulla with whatever supplies they could carry. It would take a while for Jackson to appear with his army, but their people needed them. McQueen was their chief.

Those who could travel quickly accompanied him back to the village in the north. The girl Millea had found washed up on the beach had made herself useful, and Millea insisted on taking her with them. She worked hard and was good with the horses. Besides that, the girl refused to be left.

Joie had heard the word "Ekanachatte" once before. Godfrey had told Gaspar about a treasure there. If Millea and her family were heading in that direction, then so was she.

Coincidence? Perhaps.

From what she had overheard, Joie knew that Gaspar wanted Bowles's treasure. He would find it at one of the villages near St. Marks, at one on the Apalachicola River, perhaps his father-in-law Perryman's village, or at Miccosukee, where Bowles had first taken her brothers before they made it to St. Marks. She figured Godfrey was probably safe as long as he led Gaspar to believe that he might know where Bowles's treasure was. If he could escape, it would be somewhere in North Florida.

Joie despaired of ever seeing Godfrey again. And even worse, she wondered if he cared.

McQueen packed the horses so they might move more quickly. Still, he anticipated going no farther than fifteen miles a day, as they could only travel from about ten in the morning, when they gathered the foraging animals and packed them, to four in the afternoon, when they must unpack the animals so they might eat once again.

And so they went, traveling through the Green Swamp from which the Hillsborough, Withlacoochee, Ocklawaha, and Peace rivers flowed onto peaceful lands for farming and cattle raising. They tramped north through hardwood forests, marshes, pine flatwoods and sandhills, and cypress swamps to finally arrive at Francis Towne on the Wakulla River—Millea's home.

But by the time McQueen's band made it back to Francis Towne, they already knew that the war had begun. There, they were told that the Red Stick Creeks, with their Seminole and black allies, had gathered together in the Council House at Miccosukee fifteen miles up the St. Marks River from St. Marks to discuss what to do next. Miccosukee, under the authority of Chief Kenhega, the principal chief of the

Seminoles, was a town of thousands that spread for about ten miles around Lake Miccosukee.

The village of Miccosukee was strangely quiet on the way in, though they heard the pounding of drums coming from the center of the village. Cabins along the way were deserted, and all but the drums was silent until they proceeded down the wide avenue to the village square. Suddenly, they could hear shouting and singing. At that moment, Millea's three-year-old brother Jim Earle came shooting out from a spot where she knew their mother had thought he would be safely watched by a nursemaid. Millea figured the nursemaid must be new—or distracted—not to realize that Jim Earle could move like greased lightning.

"Where is everyone?" Millea asked the little boy.

"Millie! You are just in time! Papa is about to burn the American!" he shouted, jumping up and down in his excitement.

"Burn the American?" Millea repeated.

"Yes, he'd gone fishin' and they catched him! Papa ast him lots of questions, but he don't know much. Ain't worth feeding, Papa said." Jim Earle laughed.

Millea reached out her hand and pulled her brother up before her on the horse. When they passed a frantic girl searching and calling for Jim Earle, Millea gave him a fierce squeeze and then handed him down to the her. Then, with a look of determination, she turned directly toward the center of the action.

A crowd was gathered in the center of town, where a naked white man with his head shaved was tied to a pole in the middle of the plaza. Warriors danced and shouted around him, waving their tomahawks in the air. The crowd had chanted themselves into a pulsing drive of bloodlust.

Joie followed close on her horse as Millea urged her own horse forward until they could proceed no further through the throng of people. Millea jumped down and pushed herself through the crowd. No games were played on the square today. Instead, it was a serious matter of life or death for the brutally ravaged man tied to the pole, exposed in the uncommon cold.

At least fifty fresh scalps, including those of women and children, a macabre reminder of a recent raid, along with several hundred older scalps, dangled from the pole above the man.

He was young. Hardly older than Millea and Joie. Joie saw shock and dismay written clearly across her friend's face. Just as her father commanded that the fire be lit, Millea threw herself between the brave who had lifted his torch to throw upon the kindling.

Millea braced herself, one arm raised in defense. "Take my life and spare his," she cried out to her father.

A hush settled over the crowd. The chanting ceased. All eyes focused on the drama before them.

"Millea," Josiah Francis said, "this man's life has been claimed by Grey Wolf as reparation for the death of his mother and sister at the hands of the Americans."

When Francis spoke to his daughter, Joie sensed a great bond of affection between the two of them.

"Father, you are more than a chief," Millea insisted. "You are a prophet, a spokesperson for the Great Spirit. Does the Great Spirit demand the life of a man hardly older than a child captured while fishing? Was his hand raised against you? Freeing this man would show our enemies the heart of our people."

Francis studied Millea. She was naïve. The Americans would not show their people the same compassion. That he knew in his heart. She was too young to remember the massacre of the Hillabees, who had already put themselves under Jackson's protection during the Creek War before being annihilated by East Tennesseans who were unaware of the truce. She could not imagine men who ate potatoes cooked in the oils of people they had brutally killed, as Jackson's men had at Tallushatchee.

The British were no better. He had gone to England and stood before the English prince, wearing the coat of his rank in the British army in which he had served as a colonel. He had pleaded for them to fulfill their promises to the people who had aided their cause. Their prime minister had casually told him their policy had changed. That man sat in warmth, clothed in furs and fine fabrics, with his belly full.

166

Francis's own people were ragged and hungry, hunted from place to place, while politicians with no conscience encouraged others to steal their horses and cattle and urged the relentless encroachment upon their lands. Reluctantly, Francis had accepted the gifts from his former allies and left them with Woodbine to convert into arms and bullets so they could hunt meat for his people and—should need arise—defend them.

Unless Woodbine, Nicholls, and their associates with a conscience followed through on their efforts, all would be lost.

But, looking at his daughter, he knew that Millea spoke the truth. Josiah Francis was a holy man, and it was right to show mercy. This pitiful man-child did not represent the enemy that threatened his people. His hand had not been raised in battle. He had been hungry and had gone fishing for something to cook and eat—and gotten lost.

Francis knew that Jackson would pursue them regardless of what they did here today. But killing this man would not stop him. He could not deny his daughter one gesture of humanity in a world gone crazy with hate. Still, he had to speak carefully.

"It is up to Grey Wolf to decide if he will demand this man's life," Francis told her.

Millea turned to Grey Wolf. "Look at this man, Grey Wolf," she pleaded. "I knew your mother. I knew your sister. Your mother's heart was as gentle as any I have ever known. It would honor her memory to grant this man the compassion she would herself have shown."

Grey Wolf saw the tears in Millea's eyes and thought of his own sister. She also had a tender heart. She also would have said to him that this man was innocent. As would his mother, who had once told him of two boys held captive by Savannah Jack and William Augustus Bowles for whom she had done a small favor. Those boys escaped, and the joy of that one act of kindness followed her always.

He could almost hear her words now: "A small act of kindness could have a greater impact than the thrust of the sharpest spear. The Great Spirit does not give us eyes to see the ripple of your single act. Yet he gives us a picture in the ripple of an acorn falling into the clear pond water. That single ripple can reach the farthest shore."

"Grey Wolf," said Josiah Francis, breaking into his memory. "I will sell this man to the Spanish at St. Marks if you choose to spare his life."

The crowd was quiet, a great contrast to their earlier demands for vengeance. Everyone waited to see what would happen.

Joie felt the emotions roil around her. Only a few months ago, she had played the part of corseted refinement in the most civilized environments in London drawing rooms. Today she was in the middle of a Seminole village, befriended by the same Red Sticks who had attacked Fort Mims, where they would have killed her. Today the enemy was friend. Her head reeled as she tried to adapt.

Others were confused as well by the sudden shift of mood in the center of the square.

From the back of the crowd, where they could barely hear Millea's words, someone demanded, "What did she say? What is happening?"

Grey Wolf considered Millea's words. Finally, he said, "Loose him. I will not require his blood for the loss of that of my mother and sister. It is as they would wish." Standing before the young man, he lifted his hands so all would hear. "Your life is my mother's gift. Be worthy."

Grey Wolf nodded, and Millea cut the ropes that held the man. Francis gestured to the brave holding the torch, indicating that he should take the man back to the hut. He would be confined there until someone could deliver him to St. Marks.

Grey Wolf walked proudly toward the rest of his family—women wailing but nodding. They opened their circle to surround him.

"Millea, follow me," Josiah Francis commanded.

"The girl will come with me," she said, turning to find her new friend.

Joie was related to these people. She was aware that if she told them her name, they would know her immediately, and her chance to surprise Savannah Jack would disappear.

Francis eyed her curiously but proceeded on to the Council House at the other end of the square, where the other chiefs soon gathered.

Joie looked at Millea with new respect. Her brother, Cade, had told her about Chief Cornstalk's famed sister Nonhelema, a Warrior Woman and the women's peace chief, who stood six foot six. It was said that she was a beautiful woman who rode into battle at her brother's side, covered in war paint, when their people were threatened. And yet she saw her true role as peacemaker.

These stories, which Cade had learned from his foster mother, Nicey Potts, had given him much information that helped Joie understand her people. From what Cade had told her, Millea was Nonhelema's great-grandniece. Millea was tall, though surely not as tall as Nonhelema. But Millea certainly had the same strength of character. It was nice to think that those qualities might run through Joie's own blood as well.

Millea hurried back to Joie, who was now standing with Millea's mother Hannah and her brother Jim Earle.

Looking at the faces around her, Joie could not escape the irony of her presence in that village. Hannah Moniac was the half-sister of William Weatherford. The last time Joie had seen Weatherford, he was acting as a Creek war chief, leading the attack on Fort Mims along with Peter McQueen.

"Where is Big Sister?" Hannah said, scolding Jim Earle as she dragged him off by his ear. "Didn't I tell you to stay by her side?"

Millea grabbed Joie's hand, and the two girls made their way through the crowd to the Council House. Millea sent Joie to bring in more wood to build up the fire in the middle of the room. The smoke drifted up through the opening at the center of the roof, high above the spot where the supporting poles came together and were thatched with thousands of palm fronds. The chiefs sat around the fire with their respective villages and clans, some on raised tiers. Other women brought food and drink.

An angry and agitated Chief Neamathla of Fowl Town was explaining what had happened during Peter McQueen's absence. "When Gaines called the chiefs together, I refused to go. He told those who attended that our land was part of the cession of land included in the Treaty of Fort Jackson. I sent him a message that the treaty does not apply to Fowl Town because *none* of our people or our chiefs had participated in the war or signed the treaty. He did not care. He ordered that the land should be handed over to him. He also told them that we harbor their black people among us. He said if we stood back while they rode past us to the Suwannee to capture them, then they would not hurt us."

McQueen accepted the gourd of water offered by one of the women and inclined his head toward Neamathla, signaling him to continue.

"I told General Twiggs at Fort Crawford not to cross the Flint or cut a stick of wood on my side of the river," Neamathla said. "I said that I had been ordered by the Great Spirit to defend the land. I harbor no blacks, I assured him! When General Gaines sent 250 men against our village, we were surprised! They were to bring me back with them to the fort. We resisted and fought on November 21. The Americans then retreated.

"But they returned on November 23 and killed two of our men and one of our women. They ransacked our village, taking our store of provisions for the winter. When General Gaines arrived, he burned Fowl Town to the ground."

The conversation among the mass of people who had gathered in the Council House to share the fire's warmth had quieted. Many were refugees from Fowl Town. Neamathla's words filled the room. The Red Sticks who listened to him had walked this path to war before. They had seen their villages destroyed and their people killed. They had already abandoned the land of their fathers to seek safety beyond the reach of the Americans.

Or what they thought was safety.

"From the distance, we watched the smoke of our homes and our granaries and knew that all was gone," Neamathla concluded sadly.

Miccosukee chief Kenhega said, "Word of the attack spread quickly. Within days, many from Fowl Town began arriving here at Miccosukee with the news. Hillis Hadjo and I hurried to Ekanachatte because we figured they would be next."

Econchattemicco sat cross-legged, puffing on his pipe. When McQueen looked his way, he nodded and picked up the story. "We sent scouts, but they did not report seeing another army. However, they did tell us that there was a convoy of supply boats making its way up the Apalachicola River from the Gulf of Mexico. We decided to set up an ambush at Spanish Bluff. Of course, we did not have much faith in surprise because that is the site of John Blount's town and of the plantations of the traders Edmund Doyle and William Hambly, the traitor. But it was cold then as it is now, and I guess those in the boats included women and children who were determined to reach Fort Crawford. They ignored the warnings we know were sent to them."

Francis agreed. "They'd already come over halfway up the river— over eighty miles—and had only around thirty-five more to go." Turning to McQueen he added, "The outrage at Fowl Town deserved retribution. Several villages in the area had already chosen to join the Americans and went north up the Chattahoochee into Creek country. The Mulatto King at Tomatley and William Perryman at Tellmochesses stayed in their homes, but Econchattemicco's warriors and your Red Sticks, along with many Yuchi that had settled near the old Mission at San Carlos, joined in our attack on the supply boats."

"They were having trouble maneuvering the current on the swift flowing waters of this wet, extremely cold winter," Kenhega said. "We attacked at the bend in the river when the soldiers were forced to navigate close to the east shore, where we hid, near frozen ourselves, among the trees and shrubs."

Chief Neamathla told McQueen, "We killed thirty-four soldiers, including their commanding officer, six women, and four children. A woman whose husband was killed is being held by one of your warriors at Ekanachatte."

"After that attack," said Econchattemicco, "General Gaines called the friendly chiefs together and warned them that if they choose to take up arms against the Americans, they should go to Miccosukee or Sewanee. He told them that if they are friends of the Americans, they could stay in their homes in peace. The Americans would pay them for their supplies of corn and meat, and when they are hungry the Americans would feed them. One who was there told me that Gaines warned them we might as well look to the moon for soldiers to help us as look to the British."

At this, all eyes turned toward Josiah Francis.

He sighed. Though he had known war would come again, he had done all he could to secure the aid and arms they would need for their fight. His heart clenched with the injustice. Gaines sat in a fort built on land forced from the Creeks in a treaty signed at Jackson's command—but not by Francis or any in the band of Red Sticks who had come south into Florida...or those of Fowl Town whose village was burned. Surely his friends Arbuthnot, Woodbine, Nicholls, and Armbrister would follow through on their promises.

Woodbine was organizing the expedition that would attack around the first of May. But that was months from now. What were they to do until then?

Econchattemicco spoke up, interrupting Francis's thoughts. "Perryman and the Mulatto King sided with the Americans," he reminded them. "Chenubby, one of my war chiefs, led a party against the traitors at Spanish Bluff—Doyle, Hambly, and John Blunt, who has prospered well since leaving Tukabatchee. William Perryman brought warriors to Blunt's defense. Perryman was killed in the battle, and his warriors now ride with us. Blunt escaped, but we captured Doyle and Hambly just as Arbuthnot had directed."

McQueen nodded his approval.

"Two days later," Neamathla supplied, "we heard that more boats to supply Fort Crawford were at Ocheesee Bluff under a Major Muhlenburg, whom we have learned actually commanded that Lieutenant Scott advance up the river in spite of the warning they received. About then, warriors from Chief Jack Mealy's village joined us, and we shot at those in the boats from both sides of the river. Muhlenburg's men remained anchored there for four days, not daring to peek above the bulwark of their boats or risk being shot. But then Gaines sent a specially designed boat down the river with provisions and materials that protected them from our fire. Muhlenburg used some kind of special anchor to pull himself forward in the fast current of the river."

Neamathla's voice held an element of admiration for the inventiveness of their enemy.

"It was about time, too," insisted Econchattemicco. "It was colder than a dead beaver's dick out there."

That brought a chuckle from the solemn gathering, and everyone seemed to relax, breaking into their own small groups of conversation around the Council House.

Turning to McQueen and Francis, Chief Kenhega said, "Since Arbuthnot was away when Hambly and Doyle were captured, they were brought to me at Miccosukee. The black survivors of the Negro Fort wanted to kill them immediately. I was going to send them to New Providence, but Arbuthnot returned and sentenced them to be tortured by some of the Choctaw who had survived the explosion. Arbuthnot charged them with having sold Indian lands without Indian permission— referring to that land grab, over one million acres, by John Forbes as payment for debts he claims were owed."

"Doyle and Hambly hate Arbuthnot as much as Arbuthnot despises them," Francis added. "Probably because, when Arbuthnot opened his posts, he treated us fairly and became our voice in writing to the British and Americans. He has defended us to the Americans, rightfully blaming Doyle and Hambly for inciting the violence along the border, the cattle stealing and murders. Hambly betrayed us all when he guided the American gunboat up the river and showed them exactly where to direct the shot that blew up the fort."

"Doyle and Hambly are still at Miccosukee," Kenhega said. "I have forbidden any harm to them as of yet. But I think I need to get them out of here as soon as possible. I plan to take them to the Spanish at St. Marks to ship off to New Providence with the promise that they never set foot here again."

A companionable silence set in. They were lulled by the warmth of the fire and the convivial conversations around them. McQueen drew deeply on the ceremonial pipe, blew the smoke in a spiral, and watched it rise through the opening at the top of the Council House. He then leaned closer to Francis and Econchattemicco as they sat together in the midst of the gathering now distracted by their own concerns.

"My daughters at Tukabatchee tell me that President Monroe has called Sharp Knife to deal with us," he told them in a low voice. "White Warrior, William McIntosh of Coweta, has been summoned to bring his warriors to join Jackson's forces."

Their faces remained stoic. Though they had expected this, it was nonetheless sobering. They had fought Sharp Knife before. He was a formidable opponent.

McQueen passed the pipe to Josiah Francis and then asked Econchattemicco, "How does my sister fare?"

"The cold makes old women ornery, my friend," Econchattemicco said diplomatically.

McQueen chuckled. "Everything makes Queen Ann ornery. But then, she remembers well our time of peace and plenty. She longs for the days when Alexander McGillivray was able to play British, Spanish, and American off of one another for the benefit of all our people. The fact that those were the days of our youth make them all the more memorable, I suppose."

"Yes," Econchattemicco said. "She sits with the other women, cackling at their ribald jokes, bossing the young women at their work, and nursing their bent hands, competing with one another for the most effective potion to deal with their aches and pains. But often, when the weather is warm enough, she has her granddaughter Sarah place skins in front of their cabin facing north. And there she sits for hours on end. Sarah says she plants or harvests her old fields in her mind and remembers."

Francis looked toward Joie and quietly asked McQueen, "Who is this girl who laughs with my daughter?"

"Millea calls her Niña because the girl does not know her name. Millea found her cast up like driftwood upon the shore near the Cuban Fisheries in Charlotte Harbor. She says she has no memory of who she is, and your daughter refuses to press her."

McQueen paused a moment thinking. Then he added, "Savannah Jack says she looks familiar. There is something between them. She watches Savannah Jack warily."

They all looked toward Savannah Jack, who was, as usual, whittling on a knife handle.

"His memory of who she is will come," Francis said.

They were all curious and tried to think who the girl might be.

McQueen broke the silence. "I think we should send someone to Creek country and get the word out about Sharp Knife's approach and the coming conflict. See if others would come and fight with us. I would send John Durant. He needs a distraction from the death of his brother, Sandy, but maybe we should send Jack instead."

The flames danced high in the center of the Council House. Waiting for the need for more firewood to fuel the flame, Joie had picked up a knife and brought forth the piece of river cane that she had cut on the journey from Peace River to Francis Towne. She whittled away at the cane, which was at last taking the shape of a flute like those her brother Gabe made. Unconsciously, she blew lightly into it, testing the sound and apparently startling Savannah Jack, who jerked around to stare at her. Joie's heart clenched in her chest as she caught his glance. He was close to recognizing her, she could tell. But she was not yet prepared! She desperately sought out her friend, Millea.

Instead, her glance captured that of Josiah Francis, who caught his breath.

McQueen looked his way and followed his gaze.

"Do you remember Snow Bird, Savannah Jack's first love? Granddaughter of Red Shoes?" Francis bent toward McQueen and whispered close to his ear.

McQueen nodded.

"That girl is Snow Bird's daughter with her father Jason Kincaid's eyes. I would swear it," Francis said. "I grew up with Snow Bird, and I see now that this girl is her image, just as beautiful and, with those startling blue eyes, perhaps even more lovely than her mother."

"So she is Creek and Clan of the Wind. My wife's clan," McQueen said, looking toward his wife Elizabeth's surviving brother, John Durant. That made this girl family and even more his responsibility. Though his facial expressions never changed, Francis spotted the glimmer of alarm in his eyes.

"If Savannah Jack realizes who she is, he will kill her," McQueen said with certainty. "He has never gotten over Snow Bird's rejection. And then her marrying that scoundrel Kincaid."

"You think he incited Bowles to challenge Jason Kincaid?" Francis speculated. "To give him a chance to kill Jason and then claim Snow Bird?"

McQueen nodded. "He hated their boys because they had Kincaid's blood, and Jack had wanted to have sons with her. They were fine boys who outsmarted him, and that grates as well. And then one of her sons won the other woman he wanted. He nearly killed him, too, at Horseshoe Bend."

"I think she must remember who she is and know Jack, or she would not be so aware of him," Francis said. "She follows him with her eyes wherever he goes."

"He thinks she wants him," McQueen said. "See how he preens?"

"It is a very dangerous game," remarked Francis. "The only one she really trusts is Millea."

McQueen nodded and then made a decision. He sent a woman to bring Savannah Jack to him.

"Jack," he began when the man was standing before him, "we need you to go to Creek country and gather more warriors to join us in fighting Sharp Knife once again. We also need the guns you stashed in the caves at Catoma Creek. Can you do this?"

"I will do as you say," he said, and quickly left the Council House, but not without one last look at Joie.

"The girl was bruised and thin with a great big knot on her head when we found her," McQueen said. "She looked as if she had been very sick. Now that she is getting her health back, Jack is becoming suspicious."

"The sound of the flute reminded me of her brother, Gabe, who was Weatherford's horse whisperer. That was a clue to her identity," Francis said. "He played the flute to calm the horses."

"It sparked a memory with Jack as well," McQueen noted. "The girl is indeed improving, but she still looks fragile. I heard that she and her family had left Creek Country. I know Savannah Jack has been searching for them. Her feels he has a debt to pay for Horseshoe Bend."

"How did she come to be washed up on the shore like that?" Francis wondered aloud.

Chapter 13

Caleb Connory was slipping away from Godfrey. All the courage and bravado he'd called forth from his literary alter ego had eroded as solitude, starvation, and Joie's loss ate away at him. He imagined all sorts of scenarios in which she had died or now lay suffering somewhere. He had never imagined the bliss of loving and being loved by Joie Kincaid. He was unworthy of such a gift, and yet she had given it generously, freely, disregarding the hurt he had inflicted upon her when she was a vulnerable child.

The quivering, fearful Godfrey Lewis Winkel, protected now only by the precariously affixed shell of his alter ego's self-control, was a prisoner of José Gaspar. Fortunately, Gaspar's long recuperation had benefited the near-starved Godfrey as well. Godfrey had almost regained his strength and now plotted an escape.

Gaspar was determined to steal the treasure of William Augustus Bowles from the "pagan Indians," as Gaspar called them now that he had gotten religion after his close bout with death. He was born a Spaniard and had been christened in the One True Church. He was one of the chosen. His rejection of all things Spanish, his vendetta against Spain, was now forgotten. As soon as he could find a priest, he would ask forgiveness, perform a few acts of contrition, and go with his substantial treasure to a life of luxury and benevolence in South America. He might even build a church.

Gomez indulged him by participating in his fantasy—building mansions in the air.

When originally telling the story of William Augustus Bowles, Godfrey had merely been buying time with a topic on which he considered himself an expert—pirates, particularly in the Caribbean and Gulf of Mexico. It was the curse of scholars that, whenever they found a receptive audience, they were compelled to share each fascinating detail. While the average audience was usually bored into a near-catatonic trance, Gaspar was awestruck, encouraging Godfrey's over-eager responses with question after question.

When Godfrey had finished talking about Captain Kidd and stupidly revealed the fact that his treasure was already discovered, his and Joie's lives suddenly had little value. To keep them alive, he had then begun telling the tales he had heard of William Augustus Bowles and his piratical career. That had intrigued Gaspar because he had actually *known* Bowles. Godfrey had not thought far enough ahead to suspect that Gaspar would actually want to go and find Bowles's treasure.

With the rattle and clank of a boatload of pirates sharpening cutlasses and loading pistols, it finally dawned on Godfrey that innocent men, women, and children in the unsuspecting Indian village of Ekanachatte would soon be killed by a pack of rapacious pirates.

Good God! What had he done?

He knew that it would take Jackson's army to save them from destruction. After all, he'd seen these pirates in action when they took Menendez's ship! Unfortunately, Andrew Jackson was sitting high and dry at the Hermitage, having won against the Creek in the Creek War and gone home the hero of New Orleans after defeating the British in the War of 1812.

There was no way for Godfrey to lead them up the wrong river, away from Ekanachatte. The pirate knew his way around the rivers and inlets all along the west coast of Florida. Godfrey now regretted having told Gaspar what he had read in one of Bowles's letters: that Bowles planned to leave something with "the Bully," who had been the chief of Ekanachatte before the current Red Ground King, Econchattemicco, had become chief.

Godfrey had even described seeing the Purcell map of the Pensacola-St. Augustine trail, which had included the notation of Ekanachatte that placed it up the Apalachicola River near Ellicott's line. Godfrey had been so proud of himself, puffing out his chest and declaring, "Considering what took place immediately after the days when Bowles had gone pirating, it is my opinion that it is quite probable that Bowles's treasure was left with his partisans at Ekanachatte."

Godfrey now cringed at the memory. Caleb Connory would have sense enough to keep his mouth shut, to be the strong silent type and not regret the consequences of ill-considered prattle.

He had no choice but to accompany the pirates to the Indian village. But once they left the ship, he would escape—or be killed in the attempt.

Life simply wasn't worth living without Joie.

It was freezing cold with snow flurries. And it was March! Gaspar's crew would much rather head south than north, but Gaspar had recovered his strength, listening to Godfrey recite anything from his mental repertoire that was related to William Augustus Bowles. Though Gaspar had captured Godfrey because of Captain Kidd's treasure map, Godfrey had managed to convince him that Kidd's treasure was discovered by John Jacob Astor, fur trader turned financier. By talking up Bowles's treasures, Gaspar suspected he'd only meant to distract the pirate and buy time to devise an escape.

What began as an interesting pastime started to gall Gaspar: Bowles might possibly have out-pirated him! If there was a chance that Gaspar could find Bowles's treasure, then he would have both Bowles's treasure and his own. He would ensure that his biographer made it well known that Gaspar was the most successful pirate of all time!

And then he could retire to South America.

They sailed into the Apalachicola Bay with Gomez at the helm of the *Floridablanca* and Gaspar tucked beneath layers of blankets, sitting calmly and enjoying the scenery and the brisk cold. Godfrey shivered nearby with his hands tucked into the thin coat Gomez had thrown at him.

Gomez pointed ahead and said, "The mouth of the Apalachicola River."

Looking around him, Godfrey noted, "Then that must be St. George Island. Bowles was shipwrecked there after the Spanish captured him. He escaped and made his way to England."

Just the mention of Bowles's name brought Gaspar to his feet.

"He was being returned to Florida aboard the *H.M.S. Fox* when it ran aground on the east end of the island in a storm and shattered,"

Godfrey went on. "It just so happened that Andrew Ellicott was surveying the boundary line between Spanish Florida and the United States and had sent two of his men in a small boat to fish. They spotted the ship's captain, Lieutenant Wooldridge, Bowles, and the other sailors who had survived the storm standing in over two feet of water on the island. Woodridge sent a letter to Ellicott, requesting his assistance."

Godfrey tried to tell Gaspar that he had also read reports that Bowles had later returned and buried his treasure on the west end of that island. But Gaspar discounted that, insisting, "Bowles would not have buried his treasure on a barrier island. Too vulnerable to storms!"

Godfrey truly believed that Bowles had left his treasure at Ekanachatte. He'd read reports that Econchattemicco was recognized as an extremely wealthy man. What else could be the source of such riches? Godfrey wanted to sail up the Apalachicola River as close to Fort Crawford as possible, but he did not want to cause the deaths of so many innocent people.

If he could get away, though, he would try to make it to the security of that fort.

They began their upriver journey in a fog. Snow flurries fell on a day so cold that every other living being had better sense than to be out in the open. The only indicator of life as the sloop made its way carefully up the Apalachicola River was the smoke they smelled coming from fires in passing villages.

When the time came, Gaspar secured the boat in an inlet near the sleeping village of Ekanachatte and ordered their silent approach.

The pirates spread out and circled around to the north, where they spotted men of the village who had gotten up early to check on the livestock at the head of a creek. When a horse came galloping toward them, Gaspar and his men held their breath, afraid that they had been spotted. But whatever news the rider brought led the men with the livestock to jump on their ponies and head down toward a high bank of the creek. Gasparilla ordered his men to fade back into the woods. They watched as frantic warriors loaded the six ponies with heavy bags from a cave below the ridge of the creek.

Gaspar held his group back, thinking that the men and their ponies would pass right before them as they maneuvered around the pond. Suddenly, they all realized that the Indians were slowing to throw the bags into the water rather than leading the ponies past the pond toward them.

Gaspar lifted his hand to order an attack. About then, the Indian who had come to alert the others made it to the village and cried out a warning. A thunder of horses' hooves pounded. People came running from their warm beds out into the cold, where nearly a thousand warriors led by William McIntosh erupted out of the fog.

Godfrey quickly made his decision. He evaded Gomez's grab, ducked Gaspar's effort to club him with his musket, and headed toward the warriors running to the center of the village, quickly losing himself in the middle of the action. "Old Yarbor Pond," he heard one of the men whisper to another, who kept gesturing toward where they had come from. Whatever his companion had said apparently eased the man's worry.

Gaspar and his band melted away into the woods. The village had been so surprised by McIntosh's attack that there was little resistance.

McIntosh supervised as his men rounded up the people of the village, including the women and children. Figuring he was safer in that crowd, Godfrey allowed himself to become part of the roundup. Judging by the curious looks of those around him, however, he was not as successful as he hoped.

"You're not one of us," said an old woman next to him who looked Indian but spoke English with a Scottish lilt. Snowflakes swirled around them and covered the blanket she had wrapped around her shoulders. She held herself proudly with a dignity that belied her ragged clothing. She glanced down at the cutlass still at his waist and then assessed him with curiosity in her hazel eyes. He imagined she'd been a beauty in her day. He smiled at her, acknowledging the obvious.

He was sure that his own attire had provoked her interest. He'd had little to do with the selection. Gaspar had thought it amusing to dress his "biographer" in wide, knee-length trousers, a jacket and waistcoat, a long linen shirt, and a red kerchief that covered Godfrey's long, sun-bleached hair. He yanked the kerchief off. Of course, that did little to help him blend in.

Gaspar's quartermaster had provided all of Godfrey's clothing, except his boots, which were his own. At the last minute, Gaspar grabbed a British Royal Navy cutlass from the armory and thrust it into Godfrey's hand making a spur-of-the-moment decision to trust him. Gaspar had trusted him to carry a British Royal Navy cutlass. Fortunately, the pirate had grabbed it from the armory and thrust it toward Godfrey at the last minute as they left the ship.

His curiosity piqued by the woman's accent, Godfrey nodded at her. But before he could ask a question, William McIntosh, their attackers' leader, rode toward her.

"Queen Ann," McIntosh said, looking down at her.

"*White* Warrior," acknowledged the old woman with an incline of her head and a touch of contempt in her voice.

White Warrior was obviously well fed and well clothed. From McIntosh's correspondence with Benjamin Hawkins, Godfrey knew that White Warrior had accumulated land and power and had enriched himself by his close friendship with the American agent to the Creeks. White Warrior's first cousin, George Troup (the son of Catherine McIntosh Troup, his father's sister), had attended Princeton just like Godfrey, Benjamin Hawkins, Jacob Rendel who was now the Duke, and President Madison, a detail Benjamin Hawkins had been sure to share with Godfrey. Hawkins had died during the year there was no summer, ending the three-year correspondence the two of them had with McIntosh. White Warrior's village of Coweta was on the lower Chattahoochee near where the Federal Road from Milledgeville, the capital of Georgia, to Fort Stoddert crossed the Chattahoochee River.

"We have not seen your chief, Econchattemicco," White Warrior challenged the crowd angrily. "Has he hidden like a woman?"

The Indians looked at one another fearfully. Would White Warrior take his anger out on them?

One of his warriors galloped up. "A prisoner told us that Econchattemicco left early this morning to check on a herd of cattle hidden up on the Chipola River."

"Where is your brother, Peter McQueen?" White Warrior demanded of Queen Ann.

"Talmuches Hadjo has gone to the Cuban Fisheries," she answered, using her brother's war name. "The winter has been severe, and we need supplies."

She looked toward the storehouses that held their meager supply of corn and seed for the spring planting, which were being looted by White Warrior's men. She looked back at him with disdain. "Once again you are Sharp Knife's minion?"

"And once again you Red Sticks cause a war."

"We only want security in our land and peace to plant and harvest our crops," she said wistfully, her old woman's voice cracking with emotion. "White women now plant the fields I once planted with my mother." It was more a question than a statement, but, as McIntosh wheeled his horse around to ride away, Queen Ann could tell from the look on his face that her words rang true.

"Keep a close watch on this one," White Warrior commanded. "McQueen will bargain for his sister's release."

"Excuse me," Godfrey said, waving his hand to capture White Warrior's attention.

But, at that point, around twenty of the captured warriors broke away. After a quick pursuit, they were shot down by White Warrior's men. Distracted by their flight, the guards did not see the young boy at the other end of the village whistle and beckon to Queen Ann. He moved closer, clutched his grandmother's hand, and pulled her through the crowd, which parted to see them through. They then closed ranks as they passed, shielding their escape.

But first Queen Ann reached for Godfrey's hand. "Come with us," she said impulsively.

"You are safer without me," he whispered.

Gaspar could well be watching and waiting. She did not realize that Jackson's army had probably actually saved many of their lives.

She looked at him questioningly and then slipped into the bushes.

William McIntosh, also known as Taskanugi Hatke, ordered the houses, corncribs, council house, and other structures of the village burned. Fifty years in existence, extending for one mile along the Chattahoochee River, home to at least 800 people who lived in comfortable dwellings, the village now burned to the ground. Godfrey watched enviously as McIntosh directed his men to take the warriors captured at Ekanachatte to Fort Crawford and sent the wailing women and frightened children north to villages along the Chattahoochee.

But Godfrey's cutlass had caught McIntosh's eye.

British made, White Warrior thought. This stranger had acted friendly to Queen Ann, who was now on her way north with the women of the village. Who was this man? He eyed Godfrey curiously. Dressed like a pirate at a costume ball, he could be a British spy.

Godfrey attempted to plead his case, but McIntosh was not interested in his story. "Tie him up and take him to Jackson," he commanded.

Godfrey was set upon a packhorse, trussed like a holiday goose with his hands tied to the pommel, and taken down the Apalachicola. They found Jackson amid the teeming army of several thousand men at Alum Bluff, a place with a beautiful view rising 130 feet above the river. Jackson's men were on the verge of starvation, with only three days of parched corn and pork left. He had come 450 miles from Nashville to Fort Scott in eighteen days, where he found those in Fort Scott starving. Excessive rains had rendered the roads so bad that wagons had found them impossible. Jackson had ordered the men to take their supplies from the wagons and secure them on the wagon horses. They abandoned the wagons since the roads were muddy and the streams nearly impassable. They either had to bridge or swim every fast-running stream.

Once again, the contractors had failed them. Gaines's quartermaster managed to secure 1,100 hogs along with a bit of corn that he hoped would sustain Jackson's army until provisions could arrive by water up the Apalachicola River. Fortunately, the Indians at Chehaw had welcomed Jackson and provided corn. Every able-bodied Chehaw warrior had also joined their army. The only ones left in the village were women, children, the elderly, and the sick.

With no provisions at Fort Scott, Jackson had set out immediately. Five days later, to their relief, a boat loaded with supplies had actually made it up the river.

When Godfrey arrived, Jackson's men—his Tennessee Life Guard, 1,000 Tennesseans, and 1,100 Georgians—were gorging on the remaining pork and corn while they waited for the supplies to be unloaded. The food and the news of their success at Ekanachatte created a celebratory mood in the camp.

Godfrey thought of Napoleon's comment that an army marches on its stomach. He knew that no one was more aware of that fact than Andrew Jackson.

The man to whom Godfrey was led sat erectly on a white horse, probably the horse Sam Patch, whom Jackson named for the American daredevil. After his return home after the Creek War, Godfrey had read everything he could find about Andrew Jackson. He struck up correspondence with those who knew him personally or knew about him. Writing for his father's newspaper helped open doors and justified his avid curiosity. Few realized that Godfrey was then just a boy barely out of boarding school. He'd found that his amazing memory made some people uncomfortable—especially when they realized how much he knew. He had learned to sit with an interested look on his face and let them tell him what they wanted to tell him. It was a trick that usually encouraged others to fill the silence by telling him more than they probably wanted to say.

One of Jackson's Washington friends, who was also a friend of Godfrey's father, had told Godfrey that Jackson was an avid gamesman who enjoyed fighting gamecocks. He said Jackson could quote "The Rules for Fighting a Main of Cocks," which had been transcribed by the devout Georgia Methodist, Richard Blount. Jackson had been introduced to Blount by Benjamin Hawkins, who told him of Blount's two sets of gaffs that he had personally made according to the written rules, round from one end to the other, curved, and almost as sharp as a needle.

Jackson also collected thoroughbreds, which he raced at Clover Bottom. Jackson and John Coffee built the racetrack on the bottomland of Stone's River, the site of an early settlement established by John Donnelson, Jackson's brother-in-law. Jackson once ran a general store at Clover Bottom. Though he had jockeys and trainers at his extensive stables at the Hermitage, he enjoyed training the animals himself. His two most famous horses were Truxton and Pacolet.

"He implants the will to win in them by first riding them to the limit of their endurance," Godfrey was told. Looking at the hard-scrabble men about him, Godfrey decided that was his gift with leadership of men as well.

Jackson was not a handsome man. Amazingly, his face had not suffered the disfiguring pockmarks of most who had survived smallpox, though he still had the white gash down the side of his head and on his hand where a British officer struck him when he refused to clean his boots. Jackson had contracted smallpox at fourteen when he and his brother were prisoners of the British after the battle of Hanging Rock. His mother had managed to get the two of them released, and the feverish Jackson survived the walk, coatless and barefoot in the rain, back to his home beside the horse carrying his critically ill brother that his mother led.

Jackson had been shot several times, and those bullets continually gave him pain. Yet he sat on that horse as straight as a steel rod. The same stamina and steely will that had gotten him through earlier days was evident in the way he pursued his enemies into Spanish Florida.

Godfrey had read that Jackson was freckled faced and red haired as a boy, but now the hair about his face was wiry and white. He wore a long queue down his back tied with an eel skin. Gaunt to the point of emaciation, Jackson watched as his men devoured the rations. Godfrey knew he had shared their privations. This was the hero of New Orleans.

Godfrey had been in Washington with his father when the news had arrived of Jackson's victory. The war that had gone so badly wrong in the north (Monroe and Jefferson had thought all the Americans had to do was march into Canada to conquer it) had suddenly snatched victory from the jaws of defeat with Jackson's masterful win over Pakenham and the Brits at New Orleans.

Godfrey approached the great man, his heart pounding, with a sort of hero worship.

Jackson shifted on his horse and turned his intense blue eyes upon Godfrey. He cocked his head to one side and asked bluntly, "Are you a British spy?"

"No, sir," Godfrey replied, letting loose his broadest New York accent. "I am Godfrey Lewis Winkel, a writer for a New York newspaper."

Jackson's eyes narrowed, and Godfrey recalled how newspapers had pilloried Jackson at times.

Godfrey's heart pounded, his face flushed, and he stammered a bit, knowing how much power Jackson wielded. "I...I got k—kidnapped by the pirate José Gaspar and have been held captive since September. I have only just managed to escape by telling him of a treasure at Ekanachatte that led him here. Fate led your forces to attack at a most providential time."

"Where did you get the British cutlass, Mr. Winkel?" Jackson asked, cutting straight to the point, his eyes as cold as steel.

"Gaspar took it from his armory of weapons and thrust it into my hand as we left his ship."

"I have never heard of this pirate Gaspar, Mr. Winkel," Jackson said.

"But you have heard of the pirate Lafitte, General," Godfrey said. "According to Lafitte, he and his brother Dominique You were instrumental in your victory at the Battle of New Orleans."

Jackson quirked a brow. "How did you come to know Lafitte and You, Mr. Winkel?"

"Sir, I was present at a convening of pirates who met to discuss the growing menace of the American navy in the Gulf at the island of the pirate known as Gasparvilla."

After assessing Godfrey for all of two minutes—two minutes that seemed like two hours to Godfrey—Jackson's eyes lost their chill. He'd decided to believe him.

"Isaac Johnson," he called to one of his Kentucky guardsmen. The man jumped up from where he squatted and hurried to the general.

"Sir," Johnson said, standing at attention.

"Untie this man," Jackson ordered. "Take him to my tent."

"I need your help, sir," Godfrey said. "There was a young woman kidnapped at the same time as I who is now missing."

"You've obviously got quite a story to tell."

At last, Godfrey was able to breathe. Jackson could have easily had him shot as a British spy, which was what White Warrior suspected. Godfrey still wasn't certain that Gaspar wouldn't suddenly appear to take him once again. But he supposed he was as safe from Gaspar as one could be, situated as he was in the center of an American army in the tent of the most successful American general of his time.

"We have much to discuss, Mr. Winkel," said Jackson, dismissing them with a nod.

It was a gloriously beautiful spot there on the bluff overlooking the Apalachicola River. The soldier untying Godfrey noticed him looking about them in wonder. As they walked away, he spit out a jaw full of tobacco juice. Once he was able to speak without choking on his plug of tobacco, Johnson said, "I've heard some who knew Hambly and Doyle, who had plantations here, say they told of a legend that this is the location of the Garden of Eden 'cause gopher wood grows here."

"Knew?" Godfrey asked.

"Yep. Injuns took 'em. Their scalps is probly on some pole now," Johnson said matter-of-factly.

Godfrey shook his hands and stomped his feet to bring back the circulation; he couldn't tell if the numbness was due to the ropes or the frigid air. It was so cold that the underbrush and ground cover crackled and crunched as they walked. Birds that should have been singing in the glorious tropical foliage now covered in snow were probably sitting on a limb somewhere shivering and planning a trip further south.

Curious about the shell of a fortification there on the bluff amid the palm trees and scrub oak, Godfrey asked the soldier about it.

The soldier let fly another spray of amber spittle. Godfrey sidestepped quickly and avoided collateral damage. The Kentuckian put his long rifle to his shoulder as he thought a moment. Godfrey wondered if this man had been with Jackson at the Battle of New Orleans. It was a bloodbath for the British armed with muskets, while Jackson's men were sharpshooters armed with long rifles. He'd read that the British had 2,042 casualties, while the Americans had only 71. Facts he read and always remembered, but they were dry and bloodless. This man standing beside him had served his country by braving the battle—one few actually thought they would win.

Had the British taken New Orleans, England might have asserted itself into all the land President Jefferson had acquired through the Louisiana Purchase, a transfer of land that had violated the treaty in which France promised Spain the right of reclamation for the land connecting the Gulf with Canada, blocking any American westward advance.

Godfrey could almost see the gears of Johnson's brain shifting as he pondered the wisdom of talking to the young man with the British cutlass and the fancy New York accent. He finally decided that telling a little history of the place wouldn't betray a trust.

He glanced behind him at General Jackson, known fondly by his men as "Old Hickory," who was still sitting there watching the supplies get unloaded. "In July of 1816," Johnson began, "I uz with Edmund Pendleton Gaines at Fort Scott near where the Flint and Chattahoochee come together to form the Apalachicola River.

"It used to be called Fort Crawford, but they renamed it Fort Scott after the Injuns kilt thirty-four men, ten women, and four children that Lieutenant Scott was bringin' up the Apalachicola River to Fort Crawford. We passed that spot on the way here," he added as an aside.

"We uz running out of supplies and expecting provisions coming from New Orleans that were on a schooner in the Apalachicola Bay. Supplies uz put on a keelboat to come up the river. Gaines assigned me to Lieutenant Colonel Clinch to go down and give some support to the boats coming up the river. Jackson had demanded that the Spanish roust out that ant bed of blacks, Choctaw Indians, and other stealin' lowlifes. They were so well settled we found their cornfields spreading for fifty miles up and down the river, and their numbers uz growing. They uz robbin' the Spanish as bad as the Georgians! But the Spaniards didn't have the *cajones* to do nothin' about it."

Johnson cut his eyes Godfrey's way to make sure he caught it that he'd tossed out an authentic Spanish vulgarity, and then laughed at his mastery of one Spanish word. Godfrey smiled obligingly.

"Twarn't nothing new, really. I heard one of the general's spies telling him they'd been in a large colony of so-called exiles who'd fled South Carolina nearly 100 years ago, livin' 'round where they built at Prospect Bluff, but what started off being called Fort Nicholls wound up bein' called the Negro Fort when the blacks moved in and took over. Then they uz under the leadership of a Spanish-Negro half-breed called Garcon. Some of 'em were recruits of Nicholls and Woodbine from here and Georgia who'd got organized into a British company of so-called Colonial Marines.

"Though the Brits left the fort in the hands of the Red Stick allies who come with Nicholls from Pensacola, they moved out and settled in with the Seminoles, and the fort wound up in the hands of those runaway blacks who had joined up with Nicholls in Pensacola. Under Garcon's leadership, they moved in and took control. The Brits had left the fort well armed. That made them Georgians shit bricks, I tell you!"

Johnson bit off a plug of rolled tobacco that he pulled from the pocket of his coat, stuck it between his jaw and darkly stained teeth, and started chewing. As they neared the general's tent, he nodded to an acquaintance and spat once more. He then continued, "When Woodbine and Nicholls left the Fort, Hambly, a former employee of John Forbes who owned several trading posts and also had a plantation nearby, was supposed to be in charge. Hambly left the fort on account of the company he had to keep and joined up with us Americans.

"We met up with some friendly Injuns heading this way and joined forces. Old Captain Isaacs and Mad Tiger, that fought with us when we fought the Red Sticks before, were there with William McIntosh and about 150 friendly Injuns. They galloped around the fort, shouting and threatening and getting shot at by Garcon and his men.

"Clinch had sent for gunboats, and four days later they arrived. Then Isaacs and Mad Tiger went into the fort under a flag of truce to demand surrender. But Garcon told them he'd 'blow up the fort if he could not defend it.' The Union Jack had already been flying above the fort. As they left, we watched 'em raise a red flag of no surrender above it.

"Usually the river is way too shallow there to get a shot close enough to the fort to do any harm. But the weather took a strange turn in 1816, and the water ran fast and high."

Johnson choked and coughed a spell, took a breath, and spit once more.

Godfrey tried not to look.

"We got lucky with Hambly telling us where to shoot. Hambly told Clinch exactly where to direct the shot to the magazine.

"The cook told me the sailing master named Loomis woke him up at five o'clock in the morning on Saturday, the 27th of July, and told him to build up the fire hot as he could get it and stick the cannonballs in it. Cook heated 'em up real good and then come out and said, 'Breakfast is ready.' Loomis trained one of the guns so that it wouldn't hit earthen ramparts of the fort again, wastin' another shot, and then he loaded it with red hot shot. Damned if it wasn't a direct hit on the goddamned magazine. Lord, how the earth shook! Thought we'd blowed *ourselves* to Kingdom Come! Our ears were deafened by the explosion. Smoke filled the air and covered the sun!

"It was such a awful sight, we felt sorry for the poor bastards. The lucky ones uz dead. Others got blowed apart. 334 were in the fort. 275 got killed. The explosion was felt all the way to Pensacola and skeered those here close to the Negro Fort so bad they also abandoned *this* spot they called Alum Fort. And everybody that survived and lived around there—that didn't get captured to send back to their masters or to sell or get scalped by McIntosh's friendly Injuns—fled to the swamps.

"Hambly seized the blacks that had come from Pensacola...said he uz acting as an agent for Forbes and Company and probly got a commission for returning 'em. Clinch took the American blacks to Camp Crawford for their return."

He stopped to take a breather and cut off another chaw. Godfrey had no idea how he could possibly have any left. Johnson propped his gun against a tree and then leaned against the tree himself while he cut the chaw with his knife. Waving his knife with emphasis, he narrowed his eyes and he said, "I'm aimin' on catchin' me some o' them escaped slaves." Then he leaned closer to whisper, "Hear tell there's a $50 bounty right now for each slave we capture to return to their masters."

That was chilling. Of course, Godfrey wouldn't have thought twice about enslaved blacks if he hadn't spent months with little Mo, who later demanded that they call him Andro. He was the small black child Joie and Lyssa had rescued at the same time they'd rescued Godfrey. Smart as a whip and loving as could be, that little imp had wormed his way into Godfrey's heart just as he did everyone who knew him.

Fort Mims had changed Godfrey. Before, he had looked at life and people analytically, with a reporter's removal from the emotions at play.

No more.

Godfrey wondered who Mo's parents were. Were they killed at Fort Mims? Had Mo been ripped from his true mother's arms long ago? He knew that small children were sometimes sold away from their parents. Hearing this man talk of catching a slave made him envision the child he loved and would protect with his own life. Johnson's words grated on his soul. Though his heart pounded, he kept silent.

Johnson retrieved his gun and led Godfrey on through the teeming mass of soldiers squatting about. Godfrey marveled at how Andrew Jackson could make an army out of such men.

"That ain't all," Johnson said. "Clinch had promised them Injuns the ammunition in the fort. They found a shit load. I'm afeard some of that wound up in the hands of those Injuns we's gonna be fightin'."

How the man could talk around that bulge in his jaw without choking was a wonder. But he could, and he had told quite a story.

If only the trees could talk, Godfrey thought. What a story they could tell.

"I knows that's the truth 'cause I was there," Johnson added as he pulled back a flap on the general's tent and pointed inside. "So I can tell you for certain that's why they hate Hambly and took him. And probly scalped and killed him."

Godfrey stepped into the tent and sat on the only stool. Johnson stood guard outside.

Godfrey got the point. Hambly *was* probably scalped and killed. Maybe he deserved it.

He might have been scared himself had he not already avoided being scalped and killed by Red Sticks once and then recently evaded death at the hands of the most bloodthirsty pirate nobody knew! And now he was smack dab in the middle of another Indian war—something he'd never dreamed could happen twice in a lifetime! It would probably be wise to guard his tongue before he got himself in deeper trouble.

After his last experience, he had planned to stay in fine hotels in big cities far away from the frontier. But, as Robert Burns wrote, "the best laid schemes of mice and men go often astray." Godfrey had attended enough obligatory chapel meetings at Princeton, established by New Light Presbyterians to compete with the Puritans at Harvard and the Church of England at William and Mary, to understand predestination.

He had rejected that belief—*at least until now*. Maybe he was on a path that had already been decided. Maybe he should just sit back and let things happen.

But he knew he couldn't do that, not with his beloved Joie in danger. The predestined plan—if it one existed—could play out, but he was determined to keep looking for her. And if anyone could help him find Joie, Old Hickory could. After the Battle of New Orleans, folks thought that Old Hickory could almost conjure the wind and rain.

Chapter 14

Millea had stopped asking if Joie remembered who she was. They had drifted into a companionable friendship. Millea's mother, Hannah, treated Joie like her own daughter.

Of course, Joie had no idea that Josiah Francis had identified her and told his wife. Peter McQueen's wife, Elizabeth Durant McQueen, had known Joie's mother, Snow Bird, well. Elizabeth's mother, Sophia McGillivray Durant, had actually brought Snow Bird to live with their family when Snow Bird's own mother died. Elizabeth's sister, Polly, had been Snow Bird's best friend. Indeed, the relationship between the two of them was nearly as close as Elizabeth's relationship with her twin, Rachel. They'd had a happy childhood filled with brothers, sisters, and cousins who lived close by. They all belonged to the Clan of the Wind, their mothers' clan.

They wondered how Joie ended up on the shore in such an awful condition, but they would wait for her to recall what had happened—if she truly had lost her memory. If not, then they would wait for her to trust them enough to tell them her story. The way she often fell silent and looked off into the distance as if remembering something—or someone—made them suspect that she did remember, and perhaps the memory was too much to share. Now that Savannah Jack was gone, though, Joie seemed more lighthearted and relaxed. Those who knew the truth of her identity agreed that she was wise to hide it from Savannah Jack, though they would have protected her from him if the need arose.

Joie observed their courtesy at not interrogating her, but she felt guilty for not opening up to them. Now that Savannah Jack was gone and it appeared that she had been welcomed into their family, perhaps it was time. She was obviously pregnant now. Hannah had told everyone of how bruised and battered she had been when they found her, and the women clucked about her, thinking that her man had beaten her and then tried to kill her.

She wanted to tell Millea about Godfrey. The strangest things reminded her of him. A bird taking flight took her to the rail of the ship and the memory of a lingering glance. The smell of sofkee brought back the times she had fed him during his recuperation when she was just a girl. The glimpse of a man's bare chest made her think of their one night together.

And then the baby had kicked. Suddenly, her world was caught up in the wonder and mystery of the fact that she and Godfrey had created life. A part of him lived within her. Was it a girl? Was it a boy? Would the baby have her eyes? His eyes? No more showing off on the backs of horses. The growing life was precious to her, and she would not risk it. She might never see Godfrey again, but she would have the memory of him and the life he'd given her.

She felt grateful that Millea had become her friend. For Joie, a friend was a rare treasure, and she had little experience being one. But Millea had proven herself time and time again. Joie had decided she would tell Millea her secret.

Today.

It was a special day for Miccosukee, the Spring Busk celebrated at the new moon before the full moon of March, when the shoots of new corn would have usually appeared. The cold had hindered the planting and growing cycle, but many had traveled to Francis Towne on the Wakulla and to the villages around Lake Miccosukee. The numbers of people in the area swelled as visitors arrived at their Mother Fire—their hometown. It was a time of cleansing and celebration, something that had lately been hindered by the cold weather and failed crops.

Miccosukee itself was a prosperous town. Its people had been careful of their resources and boasted a herd of 1,000 head of cattle. Times were tough, but their methods of conservation had put them in a good position. They supplemented their meat with what the men brought home from hunting. But gunpowder was short, so they had reverted to using bows and arrows for hunting game, reserving the gunpowder they might need for defense. There were always fish in the streams. Corn, beans, and squash, known as the Three Sisters—their usual staples—had not produced well in the past couple of years, but they had still managed to secure 3,000 bushels of corn. And the visitors brought additional supplies of their own.

Fortunately, during their long days of hiding from the Red Sticks after the Fort Mims massacre, Lyssa had taught Joie how to find food in the resources around them: the inner bark of cedar, slippery elm, and white birch trees; the wapato in swampy areas with roots as big as walnuts; and the bog potato, a slender vine on dry banks with as many as one to a dozen potatoes springing from its roots. Millea and her mother, Hannah, had been impressed by Joie's resourcefulness.

Today, the boys were engaged in energetic ball play on the square at Miccosukee, preparing to compete village against village. Scalps still dangled from the pole on the field, a ghoulish reminder that their playtime was the little brother of war. Jim Earle ran along the sidelines, shouting and squealing and giving Big Sister fits. The happy sounds of the children playing drifted into the Council House, where Joie, Millea, and Hannah had gathered with other women before the speakers, respected men of the village, began addressing the crowd.

Their presence in the Council House at Miccosukee was intended merely as a friendly visit. The fire burned brightly and brought warmth to all who gathered. As they waited for words from the various Creek speakers, the women shared patterns for baskets, beading, and pottery designs, something to which they had looked forward during the long winter months. Hannah Moniac Francis demonstrated her unique patterns for basketry using sweetgrass from the hillocks in the Everglades along with palmetto fiber sewn together by colorful threads.

Suddenly, the cheery companionship of the gathering was shattered from a cry outside the Council House. Josiah Francis jumped to his feet and ran to the door. The boys scattered when Econchattemicco galloped onto the square and jumped from his sweating, heaving horse. He had ridden hard from the burning rubble of his village at Ekanachatte.

Francis stepped back as Econchattemicco pushed past him into the Council House, crying, "Can Jacksa Chula Harjo conjure the weather? Ekanachatte was attacked before my people could rise from their blankets by their fires."

"Many would have been there for the celebrations at their Mother Fire, just as there are here," Hannah said aloud, looking worriedly at the women around her.

It had been days since Peter McQueen and his nephew had left to get Queen Ann, who had sent word that she was much better and wanted to be with them for the Spring Busk. And they knew of many other Red Stick refugees at Ekanachatte. Friends. Relatives.

"I returned to the village after leaving early to check on the cattle foraging on the Chipola River and found my village in flames!" Econchattemicco said, the despair clear on his face. "White Warrior's men were herding my people to Fort Crawford and the villages on the Chattahoochee!"

Heads turned as Peter McQueen stepped into the Council House just behind Econchattemicco. At least he was alive. "None of us thought an attack possible with this cold," he said. "Billy and I arrived just as the ambush was taking place and barely managed to get Queen Ann out of the village without being captured ourselves. We met Econchattemicco making his way back toward the village and alerted him. Otherwise, he would have been captured himself. Billy and some of our warriors are coming behind us, bringing Queen Ann at a slower pace. We hurried back to warn you to be prepared. Sharp Knife is coming."

Whispers spread throughout the Council House. Many slipped closer to hear more.

"Captain Isaacs, Mad Tiger, Noble Kennard, McIntosh's cousin, and George Lovett ride with McIntosh and 1,500 other Creeks against us once again," McQueen told Josiah Francis.

It was known that Isaacs and Josiah Francis were sworn enemies. Francis had tried to have the turncoat Isaacs killed, but he had escaped and fled to Big Warrior at Tukabatchee. From then on, Isaacs had fought against the Red Sticks with William McIntosh, White Warrior. Now they pursued the Red Sticks down into Florida. Captain Isaacs was familiar to Joie. She recalled someone saying that he was with McIntosh when he helped the Americans destroy the Negro Fort in Spanish territory.

"I should have killed him when I had the chance," Francis said. "Can't the damn fools see that they are not making friends with Jackson? He is using them to do his bidding now, but their lands will be next."

Everyone eyed him speculatively. Had Francis had a vision?

He answered their unspoken question. "It does not take a vision to see what is happening. In July of last year, the Cherokee signed a treaty giving the Americans their land, and in return they accepted land on the west side of the Mississippi. Those who chose to stay agreed to accept 640 acres and live as white men live. Will the land allowed the Cherokee grow crops and sustain cattle? Or will the red man only be allowed the land that no one else would have?"

"Even then, how long have you known the Americans to allow an Indian to own land?" Peter McQueen added with feeling. "About as long as the tafia rum lasts for the celebration, and then they get a signature to sign the land over to a white man. We lose who we are! We no longer rule our land or make our own laws."

"*Ecunnaunuxulgee*," Francis said. The men nodded.

Millea leaned over and whispered to Joie, "That means 'those who greedily grasp for our lands.'"

"We call Sharp Knife's friend, William Blount, who is the governor of Tennessee, 'Tuckemicco the Dirt King'!" Francis exclaimed. "They are cut from the same cloth and have a long history of stealing our lands and then profiting by selling them. They are both now very rich. They see a toothless panther in Spain and hunger for the land that adjoins what they have already taken. We are only his excuse for invading Florida." Thinking of the young black named Abraham, he added, "And those who clamor for the return of those poor wretches who have escaped their masters across the border." Nearly 300 blacks lived near Josiah Francis. They were known as his slaves, but that association was more of a cooperative agreement that they would share the product of their labor with Francis in return for his protection.

Hannah looked up, worry once again evident in her features. "Were my brothers, Sam Moniac and William Weatherford, riding with White Warrior?"

"Those who would know were gone by the time I returned," Econchattemicco answered.

Provision stores at Miccosukee and Francis Towne had dwindled. The hungry people were glad to see McQueen returning with supplies, but now there were *more* mouths to feed. The people of Fowl Town had come to Miccosukee having watched Jackson and his men burn their own stores of seed corn and supplies. Now the wealthy Econchattemicco came to their fire empty-handed, with his people dispersed. Many of those people, now Jackson's prisoners, were Red Sticks who had come with McQueen and Francis after Horseshoe Bend. Added to these were the guests who had arrived for Spring Busk. Even with the food brought by visitors, how could they possibly feed them all?

"Jackson comes for us," Francis said to McQueen.

Women who had happily shared their crafts only moments before began to wail and wring their hands.

"What is Jackson's number?" asked Chief Kenhega of Miccosukee.

"At least 3,000," McQueen responded. "And that does not include the 1,500 Creek warriors led by White Warrior."

The number was sobering. Encompassing ten miles on the western coast of Lake Miccosukee, the area had about two hundred warriors. With at least ten women, children, and older people living in Miccosukee for every warrior, there were *at least* two thousand men, women, and children who needed to be evacuated before the onslaught of Jackson's men.

Francis and McQueen had defeated Jackson at Emuckfaw and Enitachopco and had badly battered Floyd's army at Calabee Creek in the Creek War. Jackson had a personal vendetta against the two of them. As Francis once told McQueen, the fact that they had escaped him after Horseshoe Bend was a canker on the man's ass. They'd laughed about it then, glad of causing Sharp Knife some of the grief he'd caused them.

But now McQueen looked at Francis with grave concern, "How will our people be treated by White Warrior and his men?"

Francis thought back on their bloody history. "We must prepare our people and leave immediately." Turning to his wife, he said, "Hannah, spread the word among the women. Take only what you can carry, the things most necessary. We must use the horses for the old and sick and head out immediately for Bowlegs Town."

Hannah nodded and led Joie and Millea from the Council House. "Help me spread the word," she told the girls and the women who had been with them.

Chief Kenhega's wife was nearing childbirth. "I will see to our people," she said, and, rubbing the small of her back as she walked awkwardly away to prepare her own family, she turned to the boys on the field, calling them to her so that she might instruct them in spreading the word.

Josiah Francis had followed them out the Council House door. "I will return immediately to Francis Towne to prepare our people," Hannah told him. He touched her face lovingly, and her eyes filled with tears. He had survived one war. They both knew that Jackson was a dangerous opponent who wanted Josiah Francis dead. Watching her husband return to the other men, Hannah realized that he would soon be in terrible danger once again.

The men were now alone in the Council House. It no longer felt friendly and safe. Josiah Francis looked meaningfully at Peter McQueen. Both remembered well the actions of Jackson's men at Tallushatchee. It had been just five years since 186 men, women, and children were killed and burned at Tallushatchee in retribution for the attack on Fort Mims. McQueen and Francis remembered how their warriors were reduced to fighting with bows and arrows because of a shortage of gunpowder. They also remembered the massacre at Hillabee of those who thought they were safe after making a truce with Jackson.

And now Jackson approached them at a time when they were in desperate need of the supplies they expected from Woodbine or Armbrister. They were ill prepared to meet Jackson's army.

"We *know* they will come here to our towns," said Chief Kenhega. "We have thousands that must leave their homes. We will leave 200 warriors here to meet Sharp Knife while others guide our old ones, our women, and our children toward Bowlegs Town."

"If Woodbine has sent Armbrister with the supplies he promised," said Francis, "they will be at St. Marks, or, if he is blocked there, he would take them to Bowlegs Town on the Wakulla."

"Let us hope our friends Woodbine and Armbrister deliver on their promises," Kenhega said.

"After we gather what we can from Francis Towne, I will go to St. Marks and see if Woodbine or Armbrister have arrived," Francis offered. "Hannah and the children will go with our people and meet up with you in the swamps."

Millea and Joie accompanied Josiah Francis back to Francis Towne. They passed the word to the 300 blacks who lived between Miccosukee and Francis Towne on their own plots of land in their own cabins. Those blacks would travel with them. Hannah was now directing the women who had gone with them to Miccosukee to gather all they could together, rigging travois to carry supplies and the elderly and sick.

Group after group set off safely until finally only Millea and her family remained at Francis Towne. Millea's father was determined to check once more at St. Marks to see if Woodbine or Armbrister had arrived with the supplies and gunpowder they had promised. Runners came with the news that Jackson's army was fast approaching. While Millea's father prepared, Joie took her friend by the hand and led her to a bench in front of their cabin.

Much was going on about her. She would not add to their anxiety by telling of the pains in her back or the spotting she had been experiencing. But she could no longer postpone telling her story.

"I know who I am," Joie told Millea. "I am Joie Kincaid, the daughter of Snow Bird, who was the granddaughter of Red Shoes."

"I know too," said Millea.

"You know?" Joie was shocked.

"My father and Peter McQueen saw the truth the night they sent Savannah Jack to retrieve the guns he had hidden." She smiled and added, "When you blew on the flute, they recalled the flutes your brother used to make. They noticed then that you look amazingly like your mother, who was Savannah Jack's first love. They were afraid time was running out before Jack realized who you were. And then he would kill you. So they sent him off."

"I was going to kill him first," Joie insisted. "Your father saved him by sending him away."

Millea laughed.

Joie sniffed at Millea's disbelief. "You have only known me with child. I will surprise you once this babe is born."

"Tell me more," Millea said, leaning forward, eager to hear her story.

Joie's eyes darkened. "My brother Cade married Choctaw chief Pushmataha's granddaughter, Lyssa Rendel." She thought it best that she not mention Fort Mims, since Josiah Francis and Peter McQueen were both prophets who had led the attack there.

"Lyssa's mother, Malee, was married to a Virginia planter's son who turned out to be the heir to a title and estate in England. After the war, he took all of us with him to claim his inheritance. After living in England for a few years, we were all about to board the ship to return to Virginia when I decided to say goodbye to my friend Sabrina. She was having tea, and I followed her to surprise her at the tearoom.

"And there she was having tea with Godfrey Lewis Winkel, who Lyssa and I had rescued a long time ago. Damned fool! I should have let him rot that day, but I didn't and now he's the father of my child. I'll bet he doesn't care a lick at a black snake for me and the fact that he put a baby in me, and now he's nowhere to be found and probably doesn't ever want to see me again or even remember!"

"He beat you up and abandoned you!" Millea cried. "I knew it!"

"No," Joie insisted, shaking her head. "The pirate Gaspar who kidnapped us took him to his home and sent me to Captiva Island with the other women. That night, Black Caesar came to rescue a woman named Sheba, and she insisted they take me as well. The boat capsized in the storm, and I got hit in the head and wound up washed ashore on the beach where you found me. I looked up and saw Savannah Jack and remembered that he had kidnapped my brothers Cade and Gabe when they were children. He also killed my father and his wife and almost killed my little brother, Jay." By now Joie was crying. "And…Oh! I miss them all so very much. And I bet they think I am dead! But what could I do? How could I let them know? What if Savannah Jack finds out who I am?"

Millea had no chance to answer these questions. Joie hadn't expected answers. Her tears soon turned into a look of cunning as she whispered to Millea, "I have a plan. I will steal one of those knives he carves, and when he comes at me, I will stab him with the knife and then pull upward and turn the knife in his gut!"

Millea sat with her mouth open.

Joie heard a gasp and turned to see Josiah Francis of at the cabin door, with his wife Hannah beside him. Apparently, they had overheard most of her story.

"She thought she could kill Savannah Jack with his own knife!" Francis said.

"Yes, *she is* of our blood," Hannah said. She looked proudly at Joie. "I knew your mother, dear one. She was much loved. Your father…well…not so much."

"Joie, I think it best to take you to the Spanish at St. Marks," Josiah told her. "British and Spanish ships come in and out of there frequently, and they will return you to your family. Don Francisco Caso y Luengo is a friend."

Turning to Hannah, he said, "If Woodbine's ship is there, I will sail with them to the Suwanee River. If it isn't, I will catch up with you and the children in the swamp."

"I am coming with you, Father," Millea said. "Joie may need me." Hearing this, Joie wondered if Millea suspected that the pregnancy was in danger. Regardless, she would be grateful to have her friend along.

Millea's older sister, Polly (also known as "Big Sister"), had already mounted a horse. "You're bound to get into trouble," she said to Millea. "Mother agrees. She thought you would insist on going. I'm coming as well." She lifted the gun she carried.

Joie had no doubt that Polly knew how to use it. The tradition of warrior women had apparently followed this generation.

Carrying all they could retrieve from Francis Towne, the girls' father said reluctantly, "We will talk to the commandant and then you can decide." Then he turned to their mother. "Hannah, take Jim Earle and leave immediately. I have heard that McIntosh has already put the torch to some of the blacks' cabins north of Miccosukee. He will be here soon. I will meet you at Bowlegs Town"

"I hope they've all made it into the swamps," Hannah said. She took Jim Earle by the hand, leading him into the canoe that would take them through the swamps surrounding the Wakulla. They would travel east and meet up with refuges from Miccosukee.

"I want to go with Father," the little boy said, attempting to jerk his hand from Hannah's grasp.

"Go with your mother, Jim Earle," Josiah said. "You must protect her."

Obstinacy shone on his son's young face.

"A warrior obeys his chief," Josiah insisted.

Obediently, Jim Earle turned. "Follow me, Mother," he said.

They all smiled briefly before recalling the danger and urgency of the moment.

Joie mounted her horse awkwardly. She could not dally. The lives of these people who had saved her were at risk. As they rode, she would look for the herbs she knew would help her symptoms. Millea jumped up behind her.

Joie looked down toward the river where Hannah and Jim Earle were getting into the canoe with Jim Earle's unfortunate nursemaid, who had loaded the canoe with their meager possessions.

Hannah's eyes met Joie's, and she lifted her hand in goodbye. Then her gaze drifted to her husband, sitting proudly on the gray stallion and waiting for the girls to be ready to set off. Joie watched as Hannah pressed her hand to her heart when he looked at her. He lifted his own hand to his heart and then extended it, opening his hand as if sending his heart to her. After that, he turned and spurred his horse forward, lifting his head high.

Joie clenched the reins as Millea settled herself. She saw Hannah's canoe wobble as Jim Earle jumped eagerly into his nurse's arms. To him it was all an adventure. His high-pitched voice distracted her. When Hannah finally sat down, the young black man at the stern guided the canoe out onto the Wakulla River to follow the web of streams as far as they could into the swamps toward Bowlegs Town.

Homathlemicco, Josiah Francis's right-hand chief who had led the attack on Lieutenant Scott after the attack on Fowl Towne, accompanied them to St. Marks, along with a small contingent of warriors. They all followed the handsome, six-foot Josiah Francis, who had dressed in a fine grey frock coat with a linen shirt and his usual leather leggings moccasins. He rode proudly before them on the three-mile journey. Should they find the British ship at the harbor there, they would direct it to leave quickly and join the refugees at Bowlegs Town.

Chapter 15

After listening intently to Godfrey's story, Andrew Jackson sat back with narrowed eyes. "There's little chance of the woman being alive, you know," he said. "But if she is, there may be information at St. Marks through Spanish channels. You may travel with us, if you wish. Pick up a rifle and fight with your fellow Americans so that we might have peace and security on our southern border."

Godfrey found that he liked the man who was America's hero. Jackson was his best chance at finding Joie. "Thank you, General. Make me useful."

"You are a newspaper man, you say. Look and learn. And then you can return home and tell the tale of this noble venture."

They did not stay long at Alum Bluff. Jackson led them down the river to Prospect Bluff, the site of the Negro Fort, sixty miles below the United States border. Godfrey followed Jackson as he scouted about the bluff. He appreciated its strategic location. It was a beautiful spot with a stream to the north and swamps to the west.

"Little wonder Nicholls selected this spot," Jackson said, as much to himself as to Godfrey.

Isaac Johnson picked up a rusted musket nearby. "Lookie here, General. Them darkies left perfectly good guns. I can clean this up and I'll bet it's good as ever!"

"Go to it, soldier," Jackson said. "But first, find my aide-de-camp Lieutenant Gadsden and send him to me."

To Godfrey, he said, "The water bastion looks usable. I will have Lieutenant Gadsden use that as a beginning and build us a fort here. It is much easier to bring supplies to Fort Scott by water than overland."

He stepped closer to the bluff and looked down the river. "This is a definitely a strategic spot on the Apalachicola, and we must secure it. The damned British are determined to incite the natives and blacks. They've proven it over and over. This time we must exterminate the vermin who are causing the fear and unrest on our southern border and ensure that the Brits and the Greasers are put in their place."

Godfrey was shocked by the contempt in the general's voice, and evidently it showed on his face.

Jackson caught his expression and asked, "Do you know much about this fort, Mr. Winkel?"

"Only what Johnson there has told me," Godfrey responded.

"I will recollect for you," Jackson said. "For the record. I assigned Brigadier General Edmund Pendleton Gaines at Fort Scott to destroy the Negro Fort. It was built by one of our nation's greatest enemies, the blustering Irishman, Colonel Edward Nicholls of the Corps of Colonial Marines, a disreputable collection of runaway slaves, and, by then, a collection of renegade Red Sticks. He'd been in Creek Country off and on since 1804, stirring up the Indians and offering five dollars a scalp.

"You can thank the man who built this fort for what happened at Fort Mims. We found men, women, and children with their whole scalps gone, and later we found those scalps on poles and on the belts of the damned Red Sticks. The Brits formed the Corps of Colonial Marines and encouraged blacks to leave their masters and Red Sticks to join them. They offered the blacks freedom and the Indians their lands if they repudiated the treaty I had them sign at Fort Jackson. Kept stirring them up. Left them with a stash of weapons here to start a small war, but we blew it up in time.

"I sent Lieutenant Colonel Duncan Clinch with a land force to the Negro Fort, and I sent Sailing Master Jarius Loomis with a convoy from New Orleans to sail up the Apalachicola River to provoke an attack and justify our actions in destroying the damned fort. The ploy worked. Of course, God was with us since the water was higher than usual and we could get closer than normal. The low, shallow water had been a problem for us but a boon to the inhabitants of the fort. The blacks fired upon us, but they were inexperienced with artillery."

Jackson stilled his horse, and Godfrey sidestepped his own horse a bit closer. He watched the general, trying to imagine the action as he recounted it. The bluff was such a lovely place, and nature had already reclaimed much of the devastation that had occurred there. Though the area was still damp from the incessant rain and the weather was uncommonly cold, birds sang in the trees and fish jumped in the intermittent rays of sunshine that sometimes hit the river with sparkles of light, reminding Godfrey of the fickleness of fate and circumstance.

"Loomis sent Midshipman Luffborough ashore for fresh water," Jackson continued. "The crafty Garcon, the black leader, had set a trap by having one of their own in plain sight. Luffborough thought that he was an escaped slave and set out to capture him. He landed with three seamen, and they were shot upon by a party of blacks and Choctaws. Midshipman Luffborough was shot along with two others, and one escaped by swimming across the river.

"Lieutenant McIntosh, along with the old chiefs, Captain Isaacs and Mad Tiger, had joined the expedition in order to secure slaves and return them to their masters for the reward. McIntosh was ordered to station one-third of his men hovering around the fort. That was successful in that the inhabitants of the fort kept up an incessant but, due to their inexperience, unprofitable firing. A well-aimed firing of a red-hot cannonball by Loomis's man, Sailing Master Bassett, into the enemy magazine caused the terrific explosion that was felt far and wide.

"The human misery in the fort caused our battle-hardened Lieutenant Colonel Clinch to tear up, I understand."

Jackson's jaw tensed as he imagined the scene. War was a bloody horror that he'd experienced firsthand. "Lieutenant Colonel Clinch soon regretted his promise to reward McIntosh with the artillery left within the fort," the general said. "Amazingly, they found 2,500 muskets, 50 carbines, 400 pistols, 500 swords, and 163 barrels of gunpowder still intact."

He looked at Godfrey intently and shook his head. "Nicholls and Woodbine had left the Red Sticks and Negroes well armed. It is hard to understand why the Red Sticks did not take the ammunition from the fort when they left. I fear that some of it may have found its way back into the hands of the Negroes, Red Sticks, and Seminoles we will be fighting.

"Let me tell you, I have long experience with Indians. I moved to Natchez in the Cumberland as the only licensed lawyer and public prosecutor in West Tennessee in 1789. I traveled from Nashville to Nachez, sleeping in the open frequently for days on end, exposed to the elements and the Indians. I was lucky; I still have my scalp." Jackson ran his fingers through his wild hair.

"From 1780 to 1794, there was one person killed every ten days within a three-mile radius of Nashville. I *know* the suffering of these Americans on the borderlands of our country. They are encouraged in their depredations by men like the fanatical Scot Alexander Arbuthnot and the mad Irishman, Edward Nicholls. I knew George Woodbine before he was appointed a British agent to the Creeks, puffed up with the brevet rank of captain of the Royal Marines. Most recently we have been cursed with that upstart Armbrister, who, I'm told, loves to parade about in his red coat 'drilling' the Red Sticks and blacks."

The general fell silent for a moment, and Godfrey brushed debris from his shirt.

"Do you see these scars, Mr. Winkel?" Jackson finally asked, indicating his head and his hand. "My brother and I were prisoners during the War for Independence. I was fourteen years old. My brother was near death with small pox, and another brother had already died. An officer commanded that I polish his boots." His eyes were frigid with the memory. "I refused, and he slashed me with his bayonette. These bandits and murderers must be brought to justice!"

Muscles ticked in Jackson's jaw. Godfrey knew that there was much more he could tell him, but the memories and the emotions were too raw.

They had been at Fort Gadsden for nine days when Captain Isaac McKeever of the navy and Captain Gibson of the army arrived, informing General Jackson that the provision flotilla was waiting at sea. The general made arrangements to leave Captain Gibson in command at Fort Gadsden and ordered Captain McKeever to take the flotilla around the Bay of St. Marks.

"Should the enemy attempt to escape to the small islands, I order to stop them!" Jackson instructed. "I am told that Peter McQueen and Josiah Francis, prophets who stirred up the Creeks in the Red Stick war, are now doing so with the Seminoles. They are said to be in the vicinity of St. Marks. Woodbine and Arbuthnot have united with them and gathered with a motley group of slaves stolen from their masters. Together, they are stirring each other to acts of hostility.

"McKeever, you should move along the coast, and, as I approach by land, capture and make prisoners of anyone who seems suspicious. In eight days, I will arrive at St. Marks and communicate with you in the bay and receive my supplies." Jackson paused and then added, "Do what you must to capture them. Or kill them, if you must." The determination in his voice was pure steel.

"Godfrey," Jackson said, "you may go with McKeever by sea or with me by land."

"I'll stick with you, General," Godfrey said. "I've pretty much had my fill of ships for a while."

On March 29, Jackson crossed the rain-swollen Ochlocknee and sent a party of 200 men under David Twiggs to Tallahassee. Twiggs found the town deserted and set it afire.

Two miles out of Miccosukee, Jackson's spies stumbled upon men trying to herd some of their cattle to a safe place. The general added some of McIntosh's men to the vanguard and drove the Indians to a swampy finger of land jutting out into a pond. When confusion occurred in Jackson's ranks, with friendly Creeks being mistaken for the Seminoles, a tumultuous chase through the village ensued, and Chief Kenhega was able to escape to the swamps, where his family had already evacuated.

When Jackson's army entered the now-deserted village of Miccosukee, scalps taken from the attack on the Scott flotilla still dangled from the pole on the plaza outside the Council House. This evidence of the murders of women and infants enraged Jackson. McIntosh ordered his men to set fire to the village and secure all the supplies they could find. He terrorized any villagers who appeared.

Johnson explained to Godfrey that McIntosh was determined to bring the renegade Creeks under the control of Coweta, the new capital of the Creek Nation.

McIntosh's men reported that there were at least fifty *fresh* scalps in the Council House. An Indian wearing the coat of Captain James Champion, who had been killed when sent to relieve Major Muhlenberg, was found in one of the houses. Then the pocket book of a Mr. Leigh, containing several letters, including one to General Glascock, was recovered.

Jackson's infamous temper erupted.

"To think that my hands have been tied so that I could not pursue those heathen Red Stick animals before this! And now with the Scott party, they have attacked more defenseless women and children. Imagine them ripping the babes from their mother's arms and bashing their heads against the side of the boat before scalping them! And then, I'm told, they cut their mother's breasts off when they killed them!"

Godfrey's stomach turned. He'd experienced war before. He knew the sadistic depths to which men could sink because he had witnessed it firsthand at Fort Mims. He'd hoped never to see it again.

"Torch their Council House!" Jackson shouted. Then, turning toward Godfrey and his aide-de-camp Gadsden, he raged, "And to think those goddamned Greasers harbored them and put up with these activities! Francis Towne is a mere three miles from the Fort at San Marcos. The Spanish have been complicit in harboring Francis and McQueen and all of their band of cutthroats!"

When the general calmed at last, he called for his campaign desk and sat down to write a note to Don Franciso Caso y Luengo, stating that he thought that the rebel Red Sticks were headed toward St. Marks and Jackson considered it his duty to occupy the fort. "It is necessary," he wrote, "to chastise a foe who, along with a lawless band of Negro brigands, has for sometime past been carrying on a cruel and unprovoked war with the citizens of the United States."

Godfrey stood by while Jackson then penned a note to Secretary of War John C. Calhoun, justifying his march to occupy St. Marks by saying that he thought the rebels were headed there.

Godfrey was hopeful that someone at St. Marks had news about Joie. Black Caesar's involvement in her disappearance gave him the only hope to which he could cling. He simply could not bear the thought of losing her forever.

Chapter 16

New Providence bustled with the British naval presence on the Bahamian island closest to the Florida Strait. Gabe had no doubt that an occasional pirate frequented the harbor as well. Indeed, Woodbine's associate, Gregor MacGregor, might possibly be considered a pirate. MacGregor had already informed Gabe that he was "Brigadier-General of the United Provinces of the New Granada and Venezuela and General-in-Chief of the armies of the two Floridas." Luis Aury, their confederate, had finally appeared.

Armbrister relished the clandestine element of preparing for their expedition. He procrastinated in actually setting sail until he had procured the support and supplies he and the others knew they would need for their endeavor.

And so Gabe languished in the tropical paradise for months, impatient and anxious. He knew that he was being watched and followed to ensure that he did not betray their enterprise. To pass the time, he hung out down at the harbor, talking to anyone who might have news of Gaspar or the goings on in that area. Woodbine and Armbrister welcomed his activities because they felt that Gabe Kincaid's search for his sister gave them cover for gathering news that might be pertinent to their own cause.

Gabe's heart ached. Joie could very well be dead. Typhus was a deadly disease. But he clung to the knowledge that she was young and strong and spirited.

Luis Aury was nothing like Gabe had expected. He appeared to be a little older than Gabe, maybe around thirty. He had brooding black eyes with highly arched eyebrows that gave him an always-intent expression. He parted his hair in the middle and brushed it to hang down over his ears, a hairstyle that Godfrey thought only enhanced the size of his distinctive nose. Aury held a letter of marque from Cartagena and New

Grenada. He had laid claim to Amelia Island on behalf of the Republic of Mexico after Gregor McGregor abandoned it.

Gabe couldn't miss the irony that Cartagena, under which letter of marque Aury conducted his privateering, had *outlawed* the importation of slaves, though it was well known that Aury took the slaves he captured with his prizes to the Lafitte brothers at Barataria to sell in New Orleans. In addition, Aury's well-trained crew consisted of 130 mulattoes from Galveston who were known as "Aury's Blacks." Down at the docks, Gabe heard it whispered that their presence on Amelia Island intimidated the Georgians just across Cumberland Sound and led to Aury's being run out of Amelia Island by the United States Navy.

Gabe had learned a lot about Woodbine and his associates, as well as other well-known characters operating in the Gulf and the Floridas, from the sailors with whom he spoke. He made friends with quite a few of them, drinking coffee with them at the taverns near the sea. Those Yankee sea captains loved to gossip, and an ear eager to listen was welcome after months at sea with the same people.

The bartenders near the dock had become accustomed to the presence of the tall, copper-colored man who spoke English like a lord but drank coffee while generously plying others with grog. Whenever a new ship docked, Gabe arrived and took his regular seat near the bar where the sailors were most likely to stop first. If they came from Amelia Island, he anteed up for a round for all and lubricated their tongues before he asked any questions.

Much of the talk was about the goings on at Amelia Island, which was apparently a popular stop. Captain Isreal Ushur, loading rum for the trip back to New England, told Gabe that a man by the name of Black Caesar had acquired medicine for typhus for a young woman fitting Joie's description. Since that was something Gabe already knew, the information was not very helpful.

The captain tipped his hat to Gabe and went on to secure the goods being loaded onto his ship. "Got to make sure the crew doesn't drink up the cargo, you know!"

But at least his words began a discussion on Black Caesar, and a grungy-bearded sailor from another ship eagerly added, "Black Caesar has left the pirate Gaspar." He stared into an empty glass.

"Another drink for the gentleman," Gabe said. The sailor gulped the drink and then slammed the glass on the table once more. Gabe nodded to the bartender.

"The story I heard," said the man, "was that he rescued his woman Sheba in the middle of a storm." He upended the glass and drained it, then looked once more to Gabe.

Gabe nodded, the bartender poured, and the grog disappeared.

"Sheba told the cook, who told the lady of the house"—here he winked suggestively at Gabe, implying that he should know what kind of house to which he was referring—"and I overheard, though they thought I was merely sleeping off a night of overindulgence—in more ways than one, if you know what I mean!"

He elbowed Gabe and winked once more for good measure. He was truly enjoying having an audience, especially one so receptive that he rewarded each line of the tale with grog!

The glass was empty again. Gabe had only to lift a finger, as the bartender stood at the ready.

The sailor poured more grog down his throat. Some of it actually made it into his mouth.

"She said...that they had capsized in the middle of a storm, but Caesar saved her. Couldn't save the other one, though. Her friend. The dark-haired, blue-eyed beauty that had just come to the island that day."

The man looked hopefully at Gabe once more and lifted the glass.

Gabe was devastated. Joie was dead? Drowned? No! He couldn't believe it. He got to his feet before the sailor saw the tears in his eyes.

After that conversation, Gabe continued to come down to the docks and listen to the sailors, though now he asked if any had been to the Cuban Fisheries that he had heard of in Tampa Bay and Charlotte Harbor. His heart ached, but he would not give up. That Joie might have died was simply one tale of a man who had probably been so drunk that he misunderstood what he overheard from his lady friend. Gabe hadn't come so far to give up now.

Day after day he went to the docks. The barkeeps knew him so well that they sent one of their barmaids to him with a cup of coffee as soon as he arrived. The barmaids had heard the story of his search, and he paid them regularly to question sailors for any word that might pertain to Joie. They grew fond of the man who loved his sister. They petted him and coddled him, wishing he wanted more than just information.

But Gabe was finally close to despair. Was it time to give up after all? To accept that his sister had drowned in a storm attempting escape from the pirate Gaspar? Gabe swore vengeance. It was habit that now took him to the pubs near the docks.

Then one night, Carlotta at Greasy Dick's greeted him with a whisper. "Got a new friend 'as jus' come from the Fisheries." She tossed her curled blond head toward a tall, skinny man who was leering, winking, and crooking his finger at her and then pointing at his essentials, making it clear that he wanted much more than grog that evening. Carlotta threw him a beguiling smile and then turned to Gabe to roll her eyes. She pulled at the pocket of her apron, and Gabe deposited several coins there before making his way to the sailor.

"The lady tells me you've just come from the Cuban Fisheries," Gabe said, and he looked toward the bartender, who brought a bottle immediately. The man's eyes followed Carlotta.

"May I join you and offer you a drink?" Gabe asked.

The sailor licked his lips. He took the drink just poured and quickly emptied the glass. "What do you want to know?" he asked suspiciously, glaring at Gabe from beneath bushy brows in which Gabe could have sworn he saw something moving.

Fighting his digust, Gabe said, "I am looking for my sister. I heard she might have been in Charlotte Harbor when a storm struck."

"Well...I might'a heard something." He picked up the bottle, filled his glass to the top, and then bent down to lick what leaked down the side. "I heard there was a woman washed up on the beach while I was there." The sailor then turned his attention to Carlotta, who was serving others.

"Is she coming back to me?" he asked Gabe.

Gabe shrugged and gave the man a few coins.

With a nearly toothless grin, the man said, "There's some Injuns settled near the Fisheries on Peace River. Heard they picked a girl off the beach."

"Peace River," Gabe said. His heart was pounding. There was a chance.

Another sailor sitting nearby looked at the bottle and commented, "They ain't there now."

Gabe looked at the barkeep and held up two fingers. Two new bottles appeared.

"They uz Red Sticks. I fought with Jackson 'gainst those Injuns. Heard they uz headed back to villages near St. Marks."

Near St. Marks…where Savannah Jack had taken Gabe and Cade— and would have killed them.

There was no way Savannah Jack could be at St. Marks, was there? Surely if there was a God in heaven, he couldn't be!

Gabe described Savannah Jack, hoping desperately that he had not been seen among the Red Sticks near the fisheries.

But to his dismay, one of the sailors confirmed it. "Yep! Scariest man I ever saw. Never smiled. Just looked like he wanted to gut you for breathin'. Carved knives and cut himself with them just to lick his own blood. Gave me the willies, I'll tell you!"

All of their friends had gathered by now. They smiled and nodded in agreement. One or two shivered with the memory of seeing that man at the Fisheries.

"Thank you, gentlemen," Gabe said. "You have been of great help. Carlotta, please bring these men drinks all around." At that, Gabe pushed himself to his feet after tossing a few more coins on the counter.

His blood ran cold. His little sister was captured by pirates and then survived both typhus and a shipwreck only to wind up being "rescued" by Savannah Jack, who was now apparently taking her to St. Marks! Good God!

And here he was, stuck on New Providence, twiddling his thumbs while Woodbine, Armbrister, McGregor, and Aury plotted to build an empire.

He hurried back to Woodbine and informed him of the news.

"Armbrister is ready to sail to Tampa, Mr. Kincaid. And then he will proceed to St. Marks, which, according to your information, is exactly where you need to go. So your patience has not gone unrewarded." Woodbine clapped Gabe on the shoulder jovially. "I will sail to some of the other islands and talk to others with whom I have served to enlist their services in our noble endeavor."

At last they set sail and made their way to Tampa Bay. One of their crew had heard rumors of the location of Gaspar's hideout. Armbrister reluctantly detoured into Charlotte Harbor, where they found Gaspar's island deserted, his fine house abandoned, and nearby Captiva Island a wasteland. Wind and water had washed the small huts into a rubbish heap. A quick visit to the Cuban Fisheries confirmed the information Gabe had received from the sailors at Greasy Dick's.

Gabe's heart was in his throat. Would he arrive in time? Did Savannah Jack know who Joie was? After all, his sister was the spitting image of their mother, Snow Bird. Had Savannah Jack ever known their mother?

Armbrister was anxious to get the preliminary preparations accomplished. The expedition would soon be under way. He sailed further into Tampa Bay, where he ransacked Arbuthnot's store and turned his attention toward St. Marks. His goal there was to collect the Indian allies they had wooed for so long. He commandeered Arbuthnot's schooner, the *Chance*, with its black crew accustomed to the run to Suwanee and St. Marks. He carried 9 kegs of powder and 500 pounds of lead for the expedition that would wrest the Floridas from the Spanish and set up an Indian nation as a buffer between their empire and the United States. Armbrister made a last-minute decision go to the to the Suwanee River rather than directly to St. Marks. When they learned from the Cuban fishermen that there had been trouble on the American border: the Indian village of Fowl Town had been attacked.

"I think it would be prudent for us to take the *Chance* up the Suwannee to Arbuthnot's other store near Bowlegs Town," Armbrister said. "There may be news of your sister there, and if not, we will go from there to St. Marks."

The April day was clear and balmy, a welcomed circumstance since the uncommon cold of March. Gabe, standing on the bow of the ship, was hopeful that there would be news of his sister at Bowlegs Town. Before he could shout an alarm warning, the heavily loaded schooner hit a sandbar, with Bowlegs Town still 100 miles up the Suwanee River.

"It appears we now must walk," said Armbrister jauntily.

Was all of this just play to him? Did he not realize the gravity of the situation and that his sister's life was at stake?

Please God, let Joie be alive!

Armbrister said, "It is April 15. There are two weeks before the May goal for Woodbine's expedition into Florida. We can walk to Bowlegs Town and have the Indians return with us to unload the cargo and meet our target for beginning the glorious expedition." They left the *Chance* moored at the mouth of the Suwanee River and set off.

Gabe wanted to run to Bowlegs Town, but he restrained himself to walk at Armbrister's gait. He needed to be ready for what he might find ahead of him.

"We'll be there as scheduled, Kincaid. We'll have our Indian allies armed and ready for the May expedition just as Woodbine planned," Armbrister boasted.

The sailors on their dinghy took them to a path that was familiar to one of their black guides, a member of Arbuthnot's original crew. With a firm, confident stride, Armbrister, whistling "God Save the King," led Gabe north.

Chapter 17

The Spanish Fort at St. Marks bustled with activity. William Hambly and Edmund Doyle were imprisoned there, having been brought to the site months earlier by Chief Kenhega of Miccosukee. Duncan McKrimmon, who had been saved by Millea Francis, was there as well, having been sold to Don Francisco Caso y Luengo. Alexander Arbuthnot had made his way leisurely to St. Marks and was enjoying a visit with Caso y Luengo in his private quarters, though he had left his horse saddled and tied by the open gate of the fort.

Duncan McKrimmon stood on the bluff where the spring-fed Wakulla River joined the dark waters of the St. Marks for a brief journey into the Apalachee Bay. It was one of those clear-as-a-bell days where the sound carried well across the water, so Duncan was careful to tread quietly to the point of land where the two rivers came together. He'd wandered alone once before and gotten captured; and though Caso y Luengo knew he was out walking, he would not lower his guard again. While this scenery was captivating and the balmy day a rare gift after the chill of the past months, Duncan knew how deceptive such peace could be. Beyond the rivers were the unrelenting hardwood and cypress swamps, harboring wildlife and violent men. He had experienced them the hard way: as a prisoner of Red Sticks on the warpath.

His hair had grown back from being shaved, and he bore only scars on his body and nightmares in his sleep as reminders of his time as the prisoner of Josiah Francis. Though he had been brought to St. Marks and given over to Don Francisco Caso y Luengo, he would not breathe easy until he was at last on United States soil once more. He looked north up the dark of the St. Mark's waters, remembering Miccosukee and the horror of being tied to a pole and nearly burned to death. He shuddered, thinking of what might have happened if Millea Francis had not returned to the village when she did. It was such a beautiful and peaceful place that it was hard to believe what had happened to him there.

He breathed deeply, willing himself to calm down.

As he stood looking out toward the St. Marks flowing toward the Gulf of Mexico, wishing for a way to escape, a ship sailed into view, flying the Stars and Bars. His heart skipped a beat, and he blinked hard to make sure what he saw was real. He was so shocked that he glanced around him to see if anyone else noticed. If there hadn't been a rowboat handy, he'd have jumped in the cold water and swum out to the ship! Too many damned Red Sticks hung around St. Marks for his comfort. Fortunately, there *was* a rowboat handy, and he rowed quickly out to the ship.

Captain Isaac McKeever stood on deck of the *Thomas Shields*. He watched McKrimmon row toward his ship as if his life depended on it. He held out his hand as the young man climbed the rope up the side of the ship.

"Welcome aboard," McKeever said.

"Thank God you're here," McKrimmon exclaimed. He was literally shaking with relief at being with Americans once more. "I was captured at Prospect Bluff and taken to Francis Towne and then to Miccosukee. There I was nearly burned to death by Josiah Francis. I am only alive now because his daughter, Millea, begged for my life, and he granted it."

"Francis?" McKeever asked, just to make sure he had not misheard.

McKrimmon nodded.

"So Francis has returned from England," McKeever said.

"Yes!" McKrimmon said. "Francis Towne is just three miles that way." He indicated the Wakulla River to their west. "Francis has been expecting a British ship and comes frequently to check and see if it has arrived. In fact, that is who I thought you were when I saw you approach."

McKeever's eyes glittered as he remembered Jackson's command to capture Francis if he had the opportunity. "I wonder if we might encourage Francis to think that also," he remarked.

McKrimmon smiled and nodded, catching his drift.

"Lower the Stars and Bars," McKeever commanded. "Raise the Union Jack!" Turning back to McKrimmon, he added quietly, "We'll be a decoy."

"St. Marks is just beyond that bend," Millea told Joie. "The fort sits on a bluff where the Wakulla flows into the St. Marks River."

Before they could reach the bend, Josiah Francis slowed his horse, cautious of what they might encounter. He lifted his hand and indicated that they stay put. Then he dismounted and approached the bluff on foot. When he spotted the Union Jack flying from a ship anchored in the harbor, he hurried back to where they waited.

"We are saved!" he exclaimed and pounded Homathlemicco on the back. "Our friends have not failed us!"

Millea jumped to the ground from behind Joie. Joie dismounted more slowly, but Millea was too excited to notice her friend's caution.

Polly looked worried. "Father," she said. "It could be a trap."

"There is no time for caution, child," Francis told her, waving a hand at her. "Jackson nips at our heels like a hound at hunt. If it is a trap, take the southern trail to Bowlegs Town and join your mother and Jim Earle."

Francis and Homathlemicco headed down to the bank of the river, where they found canoes secreted there under some vines. Joie wondered if that was where Cade had found the canoe that saved his and Gabe's life all those years ago.

Josiah Francis hesitated a moment. He cocked his head, listening. There did not appear to be anything out of the ordinary.

"Homathlemicco and I will greet our friends, Millea," he finally said. "You and Joie stay here with Grey Wolf and the others until I send for you."

Francis and Homathlemicco pushed off and rowed quickly toward the ship.

Millea fidgeted. Polly clutched her rifle at the ready. Joie felt it too. Something was not right.

The two Red Stick leaders approached the ship warily, but they were desperate for the weapons Woodbine had promised. Lives depended on them.

McKeever had removed the coat of his uniform and presented himself as a simple sailor. He invited Francis and Homathlemicco aboard.

When they were on deck, Francis asked, "What are you loaded with?"

"Guns, powder, lead, and blankets for our red friends," McKeever replied.

Francis sighed deeply in relief and touched his friend on the arm. Homathlemicco let out a loud whoop that even Millea and the others could hear from the spot where they waited.

"Come and have a glass of wine with me in my cabin," McKeever said, continuing the ruse. "We will make plans for distributing these supplies." Then he reached for their weapons. "You won't need these," he said with a smile, and graciously gestured for them to precede him toward his cabin.

When their backs were turned, McKeever indicated that two of his men should seize them and tie them up. At that point, Duncan McKrimmon came onto the deck from the cabin below, gun in hand and aimed directly at Francis's heart.

"This is what I get for saving your life," Francis said, recognizing the young man at once.

"It is not to *you* I owe my life," McKrimmon replied, "but to your daughter. For her I will do what I can for you."

Polly paced along the bank of the river, her clear green eyes glued to where she had watched her father disappear around the bend. "That's it!" she finally said. "I've got to go and see what has happened. He must have simply forgotten to send for us."

Millea prepared to follow Polly. But, when Joie struggled to stand from where she lay on the bank, Polly gave her sister a meaningful look. "I'll be back soon," she insisted. "You would only slow me down."

Millea nodded reluctantly, eying Joie while she was distracted by collecting the reins of all four horses, which were acting strangely.

Grey Wolf was also concerned. "You should stay here and let me go alone," he said, but Polly was already halfway down the bank to another hidden canoe. Grey Wolf rushed after her, putting his gun next to hers in the bottom of the boat. They each took up an oar.

The waves were whipping up with the afternoon winds, blowing Polly's long black hair into her eyes as she rowed into the current. The canoe was difficult for she and Grey Wolf to control. When Grey Wolf looked up at the deck of the ship, he spotted an officer in the coat of an American.

"It's a trap!" he told Polly. "Those are Americans!"

"No! Father!" Polly cried out.

Grey Wolf and Polly quickly turned the canoe around and made for shore, with the wind now fortunately at their back.

"Halt!" McKeever shouted from the deck.

Grey Wolf heard the faint voice. Polly looked back, but they ignored the command.

"Shoot, but not to kill," McKeever ordered the artillery officer, who aimed the cannon. The shot went short. "Again," McKeever commanded when those in the boat ignored the fire. The Indian warrior rowed faster.

An impatient McKeever ordered yet another round of fire, and the artillery officer shot a round of grape at the fleeing Indians with no avail.

McKeever ordered three men to pursue them, and that boat quickly gained on the canoe. But the Indians made it to shore first.

At that point, Duncan McKrimmon made his way to the deck beside McKeever.

"That's the girl who saved my life!" he cried, mistaking Polly for Millea. "Cease firing! That is Francis's daughter. Call your men back!"

McKeever put a whistle to his mouth and got his men's attention, motioning for them to return to the ship.

Polly jumped into the shallow water and grabbed her gun from the bottom of the boat. Just before disappearing into the woods after Grey Wolf, she fired a round that struck the rudder of the *Thomas Shields* right under the arm of the steersman.

Chapter 18

A note from the governor at Pensacola arrived at Fort St. Marks just before Arbuthnot, informing the commandant, Don Francisco Caso y Luengo, of the approach of Jackson's army. In addition to eighteen ships of sail, the governor wrote that Jackson had more than 1,000 Indians rebuilding the fort at Prospect Bluff under the direction of his officers. He then informed Don Francisco that as soon as that was done, Jackson planned to head toward St. Marks. Jackson had written him, in fact, saying that he heard that Indians found protection and were getting guns and ammunition at St. Marks, and therefore Jackson deemed it necessary to garrison American troops there to prevent "the recurrence of so gross a violation of neutrality and to exclude our savage enemies from so strong a hold as St. Marks."

Arbuthnot immediately wrote his son John, detailing the gist of Jackson's note, and sent the message by one of Don Francisco's most dependable slaves to the store on the Suwannee. He watched the messenger slip into his canoe and row away into the swamp across the St. Marks River right before General Andrew Jackson rode up.

Godfrey rode to the fort with General Jackson. Don Francisco Caso y Luengo was at the gate, where an elderly gentleman was in the act of mounting his horse.

Don Francisco introduced the seventy-year-old Scot, Alexander Arbuthnot, to Andrew Jackson.

"Arbuthnot!" Jackson spat with contempt, his eyes flashing. "At last I meet the infamous instigator of this war! It is you who have led these poor savages in the belief that the treaty they signed in my presence is worthless! *You* have encouraged them in their depredations. It is you who claim to speak for them."

Giving Arbuthnot no time to defend himself, Jackson commanded, "Arrest this man!"

"I am now in command of this fort, Don Francisco," Jackson said.

"By what authority?" Don Francisco demanded, offended by the temerity of an American soldier trespassing up Spanish soil and daring to claim authority over a Spanish fort.

"By the authority of the 3,000 men in my army, sir," Jackson responded. The general lowered the Spanish flag himself and raised the United States flag over St. Marks.

Jackson then entered the fort, where he found William Hambly and Edmund Doyle imprisoned. "Release these men!" he ordered. "Mr. Arbuthnot, these are your new quarters."

When told of Jackson's arrival, McKeever presented himself dressed in full uniform, along with Duncan McKrimmon.

"Sir," he said, "I have the privilege of reporting to you that Josiah Francis and Homathlemicco are imprisoned upon my ship. This young man, Duncan McKrimmon, was captured and nearly burned at the stake at Miccosukee by the prisoner. Francis's daughter saved his life, and Francis had him brought here to St. Marks. When I arrived, he came seeking my protection and informed me of Francis's expectation of a British ship to arrive with guns and powder. We decided to let Francis think my ship was British. The ploy worked, and he brought himself onto the deck of my ship, whereupon I offered refreshments like a good host and they willingly entrusted their weapons to me. McKrimmon tells me that Homathlemicco led the attack on Lieutenant Scott's party."

"Then he is responsible for the mutilation of the six women the survivor, Mrs. Stewart, told us about," Jackson said, his voice trembling with rage, "and for the deaths of those unfortunate Americans who were with Lieutenant Scott. They made her watch as they tortured Scott." The general's expression turned resolute. "I have seen their scalps and the scalps of the infants he killed. Homathlemicco will hang with Josiah Francis," he commanded.

Godfrey had seen the violence Josiah Francis could incite. Francis was a leading prophet during the Creek War and had been at the vanguard of the attack at Fort Mims. Godfrey's own scalp would have been on Francis's belt if Joie and Lyssa had not rescued him at Fort Mims. The recitation of Homathlemicco's cruelty made him feel sick.

Even so, he had expected a trial of some sort.

As General Jackson prepared to leave St. Marks, he pulled Godfrey aside. "Mr. Winkel, I give you permission to stay behind and observe the execution of these villains. I would think that with your history, this would bring a form of justice for you, your aunt and uncle, and those you knew in Fort Mims who met such a horrible death at the hand of Hillis Hadjo—Josiah Francis."

Godfrey agreed. He would stand there and represent all who died by Francis's hand and by his order. With a heavy heart, he went with McKeever and McKrimmon back to the *Thomas Shields*. McKeever ordered Francis and Homathlemicco to the deck.

Godfrey was surprised by Josiah Francis. He was tall and of gentle manners, dressed in a stylish frock coat that any gentleman of the haute monde in London might have worn, except that his shirt, leggings, and moccasins were Indian with fine beading and fringe.

"General Andrew Jackson has ordered that the two of you be hanged for the crimes you have committed," McKeever pronounced.

"Like a dog?" exclaimed Francis. "Shoot me instead!"

McKeever stood as resolute as General Jackson, his lip curled in contempt for the two standing before him.

"Let me see Jackson!" Francis pleaded. Godfrey noted that he spoke in perfect English.

"The general has returned to his men and left me with the order that I will obey," McKeever responded.

Francis recognized the futility of his plea and turned to Homathlemicco, speaking to him in Creek. Homathlemicco stood stoically, giving only the slightest nod that he understood. Godfrey watched as Francis and his friend walked proud and tall to the noose looped over the yardarm of the *Thomas Shields*. Though he despised Francis for the harm he had done to the people he knew at Fort Mims, Godfrey could not help being impressed with the demeanor of this warrior.

With their last act of dignity, Josiah Francis and Homathlemicco stepped up on separate boxes for the two nooses. A bird sang out, capturing Francis's attention. He looked over the heads of the sailors gathered to watch the execution of one of their greatest enemies, and his expression softened. He put his fist to his heart, extended his arm, and opened his hand. He then began to sing an eerie chant, once again in the role of the prophet.

McKeever signaled for the boxes to be kicked from under their feet. Within seconds, Josiah Francis and Homathlemicco were dead.

The song of Josiah Francis was silenced forever.

At last Fort Mims was avenged, Godfrey thought. But the joy he expected to feel did not come. Before him hung a man who had fought for the traditions of his people and the right to the land on which his forebears had lived, planted, and hunted. Godfrey remembered Jackson's words about his experience with the Indians in West Tennessee. If Jackson and Francis had been swapped at birth, would Jackson have behaved differently?

Suddenly, a wail drifted eerily across the Wakulla, carried easily across the water from the woods nearby.

Above the sound of this painful cry, Godfrey thought he heard Joie scream, "No! Dear God! Millea, please!"

His head jerked around toward the noise, and his heart quickened. Surely he was imagining that he heard her voice.

Before he could think, he dove into the cold water from the stern of the boat. In order to follow him, Duncan McKrimman climbed down the side and jumped into the dinghy that they had brought from St. Marks.

Godfrey pulled himself through the water fiercely and powerfully, adrenaline flowing, swimming as fast as he could. When he got to shore, he sprinted into the newly green woods, searching desperately in the pines, palms, and palmettos for any sign of Joie. He found a place where those he had heard had stood watching with their horses nearby.

But he could not see them now.

Was it possible? Could Joie have survived the storm? Had she truly joined the ones who had threatened her life and survived?

McKrimmon had followed Godfrey into the woods. Godfrey took him by his shirt and demanded, "Did you see a girl with Millea Francis in that village?"

McKrimmon nodded.

"Describe her," Godfrey said.

"She looked much like Millea, though smaller," McKrimmon said, his eyes wide. "She had extraordinary blue eyes…and she was pregnant."

Godfrey fell to his knees. He lifted his head and keened, "Joie!"

"Why do you ask? Who is she, man?"

How could he answer? Joie was life itself to him. And now she would be the mother of his child. Could he could find her before some American soldier decided to avenge his anger on her?

"She saved my life just as surely as Millea Francis saved yours," he told McKrimmon. "And if what you say is true, then she is the mother of my child. She *will* be my wife if I can find her and keep her safe!"

McKrimmon held his gun at the ready, knowing that Indians could be hiding anywhere. But he put his hand on Godfrey's shoulder. "We're a sorry pair, man. I would offer for Millea if she would have me."

His own words surprised him. But now he realized they were true. She was beautiful, and she was brave. He would be a lucky man if she would have him.

"Do you remember more, McKrimmon?" Godfrey asked.

"They said she did not know her name…had lost her memory. But I saw that Francis and McQueen kept a watchful eye on her. So did Savannah Jack."

Godfrey's blood ran cold. "Savannah Jack is here?"

"No," McKrimmon said. "They sent him away to bring back weapons he had hidden back in Creek Country. They expect him to return any day."

Godfrey thought quickly. A courier from Fort Dale had brought General Jackson a report of what Jackson referred to as the Butler massacre. It occurred on March 20th, about a week after White Warrior had attacked Ekanachatte and Godfrey was taken to Jackson's camp. Savannah Jack had led the attack on a well-armed party of settlers under

231

Captain William Butler, who was taking dispatches to Fort Dale. But that was far away in Creek territory. Captain Sam Dale had been sent out after him, but no message had come to Jackson that Savannah Jack had been captured. It was now April 8th.

Dear God! Jack had plenty of time to return from his mission with the weapons he had stashed plus those he'd taken from Butler's men.

Had Joie truly lost her memory again? Could she really not know who she was...not remember him? If Savannah Jack discovered her identity, he would take revenge on Cade through her!

"I must find her!" Godfrey said. "If Savannah Jack ever recognizes her, he will kill her!"

The horses grew agitated when the cannons began firing. After stroking them and speaking softly to them, Joie was finally able to mount her horse when Millea and Grey Wolf appeared on the opposite bank. Joie guided the horses down into the river and led them across to the others.

"The Americans captured my father," Polly said with a lump in her throat. "They flew the British flag and lured him onto the ship." Tears filled her hazel eyes. "Grey Wolf, you should take Joie and join my mother. I will stay here and await news of my father."

"I will not leave you, Polly," Millea said stubbornly.

"Nor will I go," said Grey Wolf.

They made camp in the woods where they could watch the ship. Much to their dismay, General Andrew Jackson arrived at St. Marks later that afternoon. That was when the action aboard the ship increased. Polly stood by Grey Wolf. Millea took Joie by the hand and held it as they watched the sailors string two ropes with nooses over the yardarm. Then they saw Josiah Francis and Homathlemicco arrive on deck. When an American slipped the noose around her father's neck, Millea's grip became a vise on Joie's hand.

Joie could almost feel her friend's heart pounding through their joined hands. Millea struggled to make the bird sound that was the secret sign between her and her father. Polly's own call followed fast. Francis's face turned their way, and they could nearly sense his eyes on them. Millea stifled a sob, and her free hand flew to her own heart when he touched his fist to his heart and then released his heart to their care. His voice and the chanting song lifted clearly over the water. And then the boxes were shoved from beneath his and Homathlemicco's feet.

"Father," Millea whispered and fell to the ground.

"No! Dear God!" Joie cried, and then, seeing her friend crumple, she exclaimed, "Millea, please!"

Grey Wolf grabbed Millea up in his arms, and Polly pushed Joie toward the tethered horses.

Joie did not see the golden-haired man on the stern of the ship jerk around and dive into the cold waters. Grey Wolf ordered everyone to mount and then guided them through the swamps, doing as Hillis Hadjo had directed them should something happen. They would make their way to Bowlegs Town, 107 miles away. Joie followed, ignoring her cramps.

They rode hard, crossing the St. Marks south of the confluence, and then made their way, spending several nights in the flat, swampy wilderness. Fortunately, Joie found the right herbs one night before lying on her blanket to sleep, and the cramps and spotting eased for the moment.

They skirted the main road, following seldom-taken paths toward the village. Joie worried about Abraham and his people. Had Jackson burned Abraham's house as he had done those at Miccosukee?

They finally arrived to find Bowlegs Town nearly deserted. Abraham remained with Chief Bowlegs, guarding the rear of the evacuation. One of McQueen's men approached at a gallop from a different path at nearly the same time.

"What is happening?" Grey Wolf asked.

"White Warrior came upon us on the road. Jackson was close by. We fought for nearly an hour in the swamp, but there were so few of us! They followed us for nearly three hours. We lost many men, and they took our women and children, many cattle, our horses and corn. He has halted for the moment at the pond six miles west. I hurried here to tell Bowlegs."

"How did you know to evacuate?" Grey Wolf pressed.

"Alexander Arbuthnot sent his son John a note at their trading post," Abraham explained. "John sent it immediately to me to read to Chief Bowlegs. Arbuthnot had learned that Jackson's army was already headed that way and had captured two of Peter McQueen's sons and another Indian. He told his son that three ships had appeared at the mouth of the St. Marks, the largest flying an American flag. At the time he wrote, the commandant expected some communication from the vessels, but none had yet occurred. He said he thought their purpose was merely to block passage for the Indians. Twenty canoes were turned back yesterday."

It was only then that Abraham thought to ask Polly about Josiah Francis. "Your father is here as well?"

Tears filled Polly's eyes.

Millea answered for her. "They hanged Father and Homathlemicco from the yardarm of the ship of which Arbuthnot wrote."

Polly finally spoke over the lump in her throat. "Father thought it was the ship he had expected from Woodbine. He was desperate to believe his friends had arrived in time. They flew the Union Jack and lured him aboard."

"What else did Arbuthnot write?" asked Grey Wolf.

"He told his son that he had arrived at St. Marks by horseback alone and was tired," Abraham said, now with a note of sadness in his voice, "but was setting forth immediately. I remember this part vividly. He wrote, 'The main drift of the Americans is to destroy the black population of Suwany. Tell my friend Bolick that he is throwing away his people to resist so powerful a force as will go down on Suwany; and as the troops advance by land, so will the ships by sea. Endeavor to get all the goods over the river in a place of security; as also the skins of all sorts: the corn must be left to its fate. So soon as the Suwany is destroyed I expect the Americans to be satisfied....'

"Arbuthnot told his son that if the schooner had returned, he should load all the goods aboard her and set off for Mounater Creek in the bottom of Cedar Creek Bay."

"Have you seen my mother?" Millea asked. She looked desperately about her. The Americans would soon be upon them.

Abraham looked toward the swamps. "I did not see your mother among the women."

"Go, Abraham. You must see to your people. There are some children still straggling behind," Polly said.

"We are headed for the Caloosahatchee River and Big Cypress Swamp. Follow us," Abraham said. The high-pitched voices of children distracted him. "Berry pickers from my village," he explained. "I promised their mothers I would guide them through the swamp."

"I'll bet Jim Earle got loose again and Mother is chasing him down," Polly said with exasperation. She was tired and worried and needed to tell their mother what had happened to their father. She knew the Americans were close because she could smell the smoke where they had already set fire to the houses of Abraham's people at Pilaklakaha.

Abraham turned his horse and headed toward the anxious and confused children. Millea and Polly followed automatically, knowing that Jim Earle could very well have gotten away from their mother and into that group.

Grey Fox and his warriors spotted Chief Bowlegs and went to ask where he needed them.

And then, suddenly, Savannah Jack appeared from nowhere. Though Joie cried out, Jack silenced her with his hand over her mouth. She struggled frantically, but the noise and confusion was so great that no one heard or noticed, and then he struck her in the head and all went black.

Sure enough, Jim Earle was with the children, and Hannah had him by the arm with a lock-hold grip. "I was so afraid we would have to leave and go into the swamp without you!" she cried when she spotted her daughters.

Then she looked around. "Where is your father?" she asked.

Millea and Polly slid from their horses. The looks on their faces told Hannah Moniac Francis all she needed to know. She dropped to her knees and wailed. Jim Earle's little face went white, and he threw his arms around his mother to give her comfort. Millea and Polly knelt to hold them both.

"How?" their mother asked when she could speak again.

"They used a British flag as a decoy on an American ship," Millea said through fresh tears. "Jackson arrived immediately after his capture and ordered his execution. Both our father and Homathlemicco were hanged from the mast."

"We stayed until it was over," Polly said. "He knew we were there."

Millea nodded.

"Where is Joie?" Polly asked.

"She was here just a minute ago," Millea said, spinning around to look for her friend.

"She wouldn't have gone on with the women into the swamp, would she?" Polly asked.

Millea ran after Abraham, who was by now on the bank of the river, ready to swim across with several children holding on to him and his horse. Others were in a canoe beside them. Across the river, she caught glimpses of people disappearing into the cypress trees, cane, and cattails on the other side.

"Abraham, have you seen Joie?" she asked.

"I thought she might be in pain. Savannah Jack was carrying her on his horse on his way out of the village just a few minutes ago," Abraham responded. He turned his attention back to the children.

Millea blanched and rushed back to her mother.

Hannah's anguish over her husband's death took a back seat to the immediate danger of her daughter's friend. "Savannah Jack traveled this area frequently with Bowles," Hannah said. "He is well acquainted with trails and places to hide."

Millea looked about her. "There are no warriors to go with us to look for her!"

Horses galloped directly toward them. The vanguard of Jackson's men was upon them. Jim Earle pulled away from his mother and ran toward the soldiers, brandishing a knife. Millea ran after him.

Bowlegs and his men held their position at the edge of the river until Abraham made it across with the children. Once he reached the shore, Abraham looked back at Hannah, and she lifted her hand in salute and goodbye. She and her children had separated themselves from the others unintentionally, but his people needed him. Reluctantly, Bowlegs ordered his men to retreat across the Suwanee River.

Millea was once again chasing Jim Earle, who was threatening to kill the Americans. She was surprised to hear an American voice say, "Millea, we have been following you. Are you all right?"

Hearing his sister's name on the lips of the American stopped Jim Earle in his tracks. He looked from his sister to the stranger holding a knife as if he actually knew how to use it. Millea grabbed the weapon from her little brother's hands before he killed someone. Or got himself and the rest of them killed.

When Millea could finally look up, she recognized the American soldier she had saved from being executed by her father.

"We have been trying to catch up with you to offer you our help," Duncan McKrimmon said. "This man is Godfrey Winkel. He is searching for Joie Kincaid. Could the woman who was with you be the woman he's looking for?"

Horses hooves pounded behind them, along with the shouts of angry men and the smell of burning buildings.

"She has been taken by Savannah Jack," Millea said.

"Dear God!" Godfrey exclaimed. So close!

McKrimmon reached out to grab Godfrey's reins as he wheeled his horse to head into the swamps. "Now is not the time to go half-cocked into the swamps looking for Savannah Jack. From what I hear of the man, he knows every stream and chickee in this area. If he didn't kill her here, he has kept her alive for a purpose."

"Blackmail?" Godfrey said, breathing fast.

"Let's take Millea and her family back with us to Andrew Jackson. We'll keep them safe and get some help in finding Joie." McKrimmon spoke deliberately, hoping to calm the man.

237

Hannah said, "Joie's brother, Gabe Kincaid, lived with my brother Red Eagle, William Weatherford, taking care of his racehorses before the war. William signed Jackson's treaty. Perhaps Jackson will look kindly upon Gabe and Joie and will send men who know how to track."

Duncan took her tactful criticism to heart. The two of them would do well not to get lost themselves in the swamps.

Godfrey, however, looked longingly in the direction they would have taken. He wobbled on the horse, and Duncan feared he might tumble off. Catching himself in time, Godfrey dismounted. Then he put Hannah and Jim Earle on his horse, and Duncan helped Millea and Polly onto his, since their own had been confiscated by Bowlegs's warriors.

Jackson acknowledged their presence and agreed that they should stay in the camp overnight, but was too angry at Bowlegs's escape to speak to them at the moment. Godfrey and Duncan settled the women and Jim Earle at a campsite where they stood guard. In the middle of the night, the sound of a musket and then a rifle rang out. Five thousand men stood at the ready. Four men, two white and two with darker skin, had blundered into Bowlegs Town in the dark. The guards who had been set about the village brought them out of the black night and into the shadowy light of campfires. When Jackson's fire blazed up as a log was thrown upon it, they could see a man wearing the dashing red jacket of a British officer, another white man dressed less finely, and the two men with darker skin.

Jackson greeted the men coldly. A Redcoat had shown up at the moment when his enemy, who had been nearly within his grasp, disappeared. "Have you searched these people?" he asked the guards.

"Yes, sir!" the guards responded.

One produced a note and handed it to Jackson. "We found this on the slave there," he said.

Jackson read the note aloud. Millea, who was listening, recognized it as the note Abraham had quoted, the one Alexander Arbuthnot had sent from St. Marks the day before her father was hanged.

Jackson was enraged. "Because of this damned letter from Arbuthnot to his son, I dragged my cannon through the muck, my army trudged through swamps, and we lost many horses because there was nothing for them to forage—and all for nothing! The enemy escaped!"

He focused his fiery gaze upon the strangers. Perhaps all was not lost. "But then...," he began, and then turned toward Armbrister. "Identify yourself, sir," he commanded with steel in his voice and fire in his eyes.

"Robert Chrystie Armbrister, General," replied the man in the red coat. "I *am* on Spanish soil, aren't I?"

His cocky smile did nothing to calm Jackson. Godfrey found himself cringing at the man's cavalier attitude.

"Who are you?" Jackson asked the white man beside Armbrister.

"I am Peter Cook, an employee of Alexander Arbuthnot. I have nothing to do with this man. He and his men commandeered Arbuthnot's vessel, the *Chance*, and took over the crew."

Jackson clenched his fists at the mention of Arbuthnot and looked ready to attack, but he displayed remarkable control. Then, with aplomb equal to Armbristers's arrogance, he said, "Lieutenant Gadsden, take a contingent of men at first light, and find the ship that brought these men here. I have an idea that Mr. Cook will lead you right to it."

Cook was nodding and smiling for all he was worth.

"Search it," Jackson added. "We will use the ship to take our wounded back to St. Marks. But first, bind these men. They will return with us to St. Marks, where we will hold a court-martial to determine their fate."

He approached Armbrister, whose expression had changed with the mention of the court-martial. Now nearly nose to nose with him, Jackson said, "I have heard much of you, Robert Chrystie Armbrister. I know you helped build the Negro Fort. You and Arbuthnot, along with your *associates* Nicholls and Woodbine, have excited the Indians to war against us Americans and have furnished them with the arms and ammunition with which to carry out war for the last time."

Jackson rubbed his hands together in satisfaction and then pointed a finger in the prisoners' direction. "Now you are in *my* hands," he finished with a chilling smile. "Take them away, Lieutenant Gadsden."

"General Jackson," came the pleading voice of another prisoner whose face had been hidden. When the guard pushed Arbuthnot forward, the firelight finally revealed the fourth man's face.

It had been several years, but Godfrey would recognize him anywhere. In fact, if the man weren't guarded by men with rifles and bayonets, Godfrey would have embraced him.

"Gabriel Kincaid!" he exclaimed. "I never dreamed you would walk out of the darkness at this moment!"

"Godfrey! Is that you?" Gabe asked. "I have been searching for you and Joie! Where is my sister?"

"General Jackson, this is Gabriel Kincaid," Godfrey said, gesturing toward the copper-skinned man being held by Jackson's men. "He is the brother of the woman I am searching for."

"General," began Gabe. His hand went to his coat but stopped when a bayonet prodded him. "Sir, I have letters of recommendation from Lord Bathurst that might clarify how I came to be with these men. I am merely a passenger on the ship attempting to rescue Godfrey here and my sister Joie, who went missing at the same time Godfrey did."

Jackson nodded, and Gabe handed him the papers.

While the general perused them, Gabe turned his attention back to Godfrey. "Godfrey Lewis Winkel?" he said in astonishment. "You have changed!"

Ignoring this, Godfrey said, "Savannah Jack has Joie! He took her this afternoon in the confusion at Bowlegs Town. Since the night of the big storm when I was held by the pirate Gaspar in Charlotte Harbor, she has been with Millea Francis."

When Jackson looked up from the papers, Godfrey pleaded his case. "General, Gabe Kincaid is not involved in anything but finding his sister. He has been trained by the best trackers in the Creek Nation, and we need him to help us locate Joie Kincaid."

"Please release him, General," Duncan McKrimmon added. "We need him to track this man's wife." He looked at Godfrey meaningfully.

"Wife?" Gabe asked, his eyes widening.

Godfrey blushed and glanced at Jackson. "Yes, wife. I meant Joie Kincaid Winkel. And I am told that she carries my child."

"You have a lot to tell me before it is light enough for us to set out," Gabe said in an ominous tone.

Jackson handed the papers back to Gabe and said, "Go and find your sister, Mr. Kincaid. It would appear that you accidentally stumbled into this international intrigue. If I had not already had Mr. Winkel here telling me the same incredible story even before you arrived, you might be bound and tried as well."

To Godfrey he said, "It is a hell of a thing to lose a *wife,* Mr. Winkel. Good luck in recovering her. I know my wife has been the best thing that ever happened to me."

Chapter 19

When Joie awoke, she found that she was lying in the bottom of a canoe. It was black as pitch, with clouds obstructing whatever moonlight might have been cast. Though she could not see him, she knew who handled the oars with such power that they flew through the fast-moving current. She heard the echoes of the bull gators, the call of bullfrogs, and the chirrups of the cicadas hidden beneath the moss-draped oaks, along with the occasional night bird's song.

And she lay still. What choice did she have? If Savannah Jack wanted to kill her, he would have done so. As it was, her back was not hurting. The pressure on her bladder was hard to ignore, but she didn't want to think about it right then. She went back to sleep.

When it was still darker than dawn, she woke again to glimpse a ship in the waters beyond the cattails. She saw grasses that hindered their progress as they made their way through the coastal marsh. As they pushed through, Joie glimpsed a blue heron, a great egret, and other birds she could not name as they took flight.

The next time she was roused from sleep, they were in the bay where she could hear waves washing upon a beach. The sky was a powder blue, with occasional wisps of white clouds. There was no longer any way to avoid talking to Savannah Jack.

"I need to…," she began, blushing.

She could not look him in the eye. Savannah Jack skillfully found a bit of beach and held the canoe while she tended to her business. She watched him warily. This was not a place where she would attempt to venture out on her own. Savannah Jack would catch her before she could take three steps in the other direction.

When she finished, Jack surprised her by holding out his hand to help her back into the canoe. He also handed her some dried meat and a gourd filled with fresh water.

Joie lay back in the canoe, where her gaze kept returning to Savannah Jack. Never did his eyes flicker her way. She dozed and woke to see the sky change from light blue to purple. When the sun set in a glorious pink hurrah, Savannah Jack pulled into an inlet on a small island and made camp. After putting her ashore on the island, Jack gathered oysters, which he then opened with one of his infamous knives, passing her one after another until she had eaten her fill. He gave her fresh water from the gourd and berries he had picked.

That knife taunted her. She fantasized about grabbing it and thrusting it into his heart.

They spent the next day in the canoe. Savannah Jack paddled conscientiously, traveling as many miles per day as possible, yet ever alert to a sail in the distance. If he saw one, he pulled into the nearest inlet and waited until the sail was out of sight. He remained silent and vigilant. Amazingly, Joie felt no fear. If anything, her feelings were those of resignation. Maybe she'd been hit on the head too many times.

On their journey, Jack had fed her and cared for her with more sensitivity than she had ever expected from one like him. She had rested. She was stronger now. But she carried a child, and should she run, she knew she would not get far.

At last they made it to an island with a sheltered inlet where Jack helped her from the canoe. He then hid the canoe in some brush. A nearly indistinguishable path led toward the center of the island, where they came to a large, shallow pond of fresh water. With a jerk of his head, Savannah Jack indicated that she walk ahead of him down the path.

Close to the tree line in the shade, Joie spotted a raised chickee with a palm frond roof built with wooden slats a mere hands width apart. It was constructed over a twelve- to fifteen-foot deep pit. Savannah Jack prodded her into preceding him across a six-foot bridge of sorts spanned between the edge of the pit and the rickety chickee. Joie held her breath and crossed quickly. She looked around her. With a little effort, she knew that she could probably dislodge the slats of the chickee, but without the bridge the pit threatened a deep fall, and it was a wide jump for a pregnant woman to make.

243

Savannah Jack was not a builder. Perhaps he did not think the structure needed to last long. Perhaps its precarious perch was intended.

Joie turned to the interior, where she saw a table, a stool, an elevated, clay-lined basin in which to build a fire, and a bit of wood and some moss with flint. She supposed that a second clay pot on the floor was intended for private business. A hammock hung diagonally across the chickee, and it appeared as if tying the hammock had helped keep the structure's supports in place.

Joie looked at Savannah Jack. His reptilian eyes at last caught her own, and her heart lurched.

He had prepared this chickee just for her. It would be her cage. Savannah Jack closed the makeshift door and secured it with a long, rusty metal chain and combination padlock, both of which he might have scavenged from a ship she saw wrecked on the beach in the distance. The floor wobbled when Jack moved back across his tenuous bridge.

They had traveled west from the Suwannee River. Joie knew that much. She recalled passing the mouth of a river and wished she had paid attention to the tutors the Dowager Duchess had employed when they taught geography. Instead, she had daydreamed about dancing with the horses alongside the gypsies. Her favorite daydream, however, was tossing a knife close past the head of the humorless scholar—just to ruffle his feathers. His contempt for his Indian students was obvious to her, though he masked it well with Cade and Gabe, who were much larger than he was.

But Joie *had* listened to Cade and Gabe as they told of escaping from Savannah Jack when he and William Augustus Bowles had held them at St. Marks. Lyssa had thought it important for Cade to tell the story he had kept to himself for so long. She encouraged him to bring it out of the dark recesses of his mind into the bright light of day, where he was in control. Cade had taken the canoe and managed to get the two of them from the St. Marks River to the Apalachicola River. From there, he had made it far enough up the river for High Head Jim to find them.

Had she and Savannah Jack passed the St. Marks River? Were they near the Apalachicola River? If so, the Negro Fort that Abraham had mentioned was not too far up the river. Why would Savannah Jack bring her to a place so close to where he had taken Cade and Gabe?

And then it struck her! She was to be the bait to attract her brothers! The path led directly to the door of the cage.

"You think they will come for me, don't you?" Joie said from inside the structure, placing her hands on the slats.

Jack said nothing but pulled away the makeshift wooden bridge.

"I got kidnapped by pirates before Millea found me," Joie called after him as he walked off. "Don't you think that if anyone were looking for me, they would have been here by now?"

He was not gone long before he returned with dried beef, ground corn, and blackberries, along with a couple of gourds filled with water. He reattached the bridge, and Joie moved to the other side so the chickee would not tip and send her sprawling twelve feet below, burying her beneath a heap of wood. Near the bottom of Jack's improvised door was a smaller door about one foot square, and he opened this to pass the food in to her.

And then he left.

Joie drank from the gourd, mixed water with the cornmeal, and ate that with the dried meat.

Then she stood there looking around, getting her bearings. The island was narrow. Behind her on the bay side were a pine thicket and sand dunes covered with sea grass. A shallow, rain-fed, freshwater marsh lay between her and the sparkling blue ocean with its waves folding and crashing upon the white-sand beach. The hum of a thousand insects surrounded her—she slapped at a cruelly biting deer fly—mosquitoes hovered, honeybees buzzed about, and wasps had already made a nest in the chickee. She waved away the punky no-see-ums near her eyes. They were already making her miserable.

And yet the island was a beautiful place with plenty of palmetto plants, sea grapes, and cabbage palms that could provide food if Savannah Jack would only let her out of the chickee to forage. She felt like a captive bird in a cage that swayed on its fragile support with each gust of wind. With nothing else to do, she wrapped up in the hammock to protect herself from the bite of the insects and, lulled by the waves, the wind, and the rocking chickee, went to sleep.

When she awoke later, she caught glimpses of Savannah Jack working around the perimeter of her prison. As she watched, she realized what he was doing.

He pockmarked the path leading to the chickee with holes covered over with brush—a distraction, perhaps to keep the brothers he was sure would come after her from spotting the gun and bow traps he had rigged around the area.

She watched him secure a gun and barrel in stout crotches driven into the ground and standing about three feet high. He then cut a small sapling about a foot or two in length, rigging it so that someone would trip on the string and spring the hammer of the gun. But most alarming were the poison-tipped bow-and-arrow traps scattered throughout the area.

And then Jack disappeared once more. He returned sporadically, bringing her scallops, oysters, water, nuts, fruits, and always more corn. Sometimes he brought dried fish. When he did that, she knew he would be gone longer than usual. He never spoke.

Savannah Jack was in for quite a wait. How would anyone have a clue where she was?

Gabe had shed the clothes of an English gentleman and once more looked like the Creek warrior he was raised to be. Once William McIntosh, White Warrior, had vouched for him to Andrew Jackson, the general and his men had pursued Bowlegs and his people into the swamp, where they simply evaporated. Upon hearing that some Indians had taken refuge in Pensacola, however, an angry Jackson did an about-face and took his army back to St. Marks to resupply and proceed to Pensacola.

There would be no further help from Andrew Jackson in pursuing Savannah Jack and Joie. The general had grander goals than the pursuit of one lost woman. Godfrey sadly watched the last of Jackson's army disappear.

"Let's see where the tracks lead," Gabe said, clapping Godfrey's slumped shoulders.

After following an elusive trail to a creek near the mouth of the Suwannee River, where the track of Jack's horse disappeared into the muck, Godfrey and Gabe sat together around a small campfire, exhausted.

"I've been in these swamps before," Gabe said. "But I was delirious and remember very little."

"That's why I'm here!" came a voice out of the darkness.

"Cade!" Gabe exclaimed, recognizing the familiar voice. He leaped to his feet and embraced his twin brother with a big bear hug.

"Good to see it's you at this campfire, brother," Cade said, hugging him back with the same ferocity.

"I'm glad to see you, but what changed your plan about staying with Lyssa and the children?"

"A couple of months after you sailed from Falmouth, Lord Bathurst sent word to Sir Phillip Stapleton," Cade explained. "He had learned that Woodbine was involved in an intrigue far beyond anything he or Sir Phillip could have imagined. He was concerned for your safety. The Duke immediately set about finding us transportation to search for you."

"Us?" Gabriel asked, almost afraid to hear the answer.

"Whither thou goest," Lyssa said as she followed Cade into the light of the campfire.

She had lingered in the shadows to change from the dress she had worn on the ship into the traditional Indian clothing she had made of deerskin after they left Fort Mims years ago. Now she was glad she had kept the clothing.

"Lyssa was determined to get here," Cade said. "We saw the smoke of this fire, and she was bound and determined that we come and check it out. She knew it might be you, and if we waited you would disappear again. I tried to tell her it could just as easily be Savannah Jack!"

"I'm prepared this time," Lyssa said, laughing. "I've got guns and knives hidden all over my person, as the Dowager Duchess would say, though guns and knives would never be included in her sentence. You didn't think I was going to let the two of you loose in this nest of vipers once more without me, did you? While he was arranging transportation, not an easy thing with the international situation what it is, Father got a letter from Judge Toulmin saying that he had received word that Joie was among the Red Sticks in Florida.

"When Cade found out that Andrew Jackson was once more headed into a battle with Red Sticks right where Lord Bathurst said you were probably headed—and where we knew Savannah Jack could also be— there was no keeping him back."

Gabe reached for Lyssa, but Godfrey beat him to it. He swung her around while she laughed and cried for him to put her down so she could look at him.

"Godfrey Lewis Winkel, as I live and breathe! It *is* you! We have been so worried!"

Godfrey finally put Lyssa on her feet.

"I cannot believe this muscular Viking, this tall, blond god, is the skinny, pimply-faced Godfrey Lewis Winkel we managed to pull onto Beauty years ago!" Lyssa proclaimed.

Gabe then pulled her to him in an embrace. Lyssa framed his face with her hands and looked directly into his eyes. A silent communication between them. She saw that he was well but frustrated.

"So how did you get here?" Gabe asked. "How did you know where to find me?"

"Fortunately," Cade said, "Lyssa's father has maintained his friendships in Virginia. He convinced an old friend who happened to have delivered a shipment of tobacco to London to fit us on his ship headed to New Orleans. He then arranged for us to get aboard an American supply ship coming to St. Marks. We were at St. Marks when a man by the name of Armbrister was brought in. He told the Spanish commandant of the fort about a man who had accompanied him from New Providence searching for his sister. Lyssa smiled at Captain

McKeever and started dropping the names of her father's powerful American friends. She quickly succeeded in convincing him that we were worthy of his help. She's obviously been learning the art of namedropping from the Dowager Duchess! He was *so* impressed I thought I might have to hit him, the way he wound up fawning over *my wife*." Cade pulled Lyssa toward him possessively.

Gabe knew he wasn't kidding.

Lyssa blushed and said, "I only told him that Gabe was my husband's dear brother and we were all searching for Joie and Godfrey, who had been kidnapped. He simply allowed us to come with him on the *Chance* when he returned with supplies for the general and to transport more injured Americans."

"She didn't mention the fact that her father is now a *British* earl," Cade said with a grin. "We had to wait until after the court-martial of the man named Armbrister and another man that Jackson held captive at St. Marks, a man named Arbuthnot, who apparently owned the boat, the *Chance*."

Gabe listened intently. "What happened to them?" he asked.

"Jackson had Armbrister shot," Cade explained, "but he ordered that Arbuthnot be hanged from the yardarm of his own ship. McKeever told Lyssa, whom he thought was a fine American lady, that he heard Jackson say, 'My God would not have smiled on me, had I punished only the poor ignorant savages, and spared the white men who set them on.'"

"They were burying the men when we sailed with McKeever back here," Lyssa added.

Armbrister was a preening, posturing prick in Gabe's opinion, but his death still came as a shock.

"And here you are, Godfrey!" Lyssa exclaimed. "Looks like this was an unnecessary trip!"

Gabe and Godfrey just looked at each other.

"Oh, no!" Cade said, sensing that something terrible had happened.

The joy of the reunion was over.

Glancing between them, Lyssa asked, "Where is Joie?"

"Sit down, Lyssa," Gabe said.

Godfrey looked like he might cry.

Gabe took her hand. "Savannah Jack has taken Joie."

"No," she said, turning white as a sheet as she remembered her time as Savannah Jack's captive. She sat heavily on a log.

"Why do you think he took her and didn't simply kill her once he knew who she was?" Godfrey asked.

"I can tell you that," Cade said. "What better way to lure *us* back so he can finish us all off at once? It was probably Savannah Jack himself who arranged for Judge Toulmin to find out about Joie being with the Red Sticks."

"I guess Savannah Jack had someone deliver the message while he was in Creek country when he committed what General Jackson called the Butler massacre," Godfrey said.

"Savannah Jack must have felt like the Great Spirit had sent him a gift when Millea Francis found Joie washed ashore in Charlotte Harbor," said Gabe.

"What?" Lyssa said. "There was a Millea at Fort St. Marks who rejected a marriage proposal from a young man, Duncan McKrimmon, I think it was, while we were there."

Gabe allowed himself a smile and said, "So he got up the nerve. Too bad she told him no."

"You'd better start at the beginning," Cade told Godfrey.

"I haven't heard it all myself. Only Joie's story from where Millea found her," Gabe said. "I'd like to hear your part of the story."

"I am a writer," Godfrey said, "and I would never plot a novel like this. If I had not lived it, I would not have believed it myself, and I only know my part of what happened."

"I have traveled a long way in a very short time, leaving all of my children in the hands of my mother, father, and the Dowager Duchess," Lyssa said. "Forgive my impatience. I will settle back now and hear every detail."

Because of Godfrey's prodigious memory and talent for telling a good story, his tale was filled with compelling detail, but because of the late hour, he compressed the story to the essentials.

"Gypsies?" Lyssa commented once during the tale. "Was I so busy with babies that I had no idea what was happening with Joie?"

Godfrey had grown more and more agitated. His eyes were moist with emotion. And then he cleared his throat, stopping and looking at his hands.

"Godfrey," Gabe said, "I don't think you told them everything that happened."

Godfrey stood, his feet spread as Gentleman Jack had taught him to do when about to engage in fisticuffs, and hesitated. "As I told you, Joie had been very, very sick. There was only one cot, Joie was cold, and I had told Gaspar that Joie was my wife. And then—one night—the night before I was taken to Gaspar's mansion and Joie and Black Caesar disappeared, we, uh…." He stammered around, blushing all the while.

Finally, Gabe took pity on him and said, "Joie is pregnant."

Just as Godfrey had expected, Cade leapt to his feet and aimed a punch squarely at Godfrey's jaw with as much power as he could muster.

But Godfrey was prepared and dodged in time to deflect the blow and roll away with the punch. "I don't blame you, Cade," he said, panting. "I would beat *myself* up if I could. But that isn't going to help us find Joie—and the baby—which could come anytime if Millea is correct about Joie's condition."

Lyssa looked ready to leap upon him herself. "We'll settle this later," she said.

"You can hit me all you want then," Godfrey promised. "I deserve it."

Next, Gabe related Joie's story from the moment Millea had found her washed ashore. Lyssa fought back tears when he finished.

"Savannah Jack must think you have an idea of where to follow him," Lyssa said.

"I've been wracking my brain to remember," Gabe assured her, "but I was delirious most of the time."

"I tried hard to recall landmarks," Cade added, "but they kept us captive in several different locations. I hardly know where to start. And…it was fifteen years ago."

They all sat quietly around the embers of the fire that had died down during their conversation. Gabe kept his hand on his gun and remained alert to the sounds of the forest around them. He wouldn't put it past Savannah Jack to send one of his notorious knives flying at them from the darkness and then take out another of them with his gun. But somehow he sensed that was not what Savannah Jack planned.

They were all exhausted, and only a few hours were left before dawn.

"Perhaps if we get some sleep," Godfrey finally said, "then something will come to us if we're not trying so hard."

Cade had his elbows on his knees and his head in his hands.

"It's got to be something you know," Godfrey told the three of them. "I cannot be of any help. I don't know much at all about this area. The extent of my knowledge is from a book I read about a Frenchman who shipwrecked on an island near here—*Shipwreck and Adventures of Monsieur Pierre Viaud*. It was an exciting story of survival on a barrier island about three miles from the mainland—and of cannibalism." He lifted his eyebrows for emphasis.

Godfrey spread his blanket out on the ground and offered it to Lyssa, trying to make up for his own despicable behavior. He should have protected Joie! It was all his fault! He couldn't help himself. He chattered on, trying to ignore the looks—both angry and disappointed—that Lyssa was giving him.

"When I read that Dog Island was located in shark-infested waters, I vowed that was someplace I would never..."

Cade's head popped up and he exclaimed, "That's it! That's the name of the island where they kept us first! That's what Jack expected us to remember. That's where Gabe first took sick!"

Now *Godfrey* looked sick.

He sat down hard on one of the logs. "I should have known," Godfrey said. "Everything I said I would never do is now something I have done. Or will do."

"I'm too tired to think now," Cade said as he stretched out beside Lyssa, spooning her protectively. "Perhaps I'll remember more in the morning."

Godfrey lay on the cold ground and said a little prayer for Joie before sheer exhaustion took him out. Gabe leaned back against a tree with his gun propped on his knees. He knew Cade would wake after a brief sleep, revived and ready to take his turn at guard.

Joie! Gabe thought. With Savannah Jack! And pregnant. Could it get any worse?

Unfortunately, knowing Jack, it would.

In the moonlight, Joie watched the sea turtle eggs hatch, the babies all at once pushing through the sand in which they had been buried. Then the tiny creatures scurried toward the water.

Large turtles sought the high ground of the sand dunes. Seagulls flew toward the mainland. Frogs croaked so loud all night that Joie had trouble sleeping. Insect-eating birds flew low to the ground, and bees and butterflies disappeared. Even the alligators vanished to the bottom of the pond. She heard one shriek when he set off one after another of Savannah Jack's traps as he lumbered toward the pond.

The wildlife around her knew a storm approached.

Just when she thought things couldn't get worse, Joie had awakened to a red dawn sky to see Savannah Jack toss a couple of canvas bags into the pit. The hissing she heard as snakes escaped from the bags brought Joie out of the hammock's cocoon to stare into the glittering eyes of her captor. He then disappeared once more into the thicket of trees behind the chickee.

Dear God.

Her back ached, and her womb cramped. And now, looking out over the ocean, she watched as a wall of gray clouds approached the island. The sea crashed in increasingly high waves, ominously encroaching further up the beach until they nearly reached the freshwater pond. Should the waves fill the pit, the snakes would float to the top and slither easily into her chickee. Or the waves would simply disintegrate the chickee and send her tumbling into the pit.

She thought of Godfrey, cutlass in hand fighting on the deck of the ship, jumping in front of her to protect her from attack. Godfrey, climbing the mast, claiming her as his wife. Their kiss. Godfrey, whom she would never again see.

A gush of bloody water wet her thighs.

"Oh, Godfrey!" Joie cried out and grabbed her belly. She fell to her knees when a knifelike pain ripped through her body.

"I just know there are millions of sharks in there." Cade, Gabe, and Lyssa heard Godfrey mumble there on the bow of Arbuthnot's schooner, the *Chance*, which Cade and Lyssa had used to find them. "If there's one thing I hate, it's a man-eating shark."

Then Godfrey held up his hand and said, "Listen! I heard something."

Moments passed, and they heard nothing but the wind and the torrential rain.

"I heard Joie call my name!" he insisted.

Godfrey leaned so far over the side of the *Chance*, trying to peer through the grey veil of rain, that he was in danger of falling into the churning waters of the bay.

"Godfrey! Calm down, man!" Gabe said, grabbing him by the shirttails. Cade joined him, pulling Godfrey back with both feet on the deck.

"It could have been the cry of a sea bird," Cade offered.

"What birds do *you* see?" Godfrey asked. That was a rhetorical question because there was absolutely no visibility, but earlier they all had seen the sea birds flying to the protection of the trees on the mainland.

The captain of the *Chance* approached Dog Island, using his experience and instinct to guide him. He had told them there was a protected inlet on the bay side.

"The birds were smart enough to know a storm is coming," Godfrey said, "and they've all headed for the mainland. It is she, I tell you. And she's in pain."

Lyssa did not doubt that Godfrey had heard Joie. She remembered how she had sensed Cade's emotions when they were separated during the Creek War. From what she observed of Godfrey, he was deeply in love with Joie. His concern for her was evident in everything he did…as was his feeling of guilt at not having protected her.

From the story he told, however, they were lucky to be alive, and his quick wit had given them that chance. Joie's own pluck and courage had once again contributed toward her survival thus far. Lyssa prayed it would continue. They all needed a lot of luck to go with their determination.

After losing Savannah Jack's tracks on the Suwannee River, they had commandeered the abandoned *Chance* to get to Dog Island. Armbrister, who had sailed the ship in Tampa Bay, and Arbuthnot, the ship's legal owner, were both dead, after all.

It was only logical for them to use the ship to search for Joie.

Gabe was familiar to the crew, and he offered to pay them to sail with their little search party. Faced with the less desirable prospect of returning home empty handed, the sailors agreed. They knew the waters well, and soon, in spite of the rough water, they had covered the thirty-mile distance to Dog Island. The bay teemed with dolphins and porpoises escaping the stormy seas.

"Let's be smart about this," Cade said. "We know that Savannah Jack is there somewhere waiting for us. In this weather, we have few options. We must approach from the bay, and he has probably already figured that out."

Gabe looked at the height of the waves and the wild current rushing between Dog Island and St. George Island. "Savannah Jack has had time to set quite a trap," he noted. "And we know he will have set himself up in a spot where he can shoot at us when we approach."

Impatiently, Godfrey prepared to jump in, but Gabe grabbed him. "It's time to think smart, Godfrey. We will not do Joie any good if we rush into this and get us all killed."

Cade, Gabe, Godfrey, and Lyssa huddled together on the deck of the ship.

Shouting over the wind and pelted by rain, Lyssa said, "This horrible weather might actually work to our benefit. Do you think he would really expect us to be out in it?"

Gabe and Cade looked at each other, and both nodded.

"He *knows* that we will come," Gabe said. "Weather will not keep us away."

"You're right. It is never good to underestimate Savannah Jack," Lyssa admitted.

"I do think he will be looking for us to approach on the bay side, however," said Cade.

"Jack will be looking for *us*, Cade," said his brother. "He will not expect Godfrey and Lyssa."

"Now there's an idea," Lyssa said, catching on. "You and Cade should distract him. Godfrey and I can skirt along the beach while the two of you divert him."

"This rain is like a curtain," Godfrey complained as he attempted to identify some landmark. Remembering an old map he had found while doing research on pirates in the Gulf, he said, "Dog Island is about two miles from the tip of St. George Island."

The captain nodded, overhearing the conversation. "This is normally a very shallow bay. Fortunately, with no cargo we have a shallow draft on this boat and can navigate fairly close to land. We *need* a safe harbor." He glanced at the main mast, which groaned ominously.

Godfrey knew that it would take skill to navigate into the harbor. They were fortunate to have a captain who knew the area well and agreed to help them, though the cost was high. The crew had heard of Savannah Jack. They only agreed to sail the ship, not participate in Savannah Jack's capture.

Cade, Gabe, and Lyssa held their breath as the captain skillfully turned the ship into the inlet, where at last the waves calmed and the wind, broken by the trees on the island, died down a bit. They scanned the shoreline. Cade and Gabe, expecting Savannah Jack to be watching, swam ashore holding their guns aloft. Once they arrived, they headed into the thicket, taking a path toward the center of the island.

Lyssa and Godfrey, meanwhile, made it into the dinghy on the far side of the ship and rowed to the farthest point of land encircling the inlet. Then they skirted around the island, keeping to the shore as much as possible to get on the beach in front of the thicket.

The report of gunshots brought them up short. Savannah Jack had spotted Cade and Gabe.

"Move on," Lyssa said, her eyes wide and worried. "They're doing what they're supposed to do, draw his attention. We've got to do our part!"

Just as they reached the extent of their ability to circumnavigate the island, they stumbled upon a path heading toward the center. The waves crashed not far from where they stood, now covering a large portion of the island.

"Watch out!" Lyssa said. "Look at the size of that alligator!"

Godfrey jerked Lyssa behind him. They turned to run, but the gator did not move.

"Look at the arrows in his hide," Godfrey said.

"That alligator is dead. Poison arrows?" Lyssa asked incredulously.

Godfrey nodded. He stared at the giant creature, thinking. "I saw a Jacques le Moyne engraving where early Indians disemboweled a gator and used it as camouflage and a shield," he told Lyssa.

She nodded and pulled out her knife. Together, they flipped the nine-foot gator and gutted him. Then they fitted themselves inside the foul-smelling skin and crawled down the path down which the creature had come.

Joie heard shots but figured they were more of Savannah Jack's traps being set off by fleeing animals. She knew she had to act to save herself. The chickee was coming apart. With each lapping wave, the sides of the pit shifted as it filled with more water. The wind had already lifted the palm fronds from the roof and blown them away, exposing loosened vines. Joie fought an approaching contraction and loosed the hammock. Gritting her teeth during each pain, she wove the hammock between six bars of her cage and then loosed the bars from their connection to the top and bottom supports. Finally, holding the bars in front of her and praying that her handmade bridge would hold, she dropped it against the side of the pit. It barely bridged the gap, but the waves had washed some sand into the pit and it caught. Now, did she have the courage to cross over?

Her heart pounded. Before she could think, she ran over the makeshift bridge, which immediately began to slide. Joie dug her fingers and feet into the sand, clawing and climbing. Snakes hissed and struck close to her bare feet, one scraping her ankle, but somehow she made it. She dragged herself out of the pit and lay, rolling with another contraction. Fortunately, the waves had shifted the sands enough to cover most of the snakes, and those that remained were focused on getting out of the pit and onto higher land. Lyssa forced herself to lie still and get her bearings. Another severe pain had her curled on her side. It wouldn't do to rush forward and get shot.

But she had to move before a snake struck or a wave overtook her. Her babe lay in her womb beneath her heart, trusting her for shelter and protection. Godfrey's child. The boy she loved unreasonably had become a man she loved overwhelmingly. She struggled to her feet. As long as there was breath, there was hope.

Another pain and more pressure between her legs. She would not cry. Jack might hear!

She remembered exactly where she had seen Savannah Jack set up his traps. The closest gun trap was right ahead. She approached it carefully. Keeping clear of the barrel of the gun, she managed to disengage it from the string set to spring the trigger. She hoped the gunpowder wasn't wet! She now had a weapon of her own.

Behind her, the chickee crumbled to pieces and toppled into a big wave that nearly knocked her over. She clenched her teeth to stay her cry and fell to her knees with the pain of the next contraction.

A gun sounded, and a bullet whizzed past, just missing her right ear. The sand popped ahead of her. Behind her, a snake coiled and struck, grazing her heel, but she barely noticed.

Savannah Jack had spotted her. She crawled forward, ignoring the pain.

Dear God. Did you save me in the waves to have me die in this place?

To her horror, an alligator barred her path. Joie's heart plummeted. Savannah Jack behind her and an alligator ahead of her! What next?

The alligator shifted on its side, and Godfrey's voice came from beneath it. "Here, Joie!" he said. "Crawl under here!"

Another bullet pierced the thick hide of the alligator.

Godfrey? Was she delirious?

"We're here for you, Joie. Hurry!"

Could that possibly be Lyssa's voice too?

More gunfire came from behind her, and Joie saw Lyssa's hands outstretched, reaching for the gun. Joie gave it to her and, in spite of the coming contraction, she bent her elbows to protect her baby and rolled under the gator, where she was met with a fierce embrace from a kneeling Godfrey.

The erratic beat of her heart, the fear and confusion, evaporated when she looked into Godfrey's clear blue eyes, now oddly filled with tears. She lifted her face and Godfrey bent to kiss her.

"Later!" Lyssa exclaimed, handing Joie her knife in exchange for the gun. "Let's get out of here!"

Waves lapped, and the sea threatened to suck them away as it crashed around them, but they continued to crawl. They heard footsteps splashing near them and stopped. Moccasins Joie recognized all too well appeared close to her head.

Godfrey indicated that they would have to make a stand, so Joie turned to her side with Lyssa's knife in hand. Lyssa cocked the gun.

When Godfrey flipped the gator hide, Savannah Jack stood ready to shoot, but, seeing three of them, he took a second to decide where to aim. Lyssa lifted the gun, aimed spontaneously, and pulled the trigger. Misfire! The gunpowder was wet with the rain. But it was enough to distract Savannah Jack.

Joie threw the knife just as she had practiced with the gypsies, and it hit true. Blood spattered them all as Savannah Jack grabbed at the knife sticking out of his chest.

"Snow Bird!" he cried.

Incredulous, he fell back just as a huge wave crashed over the freshwater pond and sucked him out to sea.

Joie looked at Godfrey and Lyssa in confusion. Why had Jack called her mother's name? She looked out once more at the vicious sea. She would never know what motivated that horrible man.

"We must move before we get sucked out as well!" Godfrey yelled.

Joie let out a primal scream. "The baby is coming!" she insisted.

"We've got to get her out of the water!" Lyssa said.

"Don't you dare take one step without me telling you where to put your feet!" Joie commanded when Godfrey lifted her and moved forward. "Lyssa, hold on to Godfrey's belt and step where he steps!"

Godfrey held her tightly, and Lyssa followed Godfrey closer than a shadow, stepping as he stepped, her arm wrapped around his rope belt.

"Godfrey, stop!" Lyssa cried. "Joie, why is your foot bleeding?"

"Snakebite," Joie said between gritted teeth.

Godfrey knelt immediately, and Lyssa pulled out the knife strapped to her leg. She quickly cut a cross on Joie's heel and sucked the venom from her foot. Lyssa sucked and spat several times while Joie groaned with another contraction.

"Fortunately, it is only a scratch, really. The snake didn't actually puncture her heel," Lyssa assured them. She lifted a handful of salt water to rinse her mouth.

When Godfrey rose again, Joie cried, "Wait!"

"What now? I don't see anything!" Godfrey shouted over the crashing waves.

"It's the contraction, you fool! I can't watch where you're putting your feet with my eyes closed!"

"Then keep them open!" Godfrey said sensibly.

Joie cursed under her breath.

A rogue wave washed over them, and Lyssa held on to Godfrey's belt to keep from getting swept away. Godfrey was knocked to his knees as the sand fell apart beneath them, but he held firm like an oak planted on the shore. When the wave receded, he was able to step out of the oncoming water and onto firmer ground, though the waves lapped closer and closer and the soft sand made the journey slow.

Joie had to stop Godfrey occasionally just so she could bear down and then breathe; the contractions were so close, hard and frequent. The wind blew and the rain continued to pelt them. The storm raged around them, but Godfrey held her and the world was right.

Step by step, Joie guided them through the field of pits and traps, barely keeping ahead of the advancing waves. The wind wailed, and sheets of rain drenched them. Joie held him so tightly that Godfrey whispered, "I'll not let you go. Not ever again."

Joie kissed the sweet spot at the hollow of his neck, feeling secure though the wind howled and the waves crashed around them. Slowly but surely, they made their way to the path through the thicket.

"Where are Gabe and Cade?" Joie yelled over the uproar of the storm. They were finally clear of the area where she had seen Savannah Jack set the traps.

"They were going to distract Savannah Jack while we found out where he was holding you!" Godfrey answered.

"Put me down, Godfrey! Go find out what Jack did to my brothers!"

Godfrey continued holding her, feet planted firmly in the wet sand, his shirt clinging to his broad shoulders and his long hair whipping about his face.

"I don't know," he said uncertainly. Now that he'd found her, he did not want to let her out of his sight.

Joie pursed her lips. Tears spilled from her eyes. He liked it better when she was cursing.

"I'll go find them," he said reluctantly, holding her even tighter.

But then they heard a voice. "We'll be down in a minute."

It was Cade. Coming from above them?

All three looked up through the dripping branches of the huge oak tree in amazement.

"That is, if someone will cut that damned rope," Gabe yelled down.

"How in the world did you get up there?" Lyssa asked, looking up and seeing her husband and his brother dangling above them in a cage.

"Savannah Jack is better at building traps than I gave him credit for," Cade said, shaking his head. "We crawled right in. He left us laughing and saying he'd have more fun killing us all together."

Joie screamed again.

"Oh, God," Gabe said. "What has he done? Is he back?"

"No, Joie's having a baby," Godfrey said matter-of-factly.

"Baby?" Cade said. "How will she…"

"Don't start…Ohhh!" Joie cried.

"The usual way, I imagine," Lyssa said, chuckling. She squinted as the rain poured down her face and dripped from her long black hair.

"Get us down! He'll be coming back!" Gabe insisted. "This is another of his traps. He's got us where he wants us! We're all here in one place." He expected a knife to punctuate his remarks.

"No he won't. Joie killed him with his own knife. The knife Cade pulled from your father," Lyssa said proudly.

"*Joie* killed Savannah Jack?" Cade was amazed.

Lyssa found the rope suspending the cage and chopped it in two with a knife she pulled from her boot, sending the contraption crashing to the ground below.

"My hero!" Lyssa said sarcastically to the man now lying at her feet.

"'Follow me,' Cade said. And I followed him…right into Savannah Jack's trap!" Gabe grumbled, knife in hand. He sprang up from where he had toppled when the cage plummeted to the ground. "You'd think after all these years I would learn!"

With his back now to his brother, he stood ready for an attack. "Savannah Jack could return from the dead and I would not be surprised," he said.

"He told us the cage was a perfect place for us to end our lives. That was how it was to have ended at St. Marks," Cade said, his gun ready in case Savannah Jack reappeared.

"If you're finished, could someone help me here? This baby is coming! Now!" Joie yelled. "What part of 'now' do you people not understand?"

Before Cade or Gabe could react, Lyssa grabbed wet palm fronds and made a bed for Joie. Godfrey set her down gently on the makeshift bed. She gave one loud yell and a push, and the baby's head appeared.

Stunned, Godfrey removed his sodden shirt and used it to catch the child, who let out a wail.

"I told you!" Joie cried.

"A boy!" Lyssa exclaimed.

Godfrey covered his son as much as possible, sheltering him from the pouring rain. Lyssa tied off the umbilical cord with a bit of vine and then cut it. The blood from the delivery ran in rivlets off the palm fronds and onto the white sand. Joie lay back, exhausted.

Godfrey looked into the tiny face of his son and then beamed at Joie. "Caleb Connory Winkel," he said, and then he looked at her for confirmation—and approval.

His look was filled with such love that Joie was overwhelmed. And yet she knew Godfrey well enough now to realize that he truly needed her approval. She looked around at the family that had risked their lives to come and save her. And she started to sob.

Godfrey's face fell, and Joie could see his anxiety.

"If you don't like that name, we'll name him whatever you like," he said. "Just please don't cry. We can even call him *Godfrey*, but I really wouldn't wish that on anyone."

Godfrey got down on his knees with the screaming infant in his arms and pulled her to him. He held all that had meaning in his life within that embrace. Hurricane be damned.

Joie was astounded. This gorgeous, brilliant man needed *her* approval. Her sister-in-law looked on with love. And the two brave men behind them were her flesh and blood. They had all risked everything—for her! She was humbled. She who had hungered for love for so long now knew a love more powerful than she could have imagined.

Lyssa finished tending to the afterbirth and said, "I don't think it is the name that has her in tears, is it Joie?"

Joie shook her head. She reached up and pulled Godfrey's face to her. "Kiss me," she said.

And he did.

Lyssa took the wailing infant from his arms.

"There's a priest back at St. Marks," Cade said, with fatherly determination. He slipped his arm around his wife.

Lyssa laughed.

The single pure white egret on the limb above them, shining brightly through the grey sheet of rain, gave a deep, gravelly cry. Then it spread its wings to catch a powerful gust of wind that it would ride to the mainland.

Epilogue

St. Marks brought back too many bad memories for all of them and was not a place to which any wished to return. Besides, the captain of the *Chance* was determined to sail west and find Alexander Arbuthnot's son John in New Orleans. They convinced him to take them on a slight detour up the Mobile River to St. Stephens on the Tombigbee River, the capital of the Alabama Territory, where Lyssa's father still had a home near the Pebble Creek Jockey Club. There they would be close to her grandfather, the Choctaw chief Pushmataha.

The brief journey aboard the *Chance* gave Joie a little time to recuperate.

A bath and clean clothes were still a long way off, but the captain was able to give her a clean shirt. Lyssa mixed up a batch of creams from some herbs in the ship's carpenter's kit to heal the numerous bites all over Joie's body and cleaned her up fairly well with a pan of water. Now fed and clean, Joie was happily engaged with new motherhood and the joy of having Godfrey nearby.

Cade, Gabe, and Lyssa stood at the door to the captain's quarters, where Joie lay on the captain's bed and Godfrey reclined, propped on his elbow, while his son nursed at his mother's breast. He and Joie shared loving smiles at every sound he uttered and each expression on their son's face.

He was a miracle. Their being alive and together was a miracle.

Shaking his head in disgust, Cade said to Gabe, "Godfrey never leaves her side. It's like he's afraid she'll disappear."

Gabe gave Cade a look.

"No. I never acted like that!" Cade exclaimed.

Gabe looked at the woman's hand that Cade clasped tightly at his side. He quirked an eyebrow at his brother.

Lyssa smiled.

"Acted? No," Gabe said, chuckling. "Act? Yes." Then Gabe shook his head. "But *I* sure as hell will *never* act like that!" he said with conviction.

To their surprise, at St. Stephens beneath the HobucaKintopa Bluff where they planned to land, they discovered a brand new dock and a sign that read "St. Stephens Steamboat Company: Organized in 1818." The captain of the *Chance* rowed them from the ship up to the newly built dock for the steamboat company.

"I'm not gonna break, Godfrey!" Joie exclaimed as he lifted her, holding Caleb, from the dinghy and placed her in Gabe's waiting arms. Godfrey just smiled and climbed up to pull her to him on the dock.

She looked up, and he automatically bent to kiss her. They'd been doing a lot of that. It seemed that he couldn't look at her without kissing her, and if he moved an inch she lifted her face to his.

Lyssa sighed and reached for Cade's hand, which was only inches from hers.

"Disgusting," Gabe affirmed, turning to walk off the dock and up the hill to the Government Building.

"Gabe, I forgot to tell you about Sabrina Stapleton!" Lyssa called.

Gabe spun around. "What about Sabrina...Miss Stapleton?"

"Just before we left, we heard that she'd lost all of her eyesight," Lyssa said.

Gabe was surprised by the sudden clench of his heart as he thought of how devastating that would be to Sabrina. He knew it would have been to him.

Lyssa nodded toward Cade, who noted the expression on Gabe's face.

Suddenly, they heard a cry from the top of the bluff.

"Ben?" Lyssa exclaimed. "How can that be?"

And then a whole herd of children ran down the hill toward them, followed closely by Lyssa's father and mother, Jake and Malee Rendel, now Duke and Duchess of Penbrooke. The orphans Joie and Lyssa had rescued after the Fort Mims massacre, along with Cade and Lyssa's young children and Joie's half-brother Jay, surrounded them only Mo and Meme were missing.

Judge Harry Toulmin, Jacob Rendel's good friend, stood on the hill, watching the reunion.

"How did you get here?" Lyssa exclaimed, hugging each of the children in turn.

"Your father had to buy a shipping company to get us here as fast as he was determined that we should go!" Malee told Lyssa, who finally had time to embrace her mother.

Lyssa laughed and threw herself into her father's arms.

Then all of their attention went to Joie and the infant in her arms. Malee hurried to the girl who had become like her own daughter and pulled the two of them into her embrace. Joie broke into tears, and Malee soothed her.

"You have much to tell us," Malee said. A mewling sound brought her attention to the baby in Joie's arms. "I see we have a new one."

Joie's hair was matted. She had welts on her face and body from insect bites. Dark shadows circled her eyes. She was thin and weak from the ravages of the last months and from the rigors of childbirth. But she presented her child proudly to Malee.

Then she reached for Godfrey, who stood barely a hand's distance away.

"Do you remember Godfrey, GranMalee?"

Malee looked for the awkward, redheaded, pimply boy in the tall, muscular, man whose long blond hair blew loose in the wind. His hands rubbed Joie's back as if it were natural for him to be touching her. Joie leaned back into his support. Malee looked to Jake, and he gave a slight nod, acknowledging the relationship.

"Savannah Jack captured Joie," Lyssa explained. "He put her in a cage on Dog Island to lure Cade and Gabe."

"Joie killed him with his own knife," Godfrey told Malee proudly.

As Malee cuddled the new baby, Joie said, "This is my...*our*...son, GranMalee. His name is Caleb Connory Winkel."

Jake Rendel approached, with Judge Toulmin close behind. "So, Godfrey, it sounds as if it is a good thing my dear friend Harry Toulmin happens to be in St. Stephens today."

Godfrey looked him straight in the eye and nodded his agreement.

Jake saw steel in the man before him. The unsure boy he'd once known had become a man to be reckoned with.

Joie wobbled and lifted the foot that the snake had bitten. She was so tired that she could barely stand. Godfrey took Caleb from Malee and gave him to Joie, whom he then lifted into his arms.

"Joie needs rest and a doctor," he said. "She is my wife in all but name. Tomorrow, if you will arrange it, Judge Toulmin, she will be my wife in name as well."

Joie looked at him with love and trust. Godfrey smiled and planted a kiss on her forehead.

Tears filled Lyssa's eyes. Joie had the love for which she had always longed. And she had no doubt that Godfrey Lewis Winkel had become a man worthy of her love.

They all watched, amazed, as the powerful man climbed the hill toward the hotel.

"Are we sure that is Godfrey Lewis Winkel?" Jake Rendel said.

Judge Toulmin chuckled. "Remember Cade and Lyssa?"

Jake smiled and looked toward his daughter and her husband. They each had a child in their arms and another by the hand and were gazing at each other with such complete happiness that Jake could not argue with fate.

Gabe followed behind, with MaryLyssa in his arms, his face held between her hands to be sure of his attention while she chattered away about something she and those bad boys had done. Her fingers twined unconsciously in his long hair. Jay and Jace skipped along beside them, laughing and every now and then adding something to her tale.

Toulmin's expression clouded. "I received news today of a massacre on the Cheraw Indians by the Georgia militia. Their warriors had joined General Jackson to fight the Red Sticks and Seminoles in Florida. Governor Rabun called up Captain Obed Wright's company, which immediately went into the Cheraw village and began stabbing, slashing, with guns blazing away at the old women, men, children, and animals left in the town. They left the place ablaze."

Jake Rendel looked shocked. "No!"

Toulmin nodded a sad assent. "This is far from over. Jackson has already negotiated several treaties to get the Indians to divest themselves of land east of the Mississippi in return for lands west of the Mississippi. His goal is the ultimate removal of these people from their native lands," he remarked.

Jake looked up the hill at his children. Their blood was already intermingled. The destinies of two people were intertwined. They were the hope of the future.